𝓑

Briarwood Publications, Incorporated

GRAVE WITH AN OCEAN VIEW

A Long Beach Island Mystery

JAMES M. MALONEY

First Published 2003
Briarwood Publications & Sassy Cat Books, Inc.
150 West College Street
Rocky Mount, Virginia 24151

JAMES M. MALONEY
GRAVE WITH AN OCEAN VIEW
ISBN 1-892614-45-6

Manufactured in the United States of America.

Printed by Briarwood Publications, Inc.

Authority is never without hate.
                                        Euripides

A man cannot be too careful in his choice of enemies.
                                        Oscar Wilde

With heartfelt thanks to
Barbara and John Trainor
Ron Waite
Paul Maloney
and
my wife, Helen

THE GHOST STORY

Chapter 1

BARNEGAT LIGHT, MARCH 1973

When The Highland Fling capsized in Barnegat Inlet during the big March storm of '33, taking Owen Andrews and his cargo of Scotch down with it, his wife Libby witnessed it from the widow's watch on their house. As awful as that calamity was, it didn't surprise her one bit, for she had long feared something terrible would happen to one who worked so ardently in the unholy service of Demon Rum. Every year for the next four decades, Libby made a predawn climb to the watch to mark the Mister's passing.

Libby, as was her custom, left her bed an hour before dawn on a raw March morning to check the weather. Instead of dark, brooding houses outside her window, all she could see was wet, opaque fog.

"You'll not see the inlet in fog like that," Libby told herself, as she shuffled back from the window. She had half a mind to forget the vigil this year. Aye, the night climb was downright fool-hardy for someone of her years. Truth be known, her left eye was laced over a bit, and her old knees ached something dreadful these damp spring mornings.

She thought about returning to bed, but giving a resigned sigh, she pushed her cold feet into her slippers instead. Plucking the old rebozo Owen had brought her from Mexico off the peg, she wrapped it around her shoulders. There'd be no living with herself if she returned to bed.

The hallway was inky black, but she daren't put on a light, or that old gossip Delia Harris across the way who always slept with one eye open would come knocking. "Did you have a bad night?" she'd say, those round, moist eyes of hers searching for a sign of illness. Libby was wise to her long ago.

The clock in the parlor tolled four, the round notes rising through the dark like bubbles from a drowning man. Still, it was Owen's anniversary. Forty years to the day. She owed him that much.

At the stairs to the watch, Libby took hold of the rail and, working hand over hand, pulled one tired leg after the other up the steps. At the top was a trap door. She placed a hand on it and pushed. When the door lifted on the counterweight, a shower of cold air spilled down and set her teeth chattering.

The rattle of the sashes in the room above made Libby smile. The wind was rising. She might see the inlet after all, but whether it rose or no, she'd keep her vigil just the same. Her hand found a spindle of the upper railing, and she hauled herself up the last steps into the narrow room.

Light from submerged street lamps glowed outside the windows. Her "telley" stood in the center of the narrow room, its black barrel silhouetted against the radiance from the floodlights around Old Barney. She shuffled to the north end to peer out at the inlet.

The windows shook in a sustained rattle, and the gray mist shrouding the house began to unravel before Libby's eyes. Minutes later, the black water of the inlet slid into view, followed by the stretch of beach and dunes between her and the lighthouse.

Out of nowhere, a light flashed at the mouth of the inlet. It gave Libby a start. Were her poor old eyes deceiving her? She rubbed the glass to clear it and saw something move on the beach. At first, she thought it was water trickling down the glass. She eased down the top sash for a better look. Her good eye spotted the movement again, and her pulse quickened.

Without thinking, Libby turned back to her "telly," slipped off the end caps, and raised the eyepiece to her good eye. The floodlights blazing around Old Barney dazzled her sight, and she had to swing the telescope clear to keep from blinding herself. Something bobbed through the light-dazzled field of her vision. She closed her eye a moment before she sought to acquire it again.

Four shapes floated up from the pale expanse of beach like the dead rising on Judgment Day. A chill went up her spine. The figures, back lit by the glow of floodlights and weighted down with great sea bags on their shoulders, slogged slowly toward the dunes. Then as suddenly as they had appeared, they were gone, swallowed up by the brush and the dunes of the State Park.

Libby tugged the rebozo tighter around her and eyed the beach for a time longer. What did it mean? Ghostly figures crossing the beach and strange lights flashing on the water? She hadn't seen anything like it since Owen's fateful passage through the inlet. That she should see the flashes this night of all nights filled her with awe. Could Owen be calling her from the other side?

She shivered at the thought. Aye, Owen had cheated the sea day after day until the Lord's judgment came at last, as she knew it would. He was at sea meeting the trawler down from Canada when the storm roared in. She had climbed to the watch that day, too, to see the angry white caps lash the stone jetty and the beach. The inlet waters heaved and fell beneath the rising gale that worried the windows in their frames. All day long, other boats wallowed into view, rising and falling like matchboxes on an insane sea. In their turn they breached the inlet entrance and swept past the lighthouse into the bay. All but The Highland Fling.

Night came, and she began to pray, knowing full well that her words were a profanation to the Lord. The inlet was hazardous even in good weather, but through the night the winds continued to rise and made it terribly treacherous. At dawn, The Highland Fling, riding low in the water, hoved into view, its yellow mast dipping and swaying. White knuckled, she watched.

Owen timed it right. The boat surged toward the channel riding the crest of a large, boiling swell. It rode into the inlet and drew almost even with the surf. When Owen blinked the running lights to signal all was safe, she let out her breath and began to breathe again.

Libby could still see what followed next, as clearly as the day it happened. The Highland Fling began to slip down the back of the wave, and with a billow of exhaust it fought to regain the crest again. Seconds more, she told herself, only seconds more.

The wave and boat rose together as they crossed an inlet shoal. The boat careened up the side of it, shuddered to a halt, turned and with a stately roll, capsized: rail, deck and cabin sliding in turn under the waves. The hull bobbed to the surface seconds later. The next wave rolled it on its side for a moment. The starboard rail surfaced on the frothing waters one last time and then slipped under the waves. The sea broke it in pieces, but Owen's body was never recovered.

Since that awful day, she had come to realize Owen's fate had been a judgment on them both. He had made them rich, as he promised, but he had made her a widow in the doing. She wiped her eyes. The cold made them water so. Years later, they dredged the inlet and brought up Owen's cargo: dark green bottles of Canadian Scotch.

The inlet claimed him for its own. Often, she came to the watch to look out on his watery grave. Some nights, she told him her troubles, longing to feel his arms around her. She had passed her years waiting in the long coffin of her watch for time to bring them together again, and this night she had been given a sign.

The Day of Judgment was at hand. The ghosts and the light made her sure of that now. The wickedness of the world was manifest for all who had eyes to see. Hadn't the summer people grown more shameless every year? Oh, the goings on she had witnessed through her "telly."

A stippling of rain hit the metal roof over her head. Just a few at first, and then the tempo quickened. Soon the drumming rain forced her to shut the window.

Armageddon was beckoning just outside her window. The world must repent before it was too late. Libby covered her "telley" and made her way back to the steps. The wickedness of the world was no mystery to the police. Let them search the beach for signs of the unholy things she saw. Repentance has to start somewhere. What better place than with the agents of justice in this wicked world?

Chapter 2

That morning in the darkness before waking, Thomas Mahlon heard clawing at his window, resonating like the scrape of fingernails on a hollow door. The insistent tearing of talon and beak on the window frame roused him from his sleep.

He rolled from under the warm covers. With a flap of wings the tearing ceased the moment he raised the shade. Another bleak March day lay wrapped around his house and all of Beach Haven and Long Beach Island, too, by the look of it.

Rubbing his arms against the cold, he thought hard about slipping back under the warm covers. Instead, he crossed to the bathroom, the linoleum icy against the bottoms of his bare feet. A splash of cold water from the sink ended all thoughts of sleep, and afterward he dried the inch long growth of white beard on his face with a towel. Most men go gray from the top down. Mahlon's hair was still black and his beard white. He ran a hand over his face and chin. Soon, it would be long enough to trim.

He had shaved it off last September, much to Sara's disappointment. After her departure for Florida in late January, he had let it grow back again. He hoped she'd be pleased.

After dressing, he prepared breakfast. Coffee, black and hot, wheat toast unbuttered, and soft-boiled eggs eaten from the shells. The headline in the morning paper was about the Watergate trial again. The "break-in," a Republican political dirty trick, had taken place the previous June. It was just a backpage item then, but the trial in

January had it vying with Nixon's second inauguration for headlines. Between sips of his coffee, Mahlon read that McCord, one of the convicted "Plumbers," claimed that perjury was committed in the Watergate trial and all of those involved had not been exposed. How about that, now?

Mahlon stretched. There was work to do, and sipping coffee and reading the paper wasn't getting it done. Clearing the dishes, he washed and set them to dry on the rack. At his makeshift desk, a hollow core door resting on two filing cabinets, Mahlon began typing the first of two insurance reports. He was halfway done the first page when the phone rang.

"Tango Mike this is Hotel Juliet. Do you read me, over?" a gruff voice said at the other end of the line.

"Hotel Juliet?" Thomas said.

"You better load your antenna, soldier. Your signal sounds awful weak."

"Hank James, you old grunt! Where the hell are you calling from?"

Loud laughter poured from the receiver, and Mahlon had to hold the phone away from his ear.

"Up in Barnegat Light," Hank James said when he stopped laughing, "at the police station. Read about you in the paper last summer. That missing handyman case. I've been meaning to call, but you know how it is. Things are slow around here this time a year. Come on up, and we can talk for a while."

"Love to. How you been keeping yourself?"

"Oh," Hank hesitated, "All right, I guess. To tell the truth, I've got a problem, Thomas, and I want to pick your brain, if you don't mind."

"Glad to help. See you in a half hour or so."

Mahlon put down the phone. Good! The paperwork would wait. On his way to the door, he plucked his jacket from the peg and reached back to check the placement of his holster on his hip. He hadn't worn a holster for six years. The move was pure reflex and caught him by

He marveled how the body still remembered his years on the force in unexpected ways.

The morning fog had retreated above the roof tops, and a damp east wind carried the faint crash of the surf over the dunes. The air smelled of the sea and gave his spirits a lift. The thought of spending part of the day in a police station stirred a host of old feelings that he thought were dead.

Boulevard traffic was light. He passed mile after mile of homes and businesses wearing a vacant, off-season look. In Shipbottom, halfway up the island, it began to rain. An unseasonable downpour drummed on the car roof, hampering his visibility.

The rain set Mahlon thinking about when he first met Hank on a rainy spring day at Fort Dix in 1944. They had both reported for a new class at radio school. Hank's bunk was next to his. By the time they had their gear unpacked, it was raining again, so they sat across from one another on foot-lockers and talked until mess call. Hank was a lanky kid from Newark with a street-wise attitude.

Long after lights out that night something shook Mahlon's cot. A thump and a groan followed. Mahlon swung out of his bunk and found Hank standing by the foot of it with his foot on Mahlon's foot locker. Hank's fists lashed out at something. Squeezing around him, Mahlon saw another soldier kneeling on the floor. The man's hands were caught under the lid of Mahlon's footlocker, held there by the weight of Hank's foot, and Hank was pummeling him unmercifully about the face. All Mahlon could hear was the solid thunk of fist on flesh and the deep moans coming from the man's throat.

Hank delivered two more punches, and the man started to sag, but his imprisoned wrists kept him somewhat erect. When Hank drew back to punch him again, Mahlon grabbed him around the shoulders and pulled him away.

"Let go of me," Hank said, his voice icy with anger. "I'm not done with that son-of-a-bitch, yet." He struggled to break free of Mahlon's grip. Others were out of their bunks by then, and they helped subdue Hank just as the barracks lights came on.

"What's going on here?" the platoon sergeant demanded as he advanced to investigate.

"He was stealing from my footlocker," Mahlon said, nodding to the unconscious man on the floor, "and my friend caught him."

The sergeant looked at the bloody figure at his feet and gave Hank a long, hard look. "You do that to him?"

James shook himself free and stepped forward. "Yeah, sergeant. The bastard got what's coming to him."

"Oh, he did, eh?" the platoon sergeant said. "We'll see what the C.O. has to say about that."

He knelt and examined the unconscious man. The thief's eyes were swollen shut and blood from his split lip covered his chin. His wrist bore angry red groves set deep into the flesh. The sergeant rose and turned to the bystanders.

"Throw some water on this guy, so we can get him to the infirmary."

He then turned to Mahlon. "So, he's your friend, eh?"

Mahlon looked at Hank and back at the sergeant. "You bet."

"I'd be damn careful if I was you. A man with a temper like that is dangerous." With that he turned and headed off to make his report.

The net result of the whole incident was that the thief went to the brig, and Hank got company punishment. He and Mahlon were buddies from then on. Hank's fiery temper got him into a lot of scrapes, and Mahlon did his best to keep him on the straight and narrow. They went to France together, attached to a combat infantry team, and remained together until Hank got wounded and shipped home. They lost contact after that and didn't meet again until their paths crossed at a law enforcement convention in Atlantic City fifteen years later.

The rain finally eased off just beyond North Beach. The Hank he met in Atlantic City was more guarded than the one he knew at Fort Dix. When Mahlon asked about his career, Hank changed the subject. For whatever reason, he didn't want to talk about it at all.

Chapter 3

The town of Barnegat Light, at the northern tip of Long Beach Island, took its name from Barnegat Lighthouse, the island's most famous tourist attraction. The lighthouse marks one of New Jersey's most infamous waterways, the Barnegat Inlet.

Mahlon found the police station sharing a side street with the post office and rain-drenched municipal tennis courts. It was a white stuccoed structure set back from the road with a radio tower that loomed over it like a giant exclamation mark.

Inside, a female officer nodded to Mahlon as she spoke into a microphone to one of her units in the field. The conversation was punctuated by squawks and static. Mahlon took the opportunity to glance around. He spotted an empty security bench with its long handcuff pipe sitting off to one side. Another squawk followed by the words "Ten 4," and the radio conversation ended.

"Can I help you, sir?" The officer on desk duty was plain of face and official in manner. The black name tag on her blouse read "Ofc. Pamela Richardson."

"I'm here to see Hank James."

"Is it urgent?"

"He's expecting me. "

"Are you Mr. Mahlon?"

He nodded.

"The Chief will see you in a moment, sir."

Mahlon eyebrows arched when he heard Hank's title. His friend had gotten up in the world.

He sat and waited. Outside, the rain had stopped but the sky was still grimy gray. The radio spewed out ten codes and street names in erratic fits. He listened and felt a twinge of regret that the routine of station duty was no longer his. Beyond a railing was the door to the Chief's office. He read the lettering on it with interest.

BARNEGAT LIGHT POLICE
DEPARTMENT
CHIEF HENRY JAMES

Hank always hated the name "Henry." In the old days he'd punch out anyone who called him that. Responsibility has its disadvantages, my friend. Finally, the officer dialed a number and spoke his name.

The door to the Chief's office opened immediately. "Thomas! You old dog face, good to see you." Hank crushed Mahlon's hand in his large grip and rocked his friend with a swinging slap to the shoulder.

"Come in." He guided Mahlon into his office to a chair near a desk littered with paperwork. The office was small and paneled in light pine. His friend stepped back and looked Mahlon over.

"I hardly recognize you behind that beard. How long's it been? Fourteen? Fifteen years?" The voice was gruff and loud like Mahlon remembered it. His old friend looked a bit thicker at the waist, but his white uniform shirt and dark tie looked smart. Mahlon saw the gold badge on Hank's chest and remembered a time when he wore his badge with pride.

"How long you been on the island?" Hank asked without giving him a chance to reply.

"Three years, and you're up here all that time. I can't believe it." Mahlon stood there shaking his head.

"So what brought you down the shore? An officer from Trenton dropped in seven, eight years ago. Gave you top rating." Hank narrowed his eyes mischievously. "To be honest, I thought he was talking about the wrong guy. The Thomas Mahlon I knew hated lieutenants and captains and anyone else in authority." His laughter filled the small room.

"How's the missus?" Hank said when he stopped.

Mahlon busied himself removing his coat before he answered. "She died, Hank. Six years ago."

Hank straightened. "Sorry to hear that."

"Auto accident." Mahlon grimaced. "I was celebrating a promotion and drank too much." He wiped his mouth on the back of his hand like there was something dirty on his lips. "The blues on the scene covered for me. I wasn't charged with drunken driving. I fell down the neck of a bottle for a while—" His voice trailed off.

Mahlon straightened in the chair. "Anyhow, I'm a P.I., now, and I'm getting on with my life."

"Thomas, you don't have to justify yourself to me." Hank perched himself on the corner of his desk.

"Thanks." Mahlon took a deep breath. "The job was getting too damn political, anyway. I could hardly stand it."

"Hell. What did you expect?" Hank looked around his office. "I'm up to my ass in politics." He studied his nails for a moment. "But I'm not going to let them push me out." His voice was low, and Mahlon could hear the old signs of anger under his words.

"Damn! I'd rather die in uniform," Hank said, "than spend my days chauffeuring Clare to her bridge games. Though she'd hardly notice if I did." He spit out the last words as though they had gone sour in his mouth.

"It's something—" He broke off as a car drove up outside the window. A man stepped from the car and headed toward the front of the building. He wore dark rimmed glasses and an expensive tan overcoat buttoned neatly to the chin.

"There's that S.O.B. now! Coming in to ruin my day." Hank's jaw went rigid. "Trying to sabotage me. That's what he's doing." His whole body stiffened.

"Hank."

"Know what he did yesterday?" Hank's voice grew harsh. "The son-of-a- bitch switched bid papers on me. I ended up signing the highest bid." He fumed for a few seconds more, slammed his fist into his palm, and sprang from the desk.

Mahlon rose, too. He'd seen Hank's fuse light too many times not to recognize the signals.

"I'm gonna beat his ass to a pulp." Mahlon managed to block his way.

"Hank! You don't want to—"

"Get the hell out of my way, Thomas."

"Get a hold of yourself man." Mahlon pushed him back down on the desk. "Wipe the floor up with him now, and you're as good as out of here."

"I can't stand the sight of him." Hank struggled to regain his feet.

"I'll bet. Then you better beat him at his own game." Mahlon did not let go of his friend.

Hank swore and wrested free of Mahlon's grip. A vein throbbed at his temple. Mahlon wanted to get him away from there quickly.

"Isn't there somewhere we can go till you cool down?"

Hank gave the door to his office a long look. With a grim nod of his head, he scooped up the phone and dialed. "Pam,—" His voice was hoarse with anger, and he had to clear his throat before he could go on. "— we're going over to see Mrs. Andrews about that complaint. We'll probably hit Bernie's for lunch. See you around one-thirty."

Hank stood and gave the office door one last look before he crossed to a second door in the rear wall of his office. He snatched his hat from the wall rack and plopped it hastily on his head, while he fumbled for his coat. The hat landed awry with its peak to one side. The sight brought an involuntary laugh from Mahlon.

"What the hell you laughing at?" Hank said, straightening the hat on his head. "You wanted me outta here, so let's haul before I change my mind."

Not until the chief's car cleared the parking lot did Mahlon permit himself to relax. They turned north on the boulevard toward Old Barney, its red top looking sore and bruised against the gray March sky.

"What's his name?" Mahlon asked when he thought his friend had calmed down a bit.

"Sgt. David Schuyler Woodson." Hank pronounced the name with cold disdain. "The bastard wants my job. One of the 'new breed.' Came with a college degree under his belt, and nothing under his hat but—."

"He's got enough there," Mahlon said, cutting him off, "to yank your chain but good."

Hank turned to him, his lips curled in disgust. "You don't understand. He's the type who has all the theory down pat, but can't issue a damn parking ticket without screwing up." He banged his hand on the steering wheel.

"You can't even talk about him without getting upset. You keep letting yourself go off like this, Hank, and he's got your job."

"I know. I know. But he's screwing me over. If Pam hadn't noticed the switch, we'd a bought our new patrol cars at the highest bid."

Mahlon looked at his friend a long moment and said, "How the hell did you ever make chief in the first place?"

Chapter 4

Hank pulled over to the side of the road and stared out the side window as if he didn't trust himself to look at Mahlon. His jaw went rigid. The horse tail reeds outside his window swayed in the cold, gusting wind that shook the patrol car from time to time. When Hank spoke, he did so through clenched teeth.

"What's the matter, Thomas? You think I can't handle the job? That I brought all of this down on myself?"

Mahlon rolled down the side window a few inches before he an-swered. "Hell, no. But we both know you're not subtle. How the hell did you handle the politics then?"

Hank kept his eyes on the front window. When he spoke, his voice was unnaturally flat.

"After the war—" He paused and began nodding as though the truth of what he said was irrefutable. "—Newark was a piece of cake." The statement hung in the air a few seconds while Hank went off somewhere. Finally, he came back, gave Mahlon a nervous glance, and went on in a normal voice.

"I'd probably still be there walking the beat if I didn't come down the shore on vacation in '59. The job had gone sour for me, anyway, but that's another story I'd rather not talk about." Traffic rolled past the patrol car at moderate speeds, but Hank wasn't paying any attention to it.

"This place needed a patrolman. Someone to bust heads. When I came on the job, old Chief Murchison's idea of police work was catching speeders and arresting drunks. He put me on nights.

19

"The college kids in summer were no problem. But the hard drinking fishermen in the off-season gave me a run for my money. I busted my share of heads." Hank smiled and then began to chuckle.

"I'd been down here about a year or two when one night I get a call. A guy's raising hell in a joint over on Central. When I get there, the bartender points to this fat guy. Must of weighed three hundred pounds. When I tell him he's gotta leave, the bar goes quiet.

"'Ain't going nowheres,' he says and laughs right in my face."

Mahlon smiled. "What did you do?"

"I go at him with my stick in one hand and my cuffs in the other. What does he do? Gives another smart-ass laugh and puts both hands behind his back."

"He's so fat I can't reach round to cuff him. Had me looking like a fool, and the customers were all laughing."

"Yeah, and?"

"My first thought was breaking his jaw with my stick. That crowd would have been on my ass in a wink. Instead I hit him on both elbows and slapped the cuffs on him when his hands came around to protect himself. The other patrons got a laugh out of that.

"After that the bar owners started asking for the cop who could handle trouble. Chief Murchison didn't know his days were numbered—" Hank looked at Mahlon. "—but I did." They both laughed.

Hank started the car and pulled out into the flow of light traffic. "Yeah, Thomas, I like a fight as much as the next guy, but you're right. I gotta out-think Woodson. Not out-box him. And I sure could use your help."

"You got it." Mahlon looked at his watch. "After you look into that complaint, we'll talk. Where's this Mrs. Anders live?"

"Andrews, Thomas, Andrews, and she's a tough old bird."

"Andrews, huh," Mahlon said with misgivings. He hoped it wasn't *the* Mrs. Andrews. He'd questioned her last summer about the kidnaping of Sara's handyman. She had mistaken him for a police detective, and he didn't set her straight. How would Hank react when he learned he passed himself off as one of his officers?

He caught a glimpse of the dunes at the end of a cross street. The sky above them looked silver gray, and out to sea puffy dark clouds skidded over the waves.

When Hank stopped the car in front of an old Victorian house, Mahlon's suspicions were confirmed. It was the same three story house with a widow's watch that he had visited last summer. Huge bayberry bushes and holly trees hid most of the ground floor from view.

"What's this complaint about?" Mahlon asked when the motor went off.

"Old lady claims she saw a ghost," Hank said matter-of-factly as he opened his door.

"I'll wait here."

"Like hell. You'll get a kick out of this one. Come on in."

Oh, crap. Mahlon had to push his door open against the damp, cold wind. Hank was already up the steps and working the knocker. Mahlon took his time joining him. The door curtain parted and a wizened eye peered out at them.

"What do you want?" a dried old voice asked.

"Police, ma'am," Hank said pointing to the badge on his hat.

"Took your time getting here," the voice answered, and the curtain fell back in place. A key turned in the lock and the door opened.

"I see you brought help this time," Mrs. Andrews said to Mahlon. Hank gave him a strange look. Mahlon shrugged as though he didn't know what she was talking about.

"Come in! Come in! I'm not heating the whole Atlantic Coast, you know." She stepped aside as they entered, her narrow mouth drawn in the same tight line of impatience Mahlon remembered from last summer.

When Mahlon closed the door behind him, Mrs. Andrews threw a wall switch. The bare bulb above their heads cast their shadows on the papered wall long since turned brown with age. The clothes she wore on her short frame were neat and clean.

"I called five-thirty this morning about them ghosts," she said to Mahlon. "What took you so long?"

"Ma'am—," Hank said but she cut him off.

"Let your boss do the talking. You'd be here quick enough if I hadn't paid my taxes, I'm thinking." Her mouth pursed in disgust and her silver rimmed glasses rode down her prominent nose.

"Look, Mrs. Andrews—"

"Will ya tell your lackey to shut up?" Mrs. Andrews said to Mahlon.

Mahlon stifled a laugh and put a hand on his friend's arm.

"It will go easier, Hank, if you just let her have her say."

Hank eyed his friend for a moment and then nodded.

"Well, as your boss here knows, when this old body can't sleep, I climb to the third floor and watch the ocean."

"Among other things," Mahlon said out of the corner of his mouth.

Mrs. Andrews gave him a withering stare. "Terrible thick with fog it was last night. I could barely see the houses across the street." She gestured with her hand. "Anyway I was thinking to go down and brew myself a cup of tea when the fog lifted."

Her dry voice turned solemn. "That's when I seen 'em, marching in file up the beach and over the dunes. Bent over they were with sea bags on their backs."

She paused to let the significance of what she saw sink in. "Course I knew who they were the minute I laid eyes on them," she said with a triumphant nod of her head.

"And who might that be?" Hank asked cautiously.

"Why them poor souls who were murdered in their sleep on the beach so long ago. Their ghosts come back to haunt these Godless times. And do you know why?"

The men shook their heads.

"Because Judgment Day is at hand." She began nodding at the truth of her statement.

Hank cleared his throat. "What would you like us to do about it?"

"Why, go to them dunes and find their tracks and tell the sinful world what your eyes have seen. Now, off with you. I've some scones in the oven, and if I stand here jabbering any longer, they'll be burned." She began motioning them out the door with her hand like she was shooing chickens. They barely passed through when it slammed and locked behind them.

Hank went down the steps to the patrol car and opened the trunk. "I can't for the life of me think why she took you for my boss."

Mahlon's shrug brought a bitter snort of laughter from his friend.

"She's something else, Thomas. Something else." Hank pulled a pair of boots over his shoes. "I'll look the beach over just to keep her happy."

"Got another pair, Hank? I'll join you."

Hank dug out an older pair and Mahlon slipped them on.

"What's the story about men being killed in their sleep?" he asked.

"Local history. During the Revolution, a group of Tories murdered some of the local patriots on the beach over in the park."

They walked to the end of the boulevard where it intersected Fourth Street and took the path that led over the dunes to the beach.

"Hank, let's work this in separate sweeps," Mahlon said. "You cover the surf line and I'll walk the base of the dunes."

"Right." Hank glanced back toward the house and saw the small figure of Mrs. Andrews watching them from the window of the widow's watch. "A quick look-see ought to satisfy her. Then we'll warm up with a bowl of chowder at Bernie's"

The wind rode in off the sea, whipping the sand against their boots and prompting both men to pull the collars up on their coats. The beach was large and littered with the debris of winter storms: sand etched bottles, timbers, and lines of blue-black mussel shells. In the center of the beach, gray-backed Herring Gulls huddled in a great flock, and the east wind drove the waves far up the beach. The expanse was trackless but for their own footprints.

Mahlon turned and walked toward the lighthouse a quarter of a mile away, his path parallel to the dunes. Fifty yards later, he crossed the boundary of the state park. An old snow fence lay half buried along the foot of the dunes, its NO TRESPASSING signs all but sunk from sight. On the summits of the dunes, beach grass whipped and tossed in the wind. When he reached the lighthouse area, he started back. So far he had seen no sign of man nor ghost. The slopes and sand gullies between the dunes had been beaten smooth by the heavy morning rain. The boots were heavy, and his progress against the wind was slow. Near the surf, Hank lumbered along with equal difficulty.

Halfway back, Mahlon spotted something projecting from the side of a dune. He stepped through a break in the snow fence and trudged up the slope into the gully between the dunes. Three feet below the top of the dune, the front half of an old vinyl shoe poked from sand. Out of curiosity, he freed it from the sand and examined it. The inside was packed with sand and the white of sea shells a child had hidden there in the past. He dug out the shells with his fingers.

A musty smell reached his nose as he freed a gray-white object the size of a rock. He wiped the sand from it. It was not a shell at all, but porous and white. He worked his finger deeper into the shoe, pried loose several more rocks, and brushed them clean. He realized what they were a moment later.

Returning them to the shoe, he set it down gently where he found it and brushed the sand from his hand. Across the beach the dark figure of Hank stood watching him. Mahlon called to him, but the wind flung his words back over his shoulder. He signaled Hank with his arm, and his friend started toward him.

Hank cut through the flock of gulls nesting on the beach out of the wind. He walked quickly with his head down, riding the wind that swept in from the sea and sending the gulls in circling flight as he came on. Something of the tough kid from Newark remained in his walk. He held his arms out from his body, and the spring in his step rocked him from side to side. He crossed the beach aggressively, and soon stood puffing at Mahlon's side.

"Whatcha got?"

"A body," Mahlon stooped and scraped away enough sand to expose three inches of white shin bone above the shoe. The bone was clean. There was no sign of body tissue.

"I'll be damned. Been here for some time, too." Hank looked at Mahlon and then back toward the patrol car.

"I'll have to call this in. Stay here, will you, Thomas? Not that this one's going anywheres." Without waiting for a reply, Hank turned and walked back down to the beach and headed off toward the road.

Mahlon looked around for some protection from the wind and noticed a more sheltered place farther back. He made his way up the slope and hunched down out of the wind.

He eyed the top of the dune. Directly over the body, the coarse, scratchy beach grass flourished, and several runners of beach morning glory had started down the side where he found the shoe. A damn lonely place. He guessed it was a woman by the look of the shoe. Murdered, no doubt. Who was she? And who buried her in this lonely place?

A few moments later, Hank hailed him from the beach, and Mahlon stiffly walked down. When he reached his friend, Hank told him the State Police Crime Unit was on its way. Under the watchful eyes of Mrs. Andrews, they left the beach. When they got inside the patrol car, Hank banged his hand against the steering wheel.

"Just what the hell I need. A murder investigation."

Chapter 5

Chief James stood by the open door of his patrol car and watched the last vehicle disappear into the gray dusk of the March evening. The State Police Crime Unit had taken all afternoon to cordon off the area, remove the remains, and sift sand for evidence. Just when he thought they had taken all their pictures, didn't they want to take some more. And his old friend Thomas had stayed for the whole show.

James turned and caught his friend in mid-yawn. "Thomas, how about a bowl of chowder before you go? We never did get one for lunch."

"I need something," Thomas said. "One more cup of that embalming fluid the troopers served, and you'll have to put me in a body bag, too. Where's this Bernie's you been talking about?"

Five minutes later, James led the way through the front door of *Bernie's Eatery*. The walls were darkened knotty pine and the floor covered in green linoleum. He picked a table away from the door and sat. When his friend saw the bread crumbs on the red checkered cloth, his nose wrinkled.

"Not exactly a four star rating, Hank," Thomas said as he sat.

"Now, let me tell you something," James said. "In the old days you knew a good diner by the number of trucks parked outside. Right? Down here it's the number of boats. Across that dock out there are two dozen commercial fishing boats. Bernie feeds the whole damn crew."

Just then a skinny man in a blue shirt and food-stained apron approached their table. "Evening, Chief," he said barely moving his lips. "What's your pleasure?"

James smiled up at him. "Bring us two bowls of your finest and a big pot of coffee."

Bernie nodded and turned to leave.

"And plenty of those Trenton Oyster Crackers." Bernie raised his pencil in acknowledgment and went on his way.

"Sociable one, isn't he?" Thomas said. He was busy scraping the bread crumbs into the ashtray. Bernie was back a moment later with a pot of coffee, a loaf of his famous onion bread, and the salads.

"We're here to eat his chowder," James said as he filled their cups. "Not make his acquaintance. Don't let the day's happenings put you off your feed. You're about to taste the best clam chowder on the island." James started in on his salad. As he chewed it, he sat back and regarded his friend benignly. He felt bad about the way the day turned out, but Thomas could've left anytime he wanted.

"Well, here I am," James said, tearing a slice from the loaf of onion bread, "with what sure as hell looks like a murder case on my hands." Thomas nodded and went on eating his salad.

James leaned forward and gestured toward his friend with his fork. "I was watching you out there today. You were just itching to get into it. Weren't you?"

Thomas grinned and helped himself to the bread. "Yeah, I was, but that's all behind me now."

"Right. Well, I ain't ready to put it behind me yet," James said. "Been Chief here since '62. Outside of the chicken shit council throws at me about tax rates and budget items, I love the job. And I ain't anxious to leave. They'll have to throw me out. Besides, wintertime things are pretty quiet. Weather's milder. Even the snow doesn't last long."

Bernie pushed through the serving door and set two steaming bowls of Manhattan clam chowder on the table. The deep red chowder was thick with potatoes, celery, carrots and chopped clams. James raised a spoonful to his mouth and tasted it. Ahhh, yes. Tender clams, tangy tomatoes and savory seasonings — a real treat for the tongue.

"Hey," Thomas said, "this soup is great." James gave him an I-told-you-so nod of his head and went back to eating. He had no time for idle chitchat until his bowl was empty.

"So, what's this Woodson been doing?" Thomas asked when he poured himself a second cup of coffee and sat back from his meal with a contented look on his face.

"Second-guessing me behind my back. Last fall, a friend of his ran for council. Woman named Jane Sparbow. I wake up one morning and find that my budget is suddenly a campaign issue. Appropriations that had been openly discussed in council before the budget passed were suddenly questionable. Well, to make a long story short, that idiot got elected, and she's been second-guessing my every move ever since. And someone's feeding her inside information."

"How do you know it's Woodson?" Thomas buttered himself another thick slice of the wonderful onion bread and began eating it.

"When he first came here, he was always putting in his two cents. Knew the latest poop on everything. And I mean everything. Last fall it suddenly turned off. Now, he knows nothing about nothing. Leaves all the decision making to me."

James looked around and then leaned toward the table. "Take the guy we let go last week, for instance. We hired him last summer. Sent him off to the academy at Sea Girt. He came back and a few weeks later his field training officer says he's doing all right. Woodson and I both agree he's ready. Before I know it, the guy smacks his girlfriend around, wallops the hell out of a drunk one night on bar patrol, and shapes up two times with the smell of alcohol on his breath. I had to let him go."

"What did he have?" Thomas asked, "Friends in high places?"

"Uh, uh." James dug down in his shirt pocket and fished out a toothpick and set to work with it. "No, but I get called up before the Council last night for sending unqualified candidates to the academy. And that bastard Sparbow lets it drop that I hired the guy over Woodson's protest."

James shook his head in disgust and poured himself another cup of coffee. "There are other things, too, like reports getting lost. Things like that, but you get the picture. I remembered reading in the papers that you live down here and thought I'd see what you have to say."

Thomas traced the pattern on the tablecloth with the handle of his spoon for a few seconds before he looked up. "Who can you trust on your staff, Hank?"

"Pam Richardson's been with me only two years, but she's loyal and will do anything I ask. Why?"

"You better ask her to make duplicates of all new files and any important old ones. Anything that would interest Woodson. If you don't have a friend on the Council, you better get one fast. Preferably someone from the opposition. It will politicize things, but it will also keep the spotlight on them. Start meeting with civic groups. Launch a campaign to make the department more responsive to community concerns. That sort of thing. And, eh, cover your ass six ways from Sunday because Woodson sounds like he wants a piece of it."

James folded his napkin and set it on the table beside his coffee cup. "I already got Pam on the file thing, and there's a longtime supporter of mine on the Council who would be glad to help me out. I'm just not sure I want to go public on this thing yet. The community idea is good. I'll get working on that tomorrow." He gave Thomas a philosophical grin. "You come up with anything else, let me know. 'Cause I got a feeling this is going to be one helluva fight before it's all over."

With a sardonic laugh, James sat back in his seat. "Ah, crap, Thomas, Bernie's chowder always makes me see the bright side of things. Let's talk about you for a minute. What are you doing with yourself when you're not playing P.I.?"

"Oh, the usual," his friend said in an unconvincingly casual way. "I jog four times a week. Do some bird watching. Things like that."

"You sound evasive, Thomas. There wouldn't be a female friend you're not telling me about, would there?"

A sheepish smile broke out on his friend's face. "Well, now that you mention it, Hank, there is someone. Her name's Sara Speilberg. She's due back from Florida next week or so. I met her last June when she hired me to find her missing handyman."

"What she look like?"

"Oh, eh, tall. Slender." The casual tone had crept back into his voice. "And, eh, she's a redhead."

"A redhead, huh?" James said, enjoying his friend's discom-fort. "Must of been love at first sight. Right?"

Thomas shook his head. "Anything but. She was over-bearing and demanding the first time we met. But I soon came to see it as a tactic she uses in the business world."

"Now I remember," James said. "That newspaper article said she owned a bathhouse in Ship Bottom that a realtor wanted. What was her name?"

"Eva Foxworth."

"That's it. Wasn't she a former concentration camp guard or something?"

Mahlon nodded. "In the same camp where Sara was held. Eva was one of her tormentors. Thankfully, Eva's dead now and Sara can leave all that behind."

James gave a sad shake of his head. "Well, I should hope so. At least you got a social life."

"Yeah. I took her to the Brigantine National Wildlife Refuge to see the snow geese arrive last October. And you won't believe this. She took me to the opera in Philly."

James couldn't believe his ears. His laughter rang through the room. "Good, Thomas. A man needs companionship." He got to his feet and began putting on his coat. He stood there a moment. "Life is pretty empty

31

without it." To hide the bitterness in his voice, he walked away from the table.

Bernie stood by the register and took their money with a slight nod.

"Mr. Mahlon, here," James said, "is a good friend of mine, Bernie. Take good care of him when he comes back. You hear?" The man studied his friend's face for a minute and nodded again.

When they arrived back at the station, James parked next to his friend's car. They got out and stood looking into the darkness overhead. The sky was overcast.

"Thanks, Thomas, for stopping by." James held out his hand, and Thomas gave him a firm handshake.

"It's been good, Hank," Thomas said, shaking his hand. "Don't hesitate to call if you think I can help."

When his friend disappeared up the street, James got back in his car. He couldn't put it off any longer. It was time to go home.

THE DETECTIVE
STORY

Chapter 6

BEACH HAVEN
APRIL 1973

March ended with a pair of warm blue days that got Mahlon thinking that winter had left for good. Then overnight, like an April Fool's joke, the weather took a back slide into winter, and the island shivered under a twenty-four-hour assault of rain and sleet.

On the morning spring returned, Mahlon went for an early jog on the beach. Twenty minutes later, he finished the run by sprinting across the beach and up the slope of the footpath that crossed the dunes at Pelham Avenue. The slogging climb punished his thighs and left him staggering by the time he gained the top. Gasping for breath, he turned for one last look out to sea.

The waves, roiled brown with sand, curled and boomed, and the gray trailing edge of last night's storm slipped over the horizon like a newspaper falling from a table. He stood mesmerized by the motion of the waves until the loud roar of a motorcycle on the street behind him broke the moment. One of the benefits of living south of Beach Haven was the usual quietness of the place, and he resented the noisy intrusion.

The sun felt warm once he reached the street. The block and a half walk to his home would cool him down nicely. It was the kind of spring day when he wanted to get in the car with someone and ride. And he would have, too, if he had someone to ride with. Sara was almost three weeks overdue, and they kept missing each other on the phone. He didn't have the slightest idea when she'd return or if she'd return.

The helmeted driver of the motorcycle rolled up the street toward him, the motor nervously surging, blasting the house fronts with the staccato roar from its exhaust. If the guy wanted a look at the ocean, he should be over on Holyoke Avenue where the fishermen's buggies crossed the dunes to the beach. He made up his mind to ignore the idiot and kept walking.

When the cycle passed him on his left, his irritation began to mount. Then, for some baffling reason, the cyclist circled behind him and reappeared an instant later on his right.

The motorcycle crossed his path, but Mahlon kept his eyes focused straight ahead. He was afraid that if he made eye contact with the driver, he might say or do something he'd later regret. The machine circled behind him, came up on his right side, and kept pace with him for three or four strides when suddenly the ignition switched off.

"Thomas," the driver said in the silence that followed, "aren't you going to say 'Hello?'"

Mahlon's step faltered, and he looked back. The rider bent to deploy the kick stand and then straightened. The uneven smile beaming at him from beneath the white helmet and dark sunglasses belonged to only one person — Sara Speilberg. Seeing her astride a motorcycle was more than surprising. It was shocking.

"Sara," he said, "what the hell are you doing on a motorcycle?"

"I've been gone two months and that's all you can say?" Sara said in an injured tone. She removed her helmet and shook loose a spill of red hair that bounced on her shoulders. A brown leather jacket zipped to the chin, tight jeans, and square toed cowboy boots gave her slender body a look he found disturbingly attractive. She tucked the helmet under her arm.

"Well, no. I mean. Sure, I'm, I'm glad to see you."

His mind had trouble accepting the bike, and he stepped around to get a better look. Gray metal levers and black thumb switches on the handlebars. Big, dusty tires. The black mass of the motor just inches from the seat and the gas tank. It struck him as something powerful and dangerous. Something too dangerous for her.

"Women don't ride motorcycles," he said, his voice rising in disbelief.

"Well, this one does." A note of defiance crept into her voice. The helmet came out from under her arm and slipped over her head.

"Why? Why do you want to ride it?"

"I couldn't wait to see you, Thomas, but I guess the feeling isn't mutual." Sara snapped the chin strap and jump-started the cycle. While Mahlon stood there with his mouth hanging open, she pushed the bike off its kick stand. It wasn't until the bike started rolling away that he came to his senses.

"Sara, wait," he shouted as he tried to keep up with her. "Sure, I'm glad to see y—" The deafening roar of the exhaust stifled the rest. Sara, her back straight and her speed rising, left him in her dust.

Mahlon slowed to a walk. The sun was warm on his face, but he hardly noticed it because of the wintery feeling inside his chest. He'd call her as soon as he reached home. He quickened his pace. With luck, she'd answer the phone. Yeah, with a lot of luck.

Chapter 7

The April Chamber of Commerce meeting ended shortly after ten, which left Ocean County Freeholder candidate Steven Orbann plenty of time to make the rendezvous in spite of the glad-handing he had to do before he left. In Ship Bottom he joined a four-car line of traffic heading west on the causeway. A moment later before he reached the main bridge, he slowed. A solitary streetlight marked the intersection to a side road that ran parallel to the causeway on Bonnet Island. He made the turn.

The black Cadillac rolled west over the rutted road until the dark mass of the main bridge rose on his left. Doing his best to avoid the larger potholes, Orbann turned the car around and parked it well back in the shadow of the bridge. The dashboard clock read 10:55. Good. He was early. He lowered his window and switched off the motor and lights. The cool night air entered his window, carrying with it the slosh and splash of bay water against the bulkhead behind him and the occasional hum and slap of tires on the bridge.

It felt good to get out of that meeting. He stretched and yawned. What a bore. And his speech? He raised his eyes in exasperation. It didn't help much, either. Slogans and platitudes will not win it in November. He was desperate for an issue. Something to stir things up. So desperate, in fact, that here he sat, waiting for a man he didn't know to deliver he knew not what. He shook his head. Friends had warned him that the campaign would land him in strange places. He looked around. A late night meeting on a dark road. Can it get much stranger than this?

"Your campaign needs a boost, and I've something that can do it," the caller had said. I hope so. Orbann clicked on the dome light and checked his watch. Two minutes after eleven. He'd wait until ten after. That was all.

Headlights flashed through the intersection fifty yards in front of him, and Orbann straightened in his seat. A white car rolled under the yellow streetlamp and turned in his direction. A sudden stab of anxiety hit him in the gut. It had a light bridge on its roof. A police car.

Orbann drew a deep breath and exhaled slowly. He was breaking no laws. He'd simply come out here to relax and think. Let them prove otherwise, but the papers would make the most of it.

FREEHOLDER CANDIDATE
KEEPS ODD TRYST

This wasn't how he meant to stir things up.

The police car stopped opposite his open window. Orbann looked neither right nor left. He heard the whine of a servo motor as the officer lowered his window.

"Mr. Orbann?" the officer said. Orbann recognized the voice.

"You're late."

"Sorry, sir."

Orbann turned his head. The glow from the other vehicle's instrument panel showed a man in dark rimmed glasses who looked to be in his early thirties. The man's shirt sleeve bore three stripes. A police sergeant, eh? Orbann learned long ago how to handle sergeants.

"Sergeant, you have something for me?"

"Eh." The man hesitated, somewhat taken back by the use of his rank. "Yes, I do."

"Get on with it."

"I've read in the papers that your campaign is— Uh? How should I sa—"

"In trouble," Orbann said, cutting him off. "What's that got to do with you?"

"I thought I could help."

"Out of the goodness of your heart?" Orbann gave a sarcastic laugh. "What's in it for you?"

The sergeant turned and looked out his front window for a moment or two. "I want to make chief."

"Before you're thirty-five, I presume."

The sergeant nodded. "I'd need backing." He turned and looked directly at Orbann. "From someone like you."

"Provided I get elected."

The sergeant grinned and leaned toward Orbann as he continued. "There's a lot of talk about law and order in Washington these days. I see no reason why you can't use it in your campaign, too."

"The law and order thing works best where neither exists. LBI sleeps seven months a year. They'd laugh me off the ballot."

"Oh; but you're wrong. We got ourselves a big drug problem on the island, but it's being hushed up."

"Drug problem?" His ears perked up. "What exactly do you mean?"

"Off-season drug arrests are way up, and the pushers are targeting school kids. Elementary school kids."

Orbann digested this for a moment or two. "You got proof of this?"

"You bet."

"How can this be happening?"

The sergeant ran a hand over his face. "We've got antiquated police chiefs fighting this war with antiquated methods."

"Which antiquated chief do you want to replace?"

The sergeant gave an embarrassed smile. "Chief James in Barnegat Light."

"I'm interested, Sgt., eh?"

"Woodson. David Schuyler Woodson."

"You get me proof, Sgt. David Schuyler Woodson, and I'll turn up the heat in Barnegat Light. We'll put a stop to this drug problem."

Woodson nodded and rubbed his hands together. "That's exactly what I hoped you'd say. I can keep you posted on everything. Arrests. Drug raids. You name it."

"Good," Orbann said. "Get back to me as soon as you can. Bring whatever you can get your hands on. I need to get this underway as quickly as possible." He started the Cadillac and turned on his lights.

Sgt. Woodson put the police car in gear and was ready to pull away when Orbann spoke again.

"Sergeant, leave the patrol car home the next time."

"Sure thing, Mr. Orbann," Woodson said, as Orbann drove off.

Chapter 8

At noon the next day, Mahlon loaded his suitcase into the Plymouth for an overnight trip to Atlantic City. William P. Landreth, a Wall Street broker from Rumson, wanted his soon-to-be son-in-law checked out. The young man was a chemical engineer by the name of Joseph Frey. Landreth had gotten Mahlon's phone number from a former client, and he wasted no time spilling out his misgivings.

"I pulled strings to get him a position at Getty Oil," he said, his voice edged with resentment. "A graduation present, you know. After all, he is marrying my little girl. But that, that hippie turned it down. Went with one of those left-wing environmental firms that make difficulties for the street these days."

"The street?" Mahlon asked.

"Wall Street, of course. He'll be at some kind of seminar in Atlantic City. Don't ask what hotel. He doesn't deserve my Lydia. She's too good for the likes of him."

"You got a picture of him?"

"Yes. Their engagement announcement from the papers. I'll send that."

Mahlon gave his address.

"His kind always wallow in the mud," Landreth said.

"Atlantic City isn't exactly Sodom or Gomorrah," Mahlon said. "The hottest thing in A.C. this month is probably the School Superintendents' Convention. Still, a guy can find trouble anywhere if he wants to. Look what Adam did, and he was in Paradise."

Landreth was silent for a moment. "Get down there and catch him," he said and hung up.

43

On his way out of town, Mahlon stopped by Sara's house. He wanted to invite her to dinner the night after next. There was no answer to his knock. Knowing he had gotten off on the wrong foot about that damn motorcycle, he was hoping the dinner would settle things down. Unwilling to leave without a try, he wrote out an invitation on a leaf from his notebook.

Sara,

Off to AC for a couple of nights. How about we celebrate your return? My place Thurs at six. Call my answering service if you can't make it.
Thomas

P.S. I missed you, too.

He stuffed the note in her mail box and left.

Mahlon drove south on Rt. 9, that time machine to the past where lean farm houses of long ago looked on from the roadside, and the small towns he drove through still wore a tired Depression look. At the White Horse Pike, he turned east toward the ocean.

On the other side of the mud flats lay Atlantic City, a smattering of tall buildings rising square and blunt into the overcast sky, and in the middle the great hump of Convention Hall looking like a blimp hanger. In the old residential part of town street after street of close-packed bungalows looked tired in the gray light. He found a pay phone on Pacific Avenue not far from the post office and made a call to the Convention and Visitors Bureau. The Claridge was hosting an environmental seminar that week.

Inside the Claridge, Mahlon offered a pimple-faced bell hop twenty dollars to get him the number of Joseph Frey's room. Five minutes later, the bell hop returned with the room number. It was written on a paper which the bell hop dropped in Mahlon's lap on his way past to greet some new arrivals at the door.

"I'd like a room on the fourth floor," Mahlon said to the attendants at the registration desk. "Ocean view if you have it." They didn't. The best they had to offer was a room in the back hall, just around the corner from Frey's room. Mahlon took it. He spent the rest of the afternoon reading the newspaper in the lobby outside the seminar room. When the session broke up, he joined the first of the seminar group to head for the elevators. In his room he doffed his coat, rolled up his sleeves, and grabbed the ice bucket before he made his way to the corridor outside Frey's room. He stationed himself in the ice machine alcove down the hall and waited.

Ten minutes later two men in cotton shirts and faded jeans left the elevator and entered Frey's room. The older one was probably in his mid-thirties, but a receding hairline made him look older. His younger companion had shoulder-length curly hair and a thick, soup-strainer mustache. It was the same young man who held Landreth's daughter in the photo.

With his subject identified, Mahlon hastened back to his room. Guessing they would take a few minutes to freshen up for dinner, he switched ties and changed sport jackets. Five minutes later he was down in the lobby. He made a quick call to his answering service. Sara hadn't called. Great. He found a chair that offered an unrestricted if somewhat distant view of the elevator doors and waited for Frey and his friend to come down.

The rest of the evening was a bore. The men dined in one of the hotel restaurants, and Mahlon managed to get the booth behind them. Throughout dinner the older one lectured Frey on the particulars of groundwater contamination across the state. Trichloroethylene. Perchloroethylene. Schmeth-ylene. Mahlon didn't understand a word of it. Afterward they took a walk on

Pacific Avenue, downed a few beers in a nearby bar, and retired before eleven. Mahlon kept watch outside their room for an hour, but Frey never emerged.

Wednesday was the closing day of the seminar. Around eleven, the older man was paged by a bell hop. He went to the nearest phone. The worried look on his face when he returned told Mahlon there was some kind of emergency. Twenty minutes later he was down in the lobby with his luggage. The morning session had ended, and Frey was there to see him off.

After his friend's departure, Frey made a phone call and then went to the luncheon that closed the seminar. Guessing the meal would keep Frey occupied for an hour or so, Mahlon hurried back to his room. He picked up his camera and called the answering service.

His mechanic left him a reminder that it was time to take another crack at the deadbeat list. They had a barter deal. The mechanic serviced and repaired Mahlon's car, and Mahlon provided collection services twice a year. There were two inquiries about his rates and services. Mahlon took down the names and phone numbers. Sara hadn't called. His luck was still holding.

He stopped at the hotel's cafe for a coke and a ham and cheese on rye. The hallway outside the luncheon was empty except for one of the participants, who was scurrying back from the rest room. Mahlon tailed him into the luncheon and sat at a back table. Frey was seated up front, his curly head bent over taking notes.

The speaker's uncombed gray hair bounced with every movement of his head, and his brown corduroy jacket rode up his arms when he gestured. In a summary tone, he recapped the main points of his talk then paused and looked out at his audience.

"And when you're told, ladies and gentlemen, —and you will be told, make no mistake about it—by business leaders and the politicians that ocean dumping is not their problem, remember that just twelve miles from where you sat today. Just twelve miles off that beautiful beach out there—" He made a stabbing gesture in the direction of the ocean. "—is where New York City dumps its contaminated sewage every day. PCB's, cadmium, mercury, you name it. Remember and tell them: IT-HAS-TO-STOP!" He removed his glasses and took a sip of water while the applause filled the room.

She approached Frey in the hotel lobby. Straight black hair, a tan trench coat, and high heels. She walked up to him, flipped open the coat and smiled coyly. Mahlon got a tantalizing shot of her standing there in gold hot pants. Frey hastily closed her coat. With a self-conscious look around, he steered her toward the elevators. Mahlon caught the next elevator up.

He guessed they'd be occupied for the rest of the afternoon, so he skipped out of the hotel to drop off the film. He was back in twenty minutes. Room service brought the couple dinner around six. At nine, bare foot and tousled haired, Frey emerged from room for more ice. That was the last Mahlon saw of him until he checked out the next morning at eight. His companion must have left earlier.

Mahlon picked up the pictures the next morning and headed north on the Parkway by nine. Landreth wanted the dirt on Frey as soon possible, and it was a good two hour ride to Rumson. He found Landreth's house on a wide tree-lined street in the older part of town. The tan stuccoed Victorian had a four-story tower with arched windows. Mahlon parked the Plymouth on the street and followed the circular drive past the wide green lawn and manicured shrubbery up to the house.

William P. Landreth, a tall, fit looking man with well-groomed hair, answered the door himself. He wore a crisp white shirt, blue silk tie, and dark, pin-striped trousers. With barely a word, he led Mahlon into his study. With the door closed behind them and having seated himself at an antique walnut desk, he finally addressed Mahlon.

"My wife and I just returned from the Cape. I don't want her to overhear this." He leaned forward and spoke in a low voice. "Now, what's the dirt on that louse?"

"You're sure there's dirt?"

"He spent a weekend in Connecticut last summer. One of those 'est' seminars. God knows what perversions he engaged in up there."

From what Mahlon had heard the human potential seminars were more about verbal abuse and physical depravation than they were about perversion. But Landreth wouldn't want to hear that, so he kept it to himself.

"He was with a woman, wasn't he?"

Mahlon nodded.

"A streetwalker. Right? What do I owe you?"

"Your advance," Mahlon said, "covered just about everything. I'll send you an itemized statement by the end of the week."

Landreth sat back, a look of smug triumph on his face. "When I think of how close that hippie came to getting his hands—"

"On your little girl?" Mahlon asked, cutting him off.

Landreth wasn't used to being cut off. "Yes," he said, an edge of anger in his voice. "My little girl. You did get a picture of them, didn't you?"

"Yeah."

"Good. Lydia will need proof." Landreth rose. The meeting was over. "Send it to me as soon as it's developed."

"I can give it to you now."

Landreth shot him a surprised look.

"You've got it with you?" His eyes glinted with satisfaction. "Let me see the slut."

Mahlon produced the photo, and Landreth snatched it from his hand. He took a look at the picture and blinked with astonishment. "What is this? Some kind of joke?"

"No. Your 'little girl' Lydia spent the night with Frey."

Landreth let the photo drop and began shaking his head. "No," he said, "she's not that kind of girl."

"Most of us," Mahlon said, "aren't really the people our parents think we are."

Chapter 9

Around four a light rain began to fall, and afternoon
darkened into early evening. By five-thirty, Mahlon had
the shrimp peeled for the hors d'oeuvres, the salad made,
and the salmon marinating in the fridge beside two bottles
of a California grey riesling that the wine clerk had
recommended. Everything was ready.

The evening's dampness crept into the house, so
Mahlon lit the fire. Earlier, when he readied the paper,
kindling, and logs, he inserted some pine cones from his
neighbor's Japanese Black Pine. The cones burned hot and
served as a real fire starter. Certain that the fire had caught,
Mahlon hurried down the hallway to his bedroom for a
shower.

He planned to grill the salmon outdoors, but while he
showered a low rumble made him change his plans. The
night was not made for grilling outdoors. The broiler would
have to do. He toweled off quickly, combed his hair, and
trimmed his beard and mustache. Ten minutes later, he was
dressed in a blue plaid flannel shirt, tan chinos, and his
comfortable old moccasins. The crackling of the fire greeted
him when he opened his bedroom door.

In the living room, Sara stood by the fire. He hadn't
heard her enter, but the sight of her pleased him enormously.
In a white cashmere sweater and black slacks, Sara stood
warming her hands. He moved toward her, and Sara gave a
little jump of surprise when he embraced her. The clean
scent of her long red hair was wonderful, and Sara settled
back into his arms with a murmur of contentment.

"I've been waiting to hold you ever since you left," Mahlon said, his voice husky with desire. "It's good to have you back again."

Sara turned to face him and slipped her arms around his neck. "I'm glad to hear that, Thomas. You didn't seem this glad the other day, and I got worried." She made a mock-serious face and then raised her lips to his and gave him a long, welcoming kiss. When it ended, Mahlon kissed her back. When they came up for air, he slipped from her arms but kept hold of her hand.

"A glass of wine?" he asked, his words throaty with emotion. The feel of her was almost too much. His heart raced and his stomach was tying itself in knots, and here she was barely in the door. Slow down. Not so fast. You've got to make the moment last, as the poet said.

Sara smiled her acceptance and moved over to the sofa to await his return. Over at the sink, he immersed himself in the mechanics of opening the reisling, glad for the distraction it brought. He poured them each a glass and returned to the couch. She sat waiting with her legs crossed, that wonderful uneven smile on that beautiful face. Mahlon didn't trust himself to sit beside her. He'd be all over her before he knew it. He raised his glass to make a toast.

"Here's to the lovely traveler on her return."

"How nice of you, Thomas." She raised her glass and they drank.

"Stay right here," he said when he brought the glass down, "and I'll get dinner going."

"I'm not going anywhere tonight." Her smile was mischievous. Mahlon stepped away with great reluctance.

"Didn't your Florida stay last longer than you thought it would?" he asked from the kitchen end of the room after he got one of those prepackaged rice dishes going on the top of the stove. He hoped it would go well with the fish.

"I'm sorry about that, Thomas. My cousin Becky, she should rest in peace, was a lot worse than she let on over the phone. When I got there, it was clear she was dying. She's a—" She caught herself. "She was a survivor like myself. The camps left her with very bad health." She gave a sigh.

"Afterwards," Sara said after a moment's silence, "I stayed on to help the girls get things sorted out. One's just out of college and the other just started last September. Their father died last year from a heart attack. I came back as soon as I felt I could."

"I know you did." Mahlon placed the salad bowl on the table. "Do you have enough time left to remodel the course? Memorial Day will be here before you know it."

"I hope so. I got the name of an architect who designs golf courses. I called him today and asked if he ever thought about designing miniature golf courses. He hadn't, but he said it sounded interesting. He asked for a few days to think it over."

Mahlon laughed and crossed over to the couch. "He'll take the job. No one can resist that Speilberg sales pitch of yours."

"Thomas," Sara said, "are you suggesting that I twisted his arm?"

"I refuse to answer on the grounds that it might incriminate me." Her laughter rang clear and true. "May I escort you to the table, m'lady?" He made a deep bow and offered her his arm.

He refilled their glasses and toasted her a second time. The salad was crisp and the dressing piquant. The rice? Packaged. But the salmon—moist and savory. While they ate, Mahlon told her about Hank James and the body they found on the beach. When they finished, Sara helped him clear the table and set the dishes soaking in the sink. Dessert, Mahlon hoped, would come later, away from the table, in another room.

A crimson bed of embers glowed in the fireplace. Mahlon put on three branch-size maple logs and topped them with two larger pieces of peach wood that he picked up on one of his swings through Burlington County. The fragrance of burning fruitwood rose from the fire. Sara returned to the couch with their wine glasses in hand.

Before Mahlon sat beside her, he took his glass from her hand and placed it on the end table. When he was seated, he slipped his arm around her shoulder, pulled her to him and kissed her. The kiss lasted a long time. When they separated, Sara put down the wine glass she was still holding, kicked off her shoes, and came back for more. A loud pounding on the porch door interrupted them.

Swearing under his breath, Mahlon let himself out onto the porch to see who it was. A soft rain was still falling, and the drip of water from the eaves like half-heard voices filled the night around him. He flicked on the outside light, and just beyond the jalousied glass of the porch door stood Hank James, in his uniform coat and hat, hunched against the falling rain.

"Hank, what the hell are you doing here?" Mahlon asked as he unlatched the door and motioned James onto the porch.

James shook the water from his chief's cap before he an-swered. "Sorry to bother you at this hour, Thomas, but that son-of-bitch is at it again."

"Mrs. Andrews?"

James guffawed. "No. Sgt. Woodson."

"What's he done this time?"

"Could we step inside for a minute?" James asked. "I'm chilled to the bone." Mahlon saw that he had a large brown envelope in his hand.

"Yeah. I guess so." Mahlon turned and led him into the house. Sara had put her shoes back on and now sat on the couch leafing through a magazine. She looked up when they entered.

He introduced Hank to Sara and carried the man's coat and hat to the coat rack. James didn't want anything to drink, so Mahlon wheeled over the office chair from his desk for Hank and returned to his seat beside Sara. James set the envelope down beside the leg of the chair.

"What happened, Hank?"

"It has to do with that body we found."

"What have you heard?"

James gave a nervous glance at Sara. "Not a whole lot. She was Caucasian around twenty years old. She was murdered. Fractured cheek bone, and the remains of a knotted nylon scarf around her neck. Her shoes and some remnants of a light cotton blouse and walking shorts were found with the body."

"That's all?" Mahlon asked. "No wallet or purse?"

James shook his head. "You know how these girls dress in summer Cotton shorts and shirt and nothing underneath. Or haven't you noticed?"

"Yeah, Hank. I've noticed."

Sara laughed and then apologized for interrupting.

James exchanged grins with Sara. "They also found an old wedding ring on a chain around her neck. Her killer probably missed it under the scarf. The State Police Lab estimates she was in the dunes two or three years. Judging by the way she was dressed, her death occurred sometime in the summer of '70 or '71."

"Any missing person reports in NCIC or SCIC that look promising?"

"Nothing was filed within fifty miles of here at either Crime Information Center."

"The county prosecutor's got it under investigation, right?"

James shook his head and sat back. "I wouldn't be here if he did. Some pervert's been attacking young boys on the mainland, and the public wants him caught. County detectives are working around the clock on it. My Jane Doe will have to wait."

James wrinkled his nose and gave a sardonic chuckle. "Only problem is my Mr. Mayor doesn't want to wait. Had me on the phone this morning. Wants this murder solved ASAP."

"What's that got to do with Woodson?" Mahlon asked.

"Councilwoman Sparbow, Woodson's friend, got to the mayor last night. Told him an unsolved crime like this is damaging the community's image. That four-eyed robot must have filled her ear but good."

"Did you tell him the county's all tied up?"

"You bet I did, but it didn't cut any slack. The Mayor wants a quick and speedy solution, or he'll urge the council to look for a new police chief next year."

Mahlon shook his head in disbelief. "Murder investigations take time. No offense, Hank, but couldn't this have waited till tomorrow?"

"No. You got to start first thing in the morning."

Mahlon pushed himself upright on the couch. "What are you talking about? First thing in the morning?"

"You're my only hope. I can't be running around investigating with that vampire sucking the life blood out of my career back at the station. And I can't hand this over to Woodson. He'll just drag his feet."

"But Hank—"

"Let me finish. Woodson's got me between a rock and a hard place. If I don't start an investigation, the Mayor will charge me with malfeasance. If I do, Woodson'll sabotage everything he can lay his hands on while I'm out in the field. I need someone I can trust out there. Thomas, will you do this for me?"

Mahlon looked at James. He could sense Sara watching and waiting to see what he'd say. In his line of work, people played dirty little tricks on each other every day. It's what kept him employed, but he couldn't turn his back on a friend.

"Will you do it?"

"Okay. But I can't work for nothing. Half my standard fee and expenses. I'll do my best."

"That's great!" James reached down for the envelope at his feet. "I've got one of the shoes here and pictures of the ring. If you can identify where the victim bought them, it may give us a lead to her identity. If we can identify her, maybe we can identify her killer, as well."

James opened the envelope and pulled out the shoe. Mahlon took it from him and rolled it over in his hand. It was dingier looking than he remembered, and a smell of mold and decay clung to it still. Sara leaned forward to look and wrinkled her nose at the smell. With his eyebrows raised in an unspoken question, Mahlon extended the shoe to her. Sara hesitated a second and then took it in her hand.

He took the pictures of the ring from James. The first enlargement showed the outer surface of the ring. It had an intricate, filigree pattern carved around the setting, suggesting to Mahlon that it was made early in the century. The second enlargement showed a much worn engraving on the inside of the ring—K.C.J. to H.A.B. June 8, 1901. His hunch was right. Maybe the ring belonged to the victim's grandmother.

"It could be a a waitress or a nurse's shoe," Sara said. "Someone who's on her feet a lot."

"What makes you say that?" James asked.

Sara handed the gray shoe back to James. "I don't think any woman would wear it for its style. Feel the thick, cushioned sole. That's important when you're on your feet all day." She looked at Mahlon and shrugged.

"Thank you, Sara," James said, as he put the shoe into the envelope and handed it to Mahlon. "I've taken up enough of your evening. I knew I could count on you, Thomas. I won't forget this." James stood and crossed to the coat rack and put on his coat. Mahlon followed him out onto the porch.

The rain was still falling, a soft drizzle that drove the dampness into Mahlon's bones. James stood with his hat in his hands looking back at the soft glow of the window. He leaned toward Mahlon with a sly smile on his face.

"Don't stay up too late, Thomas. I want you well rested when you start gum-shoeing tomorrow."

"Go home to your wife," Mahlon said with a laugh.

"Clare will be long asleep by the time I get home." James gave a distinctly bitter laugh and turned to face the rainy outdoors.

"When I tell her about this new problem tomorrow morning at the breakfast table, she'll look up from the store ads and say, 'Whatever you say, dear.' Not much comfort in that, I tell you."

James gave Mahlon a pained look. "But you've heard enough of my problems for one night." Setting his hat on his head, James stepped out into rain and trudged to his patrol car, the stones crunching wetly under his weight. In the open doorway of the porch Mahlon stood watching him go.

Half way there, James stopped suddenly to stare at something behind the old garage that stood on the left side of the front yard. He moved over for a closer look at whatever it was and then turned back toward the house.

"Damn, Thomas. You're full of surprises tonight, aren't you?"

"What the hell are you talking about, Hank?"

"Got a lovely lady inside, and a nifty motorcycle outside. Throw a tarp over it for gosh sake. It'll be a pile of rust by morning." He continued on to his patrol car, shaking his head as he went.

Mahlon stepped out into the front yard, the cold rain hit his face and neck, sending a shiver through him. Stepping carefully to avoid puddles, he made his way to the far end of the garage. In front of its doors sat Sara's bike lit by the pale yellow light from the nearby street lamp. That thunder he heard in the shower must have been Sara arriving on her bike. It didn't look very big, but what the hell was she doing riding it in the rain?

By that time James had the patrol car backed around, and with the hissing crunching of wet stones under his wheels, he moved out of the yard. Mahlon felt cold water seeping into his right moccasin and looked down to see he was standing in a shallow puddle. He gave the motorcycle one last look and headed back.

The glow from the window lit the interior of the porch, and he spotted Sara's tan rain coat and rain hat draped over the porch furniture. He stood for a second, trying to fathom Sara's infatuation with her new toy. What was she trying to prove? With a shrug, he went inside the house.

"Thomas, I was beginning to think you rode off with your friend." She was drying her hands at the kitchen sink. She returned to her seat on the couch and drew her feet up, folded her arms, and hunched her shoulders against the chill he had let into the room.

Mahlon let her statement go unanswered. He bent over the fireplace to put the poker to the fire-blackened logs to return some warmth to the room. The fire shot up, fed by the crimson embers that had accumulated under the grate. He placed another three-inch log where it would best catch the resurrected flames and turned to Sara.

"My, you've grown quiet," Sara said. "Has your friend's request got you worried?"

Mahlon shook his head. "No, that's not what's got me worried."

"What is it, Thomas?"

"It's that bike out there." His voice was low, but the note of annoyance in it was much stronger than he intended it to be.

Her face became a stony mask. "Is it in your way?"

He shook his head. "Do you know how dangerous it is to ride a motorcycle in this kind of weather?"

"Oh," Sara said, a growing edge of indignation in her voice. "You think I should have left it home."

"Frankly, yes."

"Well, I guess I better get it there as soon as I can." She swung her feet down and busied herself putting on her shoes. He couldn't believe she was leaving. He stepped forward to stop her.

"You can't leave now. It's raining out there."

Sara stood and looked him in the eye. "Oh, can't I?"

Mahlon had more he wanted to say, but he knew he had said too much already. He stepped aside, and Sara let herself out the front door. The silence that followed was broken only by the pop and sputters of the fire. He looked at the empty couch. This wasn't how the evening was supposed to end. The porch door banged shut and a moment later the cough and rumble of the bike's motor reached him. Oh, hell, Sara, you don't have to leave like this.

He went to the door and yanked it open. Sara had the bike moving already. She completed her swing out from behind the garage and was on the street. The bike rumbled from sight before he got the porch door opened. He swore and slammed it. Behind him the fire snapped and popped, its warmth a useless cure for a very cold shoulder.

Chapter 10

The coffee tasted like it was made from the ashes in the fireplace. With a blah of disgust, Mahlon poured it into the broiler pan perched on the pile of dirty dishes in the sink. He was a long time falling asleep last night, and the rest of the riesling didn't help him either. Morning came, and he hadn't wanted to get up, but the squabble of birds at the feeder outside his window drove him from bed. The weather had cleared, and sunlight flooded the kitchen end of the room, for all the good it did.

The large brown envelope lay on the kitchen table. He leaned against the sink and contemplated the wisdom of taking on this case for Hank. Working for a friend was often harder than working for a complete stranger. Friendship intensifies the expectations, and when they're not met, the friendship usually suffers. He hoped that wouldn't be the case this time.

He pulled the envelope toward him, removed the shoe, and wrinkled his nose at the smell of mildew and decay that came with it. Mottled with water stains and flat gray in color, the shoe triggered his memory of the day he'd found it. Strangled and buried in the dunes. Not a pretty end for any young woman, and somewhere her parents were starting another day not knowing what happened to her, and the not-knowing had to be eating them alive. With a little luck and hard work maybe he could change that. Hank needed help, and so did the victim's parents. Two good reasons to take the case.

"Not just for you, Hank, old buddy. Not just for you," he said aloud to the empty room.

He raised the shoe higher into the sunlight coming over his shoulder and turned it in his hand. It was well made and not especially stylish. A modest wedge supported the heel, and sole and heel were one piece. Sara was right. The shoe was too utilitarian in style for a woman to wear on a date.

At his desk, he opened the phone book to the Yellow Pages and looked under "shoes." There were at least twenty-five stores listed there. He sank back in his chair, thought of all the women who wore shoes like it and groaned. Nurses, cleaning ladies, waitresses, medical office assistants, cafeteria workers to name a few. The leg work looked staggering. Then he had an inspiration. Maybe it came from one of those uniform stores?

He flipped back through the pages and checked the "uniforms" listing. The names of a dozen stores were listed, but only four of them sold uniforms and shoes on the island: Budget Uniforms in Beach Haven, Island Beach Uniforms in Harvey Cedars, Michelle's Uniform Boutique in Surf City, and The Shoe Shop in Brant Beach. More stores were listed for the mainland. His search had to start somewhere. Why not locally? He could expand his search to the mainland later if he needed to.

Ripping the page from the phone book, he folded it and slipped it in his shirt pocket. He was in no mood to copy stuff down this morning. The telephone sat at his elbow. Tossing the phone book aside, he swore and yanked the receiver off its cradle. His finger twirled out Sara's number with an impatient snap, and he drummed his desk while he waited for her to answer. It rang and rang.

Mahlon slammed the receiver down. In an angry huff, he took the shoe to the kitchen end of the room and found a lunch bag in one of the drawers and dumped it in. He grabbed his coat from the rack and went out, slamming the door behind him.

The neighbor's flag was snapping in the wind, and Mahlon was glad for the warmth of his jacket. The Plymouth fired up on the first hit of the starter, and Mahlon was on his way. The news on the car radio concerned former Attorney General John Mitchell and presidential aide John Dean. The two supposedly helped plan the Watergate "break-in." Mahlon smiled. My, my, my, the rot was getting closer to the top. Traffic in Beach Haven was light, and Mahlon made the turn onto Central Avenue with typical off-season ease.

Budget Uniforms was an isolated store tucked into a line of two story cottages. A female mannequin in a nurse's uniform stood in its window. The store was empty when Mahlon entered, though a buzzer in the back announced his arrival. Shelving lined with shoe boxes ran along the left wall, and racks of uniforms lined the right. Doorway curtains on the back wall parted, and the gray-haired proprietor glided into view.

Dressed in a pink shirt, gray paisley tie, and plain gray vest, the man wiped the corners of his mouth with a linen napkin. He inserted his little finger in his mouth, dislodged a morsel of food from between his teeth, and swallowed. Mission accomplished, he gave Mahlon a patronizing smile that lifted his cheeks but never reached his eyes.

"Can I help you?"

Mahlon opened the lunch bag, pulled out the shoe, and set it on the counter. "Do you carry this style?"

The man leaned forward to examine it but caught a whiff of the odor. He immediately straightened and inspected it from afar. He looked at Mahlon, eying his beard a second or two before he spoke.

"No, can't say that I do, but something just as good came in the other day." His pronunciation was crisp.

Mahlon shook his head. "Do you know where I can find it?"

"Noooo," the man said, "but I do carry a line of uniforms that will satisfy, eh, all your uniform needs. If you know what I mean?"

"Thanks, but no thanks," Mahlon said as he put the shoe back in the lunch bag. "The last uniform I wore was a cop's."

The proprietor's brow grew furrowed. "I was only asking," he said with a forced smile.

Vince's Uniform and Shoe Shop sat on the boulevard in Brant Beach. Vince turned out to be a large man in a green polo shirt and well-worn jeans. An old inch-long scar tugged at the corner of his mouth.

"What can I do for you?" Vince asked, his voice surprisingly soft and friendly. Mahlon showed him the shoe, and Vince grinned with one corner of his mouth and shook his head. "Can't help you there." Mahlon was back on the road again.

Traffic in Ship Bottom moved with it's usual slowness, fed by the line of cars and trucks coming off the causeway. Mahlon crossed into Surf City and found Michelle's Uniform Boutique in a line of one story outlets on the north end of town. The young sales clerk told him that the business had been open one year. His search was going nowhere fast.

One more stop to go. In North Beach the houses thinned, and he caught occasional glimpses of grassy dunes between the big houses that blocked his view of the ocean. The island narrowed significantly in Harvey Cedars. A decade before, a fierce March storm had battered the island and cut it in two at Harvey Cedars. He and Mary had come down a week later to see the damage. It looked like a war zone. Bushes and trees uprooted, and where the sea breached the dunes, cottages were either pushed off their foundations or upended altogether. All signs of that catastrophe had disappeared, but Mahlon knew it could happen again someday.

He spotted Island Beach Uniforms on the other side of the street before he reached the traffic light that marked the center of the old town. A break in traffic permitted him to make a U-turn, and he pulled the Plymouth into one of the empty parking slots in front. One look told Mahlon the store belonged more to the dead than it did to the living, but he left the car anyway to stretch his legs. The grimy window framed an empty interior and a display area peppered with the carcasses of dead flies. A "Closed" sign hanging on the door by one corner fluttered ner-vously in the breeze.

Sheltered by the vacant building from the breeze that had the small clouds overhead scudding out to sea, Mahlon stood for a moment watching the traffic. Well, his starting point had led him exactly nowhere. The only thing to do now was go back to the phone book and start on that long list of shoe stores. Hell.

He got back into the car, fired it up, and joined the thin line of cars heading south. Ten minutes later he was back in Surf City, and his stomach was asking if it was time for lunch. One of the old landmarks of the island lay just ahead. The Long Beach Hotel was a square four-story building with its name in standing letters on its roof. He parked in front and went inside.

The waitress who seated him was middle aged and wore a white uniform that hugged her round figure in all the wrong spots. He followed her to the table. A few customers were scattered around the room, and he could hear the voices of two men who were drinking their lunch in the bar in an adjoining room. She left him a menu and said she'd be right back for his order. Mahlon had barely scanned the lunch offerings when she was back at his table, order book in hand.

"Now, what can I get you, hon?" she asked, with a hint of Irish brogue seasoning the question. Mahlon settled on the crab cake special, steak fries, and black coffee. She waddled off to fill his order on stout mottled legs and sturdy white shoes. When she returned with his order, he waited until she had placed the dishes on the table before he spoke.

"Can I ask you something personal?"

Her brown eyes regarded him critically over the pouches that set them off from the rest of her face. "Oh, it's something personal, is it? If it's dirty, I call the manager."

"Oh, no," Mahlon said quickly. "Nothing like that. Anyone can see you're a respectable woman."

"Out with it, hon. I've got customers waiting."

It was a long shot, but he thought it worth a try. "Where do you buy your shoes?"

"So, who wants to know?"

He looked around the dining room before he answered. "I'm, eh, a private investigator working on a case. I thought you might be able to help me learn where a pair of shoes were bought."

She placed her pencil on her lips and thought for a second. "I don't know if I should tell or no. I don't want to get no one in trouble. Let me think on it." She walked back to the kitchen.

Mahlon ate the crab cakes and found them to be delicately spicy. The steak fries were thick and crisp, and he slathered them with ketchup as he ate. When the waitress returned to refill his cup, he gave her his name and asked for hers. She told him it was Agnes, and her manner began to thaw.

By the time he had almost finished his second cup, most of the other patrons had left. Agnes came back to remove his plates, when she paused for a second to look around the empty dining room and then sat on the edge of the chair opposite him.

"I want you to know," she began, "a widow like myself can't be too careful when it comes to strangers. My kids are all grown up, and I'm by myself now."

He finished his coffee and set down his cup.

"Agnes, I'm a retired police officer working as a private investigator." He flashed her a warm smile. "What I need to know can in no way harm either you or the owner of the shop where you buy your shoes."

"Retired police officer, is it?" She pursed her lips and looked down at the table for a moment.

"Okay, I believe you," she said when she looked up, and leaning forward, she took his empty cup and saucer and moved it to the top of the other dishes she had stacked before her. He pulled out his notebook to write down the name and location.

"Sammy's Shoe Shoppy in Manahawkin on Route 9 is where me and most of us girls buy our work shoes."

"Shoppy?"

"Yeah, Shoppy. You know. With two 'p's' and an 'e.'"

"Shoppy," he said again. She watched him write it down. When he was finished, she gave him a knowing nod of her head.

"Thank you, Agnes."

"Glad to be of help," she said, patting his hand with her own. "Now, come back soon and see me. You hear?"

"I'll do that." Mahlon left enough money on the table to cover his bill plus a nice tip.

Chapter 11

When Steven Orbann pulled the fusuma closed on the Asahi room, the paper-covered screen hissed in its track. His imported shoes lay at the edge of the tatami where he had left them last night. He slipped them on and walked to his office at the end of the hallway. The woven straw mat that lined the hall made each step sound like a whisper.

He had chosen the navy blue tailored business suit for the speech that afternoon because dark colors emphasized his fine posture. Image wasn't everything, but it helped win elections. He paused outside his office door and swept a comb through his black hair. It felt a little long in the back. He'd have to call Giorgio for a trim as soon as his visitor left. He entered the room quietly, the well-oiled latching mechanism making hardly a sound.

"Mr. Woodson," he said, closing the door behind him.

A startled David Woodson turned from examining the Japanese scroll painting on the wall and hastened back to his chair. An unctuous smile played on his lips as he returned the greeting and took Orbann's hand. The lack of firmness in the man's grip surprised Orbann.

"Admiring my kakemono?" Orbann asked, as he circled behind his black walnut writing table and stood admiring the art work for a second. "I acquired it last year. Adds the right touch to the room. Don't you think?"

Woodson's face took on an anxious look. "Oh, absolutely, Mr. Orbann. Absolutely."

Orbann had to smile as he sat in his chair. Aesthetics were probably the last thing Woodson was prepared to talk

about. He studied Woodson for a moment. There was something inordinately prim and proper about the man. That short, carefully combed brown hair. The bow tie. That blue sweater under his brown sport coat. He looked more like a school teacher than a police sergeant.

"Mr. Chance said you had something for me." Woodson straightened and forced a nervous smile. Orbann sat back to listen with folded hands.

"As I told you last time, what I have will win the election for you."

"Tell me more. Please."

"At the risk of repeating myself, people may not be aware of it yet, but this island has a serious drug problem."

"That doesn't surprise me, Sgt. Woodson. Most communities in New Jersey can say the same thing. After all, Long Beach Island is a resort community. How can that fact win me a seat in the State Senate?"

"The truth is incompetent leadership has let this issue sneak up on us. Some chiefs on the island think law enforcement is simply a matter of rousting drunks, catching speeders, and preventing break-ins during the winter."

Woodson smiled condescendingly and shook his head as if to say, "We know better. Don't we?"

"Barnegat Light," Woodson said, "and other communities have drug problems because, frankly, these men haven't kept up with the times."

"If what you say is true—," Orbann looked Woodson in the eye a moment. "—it must be very difficult working in such circumstances."

"This isn't about me," Woodson said. "No, sir. It's about the threat that faces our island. Those well-meaning but old fashioned bureaucrats aren't up to the battle. Modern law enforcement procedures have passed them by."

"Frankly," Orbann said, "how will this help me win?"

"Well, the people deserve the best protection their taxes can buy. When that protection isn't forthcoming, they're

being cheated. Can you afford to stand by and let that happen?"

Orbann frowned and looked out the window for a second or two before he responded. "These men have dedicated their lives to protecting the citizens of this island. They have friends and political allies who vote. Attacking them might do my candidacy more harm than good."

"You don't have to attack them directly," Woodson said, with a dismissive wave of his hand. "Focus on plans and strategies. Demand that more be done to staunch the flow of drugs onto the island. Use the information I supply anyway you see fit."

Orbann mulled this over for a moment before he answered. "As long as I make sure Barnegat Light comes in for the lion's share of criticism. Right?"

"Oh." Woodson's face began to change color. "Barnegat Light will come in for its share, I'm sure."

"Come, come, Sgt. Woodson. We're both ambitious men. If this proves to be as hot an issue as you claim it is, and if your information does what you say it will do, and if I get elected, I'll do everything to see that Barnegat Light has a new Chief of Police by the start of next year.

"But." Orbann raised a finger in warning. "I'll never use anything that would jeopardize law enforcement operations and endanger the lives of men. That has to be understood from the start. If operations, or policies for that matter, fail because of incom-petence, I won't hesitate. After all, the public has a right to expect intelligence and expertise, especially in an area so vital to the fabric of our society."

Woodson by this time was smiling broadly and nodding his head. He reached down and lifted the briefcase that sat by the leg of his chair. He undid the clasp and pulled out a manila folder.

"These are copies of directives pertaining to department activities in the area of drug enforcement over the last year. I've made notes in the margins where policy and strategic planning have missed the mark." He laid the folder on the writing table and pushed it across to Orbann.

"I hope this information is as valuable as you claim it is," Orbann said. He left the folder where it lay. "Fortunately, I have several issues to campaign on, so if this—" He nodded toward the folder. "—doesn't pan out, I still have a chance of winning."

Orbann smiled before he continued. "I assume that your own campaign is based on more than just this one issue."

"Now it is." Woodson's smirk was self-congratulatory. "The man has skeletons in his closet, and they're all about to come out and dance."

Orbann checked his watch and brought both hands down to rest on the edge of the writing table. "I'm afraid that's all the time I can spare. I've a speech to make this afternoon, and I can't be late."

Woodson closed his briefcase, reached over to shake Orbann's hand, and left. There was a bounce to his step, and Orbann guessed he was feeling good. After the door closed, Orbann remained in his chair. If he listened hard enough, he could hear the waves breaking. He closed his eyes and let the rhythm of it flow through him for a moment or two. He opened his eyes at last and picked up the phone.

"Mr. Chance," he said and waited for the bartender a floor below him to summon the man.

"Yeah, Mr. O."

"I need Giorgio up here right away. By the way, you called that one right. Tell me, how did you know he was a cop?"

"In my business, Mr. O., it all comes down to one thing. Know your enemy."

Chapter 12

Mahlon crested the top of the causeway bridge.
Ahead lay the green pinelands bright with sunlight, while
behind him clouds, dark gray with moisture, rolled in from
the ocean. The four lanes of Rte. 72 dog-legged slightly
to the left before they cut a straight path to the pines. When
he got to Manahawkin, he took the off ramp to Rte. 9
North and found Sammy's Shoe Shoppe a hundred yards
beyond the first light.

The building was a 1950's cheese box, a flat roof on
some cinder blocks with a large front window. Not exactly
what you'd expect of a "shop" spelled with two "p's" and
an "e" hanging onto the rear. There was a place for that
crap in New England, but in Mahlon's eyes the rural
ambience of Rte. 9 sure didn't support it.

Inside the store, a small glass counter on the right
held the cash register, and a double line of metal-framed
chairs divided it down the middle. Mahlon plopped
himself down on the men's side, glad to get off his feet.
He looked around for the clerk. Outside, traffic roared
past the "Shoppe" with discouraging indifference.

"Be with you in a minute," a high-pitched voice called
from the rear of the store. A short man with bottled-black
hair and a pencil-thin mustache appeared a moment later
still chewing on his lunch. He wiped his mouth with a
paper napkin, which he then stuffed in his back pocket.

Mahlon stood but the clerk waved him back into his
seat.

"You got a few minutes?" Mahlon asked.

"If you're soliciting—"

"Nothing like that. Do you sell this style?" Mahlon pulled the girl's shoe from the bag and offered it to him.

The man took the shoe and turned it over in his hands. His purple plaid shirt was buttoned to the chin, and his little paunch stuck out below his black belt. He studied the inside of the shoe for a minute before he gave it back.

"Popular number a few years ago," he said. "Company switched styles for some cockamamie reason. Went out of business a year and a half later." He shook his head at the thought of such foolishness.

"Bring her in," he said. "I'll find something to fit her. And at a good price, too."

"Eh. She doesn't need it replaced. She's dead."

The clerk's eyebrows shot up. "I see. That's a horse of a different color. So, why are you here?"

Mahlon explained that the shoe belonged to a murder victim, and he was trying to trace her identity.

"Been in a grave, has it?" the clerk said matter-of-factly. "Thought it looked shabby." The man rubbed his mustache with his forefinger and thought. "Mister, there's two things to learn from a shoe like this. Size is one, but you already have the body, so that won't be much help. The second is color."

Mahlon looked at the mottled, gray vinyl of the shoe. "Not much chance of that," he said with a disgusted look.

"Shows how much you know. I sell my share of polish to waitresses. Most like to keep their shoes looking neat. That's if they take pride in their work." The man took the shoe from him again and pointed to the crevice where the top attached to the sole. "There's shoe polish right in there. Scrape around and I'll bet you'll find something." He returned the shoe with a smug look. "You want a knife to scrape with?"

"No, thanks," Mahlon said. "Where can I find a pay phone?"

"Other side of the laundry." The man pointed his thumb over his shoulder.

"You've been a big help." Mahlon said on his way out the door.

The long distance call to Trenton put him back on the road again five minutes later. An old friend by the name of John Walters was the laboratory supervisor at the State Police Headquarters in West Trenton. He agreed to examine the shoe for shoe polish but nothing more.

An hour and a half later, Mahlon parked his car on the State Police grounds across from the old log cabin that used to be the administrative office years ago. At the lab he asked for Walters. The man was busy, but he sent an assistant out for the shoe.

Mahlon spent the rest of the afternoon grocery shopping. At closing time, he was back at the State Police Headquarters. Walters brought the results out himself. The shoe held a residue of brown polish.

"Brown polish," Mahlon said.

"What were you hoping for? White?" Walters asked with a laugh. Mahlon thought about it a second.

"No, John. Brown polish will do just fine."

"Here's an official lab report you can add to the file." He handed Mahlon a folder. "I got to be going. Me and the missus are going out tonight."

Mahlon returned to his car and joined the line of cars leaving the State Police facility for the day.

Night had fallen on the streets of Beach Haven by the time he got back. He drove past Sara's. The house was dark, so he went on home. Before he called Chief James, he got a Molson from the refrigerator and took a long, cold pull on the bottle. James picked up on the first ring.

"What the hell you doing, Hank, waiting by the phone?"

"Yeah, all evening." The note of relief in his friend's voice was hard to miss.

"Don't get your hopes up." Mahlon told him about his visit to Sammy's shoe store and his trip to Trenton.

"What did Walters find?"

"Of the five scrapings he tested, two showed traces of brown polish."

"Humph," James said, "I was expecting white. At least then we'd know she was a waitress."

"Or a nurse," Mahlon said, "or a cafeteria worker or one of a dozen other jobs where women wear white shoes. Maybe brown isn't so bad after all."

"I was so bent on her being a waitress—" He let the sentence trail off.

"Look, I'll drive over tomorrow and see what that shoe clerk can tell me. What's new at your end?"

"I'm getting bad vibes, as the kids say. This afternoon the Mayor asked for a copy of the Borough's Uniform Crime Report for last year. I sent it right over." James paused. "Woodson's got something going. I just know it."

"Sleep on it, Hank," Mahlon said. "Can we meet at noon for lunch tomorrow? I got my tip on that shoe store from a waitress at the Long Beach Hotel. I'd like to return the favor, if I could."

"Sara know you been seeing this gal on the side?" James' laugh echoed in Mahlon's ear.

Mahlon waited for his laughter to stop. "Wait till you meet Agnes, Hank. You'll be tempted, too."

"Oh, on a first name basis already?"

"At my age, I can't waste time."

"I got the time," James said. "What I lack is the energy. See you tomorrow."

"Hank?"

"What?"

"Tomorrow is a business lunch. You pick up the tab, so I don't have to list it on my expense sheet." Before James could protest, Mahlon put down the phone.

* * *

Mahlon was back at Sammy's Shoe Shoppe at ten-thirty the next morning. The clerk scurried between the wall of shoes and the line of chairs where three waiting customers sat. Mahlon watched him operate. His manner was friendly and efficient, and he knew his stock. A helper would have speeded up things, but none was in sight. Mahlon realized the store was a one-man operation. Sammy did it all himself.

Twenty minutes later Sammy came over to Mahlon. "Back already, I see." He wore the same purple plaid shirt buttoned to the collar.

"Sammy, is it?" Mahlon asked, extending his hand.

The man nodded and then stepped back and looked down at Mahlon's shoes. He groomed his thin mustache, and Mahlon had to fight the temptation to look down, too.

"I need to ask you something about this shoe." Mahlon said, as he started to pull the shoe from the bag. Sammy waved him off with his hand.

"No need to show it. I never forget a shoe, but let me ask you this. Your feet tired at night?"

"So's everybody's."

"A person eats something that disagrees with his stomach. Does he eat it again? No. But his feet hurt all his life, and he thinks it's natural." Sammy raised his arms and let them drop to show his exasperation. He looked accusingly at Mahlon.

"Well—" Mahlon searched for a response. "—the army ruined my feet. Now, about this shoe here."

"Sit down! Let me put you out of your misery." Sammy put a hand on his arm and guided him back toward the chairs.

"I really need to ask about this shoe," Mahlon said, as he backed up and sat.

"So tell me. You a masochist or something?" Sammy fetched his stool, and Mahlon put his right foot on the sloping board. Sammy unlaced his shoe and examined it. He shook his head and measured Mahlon's feet.

"You like to suffer, don't you?"

Mahlon shrugged.

"Sit here. I got just what you need in the back room." The man rose and headed for the storeroom, leaving Mahlon to wiggle his stockinged foot on the carpet.

Shoe box in hand, Sammy returned a moment later.

"These shoes were made for you. They'll caress you feet, relax your legs, and improve your posture." Sammy sat on the stool and opened the shoe box with a showman's flair. He pulled out a brown suede leather shoe and took hold of Mahlon's ankle.

When Mahlon saw the shoe, he did a double take. There was something peculiar about it. The thick sole tapered down to practically nothing at the heel. By that time Sammy had pulled its mate out of the box, and it was as screwy looking as the first one. There was no way Mahlon could see himself wearing those shoes. He tried to pull back his foot, but Sammy held his ankle in a death grip.

"I don't need a pair of shoes. I need to know about this shoe," Mahlon said, lifting the shoe he brought from the seat of the chair next to him. Sammy paid no attention to him. He had the first shoe on his foot and was busy lacing it up.

"Put your other foot up here," Sammy ordered when he finished lacing the first. "Come on. Come on. I won't hurt you."

Mahlon sighed and put up his other foot.

"Everything in its time," Sammy said, as he slid Mahlon's shoe from his foot. "Take care of the needs of the body, first, and the needs of the heart and mind take care of themselves." Sammy had the second shoe laced in no time.

"Stand up," he said. Mahlon stood and felt the back of his calves pulling.

"Walk. Don't stand there. Go on, walk."

Mahlon took a tentative step and then another.

"What do you think of them?"

"Well, I don't know."

"Of course you don't. I'm the shoe expert, and I know. Those shoes have to be walked in to be believed."

Mahlon found himself leaning forward to counteract the slope of the sole. His calves pulled, but the shoes did feel comfortable.

"Comfortable, eh? Not only comfortable, they improve your posture, too. Wear them for a week and, believe you me, you'll never go back to the others."

Mahlon circled the line of chairs. Yeah, the shoes were comfortable. His calves were pulling, but his feet felt good.

"Thirty-five dollars," Sammy said, as Mahlon walked by the cash register. Mahlon didn't answer. He walked back to his seat and picked up the paper bag with the shoe.

"Where do the waitresses wear brown shoes?" he asked.

"I'll throw in a swede brush and extra laces. It's a deal. Right?"

Mahlon sighed and looked out the window at the passing traffic. Sammy wasn't going to talk unless he bought the shoes. Hank will scream when he sees them on the expense sheet. What the hell. Buy the shoes.

"All right," Mahlon said. "It's a deal."

Sammy was already filling out the sales slip. Mahlon's feet felt pretty good. He handed Sammy the money.

"Now, tell me where the waitresses wear brown shoes?"

"Brown, you say?" Sammy said, like he was hearing Mahlon's question for the first time. "That's interesting. In June every year, the new waitresses come in looking for shoes. 'Who sent you?' I ask. 'An older waitress,' they say. May your feet be my witness. I sell only the best shoes at the best prices." He looked back at the box-lined shelves of his store.

"Only one place uses brown. When a waitress asks for brown ones, I sell her white ones and a bottle of dye. Doesn't pay to stock 'em, you know? Brown shoes, I mean."

"Yeah, sure," Mahlon said. "Which place is it?"

"Orbann's Lounge in Brant Beach on the boulevard."

"Thanks." Mahlon looked down at his shoes and flexed his toes. "My legs feel a little strange, but my feet feel comfortable. I'll say that for them."

"Sure they're comfortable. Let me tell you something." A mischievous smile played on his lips. "When you came in here today . . ." He broke off and scratched his head to hide his laughter. "I've got professional pride, too, you know. My father, he should rest in peace, told me, 'The secret to success in business is never let a customer out without a sale.' I let you go once—," He wagged an admonishing finger. "—but not twice."

Chapter 13

The underside of the overcast started to fall apart like a soggy mattress by the time Mahlon reached the island. Hanging tatters of mist trailed across the boulevard ahead of the Plymouth. Mahlon parked behind the Long Beach Hotel where a Barnegat Light patrol car was already parked. The air was raw and damp, and Mahlon was glad to be heading indoors.

His friend sat at a small table for two against the back wall of the dining room. When Mahlon sat, he was glad to give his stretching calves a rest. The look of relief on his face caught the Chief's attention.

"Something wrong, Thomas?"

"My calves are killing me."

"How come?"

"It's my new shoes, Hank." Mahlon held out his foot for James to see. James took a look and screwed up his face in disbelief.

"You didn't pay for those things? Did you?"

Mahlon shook his head. "Nope." He flashed James a smug smile and pointed his finger. "You did."

"I'm what?"

"Sammy wasn't talking unless I was buying. Anyhow, I'm just doing what you told me to do."

"What's that?"

"Gumshoing, man. I'm gumshoing." Mahlon began to laugh.

James started to protest, but he broke off and shook his head in dismay.

81

"They're a legitimate expense," Mahlon said, still laughing. "Don't worry. You'll get an itemized expense statement."

"Okay. Okay. Where's this waitress you're hot on?"

Mahlon stopped laughing and rolled his eyes in exasperation. "Hank, don't get on my back because this is costing you, or I'll let you do your own bird-dogging."

James raised his hands in surrender. "You are touchy on an empty stomach."

"Look, Agnes gave us a good tip. I merely want to return the favor."

As if on cue, Agnes appeared. Her white uniform hovered at the side of the table as she set down two glasses of water. "Well, if it isn't the private detective."

After introducing her to Chief James, Mahlon ordered the special of the day— broiled tile fish, baked potato, and salad.

James looked up from his menu. "Do you always eat like that for lunch?"

"Only when you're paying."

"What the hell," James said, handing the menu back to Agnes. "I'll have the same." After Agnes left, James turned to Mahlon with a wicked smile on his face. "How did it go the other night?"

"I was going fine until you showed up."

James recoiled when he heard that. "What did I do?"

"Showed me her motorcycle."

"Oh, I see. And you went back inside and shot your mouth off about riding that damn thing in the rain. Right?"

Mahlon nodded. "Naturally, she took offense and went home."

"She's one fine looking lady, Thomas. You best get over to her house and apologize for being a pig-headed fool. Or somebody else will catch her eye."

"I tried to call her a couple of times."

"Well, put it on your agenda for this afternoon. So tell me what did this guy Sammy have to say."

"It's only a lead, Hank. Nothing more."

"I know. I know. What did he say?"

"He said the waitresses at Orbann's Lounge wear brown shoes."

James sat back and thought a minute. His eyes looked tired and the lines on his face were deeper.

"The owner won't like you nosing around his business. I'll tell you that."

"What are you saying?"

"He's been in the papers a lot recently. Wants to be our next freeholder. Says he'll lower taxes and do some other 'feel good' things like that. He's saying all the right things so he'll probably get elected."

James drank some of his water. "Isn't it funny how the voters always want better schools, better police protection, better roads, better everything, and lower taxes." The bitterness in his tone was hard to miss.

"I'll call you tonight with whatever else I can find. Woodson—" He broke off, as Agnes approached with their salads. James waited for her to leave before he went on.

"I told you about the Mayor and the Crime Report. Didn't I?"

"Yeah. What's happened?"

"The Mayor called just before I left. The Council, Sparbow in particular, is concerned about the increase in drug-related arrests over the last three years. The Mayor thinks it reaching epidemic proportions. He's right, too. The number has more than doubled."

James studied Mahlon's face a moment. "What the hell can I say? Every summer more and more 'shoobies' come down and—"

"More what?"

"Shoobies. Summer people. Day trippers. It's an old term from when the day trippers brought their lunches in shoe boxes. Anyway, they come with their kids, their pets, and, unfortunately, their vices. Naturally, the number of misdemeanors and felonies rises in the summer, but it's the off-season increases that have me worried."

He finished his salad before he went on. "Someone's pushing drugs and pot down the whole length of this island. It's even in the elementary schools. Can you beat that? And the Mayor's demanding that I do something about it." His voice rose in indignation. "This has got to be Woodson's doings."

"Maybe and maybe not. Don't let your paranoia carry you away, Hank." A spasm of anger crossed James' face. He opened his mouth to protest when Agnes showed up with their fish platters. He held his peace.

Several minutes went by while the men concentrated on eating. The fish flaked apart easily under the fork and was moist and tender in texture. It was cooked to perfection. Mahlon was digging another forkful of potato out of its skin when he finally broke the silence.

"On second thought, Hank, you got to do something, or the mayor will be looking to replace you."

James looked up from his plate and nodded. "I'm gonna call a meeting of the island chiefs and the county prosecutor. We got to get a handle on this off-season problem now and develop some strategies for the summer."

"It's a start." When the men finished eating, Agnes brought them coffee and their bill. James took it from her and set it by his cup. The lunch crowd was beginning to thin out.

"Solve this case, Thomas, or I'm done for sure." He looked at their bill and took out his wallet. "I'll phone you tonight with what I can get on Orbann." He dropped some money on the table. Before he could close his wallet, Mahlon reached over and plucked out another bill and dropped it on top of the others.

"I pay my informants well, Hank. Get used to it."

With his brow wrinkled in annoyance, James pocketed his wallet. "I'm gonna have to start moonlighting if this case goes on any longer."

Mahlon laughed. "You always were a tight one when it came to money. I've only been on the case a day and a half, and you're complaining already."

With a dismissive gesture, James walked away. After taking leave of Agnes, Mahlon followed him out. The fog had come down over the hotel and nearby shops like a damp gray sweater. When he got into his car, the dampness sent a slight chill up his back. It wasn't a day to be outdoors. Mahlon thought about what James had said concerning Sara. The man was right. He needed to apologize. Riding a motorcycle wasn't his idea of fun, but she wanted to do it, and he had to get used to the idea.

He rode the boulevard, keeping an eye out for Orbann's Lounge. The fog turned the pastel yellows and greens of the houses dingy looking and turned the lumber framing of new structures dark and raw. He spotted Orbann's Lounge in Brant Beach, noting its location in the wide, offset area beside the boulevard. It was a long stuccoed structure with a red roof and an arched entrance.

South of Beach Haven's business district, he turned west on Berkeley Avenue. The tennis courts at the yacht club looked wet and forlorn, and out on the bay Mordecai Island was just a long black smudge in the fog. Sara's house, a white Cape Cod, lay just a couple of blocks down West Avenue, and Mahlon began rehearsing his apology.

When Mahlon reached Sara's house, there was a light inside the front window where she had her office. He trotted up the front steps. The storm door had a small white sign fastened to it.

R&S Bath Houses
Business Office

Her old business had brought her so much unpleasantness in the end that he thought she'd rid herself of all reminders of it. Sara apparently didn't think so.

He took a deep breath and knuckled the storm door. A second later the inside door swung open and Sara appeared. When she saw who it was, she gave a polite smile and unhooked the storm door. Her red hair was tied back with a scarf that matched her long-sleeved blouse of creamy white silk. He wondered if she were going somewhere.

Mahlon opened the outside door and caught a whiff of light perfume. She looked and smelled wonderful. His first impulse was to take her in his arms, and he would have, too, but when she edged back to let him enter, he caught the movement of someone else in the room.

"Thomas, nice of you to come by," she said, her tone unenthusiastic. Mahlon sensed he was interrupting something. He turned to the other person. Who's this? A square-jawed young man stood with his elbow on the top of the white filing cabinet next to Sara's desk. Aviator glasses sat perched on his head, and he held a cardboard tube in his other hand. A trace of annoyance crossed his handsome face as he waited. Sara took a deep breath before she spoke, as though bracing herself for what was to come.

"Lew, I'd like you to meet Thomas Mahlon." Sara turned to watch Mahlon's reaction. Lew stepped forward with the quickness of a tennis player moving toward the net. He gripped Mahlon's hand firmly. The muscular forearms below the rolled sleeves of his blue shirt flexed. Mahlon held his own and let a big welcoming grin spread across his face.

"Lew Price is the golf course architect I told you about. He flew into Manahawkin yesterday afternoon. He's helping me design the layout of my course." She gave Lew a warm smile.

"That's great," Mahlon said. "Designing golf courses must keep you hopping." He looked at the blueprints on Sara's desk.

"It does, really," Lew said, laying the tube across the blueprints and flashing Mahlon a condescending smile. "I've a big project that will take me to Pittsburgh tomorrow evening." He mentioned the name of a promi-nent golf pro. "We'll be working together to design the toughest course in the country.

"This is my first go at miniatures, and I'm finding it a real challenge." Lew gazed fondly at Sara. A little too fondly for Mahlon's taste. "I couldn't pass up the chance to help Sara."

I'll bet, Mahlon thought, but he wasn't going to make a scene. Nosiree. Sara's cool welcome told him he was in the dog house, and he wasn't about to make things worse. Sara was nobody's fool. She could take care of herself. He came here to mend fences, and that's what he was going to do.

"Sara, I can see you're busy, but could I have a word with you in the kitchen?"

Sara looked at Lew. "Excuse us a moment, Lew." She moved away, avoiding eye contact with Mahlon. She wore gray herringbone slacks, and he savored the sensuous swing of her hips as she strode purposely toward the kitchen.

"You were right about those shoes," Mahlon said the moment they entered the room.

Sara turned, and her eyes narrowed defiantly when she saw him eyeing the dishes piled in the sink. Mahlon guessed Lew had spent the night there.

"Did you come by just to tell me that?" she asked, crossing her arms and resting her hip against the stove. He could see her steeling herself for what was to come.

He shook his head. "No. I've gotten us off to the wrong start since you came back, and I want to apologize. I know

I didn't sound like it, but I'm really not interested in running your life. I'm just worried about your safety. That's all."

She didn't say anything for the moment, but her body seemed to relax and she brought her arms down by her side.

"Thomas, I was riding motorcycles before I drove a car. Right after the war in Germany. Before we came here. Rudy taught me how to ride. We went all over the American Zone together. In all kinds of weather, too."

Mahlon raised his hands in surrender. "Ride what you want. You won't hear another word about it from me. Scout's honor."

Sara laid a hand on his arm. "I thought you were going to say something about Lew." She nodded toward the dishes. "About his staying over."

"Where else could he stay this time of year?" Mahlon asked. "Besides, if I know anything about you, it's that you can take care of yourself."

Sara nodded in appreciation. "I enjoyed the dinner the other night very much, you know." An impish smile played on her lips. "What a shame we never got to dessert."

She slid her arms around his neck and kissed him lightly on the lips. A hot wave swept into Mahlon's belly, and he wanted to crush her in his arms.

"I better run," he said with a thickening voice. "Another one of those and I'll be showing Mr. Price the door."

Sara laughed and moved away. "Well, Lew and I have a lot to do before he leaves tomorrow night. Think you can hold out till then?"

"It won't be easy."

Lew sat in one of the white rattan chairs on the living room half of the front room, thumbing through a magazine. He looked up. The mile-wide smile Mahlon wore brought a frown to his handsome face.

"Nice meeting you," Mahlon said as he opened the front door.

"Don't fall in any sand traps."

* * *

By four-thirty that afternoon the day came to a premature and gloomy end, and Mahlon had to turn on his desk lamp. A small fire popped and snapped in the fireplace behind him. He was getting his expense sheets in order so his accountant could do his taxes when the phone rang. He'd given his answering service the rest of the day off in case Sara called, so he picked it up on the first ring. He heard a click and whoever was on the other end hung up. Ten minutes later, it rang again.

"Mr. Mahlon?" It was a man's voice.

"You got him."

"Take my advice. Don't meddle in police affairs. You could lose your license."

Mahlon stiffened. "Who is this?" Click. The line went dead.

Chief James answered his office phone on the first ring.

"Working late, Hank?" Mahlon asked.

"Yeah. Well, Claire's out so I might as well catch up on paper work." He gave a short sigh. "What's on your mind?"

"Someone wants me off the case." He told James about the phone call.

"What do you make of it?" James asked. He sounded tired.

"Your friend is trying to put a scare into me."

"Sure as hell sounds like something Woodson would try."

"Did you get anything else on Orbann? I want to see him tomorrow."

"Orbann will have to wait," James said with a disgruntled sigh. "You better make a courtesy call on Chief 'Big John' Strickland at the Brant Beach Police Station."

"Why?"

"If you're going to meddle in 'police affairs' you better cover your ass and tell Strickland you're working in his district."

"What's he like?"

"He's got a very high opinion of himself. Just down play the whole thing and hope Woodson hasn't got the word out on you yet."

"Why?"

"Strickland's the kind of guy who does things by the numbers if only to impress you with the power he wields."

"Okay," Mahlon said. "I'll play it as a routine missing person case and avoid specifics when I can. What about Orbann?"

He could hear James shifting papers on his desk. "He's from North Jersey. Bought the lounge in the early sixties. It was the 'Rancho Grande Restaurant' then. Enlarged the bar, took out the dining tables, and installed a stage. A popular place for the young crowd in the summer."

"In other words, he's a business man," Mahlon said. "I'll make the usual civic duty pitch."

James chuckled. "It might not be that easy."

"Why not?"

"The man's an aspiring politician. I told you that this afternoon."

"Politician or not, I'll see him tomorrow right after Strickland."

"Good," James said. "But do me a favor, will you?"

"What's that?"

"Wear those new shoes. You'll impress the hell out of both of them."

Mahlon cut off his friend's laughter by hanging up. An idea just struck him. Before bedtime he'd take himself a little jog past Sara's and make sure Lew Price was behaving himself.

Chapter 14

White cinder blocks and a black roof edging gave the Brant Beach Municipal Building the same sober look shared by small town municipal buildings everywhere. The police station was found at the rear, and Mahlon parked facing the public tennis courts. Despite the stiff breeze from the northwest that had flags fluttering and snapping, two tennis fanatics volleyed and served with determi-nation.

An officer sat at a desk inside the door, a radio and micro-phone at his elbow. His manner was polite and professional.

"Can I help you?"

His eyes studied Mahlon's face and person. He'll know me next time, Mahlon thought. The man's alertness spoke well for his superiors and the type of performance they demanded from their men. Routine tasks undermine an officer's vigilance faster than anything else. Mahlon gave his name and said he wanted to speak to Chief Strickland on routine business.

"Have you an appointment, sir?"

"No, but I only need a few minutes of his time. The Chief won't mind setting aside his Monthly Commissioner's Report for a moment or two. I'm willing to wait."

The officer looked at him a moment before he picked up the phone. "Mrs. Karmarz, a Mr. Thomas Mahlon is here requesting to see the Chief. Can you fit him in?" He listened a moment and then looked at Mahlon. "He can see you in fifteen or twenty minutes. Do you care to wait?"

Mahlon nodded, and the officer pointed toward a door and told him to enter.

Mrs. Karmarz, gray haired and efficient, smiled pleasantly when he entered the room. "The Chief will see you shortly. He has a full schedule this morning but I managed to slip you in." She gave an engagement calendar on her desk a tap with her pencil to emphasize her point.

He thanked her and took a seat. A brass lamp stood on a small table at his elbow. A longer table to the right of the secretary's desk held several stacks of magazines.

The phone rang and the woman lifted the receiver. "Yes, Chief Strickland, I'll be right in." She picked up her steno pad and went into Strickland's office.

Mahlon rose and stepped to the table. The magazines were national and regional law enforcement publications. Not necessarily the kind of reading Mahlon was in the mood for. On returning to his chair, he happened to glance at the open engagement calendar on the secretary's desk. The day's date was in the upper corner of the page, and the lines below it were all blank.

Ten minutes passed before the secretary beckoned him into the Chief's office. Strickland sat behind an enormous red oak desk that must have cost a fortune. Only two objects were visible on its polished top, a white designer phone and a graceful gold pen. Behind him hung silver-gray drapes that stretched from wall to wall. They matched the color of his styled gray hair.

Mahlon introduced himself. Strickland remained seated and regarded Mahlon with indifference.

"My schedule it busy. Let's get on with it. Shall we?"

He settled his big-boned torso back in his desk chair with the assurance of one who was used to giving orders and having them obeyed.

"I'm a private investigator working on a missing person case." Mahlon laid his State credentials on the desk. Strickland hardly gave them a glance. He gestured for Mahlon to sit in the chair to his left.

"And you expect us to help you?" Strickland asked in a sonorous voice. An amused smile appeared on his lips.

"No, just wanted you to know I'll be working in your district."

"Are you an outsider?"

Mahlon shook his head. "I own a home in Beach Haven."

"Where did you operate before that?" Strickland leaned forward, placing his manicured hands on the edge of the desk.

"I was a police lieutenant in Trenton."

"Well," Strickland said. "I ran one of the high rent precincts in New York City. Providing security for the likes of Henry Kissinger and Robert Kennedy was fascinating work. Someday, I'll put it all down in a book."

He checked the wafer-thin watch on his wrist. "I want a weekly progress report. If I don't get it, we'll pull you in. Understand? Your appearance will be duly noted in the day book. Now, I must get back to work."

It had gone easier than he expected, Mahlon thought as he left the room. The weekly reports would be a pain, but something about the meeting struck him as curious. Not once did Strickland call him by name.

* * *

The long beige building that was Orbann's Lounge appeared ahead on the right. Mahlon pulled onto the parallel street in front of it that was separated from the boule-vard by a narrow grass strip. One of the last vestiges of the island's old rail line, the area provided valuable parking space for nearby businesses during the summer.

The only remaining sign of "Rancho Grande" in the decor of the lounge was the wide rounded arch of the entrance and the massive wooden doors. "ORBANN'S LOUNGE" was spelled out in square brown letters high on the smooth stuccoed wall where Mahlon imagined the phony roof poles once were.

He found a parking space near the entrance. The sun felt good when he stepped from the car, and he wished he were going for a jog instead of indoors. A poster on the side wall of the entrance arch shouted at him in Day-Glo orange lettering. It heralded the triumphal return of "Rickie Gee," who was "coming home to the place where his rise to stardom began." Never too early to advertise a cultural event of that magnitude.

Behind the massive doors was a huge windowless hall with a high black ceiling. A large oval-shaped bar took up the middle portion of the floor. When his eyes adjusted to the low lighting, he saw that only one section of bar was open to noontime customers. He walked over and took a seat.

"What'll it be?" the middle-aged bartender asked while he wiped the wooden bar top in front of him.

"A bite of lunch, a few beers, and a word with Mr. Orbann in that order."

"I can take care of the first two, but you'll have to clear the last item with Mr. Chance. He'll be down shortly."

"Fine."

"The waitress just stepped into the kitchen. We only serve sandwiches. I'll send her over when she comes back. What's your poison?"

"Beer."

"Bottled is all we got. Name it."

"Molson" was Mahlon's poison of the day. After he dropped his money on the bar, he sized the place up. A dozen old men who had fled the spring sunshine for comforts of the liquid sort were watching a TV above the bottle display behind the bar. Mahlon estimated the oval-shaped bar could serve at least fifty customers. Along the walls stood small cocktail tables for those who preferred to do their drinking tete-a-tete. In the shadows at the far end, Mahlon spotted the stage. There was plenty of open space around the bar and the stage for those who like to do their drinking standing up.

A young platinum blond in a mocha brown waitress outfit and crisp white apron appeared at his side. He ordered a tuna melt and fries, and she gave an auto-matic smile and left. He noted with relief the brown shoes on her feet.

She returned ten minutes later and set his order in front of him. While he picked up some bills from the pile on the bar, he asked her a question. "Where do you buy your work shoes, Miss?"

"Sammy's Shoe Shop in Manahawkin. Why?"

"Just asking." He handed her the money.

She started to fish his change out of her apron pocket, but Mahlon waved it away. She smiled her appreciation and glanced down at her shoes. "You have to be on your guard with Sammy, though."

"How's that?"

"Last time I was there, he sold me a pair of cowboy boots." She started to giggle. "But I tell you, Mister, they're comfortable as hell."

"Know what you mean." Mahlon held out his shoe for her to see. "Bought 'em this week. Courtesy of Sammy the Shoe." She chuckled and moved onto a new customer.

Mahlon ate his lunch. When he set his empty bottle on the bar, the bartender appeared before him.

"Refill?"

"Yeah. You give good service."

"Day times are easy. Stop in some weekend in the summer. Takes fifteen bartenders to keep the bottle beer coming. Mr. O. says empties on the bar make nobody rich." The man glanced at the other customers looking for another chance to make Orbann some money.

"You said my request to see Mr. Orbann has to go through Mr. Chance. What is he? Orbann's social secretary?"

The bartender laughed like Mahlon had told him a joke.
"Hell, no. It's just nobody gets upstairs without his okay."

"Upstairs?"

"Yeah, Mr. O. lives in the penthouse." He gave another
glance up the bar. "Mr. Chance looks like a business man,
but he's run some pretty tough customers out of here faster
than you can make a ring with that bottle. When he shows
up, I'll send him your way." The bartender strode off to
uncap another beer.

When Mahlon finished his sandwich, the clock on the
far wall read twelve-thirty, but he guessed it was ten minutes
fast like all bar clocks. He nursed the last of his beer, not
caring to enrich Orbann's pocket. Then he remembered
James was paying the bill, so he drained the bottle and set it
before him. Less than a minute later, it was replaced. His
respect for Orbann operation increased.

Shortly after one, the bartender leaned across the bar
to speak to a dark haired man, who looked in Mahlon's
direction. When their talk ended, the man started toward
him. He carried his wide-shouldered body with the
nonchalance of an athlete entering a game. Beneath the
muscled bulges of his light green three-piece suit, Mahlon
recognized the slab-hard body of a fullback out for another
routine blocking assignment. The man's massive forehead
tapered down to an aggressive chin, and his nose fell
crookedly between two dark appraising eyes. He stopped a
few steps behind Mahlon's stool.

"You want to see Mr. Orbann?"

Mahlon swung around to face him and immediately
realized the move left his feet dangling. A bouncer's trick
which hampered aggressive moves by unruly customers.

"Mr. Chance, I take it." Chance nodded, a sneer curling
the corners of his mouth.

"You selling something? Mr. O.'s got no time for stuff
like that."

"No."

"He don't give to charities, either, unless they're for the island."

"I'm not after money."

"You're not selling and you're not begging. What are you after?"

"I want to ask Mr. Orbann about a waitress who worked here three summers ago."

"Mr. O.'s a busy man," Chance said by way of dismissal. "He ain't got time to waste talking about a waitress."

"I'd like to hear that from him," Mahlon said. He started to leave the stool, when Chance pushed his legs to one side. Mahlon spun sideways, and strong hands gripped both his arms and forced his upper body in the opposite direction, pinning him against the bar. Chance thrust his face close to Mahlon's.

"I'm saying you don't," Chance explained needlessly. Mahlon had already gotten the message.

"Always this nice to lunchtime customers?" Mahlon asked with a grimace.

"Chance, what's going on here?" A voice reached them over Chance's shoulder. The man eased his grip and stepped away, positioning himself where he could still keep an eye on Mahlon.

"This guy won't take 'no' for an answer, Mr. O. I was persuading him to think otherwise." Chance spoke to a man who stood at the open door of an enclosed stairway on the back wall of the room.

"Mr. Orbann, I want to ask you about a former waitress," Mahlon said, massaging his leg. "Your social secretary here decided to serve me up for lunch." Chance's face showed neither anger nor exertion. He just waited like a well-trained watchdog waiting for his next command. What was a man with his talents doing in a shore resort town?

"See to your other duties, Mr. Chance. I'll speak to him."

Mahlon slipped off the stool and walked to Orbann. The other customers followed him with their heads for a curious second or two and then went back to their drinks.

"Now, what's this about a waitress? Are you working a divorce case?"

"Nothing as simple as that," Mahlon said as he approached the stairway. "Could we talk in private?"

"I'm pressed for time, Mr.— What did you say your name was?"

"Mr. Chance never got to that question. Thomas Mahlon's my name." He extended his hand and Orbann shook it.

"Follow me." Orbann turned and led the way upstairs. He wore an open-necked sport shirt of purple silk. Following right behind, Mahlon noted Orbann's expensive shoes. At the top of the stairs, Orbann opened the door to an office that stood on the right of a short hallway. A Japanese scroll painting hanging on the wall. Orbann seated himself behind the desk before he spoke.

"I'd like to explain something, Mr. Mahlon. An establishment like this attracts all sorts. Mr. Chance keeps the peace here, as it were." Orbann smiled at his own choice of words. "Occasionally, he gets too enthusiastic, but you appear to be uninjured."

Mahlon rubbed his leg and nodded.

"Good. What is the purpose of your visit?"

"I'm a private investigator, and I'm doing some footwork for an old friend." Mahlon slid his credentials across the desk to Orbann. "It's a missing person case, and I have reason to believe she may have worked here three summers ago."

"What exactly do you want?" Orbann had a receding hairline, and his tightly curled brown hair dropped in full sideburns to the bottom of his earlobes. His face was dominated by white even teeth and dark arching eyebrows that lent his features an air of amused disdain.

"I was hoping," Mahlon said, "that you could give me a list of the waitresses who left your employment abruptly. Say from May through September of 1970 and 1971."

"Girls come and go every summer. Perhaps you could tell me the name of this missing girl."

Mahlon hesitated.

"Come, come, Mr. Mahlon. I'm a busy man. I assume you're reticent out of some desire to protect your client. Is that it?"

"I said the girl was missing." Mahlon leaned forward. "That's not exactly true. She was missing until last month when I found her remains in the dunes near Barnegat Light."

Orbann's face blanched slightly. "Murdered in the dunes?"

"That's right. On the police records she's listed as Jane Doe. I'm trying to help a good friend identify her."

Orbann wore a disconcerted look. He stood up.

"I must tell Mr. Chance something. Your little contretemps with Charles made me forget it." He started for the door. "I'll be back in a moment. Help yourself to a drink. The liquor cabinet is over there." He pointed to a handsome black lacquered cabinet under the window.

Mahlon rose and went to the cabinet and admired its oriental beauty. He parted the curtains above the cabinet and looked out. Beyond sun-drenched house tops lay olive green waters and a blue horizon lightly skirted with clouds.

He opened the cabinet and helped himself to ice and club soda. Orbann's steps on the stairs reached Mahlon, and he turned to face the door.

"Good, you've made yourself a drink," Orbann said upon entering.

Mahlon reseated himself and took a sip of his drink. "Will you help me?"

"Let me explain something," Orbann said as he sat behind the desk. "No businessman is anxious to open his records to a complete stranger. I have a duty to protect the privacy of my employees. Furthermore, to put it bluntly, what's in it for me? A rather selfish attitude, you think, but the man who gives and gets nothing in return is a fool."

"I'm sorry you see this as a business transaction," Mahlon said. "When it comes to murder, people don't usually think in terms of profit and loss."

"Have you always been a private investigator?"

"No, I used to be a cop."

"You won't believe this," Orbann said as a smile crossed his face, "but we do have something in common. I served with the army CID in Japan during the Korean War. Spent almost three years investigating murders and thefts among the enlisted breed over there. My experience taught me one important lesson. Don't meddle in someone else's trouble because it may soon become your own." He sank back in his chair. "I'm sorry someone murdered this Jane Doe, as you call her, but until you convince me otherwise, my business records will remain closed."

"Would a subpoena convince you otherwise?" Mahlon asked grimly.

"Subpoena?" Orbann gave a short laugh. "Where would you get such a thing?"

Mahlon stood. "We'll see," he said and left the room and went down the steps.

In the dim light of the hall below, elderly men watched the preseason game from Florida. Their money and drinks lay before them like a solitary repast. Something incongruous about the scene struck Mahlon. These old, worn threads of Brant Beach's senior citizenry looked out of place in Orbann's nightspot. Apparently, the man's money machine could cruise along all summer on a diet of tall drinks, loud rock, and rampant sex among the single and not-so-single set and limp through the off-season on the pocket change of pensioners. All arguments among them, no doubt, were refereed by Mr. Chance.

Mahlon drove away from Orbann's Lounge in search of a pay phone. He knew how he could get what he wanted, but it would take a meeting between his friend Del Shannon and Hank James to get it done. What he didn't know was how willing Hank would be to talk to the press.

Chapter 15

The sun had almost set by the time Chief James showed up. The crunch of tires on the gravel outside brought Mahlon to the door. He took his friend's coat and hat, and James went over to the couch and flopped down. Rubbing the exhaustion from his face, James waited a long moment before he spoke.

"So how did things go?"

"Well, I saw Strickland this morning," Mahlon said, standing over his friend. "Kept me cooling my heels for over fifteen minutes while his secretary squeezed me in. The only squeezing she did was to write my name between the empty lines on his appointment calendar." Mahlon told him the details of the meeting.

When he reached the end, Mahlon shrugged. "So I send him a report every week. God! The man's ego is enormous."

"Reminds me of someone," James said, stifling a yawn. "Remember that village outside Falaise? The one where we spent the night in the wine cellar."

"Yeah." Mahlon grinned at the recollection. "My head ached the whole next day."

"Right. When we were moving out, the Frenchies were having a commotion. The elected officials were all dead, and the town hall janitor proclaimed himself the new mayor. He was strutting around in a tricolor sash shouting at everybody. The townspeople just shook their heads and ignored him. Lt. Williams came by, and I filled him in. Remember him, the Yale guy?"

"Yeah."

"The lieutenant watched for a moment and said something in French. 'What's that,' I say. So he says it again. 'Folly de grander,' or something like that. He said it's a craziness that makes people think they're more important than they really are. 'Big John' Strickland sounds like he got bit in the ass by the same bug."

Mahlon laughed and nodded. "How right you are."

"So what about Orbann, but don't tell me how much it cost. I don't get paid until next week."

"Then neither will I." Mahlon pulled over his desk chair and sat. He took a deep breath and went on.

"We got a problem, Hank."

"A problem?" James shot upright on the couch. The lines of strain around his eyes looked deeper. "What kind a problem?"

"Now, don't panic. I know someone who can help us."

"Who?"

"I'm expecting Del Shannon any second."

"The newspaper reporter?" James shouted. "Are you crazy?"

"Let me explain what happened, will you?"

With a scowl, James folded his arms and sank back in the couch. Mahlon gave him the run down on his encounter with Chance and Orbann's refusal to cooperate.

"How are we gonna get a subpoena, Thomas?"

"We don't need one. I just said that. He's running for office, right? We can pressure him, and Del Shannon will help us do it."

"And I'm supposed to tell her I hired a private investigator to do my police work?" James shook his head. "No way. I'm not doing it."

"Better the papers hear it from you. After that call last night, who knows what twisted story Woodson is cooking up?"

James grimaced and nodded reluctantly. At that moment, a car crunched to a stop in the front yard. His head snapped in the direction of the sound. A second later a car door slammed. Mahlon got to his feet.

"What'll it be, Hank?"

James waved Mahlon toward the door. "What the hell," he said, his face twisted in disgust.

The porch door opened, and by the time Mahlon reached the front door, the inside handle was turning. Del Shannon stepped in, the miniskirt of her dark green business outfit showing more leg than Mahlon ever dreamed she had. Under the brunette bangs of her page boy her dark eyes twinkled with humor.

"I tell you, Mahlon, you know how to break a girl's heart," she said, punching him playfully in the arm.

"What are you talking about, Del?" Mahlon was unable to keep from laughing.

"I finally get an invite to this place, and you got a cop car parked out front." She cocked her brunette head and put a hand to his bearded cheek. "When's it gonna be just you and me?" Her pert mouth curled in a sly smile, and she gave his beard a playful tug.

"I know. I know," she said as she pushed past him. "There isn't any 'you and me.'"

"Del Shannon," Mahlon said, "this is my good friend, Chief James of Barnegat Light." She strutted over to where James was standing and shook hands.

"Since this isn't a love tryst," Del said, turning back toward Mahlon, "what did you drag me out here for?"

Mahlon grinned and motioned both of them to sit. Del claimed a seat on the couch opposite James and crossed her shapely legs.

"Hank and I need your help." Mahlon explained that he'd been helping Hank identify the body found in the dunes last month. Hank chimed in with an explanation about how the hunt for the sex maniac on the mainland had the County detectives all tied up.

"I wanted the investigation to go forward," James said matter-of-factly. "So I asked Thomas, here, to take it up."

Del reached down into her purse and pulled out her note pad.

"Is all this off the record?" she asked.

"No," James said, "I want the community to know that this murder has not gone uninvestigated."

"Can I quote you on that?"

"Certainly."

"You could have called this into the news desk. Why didn't you?" Her leg bounced all the time she talked, and Mahlon had trouble keeping his eyes elsewhere. The effect wasn't lost on Del.

"Our investigation has hit a snag," Mahlon said, and he explained how he traced the victim's shoes to Orbann's Lounge. "Our problem now is that Orbann won't let us see his employee records for that summer. He's protecting his employees' privacy."

"And you want me to make that known, so our Freeholder candidate is pressured to cooperate. Right?"

Mahlon grinned at James and said, "Damn, Hank. She's got looks and brains, too."

Del reached over and swatted him with her note pad. "For all the good they do me with you."

"If you think it's newsworthy," James said, "and doesn't violate your professional ethics. Yeah, we'd like you to run that."

Del thought it over for a moment, her leg bobbing away the whole time. "Okay," she said finally. "I know you haven't told me the whole story, but it isn't every day that a police department hires a private detective to do its investigation. That's more than newsworthy. The facts about the shoe being traced to Orbann's Lounge and your belief that Candidate Orbann will be forthcoming shortly will just be a report on your progress to date. How's that sound?"

James looked at Mahlon, and they both nodded their heads.

"Of course," Del said. "I want an inside line on the rest of the investigation. You know that, don't you?"

Mahlon raised his eyebrows and smiled. "Would a weekly progress report keep you happy?" James stifled a laugh.

Del looked at Mahlon suspiciously. "Why do I have the feeling you two are setting me up?"

"It's an inside joke, Miss Shannon," James said as he got to his feet. "I better be heading home, Thomas." He went to the coatrack.

"For a man who's about to be in the spotlight," Del said to James, "you're awful calm."

"If it will help find the killer of that woman, I can put up with it." James slipped on his uniform coat and set his officer's cap on his head.

"Oh, I wasn't talking about this," Del said, waving her note pad. "I heard this morning that Orbann's worked a new wrinkle into his campaign."

James looked at her in surprise. "What's it got·to do with me?"

"He's about to announce a new campaign issue. Law enforcement authorities are not doing enough about drugs and violence on the island. He's named Barnegat Light as one of the three island locations where drugs and assault statistics are up."

James's face went ashen, and he looked about wildly. Mahlon was at his side instantly.

"That son-of-a . . ."

"Don't say it, Hank." Mahlon gripped his friend's arm, spun him around, and shoved him out the door.

"She's got one story, Hank. Don't give her another."

James, muttering a stream of obscenities, wrenched free of Mahlon's grip and began pacing the porch like a caged animal. He pounded his fist into the palm of his hand a couple of times. More than a minute passed before he calmed down enough to nod his head. Without another word, he went out the door, letting it slam behind him.

"Don't do anything foolish, Hank," Mahlon called after him.

James backed the big patrol car out of the yard and smoked a yard or two of macadam as he sped away. The acrid smell of burnt rubber chased Mahlon back into the house.

Del still sat on the couch. "I didn't exactly make his day, did I?"

"He's under a lot of pressure," Mahlon said as he put his desk chair back where it belonged.

"You and that bath house lady still an item?"

"Sara's sold the bath house. She's the miniature golf course lady now."

Del stuck her note pad back into her purse and got to her feet. "Why do I always fall for guys who are taken?" She stood looking at him, waiting for him to say something.

"I can't answer that," Mahlon said. "The only thing I know is you're a good friend."

"Good friend, huh?" Del marched over to the door and opened it. Mahlon followed her. They stood opposite each other in the open doorway.

"I hope your golf course lady knows what she's got."

Mahlon didn't say anything. He just smiled.

Del slung her bag over her shoulder. Taking hold of the open neck of his shirt with both hands, she pulled his face to hers and kissed him.

"That's a deposit that will be returned with interest," she said with a rueful smile, "if she's crazy enough to let you go."

Mahlon opened the porch door. Del was about to step out when she hesitated. She pointed to his front yard.

"You've got company, Mahlon. No, wait. It's just someone turning around."

Mahlon looked past Del's retreating figure at the car backing into the street. It wasn't until it began to move away that he recognized it was Sara's car. He ran out into the yard, but she was gone before he could stop her.

He stood there scratching his head. Why didn't she come in?

Instantly, he knew the answer. She'd seen Del kissing him. Lately, when it came to Sara, if he didn't have bad luck, he'd have no luck at all.

Chapter 16

A luncheon speaking engagement and a long meeting with his campaign manager kept Stephen Orbann on the run most of the following Wednesday. He returned to the lounge just after five, checked the day's receipts in the one register in use, and went up to the penthouse. In the upper hallway, he exchanged Italian leather shoes for straw sandals. The embellished parchment door to his "yuhi" or sunset room slid aside with a slight hiss. The drapes on the large picture window were still drawn, but the room was still suffused with light.

"Good," Orbann said aloud when he saw that the flower arrangement in the "tokonoma" had been changed. The alcove hung on the north wall beneath an Amano woodcut print. A small pile of newspapers rested on the arm of the solitary chair in the room. He needed time to unwind and enjoy the sunset before he tackled them. Afternoon sunlight filtered through the delicate greens and browns that adorned the silk drapes.

At the black lacquered cabinet to the left of the doorway, he poured himself a Glenlivet and water. With glass in hand, he stepped to the window and opened the curtains. Over the mainland, thin cirrus clouds burned a bright lemon-yellow that lit the delicate bamboo pattern on the walls of his room with a warm glow. The edge of the horizon was just beginning to bleed to a deep pink, but the tops of two bronze sculp-tures floating on the white sand carpet still glowed with a golden hue.

Sipping his Scotch, Orbann nodded his approval of the room for the hundredth time. The pristine carpet, the solitary chair (no one else ever used the room), and the sculptures captured something of the tranquility of the formal gardens he had loved so much in Japan.

When the light in the western sky began to dim, Orbann turned to his chair to catch up with the island news. He had launched his antidrug campaign with a press conference on Monday, and he was eager to see how the papers reacted to it. A headline on the front page of the Beach Haven *Times* interrupted his search.

> MURDER PROBE STYMIED
> Barnegat Light - County efforts
> to nab child molester has forced
> Barnegat Light Police Chief Henry
> James to improvise . . .

The story carried over to a back page, and Orbann read it all carefully. Chief James' summation of the investigation to date brought a scowl to his face.

He set the paper down when he finished the article. The private detective was more resourceful than he expected. The man had called his hand, and there was nothing to do but show his cards. Orbann rose from his chair and closed the drapes against the darkening sky on his way out of the room.

Information gave him Mr. Mahlon's number, and he dialed it. As though he was awaiting the call, the man answered the phone on the first ring.

"This is Stephen Orbann."

"What can I do for you?" the private detective said, the note of triumph in his voice painfully obvious.

"The question is what can I do for you? My employment records are at your disposal. Can you stop by tonight before nine?"

"I'll be there in an hour," Mahlon said.

"No. I need time to get them ready. Make it after eight."

Orbann put down the phone and went downstairs to the business office. It took him two minutes to locate the files in question and the one for the year before and after it. The list of names would be scrupulously accurate. That's not all it would be. It took Orbann forty-five minutes to put the information in the form he wanted. He was not a very fast typist. When the task was completed, Orbann felt better and went to the kitchen and prepared himself a light supper.

Eight o'clock found him back in the business office. He had changed into brown leisure slacks and an open neck body shirt of burnt orange with full sleeves. He sat at the desk which was bare except for the Beach Haven Times. The office door was open enough to give him a view of the bar. The television behind it was showing a rerun of Archie Bunker and his dingbat wife Edith. Two men in denim construction clothes sat by themselves nursing their bottled beer and exchanging tired looks. A man and his woman at the near end sat with their legs touching and heads bent in that oblivious absorption only lovers know.

When the private detective entered, the bartender approached him with the lassitude of one who knows the night will be endless, as only Wednesday nights can be. Orbann made a mental note to reprehend the man. Mr. Mahlon spoke, and the bartender, stifling a yawn with the back of his hand, pointed toward the office door.

His visitor knocked twice before entering the room. Orbann made a show of looking relaxed. He crossed his legs with the unmindful ease of a slender man and let his arms rest on the arms of his chair. He motioned to the private detective to sit and studied him a moment before he spoke. When he finally spoke, it was in a mock newscaster's voice.

"Chief James believes that the victim may have worked at Orbann's Lounge prior to her murder. The popular nightspot is owned by Stephen Orbann who is currently the Republican candidate for Ocean County Freeholder."

Orbann nodded his head in tribute. "You surprise me, Mr. Mahlon. It's not often someone gets the best of me so easily."

"You wanted to know what was in it for you, and I showed you."

"Yes, and all of Long Beach Island that cares to read it, too."

"Only we know what's involved in this little game of ours," the private detective said.

"Don't patronize me, Mr. Mahlon. What exactly do you want?"

"The names and addresses of all the waitresses who left your employment unexpectedly in the summers of 1970 and 1971."

"What do you mean by 'unexpectedly?'"

"If I'm not mistaken—" Mr. Mahlon seemed to sense he was being badgered but appeared unsure of its direction or intent. "—most young people take on a job for the entire summer. So any waitress who left before, say, the last week of August should be included."

"That's what I hoped you'd say." He pulled open the top drawer of the desk and removed a folder. "I prepared a list. I hope you find it satisfactory. My accountant's out of town and I had to compile it myself. He's better at this sort of thing." He extracted a single sheet from the folder, studied it a moment, and with a grin slid it across the desk to his visitor.

The private detective looked at the list and his eyebrows shot up in surprise.

"Something wrong, Mr. Mahlon?"

"I didn't expect thirty-two names."

"Take it or leave it. It's all the same to me." Orbann picked up the newspaper from his desk with two fingers and made a show of dropping it in the wastebasket.

His guest folded the list and slipped it into his coat pocket. He thanked Orbann and rose. When he got to the door, Orbann spoke.

"I'm an exacting employer, Mr. Mahlon. Many girls start the summer here but end it somewhere else. Do I make myself perfectly clear?"

His guest spoke to the door when he answered. "Perfectly clear, Mr. Orbann. Perfectly clear." Orbann's laughter followed him out of the room.

"That should keep him busy for a while," Orbann said to the empty room, and he started laughing again.

Chapter 17

The wet sand was firm underfoot, and for a change his bum knee hardly complained, but a lone gull on a nearby beach house greeted his jogging form with raucous laughter. The morning tide was out, and a solid gray bowl of clouds arched from horizon to horizon.

Mahlon pushed all thoughts of Sara and the list from his mind and focused on covering as much distance as his knee would allow. The weather report last night had called for a partly sunny morning. Missed it by a mile. He wondered if they'd have any better luck forecasting night fall.

Forty minutes later, he was back walking Pelham Avenue toward his house. The run had given him the lift he wanted. When he reached home, he saw two house finches skittering around the eave. Their clear warbling filled the yard as they built a nest on a ledge under the soffit. When they saw Mahlon, they sailed away, but a second later the male returned to give him the once over. He had a streaked brown coloring like a sparrow, and a head hooded in soft red that gave him a look of curious alertness. Mahlon knew the small birds usually returned to the same nesting site every spring. It was something to look forward to, Mahlon thought. Their intrusion on his day was a reminder of just how long it had been since he'd been birding. Too long, that's for sure.

Before he undressed for the shower, he switched on the Faberware pot on the kitchen counter, and the aroma of brewing coffee followed him into the bedroom. He trimmed his beard with a scissors and cleaned up the neckline with shaving lather and a safety razor before he showered. Afterwards, he put on a blue plaid shirt, jeans, and loafers for his luncheon meeting with Chief James. Maybe the two of them could come up with some strategy for Orbann's list.

Mahlon took his first sip of steaming black coffee and heard someone knocking. He set his coffee mug down and went to the front door. Sara stood outside the porch on the walk. She wore pale green sweats and had her hair pulled back in a pony tail. Oh, oh, he thought, here it comes. Mahlon opened the door and invited her in.

"Care for a mug of coffee?" he asked.

"Thank you, Thomas," was all Sara said.

In the kitchen, Orbann's list still lay on the table where he had been working with it the night before. He pushed it aside and took down another mug and the sugar bowl for Sara. When he had poured her coffee and taken his seat across from her, he drew a deep breath and launched into an explanation of the other night.

"About what you saw the other—"

"You needn't explain," Sara said, cutting him off, "Miss Shannon called me last night and explained everything."

"She did?" His look of disbelief brought a small smile to Sara's face.

"Yes, she said she flirted and gave it her best, but you resisted her advances—" Sara paused. "—as usual."

Mahlon shook his head. "Del actually called you?"

"Yes, she did and apologized for causing trouble."

Mahlon couldn't help but laugh. "I'm glad she did. I was beginning to think we were jinxed. Del's a damn good reporter, and she's helped me a couple of times. When she comes on to me, I can't take her seriously. She not my type."

"What is your type, Thomas?"

He hesitated a second and grinned back at her. "Oh, I go for tall redheads with an independent streak. If you know any, tell 'em I'm available."

"Oh, you are, are you?" She reached over and slapped his arm. "You're not 'available' if I have anything to say about it. Too bad I've an appointment with the contractor in an hour or . . . " She broke off and began to blush.

"Or what?" Mahlon asked with a grin.

"Or," Sara said softly, "I'd put my mark on you good and proper, but that's something I don't want to rush."

"Whew," Mahlon said taking hold of her hand. "Is it the coffee, or is it getting hot in here?"

Sara pushed his hand away with a laugh. "So, where are you off to today?"

"I've a meeting with Hank." He told her about tracking the dead woman to Orbann's Lounge and how, thanks to Del's help, he got Orbann to hand over the list.

"But I completely forgot that fired waitresses leave unexpectedly, too. So the list is loaded with a lot of dead wood." He slid the paper across the table to her. "My problem now is how to narrow it down? And when I'm all done, she might not be on the list, after all."

Sara ran her eyes down the list and then gazed out the window in thought.

"I did a quick count last night. Eighteen live in Jersey, or at least they did three years ago. Six in Pennsylvania, and eight listed Long Beach Island as their address. Thirty-two women spread all over the place, and I got to weed them out as fast as I can."

"I assume," Sara said, "there's no harm in using our imagination to do this?" Mahlon shook his head and raised his hands as if to say, "Anything goes."

"One thing I learned early in the bath house business is that money always gets people's attention. Or the promise of money."

Mahlon put his elbows on the table and leaned forward in interest.

"What if some payroll irregularities at Orbann's Lounge just came to light? And these women have all been identified as former employees who may be due to receive some kind of refund."

"Yeah," Mahlon said. "Go on."

"But the accounting firm of Speilberg and Mahlon needs a current address. You could enclose a postcard for that purpose, and those that respond are still numbered among the living."

"You're a genius!" Mahlon stood and leaned across the table. Taking her head in both hands, he planted a kiss on her lips.

"I love the idea," he said and kissed her again, this time more passionately. Sara put her arms around his neck and returned the kiss. A moment later she was easing herself out of his arms.

"Tonight, Thomas. Let's save it for tonight." She gestured toward the door. "I do have to be going."

Mahlon made a sad face but came around the table and took her arm in his. Together they started toward the door.

"You know," he said, "something just occurred to me. Del was the woman your friend Lois saw me with last summer. The day I first knew I loved you. Now she's got us back together again."

Sara nodded but kept her thoughts to herself. When they got out on the porch, she faced him and looked into his eyes. "I don't know if I should tell you this," she said. "It might go to your head."

"Tell me what?"

"Del said you're one of the good ones, and if I was crazy enough to push you away, she'd be right back knocking on the door to your life."

"She said that, did she? I owe her a lot more than I thought."

Sara kissed him lightly on the lips. "Don't get too grateful, Thomas."

Chapter 18

Chief James entered the Long Beach Hotel dining room with the fury of a thunderstorm. His face was threatening, and his eyes forked lightening. When he reached the back table, he didn't remove the blue car coat he was wearing but just threw himself onto the chair, his hand and elbow booming against the table top like thunder. Heads turned, and James answered the looks with a belligerent stare of his own.

Thomas was nowhere in sight and that didn't improve James' disposition. He'd left his uniform coat and hat back at the station so he could get a drink. Pronto. Where was that waitress? Why the hell do they always hide when you need them?

He spotted Thomas trotting through the door a minute later with a manila folder in his hand. James looked away without raising a hand. Let 'im find his own way. Thomas wouldn't approve of his drinking, but did he care?

"Where's this waitress friend of yours?" he asked Thomas before the man had time to sit.

His friend slid into his seat and looked at him closely. "What's wrong, Hank?"

"I can't talk about it until I've had a drink."

Thomas looked him over. "You're still in uniform."

"Don't you think I damn well know that? Where's this Alice friend of yours?"

"Her name's Agnes."

"Whatever. I want a Manhattan. I ain't drunk one of them bastards in thirty years, but I'm having one today."

He thrust out his chin and waited to be challenged. "Make it double."

"A double?"

"Do I have to kick ass?"

"Right, a double." With a shake of his head, Thomas looked around. Agnes came out the kitchen door at that moment, and he waved to her. She waddled over to their table.

"Where you been, Hon?" she asked, smiling at him. "Why haven't you been around to see me sooner?"

"Agnes, my dear," Thomas said, giving her big arm a friendly pat, "duty has kept me from your side."

Agnes sighed. "You and all the other men in my life."

"Bring us a double Manhattan and a beer."

"Double, eh?" She shook her head as she wrote it down. With a sigh of long sufferance, Agnes went off to the bar. Neither man spoke until she returned and plopped the drinks down disgustedly.

"How about something to eat, Hank?" Thomas asked. James shrugged indifferently. "Two bowls of chili, Agnes."

Agnes dropped her hands to her sides in disbelief. "This ain't your corner diner, you know."

Thomas laughed. "Make it two cheese steaks and fries, then." James didn't care what he ordered. He just wanted to get to his drink.

She looked at the ceiling and began tapping her foot.

"That's not on the menu, either?" Thomas asked.

"I'd go with the crab cake special." Agnes' voice held a note of impatience.

"Okay, two orders then."

She jotted it down and left the table with her hands still down by her side. Thomas pushed the drink toward him. James removed the two maraschino cherries and set them in the ashtray. He took a large sip and grimaced at the syrupy sweetness of it. After his second swallow, James nodded toward the manila folder at Thomas' elbow. "Is that what this meeting's about?" Not that he really cared.

Thomas opened the folder and withdrew a paper, an envelope, and a postcard. With a frown, James took them from him. He stared at the envelope over. *Speilberg and Mahlon Accounting*

What the hell? When he saw the same thing on the front of the post-card, he dropped them on the table and gave Thomas a disgusted look.

"Is this your way of telling me you're going out of the P.I. business? 'Cause if it is, I don't appreciate it one bit."

"No, you idiot." Thomas's voice was low but sharp. "Just read the damn letter. What the hell's eating you, anyway?"

James ignored the question and looked down at the letter he was still holding in his hand. He took another drink before he read it.

> Dear Former Employee of Orbann's Lounge:
>
> A back audit of the Orbann Lounge account has revealed the possibility of some payroll irregularities. Our audit is almost complete, and you have been identified as a former employee who may be eligible for a refund.
>
> Please fill in you name and current address on the enclosed post card and mail it immediately. In the event you deserve a refund, a check for the correct sum will be mailed to your verified address.
>
> We urge promptness, as state statutes require us to complete this audit in the swiftest manner possible.
>
> Sincerely,

Feeling like a fool, he picked up the envelope again and noticed the notation "PLEASE FORWARD" in capital letters in the lower left corner and

Refund Information

Open Immediately!

in the lower right. He passed everything back to Mahlon, avoiding eye contact as he did. Folding his hands and propping them under his chin, he looked down into his drink. Anger burned inside him, but a sense of exhaustion was settling over him, too.

"Who's gonna answer that?" he asked. The sound of defeat in his voice was obvious, and he hated himself for feeling that way.

Thomas didn't answer him. The two of them sat listening to the voices around them. The steady clink of forks and knives against dinner plates rose from all directions.

"Does this mean," James asked, "that we're gonna sit around for the next week or two waiting for the mail to come in?"

Thomas gave him a long hard look. "You're right," he said flatly.

"How's that?"

"It's a half-assed idea." Thomas was looking around for Alice or whatever her name was. "Forget the whole thing."

"What? That's all you got to say?"

"I'll send you my bill and—"

That wasn't what James wanted to hear. He gripped Thomas by the arm to stop him from going on.

"What the hell are you, Thomas? A quitter?" The words exploded from him. "I never quit anything in my life, and I'm not starting now."

Thomas smiled and pulled his arm free.

"It'll work," James said, and he tossed down another mouthful of his Manhattan and grimaced. "Hell, it has to work." He raised his glass to eye level. "Even with good bourbon, it's a lousy drink."

Agnes appeared, and Thomas gathered up the letter and the other pieces and stuffed them back in the folder. As she was setting down their platters, she spotted the Manhattan sitting in front of James. She put a hand on her hip and turned to Thomas.

"What's the matter with Bashful. He can't order his own drink, or does he think I'm Snow White or something?" She spun on her heel and with a dignified toss of her head walked away.

Thomas thought it was funny, but James was annoyed. Why couldn't she just serve them and keep her mouth shut?

"It's inspired," Thomas said tapping the manila folder with his forefinger. "Sara came up with the idea. No one can resist the promise of money. Orbann's ex-waitresses will rip their envelopes open. As far as my sitting around waiting for the mail goes, I'm starting on the L.B.I. addresses this afternoon. How's that sound?"

James had his mouth filled with crab cake by this time, so he just nodded. While they ate, Thomas filled him in on last night's visit to Orbann's Lounge. James barely listened. It wasn't until they had finished eating, that Thomas finally got around to the question James knew he was dying to ask.

"What's got you so uptight, Hank?"

James took another swallow from his drink. "When I think about it, it makes me crazy."

"I can see that. It might help to talk about, though."

"You called this morning as I was about to go into my files for something. I keep my personal files locked."

"Personnel?"

"No, 'personal' as in mine. The drawer where I keep all my confidential reports, resumes, interview evaluations, and the like had been disturbed. Don't ask me how I know, I just do. I was in that drawer yesterday and everything was okay. This morning it looked as though someone had gone through it."

"Woodson?"

"That's just it. Woodson wasn't on duty last night. Patrolman Sanders was. Until today I'd trust him with my life. Damn it." James drained his glass. He was hardly aware of the taste. "Sanders is a very competent officer, though he chases the skirts a bit too much for my taste."

"So what's in the drawer?"

"Damn it, Thomas," James said, "let me tell the story. Yesterday afternoon, the copy machine was serviced. The repairman didn't finish until after my secretary was gone for the day. He reset the counter. I checked it this morning and three copies had been made."

"Maybe your secretary used it this morning."

James shook his head. "I asked her. She hadn't used it up to that time. Somebody made copies of papers from my confidential files. How the hell do you like that?"

"I don't," Thomas said. "What's in those files that could be used against you?"

James hesitated. "Nothing."

"Then why all the fuss, Hank?"

"I don't like having my privacy violated. That's all." James avoided meeting his friend's gaze. There were things in that file even his wife Clare didn't know.

He fished his wallet out of his pocket and paid the bill.

Thomas asked for money to pay the printer, and James dropped it on the table without a squawk. He felt listless. The last place he wanted to go was back to work. He could go home, but Clare would be there with her friends, prattling away. It was enough to drive a man over the edge. Outside the hotel, they said their goodbye under an overcast sky.

Chapter 19

The line at the post office was short, and after buying the postcards, Mahlon was back on the road heading for the causeway. He couldn't get Hank's missing file off his mind. Hank's refusal to reveal what was in it was bad news. If something didn't break in Hank's favor soon, Mahlon was afraid he'd do something desperate.

Early afternoon traffic shuttled over the causeway and onto Rte. 72 beneath thickening clouds that brought a dark-browed dreariness to the day. In Manahawkin he took the ramp down to Rte. 9 North, and a mile later, he spotted a bright yellow sign with red lettering.

LOGAN PRINTING

It stood in front of a one-story building that in a former life had been a gas station. He parked alongside the old service island in front. All that remained of the gas pumps were amputated pipes, anchoring bolts, and twists of wires, all severed just above the concrete platform.

Inside the gas station office a tall woman in her forties stood behind a yellow counter reading a newspaper. His arrival had apparently interrupted her afternoon reading. The face of the counter was decorated with bold red lettering:

LOGAN PRINTING
No job too small!
No deadline too short!

She wore a long-sleeved top covered with blue flowers. She hastily put the paper aside and a smile wrinkled the dark skin under her eyes. Beyond the open doorway to the old service bay on the left, a young man in his late teens sat at a layout table with his nose buried in a magazine.

"What can I do for you this afternoon?" she asked. She shot a nervous glance at her junior partner in the other room and shouted. "Joey, isn't the Billups' job ready to staple now?"

Joey sighed and dragged himself out of the chair and disappeared, giving Mahlon a glimpse of the magazine cover as he went. PLAYBOY. Researching staple placement in the centerfold, no doubt.

He set the pack of postcards on the counter, removed the letter and envelope from the folder, and explained what he wanted done. She showed him samples of paper stock and envelopes, and Mahlon made his choices. She named the price, and Mahlon gave her a deposit.

"When can I pick them up?"

The woman did some schedule calculations and said, "Tuesday morning all right?"

"I was hoping for later this afternoon."

"Well, I don't know."

"Your motto says, 'No deadline too short.'" Snap, snap went the stapling machine in the other room.

"Well, we'll have to put aside our other work."

Sure, Mahlon thought, the woman's page will have to wait until this evening. Snap, snap. Joey must be working up a sweat.

"Expedited work costs extra, you know," she said with a straight face. He noticed the pale black shadow of a mustache on her upper lip.

"How much?" Snap, snap.

"Twenty dollars. Payable in advance."

"What time do you close?"

"Six," she said. "We're on summer hours." Snap, snap.

He fished a twenty from his wallet, dropped it on the counter, and headed for the door when she was through modifying his bill of sale.

"Oh, mister," she called on his way out the door, "don't be late. We close on time."

Mahlon turned to acknowledge the advice and caught a glimpse of Joey in the other room. He was leaning against a back work table. One hand held the PLAYBOY while the other triggered the electric stapling machine with a piece of card stock.

"I'll be here," Mahlon said. He nodded toward the young man. "He shouldn't play with that machine. You might need it for a real job one of these days."

The woman blushed and started toward the workroom. Mahlon went out to his car. If he hurried, he had time enough to check one or two of the island addresses on Orbann's list.

* * *

The earlier promise of bad weather did not go unfulfilled. Before Mahlon reached Rte. 72, the rain started. The weather report on the local station said it would carry on into the night. When he reached Ship Bottom, he made a quick right off the causeway into the area abutting the east end of the bridge. The depressions in the gravel parking area gathered the rain like miniature catch basins. Mahlon avoided the larger puddles and brought the Plymouth to a stop on a stretch of gravel that stood above the rising water-line. The drops pelted the windshield as fast as his wipers could slap them off.

On his way out that morning, he'd put Orbann's list and a Chamber of Commerce map of the island in the folder. He got them out and underlined the LBI addresses with a ballpoint pen. Two were located in Harvey Cedars, two in Brant Beach, and there was one each in Barnegat Light, South Beach Haven, Ship Bottom, and Cedar Bonnet Island. Eight in all. Summer rental addresses most likely. Did

Orbann hold back their home addresses? Mahlon wouldn't put it past him. Anyway, the realtors should have them. Ship Bottom and Cedar Bonnet Island were the closest. He raised his eyes from the list and looked out on the bay. A boat channel stood between him and the south end of Cedar Bonnet Island, where the red and blue backs of the houses had turned gray in the falling rain. The name was Tammy May Durham and the address was on Second Street. The island was small. He should be able to find the house in no time. He returned the list to the folder and pulled the car out onto Shore Drive.

In no time at all he was back in the west-bound lane of the causeway. He crossed the short bridge to Cedar Bonnet Island and pulled off into The Dutchman's parking lot. The dark brown front of the restaurant stood at the right edge of the lot, blocking his view of the north side of the island. Partly screened by shrubs and trees and tucked under the causeway was the crossover to the south side of the island.

Wide enough for one vehicle and hemmed in by a rusting guard rail backed by a hurricane fence, the lane was like a cattle chute that led under the bridge connecting Cedar Bonnet to the island west of it. The crossing to the other side was regulated by a traffic light mounted high on a streetlight. Mahlon waited for the light to turn green and a moment later he was driving under the bridge. In the shadowy light he noticed that just the guard rail and the fence stood between the Plymouth and the choppy waters of the boat channel on his right.

On the other side, the lane veered left a short distance along the flank of the causeway, passed beneath a traffic light, and turned right. A sign identified the road as "First Street," and it widened to two lanes. Houses lined both sides, completely blocking any view of the nearby bay. Not that there was a whole lot to see out there today. He found Second Street one block over. A Cape Cod with a screened porch sat on one corner and a sand lot with a post and rope fence stood on the other.

He made the turn into Second Street and saw immediately the street had no outlet. Forty yards or so ahead of him rose the shrub-covered embankment of the causeway. He pulled over to the post and rope fence and stepped out into the steadily falling rain. The street had no sidewalks, so he hunched his shoulders against the cold touch of the rain and trotted down the middle of it, looking at the house numbers. On the causeway, trucks and cars shot past the end of the street, their tires zinging over the wet roadway.

The dark green house was a narrow one-story structure with a screened porch. It sat on the west side a few doors from the end. The screen door was missing, so Mahlon stepped up onto the porch to get out of the rain. His hair was wet and his beard dripped. Whoever took down the screen door hadn't carried it far. It lay propped against the green clapboard under the front window. One look made it clear why it had been taken down. The screening was gone from it entirely. He knocked loudly on a battered door panel and stepped back.

The door opened and a huge form on bare feet shuffled into view.

"What do you want?" The voice was hostile and its owner mountainous.

"Is Tammy May Durham home?"

"You from welfare?" With a sidestep the speaker oozed its stomach out the front door onto the porch, the boards sagging under the added weight. It was a woman wearing a bright green muumuu, a tent-sized, ratty looking thing that reeked of stale sweat.

"No, ma'am," he said as cheerily as he could.

She had no neck at all. Her head with its stringy blond hair sat atop the fat slope of her shoulders while the large pale moon of her sweaty face with encircling double chins studied him warily.

133

"Who's askin'?"

"Who is it, Ma?" called a young woman's voice from inside the house. A young child started to cry.

"Tammy?" Mahlon wanted to see who was speaking. The woman had other plans. One moment he was trying to get a peek in the door, and the next he found himself wrapped in her sweaty arms and hugged to her voluminous bosom.

He tried to push free, but her gelatinous body afforded him no purchase. The flesh just rolled away under his hands. She had the arms of a sumo wrestler. With a grunt she tightened her grip, and his head sank into the great rift between her breasts.

"Stay inside, Tammy May," she yelled. "I got this 'un all tidied up."

The unwashed smell of her gagged him. He had to break free. Then remembering her bare feet, he did the only thing he could, rammed his shoe into her bare toes as hard as he could.

The woman exploded like a bomb. Her arms flew out and her belly rose with enough force to send Mahlon, like he was shot from a cannon, back into the doorpost. She made a grab for her foot and started staggering like a one-legged hippo. Mahlon bounced off the doorpost right back into her. Over she went. Her backside hit the floor with a detonation that rocked the porch and rattled the window.

Mahlon managed to keep from falling on top of her. He backed away from the flailing form. It had all happened so fast. His head throbbed and his hip hurt. A young slovenly woman poked her head out the door, and a wet-nosed child stuck its head around the door frame.

"Ma, what's goin' on?"

"Tammy?" Mahlon asked through grimacing teeth.

"Yeah, what's it to you?" she said, with a belligerent look. Then she saw her mother rolling on the porch, and her eyes widened in shock.

"Nice meeting you," he said and turned to leave.

"Why, you . . . "

He didn't stay to hear the rest. Leaping from the porch, he started toward the car as fast as his ailing hip would let him, rubbing the sore spot on the back of his head as he went. The motor started on the first try, and he quickly reversed the car out of the street. His heart was still racing, and his hip complained. Damn! Verifying names can be hazardous work.

In Ship Bottom, he drove to the drugstore at 21st and the Boulevard to buy some aspirins. Back in the car, he shook three tablets out of the bottle and swallowed them. A check of the time showed it was almost four. His hair was wet and his clothing damp. He wanted to call it a day. A nice hot shower would feel great right about now, but he'd no sooner get home than he'd have to come back for the stuff at the printers. While he waited for his aches to subside, he opened the folder to check the Ship Bottom address. God, he hoped this one was easier.

The address turned out to be an aging one story bungalow on 25th Street opposite the municipal parking lot. It was one of those places college kids rent for the summer. A realtor's sign nailed to a wooden stake stood in front. The rain was coming down hard, and Mahlon remained in the car while he copied the realtor's address in his note-book.

The realtor's main office was just off the causeway below Barnegat Avenue. A middle-aged, heavyset man waited on him, and he looked at Mahlon's rain-soaked hair and damp clothes with some disdain. When Mahlon told him what he wanted, the man said it was out of the question. That was confidential information. Mahlon called Chief James and let Hank talk to him. With reluctance the realtor complied.

As Mahlon left the real estate office, he got to thinking he would need help addressing and stuffing the envelopes if he expected to get them in the mail first thing tomorrow.

He found a pay phone inside the QUARTER DECK, a grey, two-story restaurant/motel that was one of the first landmarks motorists saw as they approached the island over the causeway. Happy Hour was already in full swing, and women's laughter and voices carried out into the foyer where the phone was.

Sara answered on the first ring.

"You still want me to stop by this evening?"

She hesitated. "You're not going to stand me up, are you?"

"No, of course not."

"Good. I've just come in from the store with something for our supper."

"I called to ask if you have an hour to spare after supper."

"Thomas," she said in a voice just above a whisper, "I have a whole night."

With a grin that went from ear to ear, Mahlon turned away from the call box and rested his back against the wall. "I'm glad to hear that."

"I hope you are."

"But I need your help to stuff and address a couple of dozen envelopes first. Hank bought your idea about the payroll problem, and I need to get the letters in the mail tomorrow."

"I'll help."

"I've got to go to Manahawkin first and then shower." He looked at his watch. It was just after five. "I'll be knocking on your door by six-thirty."

"I'll be waiting."

Chapter 20

True to his word, Mahlon knocked on Sara's door at six-thirty that evening with a chilled bottle of chenin blanc in hand and the bulging manila envelope from the printer under his arm. Though the rain had stopped, the eave above the steps continued to drip, its wet licks cold against his face. When the door opened, he entered, glad to leave the chill and dampness behind. It wasn't until he closed the door and set the envelope and bottle on her desk that he got a look at Sara.

Her hair glowed with the soft light from the dining room fireplace, and the mandarin collar on her jade green dress made the slender whiteness of her neck very striking. There was a tantalizing glimpse of white visible beneath the silk where it was slit at her thigh. And her eyes were shining. The line of her cheek and mouth looked so enticing, his breath caught. He took her face in his hands and kissed her.

Sara's murmur of surrender set his heart beating in his ears. The kiss broke off, but they stood holding each other. Her perfume, a distillation both exotic and sensuous, worked its heady magic, and his mouth was back seeking hers again.

"Thomas," Sara said, when they came up for air, "this is wonderful, but our lovely dinner will burn if you don't set me free."

"We really have to eat, eh?"

She smiled. "There's work to be done. You'll need your stamina."

"Oh, I will, will I?"

Breaking free of his arms, she started toward the kitchen. "Yes, there's all those letters to fold and envelopes

137

to stuff." Her laughter carried over her shoulder as she disappeared from view.

Chuckling and shaking his head, Mahlon retrieved the wine bottle from the desk. The dining room table was set for two, and a crystal vase of yellow daffodils stood between white candles off to one side. The fire would soon need tending. He entered the kitchen in search of an opener.

Ten minutes later fresh logs were snapping and popping in the fireplace. At the table Mahlon and Sara toasted each other with the wine. While they ate, Mahlon described his afternoon misadventures with Tammy May Durham's mother and started Sara laughing. She apologized and tried to stop, but when she asked if he'd been hurt, her laughter started again, drowning out his denial. Mahlon suffered her mirth until she finally caught her breath.

"Can I go on?" he asked. She nodded and managed to control herself. "For someone whose eaten too many meals from a can, Sara, this one is magnificent. Burgundy vinaigrette on the salad. Asparagus in a mustard-lemon sauce, and filet of sole under lemon butter. You've outdone your-self."

Sara smiled with pleasure when he raised his glass to her again. He was about to tell her about the folder missing from Hank's file, when Sara gave a little jump in her seat as if she had just remembered something important.

"I meant to tell you this when you first came in, Thomas, but your greeting drove everything from my mind." Mahlon laughed.

"Lois Zaifman stopped by this afternoon."

"And what did that dear gossip have to say?"

Sara wrinkled her nose in displeasure. "Keep your snide remarks about my friends to yourself, or I won't tell you."

Mahlon raised his hands in surrender.

"She told me something about Chief James you might find interesting."

"Go on, I'm listening."

"I'm only reporting what she said. It doesn't mean I believe it." He nodded but didn't say anything.

"The rumor going around is that Chief James made his first wife so unhappy she took to drink."

First wife? Hank married before? That was news to him. "Anything's possible," he said. "Hank was no saint when I knew him in the army, but that's ancient history as far as I'm concerned."

"There's more," Sara said with a serious face. "They're also saying he couldn't stand being married to a drunk, so he used her weakness for alcohol to arrange the auto accident that killed her. Her insurance money bought his house."

"I'll be a son-of-a." He caught himself. "That's a vicious lie!" Mahlon put down his fork. He could feel the anger beginning to well up inside him.

"Lois' friend, Flo Sanders, swears it's true. She got it straight from her brother Greg who works for him. He claims there's a lot more going on up there than meets the eye. If it all comes out, his boss is history."

Mahlon scowled as he listened to her. Had Woodson pressured Sanders into doing this? Or was Sanders a willing participant? If so, why? Mahlon sat back and rubbed his bearded chin in frustration while he thought this over. A moment later he knew the answer: ambition.

"Yeah," Mahlon said, breaking his silence at last, "Hank will be history, all right, and Patrolman Sanders is doing everything he can to make sure it happens."

"What are you saying, Thomas?"

"Someone got into Hank's personal file while Sanders was on watch, and that someone was Sgt. Woodson. This rumor is his doing. Woodson wants to be chief, and my guess is that he promised Sanders his job if he helps him."

Mahlon fell silent again. It made sense. Hank had to be told, but Mahlon wanted to hear the story about his wife's death, first.

"Let's change the subject," Sara said in a worried voice. "I didn't mean to upset you, Thomas. That's the last thing I want to do tonight."

"Okay." He gave her a reassuring smile and cast around for another subject to talk about. "So, how are things going with the golf course?"

Relieved, Sara launched into an explanation of the headway she was making. Lew Price, as promised, had sent her a complete set of architect's drawings, and she had found a construction firm in Philly that specialized in projects of that sort.

"The land is undeveloped," she said, passing the vegetables, "so there's no demolition involved. Construction will start next week. Isn't that great?"

"Wonderful. But will you be open by Memorial Day?"

"I think I'll just make it."

"Great. I'm looking forward to playing the course."

Sara laughed. "Why, Thomas, I didn't know you played golf."

"You didn't?" he asked with a smile. "Why, I can slurp ice cream and putt a golf ball along with the best of them."

The image of him with an ice cream cone in one hand and a putter in the other tickled her. Her glee bubbled to the surface, giving Mahlon another chance to watch her lovely, laughing face.

"There's something I've been meaning to ask you," Sara said when she was herself again. "Don't get angry, now. That day you came and found Lew here. I was sure you were going to raise an awful row. You didn't. Why?"

Mahlon took a sip of wine before he answered. "And if I had? Would we be sharing this tonight?" He gestured at the table and fireplace.

Sara cocked her head before she answered. "Definitely not."

Mahlon nodded. "I knew I pushed all your wrong buttons over that motorcycle. The worst thing I could do

140

that day was make a scene. I kept telling myself Lew was just another friend, because if he were something more than that, you would have told me."

He rested his arms on the table and leaned toward her. "My dear, I've learned a lot about you this last year. You're honest to a fault, you do your own thinking, and you've too much pride to be that kind of woman."

Sara reached for his hand and gave it a squeeze. "Thank you, Thomas, for saying that."

They finished the meal and sat talking while the logs in the fireplace burned to a crimson heap and the pale wine dwindled.

Mahlon placed his hand over Sara's. "I'm hoping it's time for dessert." The gleam in his eye was unmistakable.

"Why, Thomas, you've forgotten. We have a table to clear, letters to fold, and envelopes to stuff." He made a wry face.

"The letters and envelopes were your idea," she said, her eyes sparkling with humor. "Remember?"

"Hoisted on my own petard," Mahlon said, pushing back from the table. He stood and began stacking the plates so he could carry them to the kitchen. When both his hands were full, she came to him and gave his white beard a playful tug.

"My after-hours secretarial services aren't cheap, but I'm sure we can think of some way you can repay me."

Chapter 21

Mahlon caught himself whistling on his way to the car from Sara's house the next morning, something he couldn't remember doing in years. He stood for a moment to take in the day. A northwest wind had cleared out the clouds, and the blue vaulted bay and faraway houses of Tuckerton seemed to stretch to infinity.

The nearest address on Orbann's list was in Beach Haven Manor, a mile or so to the south. Even with the map he had to stop at a Bait & Tackle shop to get directions. The address was in a bayside trailer court at the end of a horrible gravel road.

Puddles, murky brown with silt, rutted the entire road, and small dark-windowed cabins waited shoulder to shoulder to watch him splash past. The Plymouth would need a washing when the day was over. A huge pool of brown water lay across the entrance to the trailer park. Since the only way in was through it, he eased the front wheels into the water, hoping the unseen bottom held no surprises. When the tires were on dry land again, he stopped and looked around for the manager's office.

The center court, cratered and puddled, separated two lines of mobile homes, their wheels sunk deeply in weeds, corrugated bodies pitted from the salt air. In the gap where the two lines ended, the rusting corpse of a 1950 Dodge stood facing Little Egg Harbor Bay, waiting for burial at sea.

He spotted a small, sun-faded sign on the end of an old brown trailer in the middle of the left-hand line:

SUNSET TRAILER PARK
Rentals by Week or Season

An "Office" sign hung like a bandaged eyebrow over one of its windows. Mahlon turned the car around, spotted a reasonably dry stretch of ground, and parked.

Skirting puddles, Mahlon made his way to the trailer. Dents and scratches from past assaults scarred its aluminum door. Where the handle should have been, the round hole offered a short length of rope knotted at the end. Just above the hole was a hasp and staple for a padlock. He knocked twice.

The inside bolt slid aside, the door opened, and a bear of a man clad in a grimy T-shirt and ragged jeans looked out at him.

"We're not open, yet," he said through a mouthful of crooked teeth. He was in his early thirties. What little of the trailer's innards that Mahlon could see told him the bear feasted exclusively on fast food. Empty milk shake containers two and three deep stood on a narrow table beside the door. The top of the small metal desk just beyond the table held half a dozen white fast-food bags, neatly balled up and sitting in a row awaiting the afternoon maid.

"I need information on a former occupant," Mahlon said.

"Sure, and I need this week's lottery number," the Bear said with mock sympathy. His face was fleshy with heavy lidded eyes that squinted out at the bright morning light. An enormous mouth hung open as though the weight of the lower jaw was too much to hold up.

Mahlon thought he would try another approach. "I'm trying to identify a girl murdered up at Barnegat Light."

"Buddy, I don't know nothing about no dead girl. People die every day. What's it to me?" He gestured to show his lack of concern.

"Which leaves the living to earn a few bucks any way we can, right?" Mahlon said, knowing cooperation was always for sale with men like this. He gave the Bear a moment to think it over.

"Well, now that I think of it, maybe I can help," the Bear said as he moved aside. Mahlon entered the trailer and his nose was immediately assaulted by a mix of B.O. and spoiling food. He stopped just inside the open door and had everything he could do to keep from pinching his nose in disgust.

"So, how much is this info worth to you, buddy?" the Bear asked as he scuffed his way across the paper-strewn floor to his filing cabinet.

"How's ten dollars sound?"

The Bear laughed deeply. "My time ain't cheap. Twenty-five."

"Fifteen. That's as high as I go."

"Twenty."

"Forget it," Mahlon said. He turned to go. "I don't need it that bad."

"Fifteen it is. Drop the bills on the desk. I wanna see the color of your money."

Under a watchful eye, one by one Mahlon removed three fives from his wallet and dropped them atop the clutter of screwdrivers and lock parts spread across the desk top. Mahlon gave him the girl's name, and the Bear's immense hands and spatulate fingers began riffling through the file folders.

"It's here somewheres. I never throw nothin' out," the man said as he closed a drawer and opened another. "Might be worth somethin' some day."

Sure, Mahlon thought as he took a quick look around at the dirty hot plate across from him and the gray linen on the unmade bed behind the door. When the demand for refuse goes up, this place will be worth a million.

"Here it is," the Bear said as he fished the card out of the file. "She stayed here, all right, but anythin' else is gonna cost you another fifteen." A grin raised the drooping ends of his mouth. "Unless you got the cajones to take it from me."

"You got your fifteen."

"A finder's fee. What can I say?" He pulled a butane lighter from his pocket. "You don't pay, I don't read." He began flicking the lighter on and off.

The idea of letting this bum beat him out of another fifteen dollars was unthinkable. He had to do something, and what he spotted on the Bear's desk would come in handy if he left in a hurry.

"Okay," he said and withdrew a ten and a five from his wallet. "I don't want any trouble. Give me her home address and telephone number. I got to call her as soon as I can." He tossed the bills on top of the other money and put his wallet away. Taking out his notebook, he bent over the edge of the desk, prepared to write.

"What's the home address?" He copied it down as the Bear read it off. "And the phone number?"

"That'll cost fifteen more." The Bear held the card and lighter out in front of him.

"What the hell is this?" Mahlon asked angrily. He watched for the guy's reaction.

The Bear flicked the lighter and put the flame to a corner of the card. Mahlon made a lunge for it. The Bear laughed at him and spun out of reach, the now flaming card still in his hand. Mahlon's lunge missed by a mile. His right hand slapped down on the desk, grabbing two bills off the pile of money and snatching up the screwdriver at the same time.

The Bear saw his money go and roared. At the same instant the flames licked his finger tips. He flipped the card away and stuck the burnt fingers in his mouth.

As Mahlon slid out the door, he saw the burning card bounce off the filing cabinet and drop to the floor. His left hand grabbed the rope and yanked the door shut. Something thumped against it, and the rope slithered from his grasp. A hand slap put the hasp over the staple and the screwdriver fell in place. The Bear's finger appeared in the lock hole and he shook the door. The hasp held. By the time an angry roar issued from the trailer, Mahlon had leaped the puddles and got himself behind the wheel of his car.

A door in the opposite line of trailers flew open just as the motor fired. A dark complexioned man with tousled hair came out. By the time Mahlon got the car in gear, the man was trotting barefoot across his path toward the office trailer. His pockmarked Latin face glared at Mahlon in passing. A few seconds later the wheels entered the entrance puddle, and Mahlon glanced at his side mirror. Gray smoke poured from the trailer. He splashed through the water and pushed the Plymouth along the rutted road as fast as the suspension would allow.

Minutes later, he pulled into his front yard. The wail of a siren rose into the bright blue sky, summoning volunteer firemen to one small trailer fire. Mahlon stood in the yard and listened a minute. He felt a twinge of conscience and told himself the fire was the result of the Bear's larcenous soul and filthy living habits. After all, every life style has its inherent risks.

He stuck his hand into his pocket and pulled out two crumpled bills— a ten and a five. Well, that beat down the rising cost of information, but he sure as hell didn't need any more adventures like this.

The stuffed and addressed letters that were readied last night stayed in the car for mailing. He took one of the dozen or so unaddressed ones into the house. At his desk, he took a moment to write on it the address he'd just gotten. He removed Orbann's list from his pocket and studied it a moment. The next address was in Brant Beach, so back to the car he went.

Just then, the shrill wail of a fire engine roared past on the boulevard. He didn't expect there was much of the trailer left. The Bear and his Latino friend must be having a real fit right about now. It was a satisfying if not malicious thought.

* * *

Barnegat Avenue was a short street that ran parallel to the boulevard out by the bay. The house turned out to be a one-story Pullman, narrow and long as the name suggested. There was no visible realtor's sign. He hoped it wasn't shut up for the season, or it would be a dead end as far as his investigation was concerned. He could ask the neighbors, but only as a last resort. He pushed the doorbell.

A second later the sound of running feet approached, and the door swung open. A small boy with dark, curly hair, serious eyes, and a runny nose looked up at him.

"Does Myra Gunther live here?" Mahlon asked, leaning down to the lad. The boy, wearing blue overalls, grabbed the doorknobs and swung back and forth on the door, his knees raised to keep his feet off the floor. He stopped after two swings to wipe his runny nose on his sleeve.

"Does she?"

The lad faced Mahlon and delivered his words with the exaggerated importance every child with a message conveys.

"She can't talk now. She's on the toilet."

Mahlon turned away and smothered his laugh with his hand.

"Max," called a woman's voice from inside the house, "what did I tell you about opening the door to strangers?" The boy turned to watch the woman walk into view. As soon as she arrived, he ran back into the house.

"I'm trying to find Myra Gunther."

She looked to be about thirty. Black curly hair fell below her shoulders. Her drawn face carried a modest nose, full lips, and dark ravaged eyes. She wore voluminous black slacks and a red blouse.

"Who wants to see her?" Her no-nonsense tone was unmistakable.

Mahlon showed her his license and explained that he was trying to identify a murdered girl who may have worked for Orbann's Lounge.

"And you thought I was her?" Her eyes widened in disbelief. Mahlon nodded. "Well, I'm Myra. Would you like to tell me about it over a cup of tea?" The clunk of a falling chair and the wail of an injured child rang out from the depths of the house.

"Oh, my God." Myra raced back through to house. "Close the door after you," she said over her shoulder.

Closing the door behind him, Mahlon walked toward the rear of the house. The living room's black and white TV carried some children's show that his visit must have interrupted. In the next, piles of washed clothing lay on the small dining room table. Past the bedroom and bathroom, he found the kitchen.

Myra sat holding the boy and solicitously rubbing a growing red spot on his knee. Large tears coursed down his pink cheeks. Max sobbed piteously and hugged her neck when Mahlon entered.

"He's always after the cookies," she said with a shake of her head, "any chance he gets. Today, he was in too much of a hurry."

"I hope he's okay," Mahlon said.

Nodding, she perched the boy on her hip and set about putting the kettle on the stove and bringing two cups and a child's mug to the table. Mahlon slipped off his jacket and sat at one end of the table. With an economy of motion that comes with countless repetitions, Myra pulled the highchair over to the table and effortlessly deposited the boy in his seat. In no time, his mug was filled with milk and half a peanut butter and jelly sandwich clutched firmly in his small hands.

Shortly, she placed a mug of tea before Mahlon and sat across from him. She nodded for him to begin and drank her tea. Mahlon told her about finding the body in the dunes.

Between mouthfuls of tea, he related the main points of his effort to identify her. When he reached the part about Orbann's list, he asked her how she left her job at the lounge.

"I was fired," Myra said matter-of-factly, as she wiped her son's mouth while he squirmed to avoid the wash cloth.

"This guy, Chance, wouldn't keep his hands off me. So I fixed him."

"Mr. Chance? The head bouncer?"

Myra laughed when she heard that. "Head bouncer? He was only around one or two nights a week. Too often, if you ask me." The memory angered her, and it showed in her voice.

"Thought I was an easy make or something." She lifted the young boy out of the highchair and held him on her lap. "I just started work two weeks before. I got the neighbor to sit with Max. I didn't make a secret of not being married, and everybody at work knew it. Know what I mean?"

Mahlon nodded and watched her fuss with the boy's hair while she talked. Max had a finger in his mouth. He sat staring at Mahlon, and his eyes began to glaze over as his mother spoke. Mahlon couldn't tear his eyes off the delightful but losing battle Max was fighting against the approaching sleep.

"Chance kept pawing me. One night I'm at the bar getting an order when he comes up to me. The creep put his hands all over me. The place was crowded, and I got two bottles of beer in each hand. Must have thought he had me cold, until I dumped two of them on his head." She started to laugh softly to herself.

"He had this startled look on his face for a second. Then he wanted to kill me. I was fired on the spot." Her chin firmed. "It was worth it. No one touches me unless I want them to."

Max's mouth fell open and his whole body relaxed as he sank into the innocent sleep of childhood.

"Orbann," Mahlon said, "gave me the impression that Chance was his head bouncer."

"No way. They hired college football players for that when I worked there." She shrugged. "But things change."

Why did Orbann lead him to think otherwise? Mahlon filed that away for future thought. He pulled Orbann's list from the folder and pushed it across to Myra. "Do you know any of these women?" She leaned forward, studying it over Max's curly head, and shook her head.

Mahlon thanked her for the tea. Gesturing for Myra to stay, he rose. At the front door he looked back. Max lay asleep in his mother's arms. Mahlon went outside and closed the door softly behind him.

The second Brant Beach address was on Bayview Avenue opposite High Island. The house was on the bay side of the street and jammed up against the tarred bulkhead that formed a seawall along that stretch of bay front. A realtor's sign stood by the steps. The firm had its office on the causeway. At the realtor's office, he had the agent call Chief James to verify he was investigating a murder case. When the agent was satisfied, Mahlon asked for the phone.

"We need to talk tonight," Mahlon said. "Something's come up."

"What's on your mind?" Hank asked.

"We don't want to discuss it here."

Hank promised he'd call around seven.

The agent gave him the address, and Mahlon copied it onto another stuffed envelope. Ten minutes later, he dropped all the letters in the mail and pointed the car north on the boulevard. There were just three addresses left: one in Barnegat Light, and two in Harvey Cedars, but they would have to wait until he had a bowl of clam chowder at Bernie's.

Chapter 22

Mahlon was two blocks from Bernie's Chowder Hut when he spotted the cross street listed in the Barnegat Light address. On impulse he entered it and, driving slowly, searched for the house number. The small green bungalow sat next to a lot overgrown with bayberry bushes, and his heart sank when he spotted the realtor's sign in the window. He had visions of another hassle with a suspicious real estate agent.

The realtor had a local office in Barnegat Light. Knowing he'd enjoy his chowder more if the hassle was out of the way, he drove there. To Mahlon's delight, the agent had read about the discovery of the body in the dunes and was only too happy to cooperate.

In less time than he anticipated, Mahlon arrived at the Chowder Hut. Five motorcycles, side by side, spanned two of the four parking spaces in front of the place, but a pickup at the end of the line was backing out just as he arrived. Mahlon pulled the Plymouth into the parking slot as soon as the truck cleared it. On his way inside, a yellow Day-Glo poster in the front window caught his eye. What do you know? Ricky Gee's return was being touted even at this end of the island.

The five bikers sat at two tables near the window, keeping a watchful eye on their hogs. They were big surly men trimmed out in shaggy beards and broken noses. Each wore a well-chewed armless denim jacket with hand-painted tribal markings, grimy Levis, and heavy oil-soaked people-stompers. One look at them and no one in his right mind would dare lay so much as an envious thought on those bikes parked out front, let alone a thieving hand.

Bernie's skinny figure was nowhere in sight. The lunchtime crowd had left, and the only customers beside the bikers were a young couple sitting in the far corner with their heads together. The young man eyed the bikers warily, but they drank their bottled beer with the ease of men who had no fear of their surroundings.

Mahlon harvested a crop of bread crumbs from his tablecloth and dropped them in the ash tray. Bernie appeared wearing a white shirt beneath another soiled apron. He carried a tray of soup bowls to the bikers' table and fetched them another round of beers before he came over to Mahlon's table.

"New England's all I got left," he said. through motionless lips. Mahlon was tempted to ask for the name of his ventriloquist but thought the better of it. Why insult the maker of the best chowder on the island? He ordered a large bowl and a Molson to wash it down.

While he waited, Mahlon thought about the letter scam he was working for Hank. If it didn't turn up anything positive, Hank would have to search motor vehicle files to see if any of the missing names were still licensed. Meanwhile, they'd just have to see what results the letters would bring. Two weeks should do it. He knew Hank would be one impatient man.

Bernie set the bowl of chowder, a basket of fresh-baked bread, and a bottle of Molson in front of him. Mahlon buttered a slice and began to eat. There was a delicious simplicity about the meal that appealed to him. He had an instinctive distrust for the ornate and the decorative. The straightforward and plain were more to his liking. There was less to go wrong, less to peg your ego on, and less to cloud your vision. Simplification was the real aim of life, and the discovery of Bernie's chowder was a small but very enjoyable step in that direction.

As Mahlon finished the last of his chowder, the bikers paid their bill and filed out the door with casual arrogance. The young couple had disappeared some time ago. Bernie wandered by his table, and Mahlon paid his bill. The raucous roar of engines spared Bernie the acknowledgment of Mahlon's compli-ments on his soup.

The flashing lights on a Barnegat Light patrol car stopped Mahlon in his tracks when he opened the restaurant door to leave. Out on the street, the five bikers sat astride their bellowing machines while a police sergeant wearing mirrored sunglasses motioned them to shut down their bikes. It took Mahlon a moment to recognize Sgt. Woodson in his tailored shirt and immaculate uniform.

The pack leader, seated on an old but beautifully maintained Harley, studied Woodson with an indifferent tilt of his head. Each time Woodson tried to speak, they twisted their throttles and drowned his words in a roar of exhaust.

Woodson's irritation mounted as the bikers played their game with consummate skill, easing back on the throttle until he tried to speak and revving their engines again. With nostrils flaring Woodson's whole body stiffened, and he brought his hand to the butt of his gun. Mahlon couldn't believe what he was seeing. Woodson looked like he was going to draw.

Apparently, the bikers had played this game before. With a well-timed wave of the leader's hand all the engines died at once. Woodson, trying for over a minute to outshout the roaring engines, bellowed in the sudden silence that followed.

"Where're you going—" Woodson caught himself and lowered his voice. "—without protective head gear?"

"No need to yell, officer," the leader said. "We hear just fine." His companions snickered.

"Town ordinance requires protective head gear for motorcyclists. I've a mind to run you in."

The snickers disappeared and a sullen tenseness descended on the men.

"We're just crossin' the road," the leader said with all the amiability of a rattlesnake. "Wanted to look at them boats over there." With that said, he shoved his stand down and swung off the bike. The others dismounted, too.

"My protective head gear's hanging right here on my saddle," the biker said, his words parodying Woodson's phrase. He reached over and unhooked his helmet and held it in his fist like a weapon. The other bikers followed suit. Grim faced, the five men stood shoulder to shoulder confronting Woodson.

My, my, Mahlon thought, there really is a just God. Woodson's about to get his ass kicked, but good.

Sensing the menace in the situation, Woodson backed away. "Well, maybe I was a bit hasty," he said, giving the men a sick smile. "I didn't see your helmets. You're free to go." With that, he withdrew from the bikers and went to his patrol car.

"Yeah," one of them said after him, "that's what you were, all right. A bit hasty." They all laughed and remounted their bikes. They drove off with all five helmets strapped snugly to their saddles.

Mahlon walked over to the patrol car. Woodson looked pale and shaken. When Mahlon spoke, Woodson gave a start of surprise.

"Best display of bad judgment I've seen in some time. Congratulations, Sgt. Woodson."

A spasm of irritation crossed Woodson's face. "You're that bearded P.I. who's helping the Chief. Aren't you?" With a bellow from their exhausts, the bikers disappear around the corner.

"It was good seeing you eat crow." Mahlon leaned closer to the open window. "You're damned lucky you didn't eat teeth, too. And you want Hank's job? What a laugh. You're just a rule-reading coward. You couldn't fill his shoes in a lifetime."

Woodson's face flushed with indignation. "I won't forget this, Mr. Mahlon. My turn will come one of these days." He put the patrol car in gear and sped away.

The addresses in Harvey Cedars were located just a block from each other, and as luck would have it, the owners rented them through the same real estate firm. He found the office in the center of town under the shadow of the water tower. He got the last known addresses for the two waitresses, but only after he spent twenty minutes trying to convince the agent that his request was not a new wrinkle designed to steal potential clients. Again, it took a call to Chief James's office to confirm his story. Mahlon watched with satisfaction as his friend's familiar voice boomed from the ear piece. The agent jumped in his chair. Five minutes and several apologies later, the Plymouth was heading south on the boulevard toward home.

Mahlon mailed the last three letters in Ship Bottom. The island part of the investigation was done. He hadn't much to show for his work thus far. All he and Hank could do now was wait, and waiting wasn't something Hank was very good at.

* * *

Mahlon had made arrangements to go over to Sara's house as soon as he finished talking to his friend. He was waiting at his desk when the call came through. Hank wasn't on the other end of the line, though. His wife was.

"Is this Thomas Mahlon? Henry's old army friend?"

"Yes," he said. "How do you do, Mrs. James?"

"Oh, call me Clare. All my friends do." She spoke in a bubbly fashion. "Henry has been in the worst mood lately. Why last night when I got home, I found him sitting in the dark. Well, I shooed him right off to bed, Mr. Mahlon. A working man needs his rest, I always say."

"He does indeed," Mahlon said lamely.

When she spoke again, her voice was lowered. "Give him a good talking to for me. Tell him to pay no mind to what people say." Mahlon was about to ask her what people were saying but she went on talking.

"I want to have you over for dinner next Thursday. I know how much help you've been to Henry, and I'd like to show my thanks. My Thursday bridge club's been canceled, and we'd both appreciate your company. Henry says you have a lady friend. Bring her along too."

"Thank you. Sara and I will look . . . "

"Oh, dear," she said, cutting him off, "there's my ride. Please excuse me, Mr. Mahlon. I'll tell him you're on the phone. Bye." She put the phone down and he heard her walking away. Mahlon knew Hank hated the name 'Henry.' Apparently, Clare didn't.

Hank's gruff voice came on the line. "Did he give you that address?"

Mahlon laughed. "You scared the wits out of him. He was still apologizing as I went out the door."

"Good! I'm sick of piddlin' little farts standing in the way of our investigation."

"The island part of it is finished," Mahlon said. "I mailed all the letters today. Now, we just wait and see."

"Wait, eh? I'm no good at that."

"Don't I know it. I saw something today I know you'd like to hear." Mahlon told James about Sgt. Woodson's encounter with the bikers.

"They'd have stomped him," Mahlon said as he finished his story, "if he didn't turn tail when he did."

James's laughter rang across the phone line. "I'd a loved to see that. Isn't it like him, though? He's got the law book under one arm and his diploma under the other, but nothing under his hat but his empty head." They both laughed at that.

Mahlon hesitated a second before he went on. "Hank, there's some nasty rumors going around about you. I think Clare's heard them, too."

James cursed at the other end of the line. "Damn it, Thomas. It's that file I was telling you about." James fell silent for a second, and Mahlon guessed he was hunting for a way to begin.

"I was married back in Newark. Met her at a party shortly after I left the army. To make a long story short, that fun-loving lady turned out to be a LUSH in capital letters. I did what I could for her, but she wouldn't give the bottle up. I was angry at myself for falling for her and angry at her for what she'd become. I'll spare you the details, but it ended when I left her. Two weeks later, she killed herself in a crash."

"They're saying you juiced her up that night and put her on the road."

"That's a damned lie. The accident investigation discovered she'd been boozing it up at a crosstown bar and was on her way home when it happened. The report was in the file, but Woodson wasn't interested in it."

"Patrolman Sanders isn't either," Mahlon said, and he explained how he learned Sanders was the source of the rumor. "Woodson didn't have to coerce him that night, he just promised him a promotion if he'd help."

James fell silent. When he spoke again, he sounded tired. "Woodson's got me surrounded, Thomas. He's ruining my good name and turning my men against me. Where the hell can I turn?"

"I'm still working for you."

"Glad to hear that. I need someone I can trust."

"What about Clare?"

"Oh, she knows the whole story. I told her before we got married. If the rumors start interfering with her socials, she won't be happy. I'll tell you that. Otherwise, who knows?" He took a deep breath and let it out with an audible sigh. When he spoke again there was a note of forced enthusiasm in his voice.

"Well, Clare made the invite for you and Sara to come for dinner, didn't she?"

Mahlon said that she had.

"Well, I got another invitation for you," James said. "Why don't the two of you come with us to the Police Chief's Dinner Dance three weeks from now?"

"I don't know."

"What do you mean, you don't know? I got a table and I owe you both. Eat a good dinner, drink a little, dance a little. Who knows? You might enjoy yourselves. What do you say?"

"It's the dancing part that worries me," Mahlon said.

"How's that?"

"I've got two left feet when it comes to dancing, Hank. I'll be all over Sara's toes. I'll make an ass of myself. I know I will."

"Take some dancing lessons. All I know is that you two better be there. You hear?"

Mahlon felt his stomach tighten. "If Sara's free, I guess we can make it."

"Damn right you will," James said, and he hung up.

Chapter 23

Construction on Sara's miniature golf course was to begin on Monday of the following week. Getting her business up and running by Memorial Day was Sara's top priority, so Sunday evening Mahlon expected her to put off the invitation to the Jameses. They lay in her double bed catching their breath when he thought to ask her.

"Thomas," she said, rising on her elbow and hooking a leg over his, "he's your friend. Certainly, I'll be there." He expressed his gratitude with a long kiss.

Monday morning brought thin silver-white clouds that slid seaward as the day progressed. The day promised to be a warm one that would give Sara's construction a fine start. A large manila envelope and three post cards came in the morning mail. One ex-waitress had written a note at the bottom of her card:

"That creep Orbann owes me two days pay."

I'll bet, Mahlon thought, as he crossed the women's names off Orbann's list. Counting Myra and Tammy May, the list of waitresses was five names shorter.

The return address on the manila envelope read Wood Court Casualty Insurance, a North Jersey firm that used Mahlon to investigate claims in the southern end of the state. The enclosed letter concerned three recent auto injury claims for severe whiplash. All three were being treated by the same physician and the same chiropractor. Insurance outlays for the claims were piling up rapidly. Accompanying the letter were photocopies of the claimants' insurance applications and accident reports, the police accident reports.

WoodCourt's own people were investigating the medical professionals. Soft-tissue injuries were favorite targets for insurance scams because they were so difficult to verify, and, consequently, the easiest to fake. The company wanted Mahlon to investigate the claimants. Were they really disabled? If not, he was to get proof they were faking it.

The claimant's addresses sent him searching his files for a state map. The map showed that all three lived in small towns south of Millville. Holly Brice, age 20, lived in Port Elizabeth; Martin Benford, age 36, in Mauricetown; and the Reverend Darwin Parrish, age 62, in Port Norris.

A couple of things about the situation struck Mahlon as odd. For one thing, physicians usually looked down their noses at chiropractors. Their philosophies of healing were worlds apart. For another, if the two were in collusion and deliberately over-billing, why would they work their scam three times in three months on the same insurance carrier? Thieves were usually smarter than that.

Mahlon packed toilet articles, a change of clothing for a couple of nights on the road, and his Canon 35mm. in his gym bag. Photographs were invaluable in cases like this. He made a liverwurst and onion on buttered rye and washed it down with an ice-cold Molson before he left.

A half hour later, Mahlon was driving south on the Parkway. The Plymouth's AC barely held its own against the midday heat. Well past the green mouth of the Mullica River at the 322 inter-change, he turned west. At McKee City near the Atlantic City Race Track, where his friend Smokey Harris spent his time when he was in this part of the state, Mahlon took Route 40 to Mays Landing. On the other side of the Great Egg Harbor River, Route 552 took him through the pines all the way to Route 47.

Known as Delsea Drive to those who live near it, Route 47 sliced through the heart of South Jersey from Camden to Wildwood. Mahlon rode it through Millville, and eight miles later he crossed a feeder of the meandering Maurice

River into Holly Bryce's hometown. The drive took under two hours.

Port Elizabeth had six or seven streets and a few hundred souls to call its own. The address was Second Street which intersected Delsea Drive on the left, and two blocks in he found Holly's house, a butter cream clapboard bungalow with green trim. On the porch next door, an older woman in a blue housedress sat smoking a cigarette. Mahlon parked and got out.

"Afternoon, ma'am," he said, approaching her porch. "Does Holly Brice live around here?"

"Right next door," the woman said, tipping her cigarette in that direction. Her voice was hoarse. She looked to be in her sixties and had the deep lined face of a lifetime smoker. "Won't find her in, though. Just left with her father for one of them chiropractor treatments up in Millville."

"Oh, something happened to her?"

The woman gave a rueful chuckle and shook her head. "That poor girl has the baddest luck. She got rearended up at Broadway and Delsea." She pointed up the street. "Oh, three months ago. I guess it was. Bad case of whiplash. In constant pain. Would you believe it? Poor thing even had to postpone her wedding."

Her rising indignation over the fate of her young neighbor started her coughing. As her hacking went on, Mahlon grew alarmed, but the woman fought back gamely and finally stopped. She was red faced from the effort and sat a moment catching her breath.

"Afternoon, Mrs. Stout," the mailman said, making his rounds. She nodded in return. Mahlon took her mail, noted the name Miriam Stout on the top letter, and passed the letters to her. She had her breath back by that time. She set the letters on the nearby rocker and calmly lit herself another cigarette.

"I'll come back later," Mahlon said.

Broadway crossed Second Street two blocks farther on. When he got around the corner on his way back to Delsea Drive, he pulled into the shade of a great Norway maple and parked. He wrote down what Mrs. Stout had said, noting the date and time of their talk. Mahlon had a warm place in his heart for gossips. They certainly made insurance investigations easier. One down, two to go.

He checked the address of the next claimant, Martin Benford. According to his application, Benford operated a gas station in Mauricetown. He found the turnoff just two miles south on Delsea Drive and rolled into the small river town a little after three. Benford's gas station occupied one corner of the town's only intersection. He brought the Plymouth to a stop at the gas pumps. An attendant in a blue workman's uniform came out of the station wiping his hands on an orange rag. Mahlon told him to fill her up.

Inside the office an overweight man in a khaki T-shirt and a grimy neck brace sat at a desk behind a low wall of automotive manuals. His broad face, filmed with sweat, glanced at Mahlon before he made a stiff-neck turn in the direction of the repair bay. He shouted something to a mechanic working under the hood of a red Dodge pickup and made another stiff-neck turn back to his paperwork.

Mahlon dropped some change in the soda machine, and a can of lemon-lime clunked down the chute. Popping it open, Mahlon turned to face the desk and took a long drink.

"A little warm for that neck brace," Mahlon said between swallows.

"The heat ain't the half of it," the man said, making another stiff-neck turn toward the repair bay. "What torque you putting on those bolts?"

"Forty foot-pounds," the mechanic said.

"What's the manual say?" The mechanic straightened and shrugged.

The man pounded his fist on the desk and winced. "Why the hell do you think they print manuals?"

The mechanic sauntered into the office, his face a sullen mask. He selected a Chilton's manual from the collection on the desk and carried it back to the repair bay.

His eyes afire with anger, the man turned to Mahlon for sympathy. "I'm paying that idiot ten bucks an hour, and he wouldn't know a clutch plate from a cotter pin if it bit him in the ass."

"Some things you just got to do yourself," Mahlon said.

"Be in there in a heart beat, but I can't risk it." He pointed to his neck brace. "Who'd a thought a little old case of whiplash could ruin a man's life? Hell, I'm lucky to be doing the billing, and if the wife don't get some loving real soon, my marriage is in trouble, too." He gave Mahlon a wry grin.

The young attendant came through the door. "Twelve-fifty in gas," he said to Mahlon. "The oil's okay. Pay Mr. Benford. I got to go to the bathroom."

Mahlon paid his bill. "Hope your luck changes," he said on his way. When he got in the car, Mahlon looked as his watch. It wasn't three fifteen, yet. He had to smile. Sometimes the direct approach worked best. Two down, one to go.

At the edge of town, he pulled over and wrote up the encounter in his notebook. By the time he started up again, the air inside the car had grown decidedly hot. He switched the blower to high, but only hot air blew out of the vents. The AC had quit for good this time. He opened the windows and hoped for the best.

Less than a mile down the road, he took a left for Port Norris and got a view of the southwestern sky, where white thunderheads were piled up like snowdrifts. Three miles later he was rolling into Port Norris along North Street.

Fittingly enough, the address for Reverend Parrish was on Church Street. When Mahlon reached Main Street, he turned east and began searching for it. Four blocks later he turned around at the edge of town and started back in the opposite direction. Church Street lay six blocks west of North Street. Port Norris was the biggest of the three river towns he'd visited that day, but by no means was it large.

The houses on Church Street, mostly one story bungalows built before the war, were in need of paint, but the tree-lined street had a solid residential look that said it wasn't the worst place in the state to live by a long shot.

St. Ethelbert's Church, a modest red brick structure that could hold a hundred or so of the faithful, stood on the next corner. At the peak of the facade, the front wall formed a bell tower like that on the old Spanish Missions. Near the front steps, a glass-encased bulletin board listed the Rev. Darwin Parrish as Pastor. Beside the church stood the parsonage in matching red brick.

Since it was a member of the clergy, Mahlon opted for the direct approach again. The sunlight disappeared as he climbed the parsonage steps. Welcoming the relief it brought, he rang the bell. A gray haired house-keeper, her full cheeks red as cherries, opened the door.

"Is Rev. Parrish in?"

"No," she said with a good-natured smile. "He's working on the parish youth hall on Main Street. Two blocks down to your left."

He thanked her. Working on the parish youth hall was he? Mahlon didn't like the sound of that. A distant grumble of thunder punctuated his suspicions. The breeze picked up. The trees on Main Street tossed and swayed.

A stack of wallboard stood against the front of a one-and-a-half story wooden structure that had been a train station in a former life. Two youths in cut-offs and white T-shirts and a middle-aged man in a collarless white shirt and black trousers were hustling to get the wallboard inside before the storm broke. Mahlon parked two car-lengths away and watched the man work. The Rev. Parrish's neck seemed to be just fine. A crack of thunder to the west stepped up the work crew's pace.

Taking his 35mm. from his overnight bag, Mahlon took several candids of the Reverend in action. Leaving the camera behind, he got out of the car. The prestorm darkness deepened. The Rev. Parrish, having returned, looked around impatiently for one of the young men to help him. Four pairs of wallboard still had to be moved.

"Need a hand, Reverend?" Mahlon asked.

The man gave a start of surprise and then nodded eagerly. Together they lifted the top pair and started a fast shuffle into the building. Voices echoed from the darkened depths of the gutted building, but Mahlon couldn't see who was talking. The other two had the next pair on the move by the time Mahlon and Rev. Parrish got outside again.

Big raindrops splattered the sidewalk, bringing with them the smell of ozone. They lifted the next pair and hurried it inside. The teens got the last pair through the door just as the skies opened up.

They all broke out laughing at the race they'd won, and Rev. Parrish took Mahlon's hand and pumped it vigorously. Above their head, the torrent beat loudly against the tin roof.

"Thanks," he shouted over the rising din. "You're the answer to my prayer." We'll see about that, Mahlon thought.

Walls of advancing rain swept by the open doorway, driving blasts of cool air into the depths of the building to the sweating group's delight.

"Glad to help, Rev. Parrish," Mahlon said loudly. The teens stopped talking and gave him an amused smirk.

"Beg pardon?" the man said.

"Rev. Darwin Parrish. Right?"

"Yes, what can I do for you?" said a voice directly behind him.

Mahlon's stomach sank as he turned to the speaker. He hadn't heard the man approach. A thin, balding man in black clerical garb with a neck brace where his clerical collar should have been stood at his elbow. A rush of heat went to

Mahlon's face, and he tried to think of something to say that wouldn't make him look stupid.

"What can I do for you?" the real Rev. Parrish asked again.

"I'm an insurance investigator," Mahlon said with a sheepish grin. There was nothing to do but bite the bullet. "I thought this gentleman, here, was you. Obviously, I was wrong. I see you're still incapacitated."

"Actually, I'm not," he said, touching the neck brace. "The doctor gave me a clean bill of health yesterday, but I wear it here to be on the safe side." At that point, the other man spoke up about Mahlon's help.

"This is Fr. John Winters," Rev. Parrish said, shaking Mahlon's hand, "my good friend from across town. I'm afraid you came all the way down here for nothing."

Mahlon shrugged. "I'll get paid for my time just the same." He looked out the door. The rain was already easing off. There was something he wanted to know before he left, though.

"Tell me," he said. "How did your doctor ever team up with a chiropractor? They are strange bedfellows, if you'll pardon my saying so."

"Strange bedfellows, you say. A wonderful idea, I say. As for how they got together, Dr. Janson and Dr. Haden are lifelong friends who decided to give it a try a year or so ago. Frankly, I found the arrangement very therapeutic."

Mahlon nodded as he thought it over. "Thanks. I'll put that in my report."

He wrote up his notes on Rev. Parrish while he ate dinner at a diner on Main Street. The sky had cleared and the evening turned cool. On his way up to Mauricetown, he caught a glimpse of the sun burning a hole in the horizon and wished Sara were there to share it.

Well, he had clothes for an overnight stay, but he wouldn't need them. Holly Brice and Martin Benford were still disabled, and the Rev. Parrish healed. Mahlon couldn't help but smile. He'd knocked them off— one, two, three. As easy a day of insurance investigation as he'd had in a long time. Except for the fact that he hadn't seen Holly Brice. When he reached Delsea Drive, he decided to pay her a visit. It wasn't really out of his way, and he'd feel better about it tomorrow when he wrote up his report.

It was almost dark by the time he parked on Second Street, a few houses down from Holly's. The trees overhead rustled in the soft night air. Mrs. Stout's porch was empty, but someone was sitting in the shadows on Holly's. When he drew opposite her porch, he stopped. A young woman on a rocker sat lost in thought, entirely oblivious of his presence.

"Miss Bryce," Mahlon said loud enough to penetrate her thoughts.

Holly gave a jump and snapped her head in his direction. "Yes, who is it?"

Mahlon went to the bottom of her steps. "I'm sorry if I startled you." He could see her better now. The neck brace hung loosely from her neck, the Velcro strap unfastened.

"What do you want?" Her words were edged with impatience.

"I'm an insurance investigator, Holly."

Her hands flew upward, and she quickly refastened the brace. "I-I was just cooling my neck," she said, her voice quavering with anxiety. "You can't imagine how uncomfortable it is."

Mahlon didn't speak. Something Mrs. Stout said that afternoon started him shaking his head.

Holly cleared her throat. "Is something wrong?"

"It's got to end, Holly."

"Whatever do you mean? What's got to end?"

"Tell the guy you don't love him. You can't go on faking your injury this way."

"How dare you!" she said, her words rising hysterically.

"When I surprised you just now. You turned so fast, I thought your head would drop off. Whatever trouble you have, it's personal and not physical, and you know it."

She opened her mouth to protest, but the effort quickly collapsed in a flood of tears. Mahlon stood on the sidewalk and let her cry it out. A few minutes later she got control of herself.

"I'm ashamed of myself. I didn't mean to do it. My neck's been better for two weeks. I just don't want to marry Harold."

"We've all got troubles," Mahlon said. "You better tell him quick because your game's over. Give me that neck brace, please."

With trembling hands she undid the velcro strap and tossed it to him.

"The most wonderful thing has just happened, Holly. It's a miracle, in fact. Your neck feels so good, you just threw your neck brace away. Understand?"

She lowered her eyes and nodded.

"No more doctor visits and no more treatments. It isn't fair to the insurance company, and it sure as hell isn't fair to Harold."

Halfway back to his car, Mahlon spotted a garbage can beside a house. He tossed the neck brace into it, and let his thoughts turn to home. How many postcards would he find in tomorrow's mail and would the one he was waiting for be among them?

Chapter 24

Four postcards arrived the next day while he was writing up his report on Rev. Parrish, Mr. Benford and Holly Brice. He made no mention of Holly's little game. Two postcards arrived the following day, bringing Orbann's list of waitresses down to twenty-one names. Sara was right. There was nothing like the promise of money to get people's attention.

Mahlon arranged to get the Plymouth's AC repaired on Thursday. He had acquired the car from Sam, his mechanic, over a year ago in exchange for a twice-yearly go at Sam's deadbeat list. The black Plymouth was due for its yearly tune up, and Sam agreed to look at the AC, too.

The parts for the AC were slow arriving, which left Mahlon twiddling his thumbs at the garage the entire day. He spent most of the afternoon on the phone, running down customers on Sam's most recent list of deadbeats and cajoling them to pay up. It was twenty to five when he finally backed his car out of Sam's garage and started for Beach Haven.

The night before, he told Sara that he'd pick her up at five-thirty. A fender-bender on the causeway delayed traffic, and it was after five when he pulled into his front yard on Pelham Avenue. He emptied his mail box on his way into the house and gave it a quick look. The bills he dropped on his desk, and the junk mail got tossed on the mantel as he headed for the shower.

Sara was waiting on the side porch when he pulled up at her house. She came down the steps wearing a sage green tunic and pants. The cloth was knit and the lower hem of the tunic and sleeve ends were fringed in a lacy pattern. Around her neck hung a pendant of white stones leading to a bead of rich dark cedar. Her hair hung loose around her shoulders, and her eyes held a warm smile as she got into the car.

"Wow," was all he said before he greeted her with a kiss.

"Do I pass inspection?" Sara asked with a quizzical grin.

"Pass inspection? My dear, you set the standard."

On the way up to Barnegat Light, Sara brought him up to date on her miniature golf course. The land had been bulldozed, and the terraces for the final three holes had been raised and shaped along the back property line. Tomorrow the forms would start to go in for the putting greens, and the wiring for lights laid out in conduits.

"I can't wait to see it all finished," Mahlon said. "It sounds grand."

Fifteen minutes later, Mahlon parked the Plymouth in the driveway of his friend's oceanfront home right behind a Barnegat Light patrol car. Beyond the rim of the curving driveway, the two-story, gray house sat amid bayberry bushes and Japanese pine. Chief James hailed them from the far side of the house, and they followed the path around to a deck that faced the ocean.

James greeted them at the top of the steps with a handshake. "Clare's just around the corner. Let me introduce you."

Clare James, wearing a loose hostess gown of soft blue, was seated under a white canvas canopy that shaded a large area of the deck. She rose and swept across the deck toward them. There was an air about her of beauty unsuccessfully reclaimed. She wore her dark hair in a pixie cut that emphasized her large, mascaraed eyes. High cheek bones sloped in the echo of a once full line to an attractive jaw and small full lips. A note of self-preoccupation showed in her face. Mahlon imagined that her losing battle with age must provoke no end of anguish in the girl-like breast beneath her gown. Beside her flowing figure, James hovered patiently, waiting for his wife to complete her greetings.

"Mr. Mahlon," she said with forced gaiety. "How very nice to meet you at last." She extended a cool slim hand which Mahlon shook gently.

"The pleasure's mine." He took Sara's arm and brought her forward to introduce. While the women exchanged pleasantries, he turned to James. "Hank, you're a lucky man." James lifted his glass to Mahlon and hid his forced smile behind the rim of the glass.

"Henry," Clare said, "mix our guests a drink and refill mine." Mahlon winced at the sound of that name. He knew how much Hank disliked it.

Clare took Mahlon's and Sara's arms and began walking them back to the cluster of chairs where she'd been sitting when they came in.

"What's your pleasure?" James asked.

"White wine for me," Sara said.

"Scotch and soda," Mahlon said.

"Club?" James asked as he moved to a small white table by the doorway, where the makings for drinks had been set.

"No, make it ginger ale."

"Are you crazy?" James roared. "Ruin perfectly good Scotch with ginger ale? Is that what happens to a man when he lives alone?"

Mahlon laughed. "Hank, I love Scotch for the morning after, but I can't get it down the night before mixed with water. I just never developed the taste."

"It's a crime, I tell you, but you're my guest so Scotch and ginger it is." James gave a shake of his head as he carried drinks to the women.

Out of his uniform, James looked strangely smaller. He wore a dark blue sport shirt, white summer trousers, white belt, and soft leisure shoes. The selection was probably not his own, Mahlon guessed, but something Clare took care of between bridge sets.

When James returned, he handed Mahlon his drink. Taking a step toward the ladies, Mahlon toasted them and the evening. They all raised their glasses.

"Excellent ginger ale," Mahlon said to Hank, and his friend laughed. The air still held some of the day's warmth. Mahlon looked at the dunes and the ocean beyond. A pair of piping plovers flitted across the dunes toward the distant surf line. The tide was out. When he turned back to the deck, he spotted a table set for four and beyond that a gas grill against the far railing.

Clare must have noticed the direction of his gaze, for she spoke up immediately. "Henry." Mahlon winced again. "Light the grill and put on the steaks. Let's get dinner started before it turns too cool to stay out here." She got to her feet and turned to Mahlon. "Will you help me bring things out, Mr. Mahlon?"

"Stay where you are, Sara," she said, "and enjoy the view. We'll only be a minute."

Clare, trailing wisps of soft gown, entered the house through the patio doors. Mahlon followed her. The kitchen was immaculate, the countertops unblemished. Mahlon couldn't help but wonder just how much it was used.

"I got home a bit late this afternoon and found I was out of tomatoes. Henry loves tomatoes in his salad, but I'm afraid he won't get them tonight. Hope you and Sara don't mind." She removed a large bowl of crisp salad from the refrigerator.

"I'm glad you two could come," she said, handing the bowl to Mahlon. "It's not often Henry and I entertain. He's been so moody lately with all this nonsense going on at work." She poked four potatoes with a fork, placed them in the oven, and set the timer.

"I say if a man can't handle his work problems, it's time for him to get out."

Mahlon bristled when he heard that. "That's one way to look at it," he said, trying to hide his irritation. "Then again, if Hank had a little more support, he might not be so moody."

Clare stopped what she was doing and turned to him. "I have my own disappointments, Mr. Mahlon, and he has his. And while I'm at it, I've never been crazy about that name. It's always sounded so tough to me."

"He's been Hank to me for so many years, I doubt if I can call him anything else." She looked at him a few seconds longer, pursed her lips in exasperation, then turned away to tend to the potatoes. Mahlon carried the salad bowl outside. Sara had joined James at the grill, and the two of them were talking and laughing like old friends.

The meal was excellent. James had grilled the steaks to perfection, and the salad tasted great even if it lacked tomatoes. The exchange with Clare left the air between them decidedly cool for the remainder of the evening. A devilish streak led him to call his friend "Hank" more times than necessary in the course of the meal. Following dinner, James and Clare cleared the table which left Mahlon alone with Sara.

Unable to get the name business off his mind, Mahlon said, "You know, Hank always hated the name 'Henry.'"

Sara turned to him. "Is that why you've been calling him 'Hank' every chance you get?"

Mahlon nodded guiltily.

"If that's what she wants to call him, Thomas, then it must be all right with him."

He thought that over. "Maybe, but I still don't like it."

The air turned cool once the sun went down, and Clare and Sara retired to the house where it was warmer. James and Mahlon, after dinner drinks in hand, slowly paced the length of the deck. They walked in silence for a few turns, before Mahlon thought to update his friend on the status of Orbann's list.

"Has Woodson's rumor mill turned out any more garbage?" he asked when he was done.

James' answer was an unconvincing "no."

Mahlon guessed he'd hear whatever was on his friend's mind sooner or later. The phone rang, and James went inside to answer it and returned a moment later with a worried look on his face.

"There's been a shooting over by the bay. I've got to go."

"We'll go with you, Hank," Mahlon said, checking his watch. "Sara's got a long day tomorrow, and it's time for us to leave." Mahlon went into the house. He and Sara made their hurried goodbyes to Clare, and a few moments later, they were following James' patrol car through the dark streets of Barnegat Light.

The crime scene was only four blocks away, and when they got there, two police cars with flashing red and blue lights had both lanes of Bayview Avenue blocked off. Mahlon pulled off the road and parked right behind James. His friend was out of his car already, speaking to one of the patrolmen.

The porch lights on the few houses that faced the crime scene burned brightly, and small groups of residents stood on their front steps talking and watching. On the opposite side between the road and a wall of horsetail reeds, two men stood over a draped form half buried in ankle-high weeds. The strobing patrol car lights tinged their clothes and faces an eerie red. Something about their stance suggested impatience. Behind them the reeds shook in the cool breeze coming off the bay.

"I'll only be a minute," Mahlon said to Sara. "I hope this doesn't bother you. Being near a murder scene, I mean."

"Thomas, the dead lost all power to frighten me when I was in the camps. Do what you have to do. I'll be okay."

James came over to the car. "Come with me, Thomas." Mahlon followed his friend across the weeds and stubble to the body.

"What happened, Hank?"

"A resident across the road said she heard a voice yelling something in broken English. Then she heard two loud bangs and the sound of a car driving off. When she came to her front door, she couldn't see anything, until the lights of a passing car lit up the body."

"What time was that?" Mahlon asked as he tried to keep pace with his taller friend.

"Eight-forty. There abouts. She called it in as soon as she saw the body." James broke off and spoke privately with a plainclothes man who turned out to be a county detective. He showed James something in a plastic bag. Mahlon checked his watch in the pulsing red light of the patrol car. It was almost nine-thirty. Someone had taken his sweet old time notifying James about the murder.

The man beside James bent, lifted the cloth from the body, and switched on a flashlight. Mahlon and James squatted for a better look. The body lay face down in the weeds with the hands together behind the back. The male victim wore a soiled white sports shirt and dark trousers. The back of the head was moist and red. In spite of the one sightless eye that bulged grotesquely, and the stem of a stout weed poking into his open mouth, the man looked strangely familiar.

Mahlon looked closely at the man's face and realized he was looking at the same man who came to the Bear's aid at the trailer park.

He rose to tell Hank, but James was speaking to the second man who was the coroner. The man pointed to the victim's hands which Mahlon now saw were tied together by the thumbs. The cord had dug in deeply, and the thumb pads looked swollen and discolored.

James looked around at the patrol cars before he spoke, his voice tired and flat. "Something else to worry about, Thomas. The county detective believes it was a hit. They recovered a .222 Remington Magnum cartridge near the body. We won't know for sure until we identify the victim and see if he has any priors. Right now we're waiting for the State Police Criminal Investigation Unit."

"Is Sgt. Woodson the officer on duty tonight?" Mahlon asked in a low voice after drawing James away from the other two.

"No, Sanders is. The first officer on the scene was my rookie. He just graduated from the academy last month. Why?"

"The patrolman said the woman called in around eight-forty. You weren't notified until nine twenty-five or so. Sanders took his time letting you know. You ought to rack his ass for this."

"You got something there." For the first time since they left the house, James relaxed a little before he went back to the others. Mahlon left the crime scene and drove Sara home.

Chapter 25

Over breakfast the next morning, Mahlon read about the murder in the Ocean County *Press*. The victim was Carlos Diaz, a petty thief with a long record. The paper carried his picture, taken after one of his arrests. The article listed his last known address as Sunset Trailer Court in Beach Haven Manor. Mahlon took a closer look at the picture. He was sure that Diaz was the Latino man who rescued the Bear from his burning pigsty.

The last week of April passed uneventfully. Five more postcards arrived, and Mahlon dutifully crossed off the names. He spoke briefly with Chief James. He didn't think they were ever going to identify the woman. The town council wanted the murder solved before the summer tourist season, and Hank was in one angry mood. Sunday Mahlon gave Sammy's shoes a sustained workout when Sara and he walked into Beach Haven. They strolled the streets of the town, admiring its old Victorian houses, and dined in a small restaurant when evening fell.

On Monday morning he straightened the house. Sara was coming over for dinner the following night, and he wanted the place presentable. While he worked, he listened to the morning news. Haldeman, Ehrlichman, and Attorney General Kleindienst had just resigned, and the President was accepting full responsibility for the Watergate scandal. Mahlon had to laugh. Would Nixon also accept the blame? Not if he could help it.

When he was clearing the mantle of junk mail, the pile squirted from his grip and splattered all over the rug and hearth stone. A stray piece or two landed in the fireplace, and another one wafted away, landing under the nearby kitchen table. Muttering a curse, he squatted, scraped the ones at his feet into a pile, plucked the ones from the dark ashes, and with a groan went down on hands and knees to reach the one under the table.

To his surprise, it turned out to be one of his postcards. Scrawled on the back was a woman's name and address, plus a post-script that read,

> *Keep your damn money.*
> *Just give us our daughter back.*

Mahlon took the card in both hands and stared at it in disbelief. It was her! He'd have to confirm it, of course, but he knew in his soul it was her. Stuck in with the junk mail, the postcard had been sitting on his mantle since God only knows. He read the name: Karen Beauchamps, Brookside Avenue, Pennington, N.J. The body in the dunes finally had a name.

He went to his desk and called Chief James.

"I found her!"

"Is that you, Thomas?"

"Who the hell else is looking for her?" Mahlon said. "Her name's Karen Beauchamps, and she lived in Pennington. Can you believe it?"

"Oh, this is great news. Maybe it'll get the council off my back for a week or two."

"I'm heading up there as soon as I change." Mahlon described how he had discovered the card. "I'm sorry, Hank. We could have had her address a week ago, if I didn't screw up."

"Spilt milk. Nothing we can do about that now."

"What's new in the Diaz case?"

"So you do read the papers after all. It was a professional hit just like we thought. Two .222 magnum slugs in the back of the head."

"Learn anything new from the residents around there?"

"Nothing. The principal witness, if that's what you call her, heard a loud voice yelling in broken English. The only words she recognized were 'Si, Si.' Then the guy said something else and 'Si, Si' again. 'Si' means 'yes' in Spanish in case you didn't know."

"Next time I go to Mexico, you can come along as my translator. By the way, you sound in unusually good spirits today."

"Oh, I am. I am. Ofc. Sanders is currently suspended for three days without pay for lax performance of duty. He let more than thirty minutes pass before he notified me last Thursday. He said my line was busy. Hah. With a rookie on the scene, I had a perfect case. My guess is Woodson was there prowling around my office and had to clean up in case I dropped in for something. I can't prove it. Anyway, I ran Sander's ass up one wall and down the other. Believe me, Thomas, it really feels good to be on the offensive for a change."

"Great. Don't let your guard down. I'll call as soon as I can, then you can notify the papers."

"I'll be waiting."

"By the way," Mahlon said, "I meant to tell you this sooner. Remember my adventures in the Sunset Trailer Park? Well, the guy who let the manager out of his burning trailer was none other than Carlos Diaz."

"Interesting."

"Every rat has his hole, and Sunset Trailer Park happened to be Diaz's, I guess."

"Good luck, Thomas."

Fifteen minutes later, Mahlon backed the black Plymouth out of his front yard. Beside him on the car seat lay the envelope with the pictures of the ring found on the body. His sense of elation began to wane as each passing mile brought him closer to Pennington. A growing knot in his stomach replaced it. How would he tell a mother and father that someone murdered their daughter? He wished now that he'd let Hank handle it. He'd forgotten that in police work triumph usually comes at the expense of someone else's suffering.

The drive to Pennington seemed to take forever. The edge of tension that started in the pines grew and grew, and by the time he drove along Main Street, he was wishing he could turn around and drive back. Brookside Avenue intersected Main at the bottom of a hill on the north side of the town. The Beauchamps lived in a modest dark green house on the right-hand side of the street. Mahlon turned his car around and parked it alongside a lumberyard across the street.

Mr. Beauchamps in a light green sport shirt and a beltless sport slacks answered his knock. Mahlon told him his name and said he was following up on the letter he mailed them about owing their daughter Karen back wages.

"I don't care if you owe her money," Mr. Beauchamps said.

"I won't take long," Mahlon said.

With a disgruntled sigh, Mr. Beauchamps led the way down a narrow hallway past a stairway to a door that led into the dining room. His short hair was dark gray on top but fell to almost pure white around his neck. Mrs. Beauchamps, wearing a white sleeveless top and a dark blue pleated skirt, sat in an easy chair watching an afternoon soap. The room had been converted to a sitting room, and the large oak pocket doors between it and the front room were closed.

"Margaret," Mr. Beauchamps said as they entered, "this is Mr. Mahlon. He wants to talk to us about some money that is still owed to Karen."

The woman give Mahlon a strained look before she rose and turned off the TV. She was slight of build with dead black hair, small tired eyes, and a pallid mouth. When she returned to her chair, she sat uncomfortably straight with her bony arms rigid on the arms of the chair.

Mr. Beauchamps directed Mahlon toward a seat opposite his wife while he sat on the stool in front of the old upright player piano nearby. The rounded hump of the man's shoulders testified to a lifetime of desk work. He gave his wife a worried look before he turned to Mahlon.

"Please explain what this is all about."

"Under what circumstances did your daughter leave her employment at Orbann's Lounge?"

The man studied his neat fingernails for a moment and then looked down at the floor.

"We haven't seen Karen since August 1970." His voice was flat and devoid of hope.

"Hasn't she written or anything?"

"No. Why do you want to know?"

"Mr. and Mrs. Beauchamps, I'm not an accountant. I'm working with the police on an investigation."

"Has Karen done something wrong?" Mrs. Beauchamps asked.

"No, she hasn't." Mahlon hesitated. "I wish I could tell you this in a less painful manner. More than a month ago, a body was found in the dunes near Barnegat Light."

Mrs. Beauchamps gave a startled gasp. "You've no proof it's Karen." The panic in her voice stabbed Mahlon's heart.

"Now, mother." Mr. Beauchamps went to her side and placed a protective arm around her.

Mahlon withdrew the photos from the envelope and glanced at them. Mrs. Beauchamps snatched them from his hands. She turned them around.

"Why, these aren't pictures of my—" The next word caught in her throat and her eyes widened with recognition. Her body jerked upright as if she'd been shot, and the photos spilled to the floor. She gave one long, strangled cry and buried her face in her hands.

Above her sobbing head, the ash-white face of her husband stared uncomprehendingly at the photos scattered at his feet. Mahlon rose and walked to the window.

Someone else killed their daughter, but he was the one who ripped the hope from their hearts.

Almost an hour later, after the doctor arrived to sedate her and Mr. Beauchamps put his wife to bed, after the woman next door entered and disappeared up the stairs, after Mr. Beauchamps succeeded in bringing his own grief under control long enough to call Karen's brother at college to break the sad news, Mahlon stepped forward and offered his own inadequate expression of sympathy, with the hope that the grieving man would find enough strength to carry them both through the painful days ahead.

The man spoke distractedly, as much to himself as he did to Mahlon. "Until you know for sure, you always hope. Now, that's gone, too."

"I'm sorry you had to learn this way."

"You did what you had to, Mr. Mahlon. Neither Margaret nor I blame you."

Mahlon gave him a brief rundown of the facts in his daughter's death and his own effort to identify her. "Chief James of Barnegat Light will contact you tomorrow to confirm your identification of the ring and tell you where your daughter's remains are buried. One thing puzzles me. Why didn't you file a missing person's report with the police?"

"But we did. We went to Brant Beach two weeks after we last heard from her. We talked with her roommate and filed a missing person's report with the Brant Beach Police. My wife had a relapse that night and had to be hospitalized. I spent the next three months nursing her. I never followed up. By the time I came up for air, it was November, and Karen was gone for good." He fought back the tears.

"What was her roommate's name?"

"Oh, I don't remember," Mr. Beauchamps said with despair. "Rhonda something, I think. I must get back to my wife. She needs me."

Mahlon shook the man's hand and turned to leave. Mr. Beauchamps grabbed his upper arm and said with a rage-filled voice, "Mr. Mahlon, don't let Karen's death go unpunished."

"I won't," he promised.

THE REVENGE STORY

Chapter 26

MAY 1973

Mahlon called Del Shannon from a pay phone at a garage on the Pennington Circle and told her to get over to the station. Chief James had an exclusive for her. She started to ask questions, but he hung up. He called James next and reported that the body in the dunes had a name at last. The Beauchamps had recognized the wedding ring. It was a positive ID. The man let out a whoop that stung Mahlon's ear on the other side of the state.

"That's the first good news I've had in a long time," James said.

"Del Shannon will be knocking on your door any minute," Mahlon said. "With luck the story will make tomorrow's edition."

By all rights Mahlon should have felt elated, but the trip home from Pennington was a melancholy one. The afternoon turned sour by the time he reached Trenton, and the rain started in Allentown and battered the Plymouth all across the desolate stretches of Route 539. The road was empty for long periods of time, and he had only the brooding pines and somber pin oaks for company.

When he splashed through the puddles in his front yard, the house stood dark and empty. Sara had a meeting that evening, so left to himself, he heated a can of stew for supper. Nightfall came early as the rain continued. He retired early. The release of sleep was a long time coming.

The grief-stricken faces of the Beauchamps were still on his mind when he awoke the next morning. Had he yielded to the temptation, he could easily have spent the morning in bed, but he'd made a promise to Mr. Beauchamps, and his first step in keeping that promise was to see Chief "Big John" Strickland about that missing person report. It wasn't until ten, however, that his sense of discipline finally roused him from the cool sheets and sent him on his way.

The officer on duty at the Brant Beach Police station recognized him immediately. "Mr. Mahlon, what brings you here?"

"I'd like to see a missing person report filed in August of '70."

"You'll need the Chief's permission." The officer dialed his phone and spoke to Strickland's secretary. "Mrs. Kramarz will fit you in if you can wait."

"I got the time," Mahlon said, remembering Strickland's empty appointment calendar on his previous visit. He entered the adjoining room, smiled at Mrs. Kramarz, and busied himself with the magazines on the table. Right on cue, the woman ushered Mahlon into the Chief's office exactly fifteen minutes later.

Strickland sat behind his large desk, his well-groomed gray head as impressive as ever, as was the width of his chest beneath his white uniform shirt and gold badge. There was nothing about the man to show life had touched him in any way since Mahlon's last visit. Like the proverbial fly in amber, Strickland's type survived everything.

One change in the room did catch Mahlon's eye. Only a blind person could miss it. Framed photos covered the paneled wall on the left like a tapestry in black or white. Each one featured Strickland in the act of glad-handing various well known personalities. Mahlon sensed that his attention to the photos pleased the man behind the desk very much.

"My little display has caught your eye, I see," Strickland said. "That's just a fraction of my collection." He eyed the wall with obvious pleasure.

"All my crime related photos will go over here," Strickland said pointing to the opposite wall. "Worked some pretty big cases in my day." Giving the wall one last appreciative glance, he turned to Mahlon. "But you didn't come here just to see these. Did you?"

"There's a missing person report in your files I'd like to see."

"I read about your exploits in this morning's paper." A tiny note of envy was evident in his sonorous words. "You think there's a report in my files on that woman you found in Barnegat Light?"

Mahlon nodded.

"You must know that all reports are filed with the State and National Crime Information Centers within twenty-four hours after we get them?"

"But the woman's parents claim they filed one here right after she disappeared."

Strickland bristled at Mahlon's words. "They are mistaken. This office meets it responsibilities, and I don't appreciate this slur about its performance one bit."

"No slur intended," Mahlon said. "I merely stated a fact. Have your secretary bring in the file for August 1970. Let's see whether the Beauchamps filed a report or not."

Strickland regarded Mahlon with hostility for a moment. With an angry stab of his hand, he picked up the phone and dialed his secretary. During the time it took her to find the file and bring it into the office, they faced each other in silence.

"Remain here, Janey," Strickland ordered when she handed him the file. "Our visitor here claims we failed to report a missing person to the SCIC." He turned to Mahlon. "What's her name, again?"

"Karen Beauchamps."

Strickland did a quick search through the file and smiled smugly at Mahlon.

"No Beauchamps. Karen or otherwise. You owe this department an apology."

"May I?" Mahlon extended his hand.

"See for yourself." Strickland dropped the file on the desk. Mahlon retrieved it and began his own search. A moment later, he removed a report from the file.

"Papers have been known to stick together," he said. The man snatched it from his hand, read the name on the report, and settled back in his chair.

"You need to see an eye doctor. The name on this report is 'Ayres.'"

"Look at the sheet that's stuck to it."

Strickland separated the two sheets, which were held together by a morsel of Danish by the look of it. He checked the name on the second one, and his face hardened.

Mahlon could have said that things like this happen in the best of operations, but Strickland had made it such a personal thing that he decided to let the man stew in his own juices.

Strickland turned to his secretary. "I find this most embarrassing." He scraped off the offending morsel with a manicured fingernail and held it up for inspection. "How many other things have you misfiled? I have become the subject of ridicule because you decided to eat at your desk. I will not have it."

Mrs. Kramarz trembled with embarrassment, and a blush swept over her face. "I—I don't know how something like this happened, Chief—"

"I want all files," Strickland said, cutting her off, "checked before you leave today. Do you understand? All files. Now go." The woman nodded and, avoiding Mahlon's eyes, left the office.

Strickland turned a cold eye on Mahlon and asked, "What did you expect to find in this report?"

"The name and address of Karen Beauchamps' roommate."

"I'm under no obligation to share that with you."

"I understand that," Mahlon said, knowing instantly how he would call the man's bluff. "Naturally, I'm under no obligation to keep your refusal from reaching the press."

Strickland's eye brows shot up in surprise, and it took him a moment to think that over. When he finally did speak, he was in control of the situation again.

"Let me tell you how things are run in my jurisdiction, Mr. Mahlon. So there's no misunderstanding later on." He leaned forward, and his voice had a hard-edged quality.

"If word of this embarrassing lapse in procedure becomes public knowledge, you'll wish you never set foot in this station. Is that clear?"

Mahlon nodded. The mistake was unfortunate but hardly of interest to anyone outside the room.

"Furthermore, since your investigation of this woman's death is being conducted within the boundaries of Brant Beach, I expect to be informed of all major developments. In short, if any arrests are to be made in Brant Beach, I expect to be the one to make them. Understand?"

"Absolutely."

Strickland peered down his nose at Mahlon a second or two and then read off the name and address in a flat voice. Her name was Rhonda Black, and she lived in Red Bank. Mahlon wrote it in his notebook.

"I have one more question," Mahlon said as he rose from his chair. "How much advanced notice does your photographer require?"

Strickland gave him a venomous stare. Mahlon left, knowing full well his sarcasm had cost him the man's future cooperation. He'd just have to solve this case without it, and he prayed that what Rhonda Black had to say about Karen would help him.

Chapter 27

When he reached the boulevard, Mahlon looked for a pay phone. He finally spotted one against the sun-drenched front of a laundromat. Information gave him Rhonda Black's phone number, and when he dialed it, Mrs. Black answered. Mahlon introduced himself. Yes, she remembered her daughter talking about Karen's disappearance, and she gasped when she heard about the murder. Rhonda was now a senior at Montclair State College. When Mahlon asked for her campus address, Mrs. Black explained that her daughter was taking exams and might be hard to find. She offered to call Rhonda and arrange a meeting with him for the following day. Mahlon accepted and told her he'd call back that eve-ning.

Mahlon was sweating by the time he stepped from the phone booth. Everywhere he looked he saw teens in T-shirts and cut-offs. By the calendar, summer was more than a month away, but warm weather brought it to the island sooner than any where else. The breeze sweeping down the side street from the ocean brought some welcome relief. The cool waters offshore kept the day temperatures moderate and the nights cool at this time of the year, which was just the way Mahlon liked it.

He stopped by Sara's golf course on his drive back to Beach Haven. The site was a maze of cement forms, and red-topped survey stakes. A half-dozen workers were busy digging footings, and the loud whine of a handsaw drew his attention to two carpenters who were constructing the framing for the admission booth. The foundation had already been poured and the sill plates bolted in place. Sara, however, was nowhere in sight. He waited a half hour for her to return and then went home. He was having her over for dinner that evening, and he had shopping to do.

The late afternoon sky over the bay was the deepest blue by the time Sara arrived. Mahlon happened to be looking out when she crossed the gravel yard to his front door, her back straight and her stride confident. Her tanned skin positively glowed against the white sleeveless dress. She wore large white earrings and a pair of white, strappy sandals on her feet. The only thing not white was the striking red of her hair. Mahlon met her at the door with a kiss

She seated herself on the couch, and he poured her a martini from the shaker he had waiting in the fridge.

"I saw the paper this morning," Sara said after tasting her drink. "You must be celebrating."

"Any dinner with you is a celebration," Mahlon said with a smile. "But to tell the truth, I feel like celebrating. Identifying that body was a real long shot."

"Chief James must be pleased."

"Yeah, Hank's happy, all right."

"You must be glad, too. Your part is over."

Mahlon started to say something but changed his mind. He busied himself with the final dinner preparations instead. His menu was simple: a salad topped with thin slices of Spanish onion and a homemade vinaigrette, grilled sirloin steaks, foil-wrapped early corn cooked on the grill, baked Idaho potatoes and sour cream. He opened a bottle of Cabernet Sauvignon and invited Sara to the table.

The meal was a success, and when they finished, Mahlon suggested a walk on the beach, as there was plenty of light left in the cloudless bowl of the sky. Sara had brought a sweater with her, and she wrapped it around her shoulders as they left the house. Over the bay the sky glowed yellow and pink where the sun had just set. Mahlon turned his back on it with hardly a look and headed for the beach.

The pauses in their conversation grew and grew until Mahlon lapsed into complete silence. They removed their shoes at the beginning of the footpath over the dunes. The sand had lost its heat and felt cool under their feet.

When they descended into the lengthening shadows on the other side of the dunes, Sara spoke but Mahlon didn't respond. She touched his arm to get his attention.

"Something troubling you, Thomas?" Embarrassed at his preoccupation, he took her hand and gave it a squeeze to assure her he was all right.

"When I told you Hank was happy we identified the body, that was only half the story." He looked out over the dark green ocean and watched the edge of darkness slide closer on the water. "The young woman's parents weren't happy at all."

He told her about his trip to Pennington, describing the reaction of the Beauchamps to the awful news in detail.

"Sara, I can't get the look on that poor woman's face out of my mind."

"It's what I like about you, Thomas," Sara said, grasping his arm and holding it to her side. "You feel for people. I hope you never change."

He shrugged. "I don't know. Maybe so."

He took her hand and started walking toward the jetty. When they reached it, Mahlon helped Sara up, and they walked out along the top of the rocks to where the water surged and ebbed among the boulders. Black colonies of mussels clung to rocks at the water line. They stood a few minutes watching the rollers build and crash on the dark brown stones.

"I don't know if that's true," Mahlon said after a few moments. "Feeling for people, I mean. Up to yesterday, the body I found was just another Jane Doe to me. I didn't know what she looked like, and you can't reconstruct a personality from some sand-caked bones. But those two people this after-noon. I watched my words break their hearts. I keep wondering why I don't feel something for their daughter. After all, she was the one murdered. Hasn't she as much claim to my compassion as they do?"

"What exactly do you feel for her?"

"To be honest, all I have is a professional interest. Her death is a riddle I'd like to unravel."

Sara didn't say anything. She took Mahlon's hand and started back. The light was fading rapidly from the sky and the long vista of the beach line shrank in the growing gloom.

"I think, Thomas," Sara said after he helped her down from the rocks, "that you ache for the Beauchamps because their grief was tangible, and you feel guilty for adding to it."

Mahlon nodded.

"I learned in the camps that compassion is wasted on the dead. They no longer have need of it, but the living do. And right now it seems there isn't enough to go around. So don't punish yourself. You gave it where it was really needed."

He put his arm around her shoulder and pulled her close. "Thanks for saying that. You know how much I've complained about working this case for Hank." Mahlon said as they started up the path over the dunes. "I did something strange yesterday."

"What?"

"Just as I was leaving, Mr. Beauchamps begged me not to let Karen's death go unpunished—" He gave a sheepish grin. "—and for some reason I said I wouldn't." Sara smiled.

"And you said you couldn't wait to be through with this case. Why you're as unpredictable as me."

"Maybe so. Anyway, it's not like Mr. Beauchamps hired me or anything. I've done what Hank hired me to do, and if I work on it for a bit more who knows what I'll turn up."

They reached the spot where they had left their shoes. Mahlon was about to pick them up when Sara took his white bearded face in her hands. "Tell me, my fine bearded detective, where will your hunt begin?"

"At Montclair State. Tomorrow." He put his hands on her waist and pulled her toward him. They kissed as the last blush of daylight faded in the west.

Chapter 28

At eleven-thirty the next morning, Mahlon turned off Valley Road onto Montclair State's hilltop campus. The guard at the visitors' information booth on College Avenue handed him a temporary parking permit and directed him to a parking area near the amphitheater where Mrs. Black said he would meet Rhonda.

The original administration building in a Spanish mission style replete with white walls, bell tower, and red tile roofing slid by on his right. Mahlon parked and on foot joined the straggling line of students humping books across the campus. A sign for the amphitheater pointed him toward a cluster of trees.

An opening in the dense wall of poplars led him onto the stage of a natural stone amphitheater set in a hillside. Tier after tier of dark stone seats rose through dappled shade into the warm May sunlight. A second border of poplars screened the rear. The lower seats held a smattering of students. A few were engrossed in books while the majority worked diligently on this year's tan. Mahlon searched for someone matching the description of Rhonda that Mrs. Black had given him last night. No one did. He sat on the sunny side and tipped his face to the sun. When in Rome . . .

"Mr. Mahlon?" a female voice asked a few minutes later.

"Miss Black?"

A young woman in a white cotton tank top and bib overalls stood before him. Rhonda was short with long black hair as her mother described. One hand clutched two paperbacks to her chest, while the other was in her mouth having its nails trimmed. Mahlon rose.

"When I heard about Karen's murder," Rhonda said in an excited voice, "I mean, I totally flipped out. Hey, no one I know was ever murdered before."

"Lucky for your friends, I'd say." Mahlon looked around. Her comment raised a few heads, but the weight of gravity pulled them down again. "Miss Black, do you want to talk here or go for a walk?"

"Here's okay," she said with a shrug. "You can call me Rhonda." The hand holding the books gave a nervous jump. "My exam's in an hour."

They sat. She wore no makeup. Her large eyes, gumdrop nose, and sensual lips struck Mahlon as a nice combination. Whatever figure she had was well hidden beneath the overalls. She set her books on the stone seat between them.

"How did you come to room with Karen?"

"Met at the realtor's in May. We both had summer jobs and were looking for roomies."

"What was she like?"

"I really didn't see much of her. I worked days and she worked evenings. At first she tried to skate on the chores, but I got up her crack about it. We got along all right after that."

Mahlon reached into his coat pocket and took out his notebook. "Did she date a lot?"

Rhonda made a little face. "Well, she wasn't a gagger, if you know what I mean. She wasn't beautiful, either. Nice skin. Large eyes." She batted hers. "Like mine. Only hers were too large. Almost."

A disgruntled look stole across her face. "She must a had something. She got a date the first week of June." Rhonda gave a bitter snort. "It took me another week." A "Can you believe it?" note stole into her voice.

"What kind of guys did she date?"

Rhonda looked down at her hands. "What's that matter, now?"

"Oh, it does."

Rhonda looked him straight in the eye. "I don't speak ill of the dead. Understand?"

"What you tell me won't get back to Karen's parents. I promise, Rhonda." Mahlon leaned toward her and lowered his voice. "Her parents are desperate. They want her killer found."

Rhonda turned away. Her finger went into her mouth. Mahlon gave her time to chew it over. He stole a look at her books. *Everything You Always Wanted to Know About Sex, But Were Afraid to Ask* and *The Sensuous Woman*. He'd like to see the homework assignments for that one.

"All right," Rhonda finally said with a sigh. "Karen wasn't big chested or anything like that. She was thin, and she didn't stand too straight, either. If you ask me, she looked like a hank."

Mahlon wished he had a foreign phrase book. "A hank?"

"Yeah. You know. An easy lay."

"Was she?"

"I don't think she was doing the wild thing with everybody, if that's what you mean. But she was out all night, two, three times a week. I asked her who her main squeeze was. 'It's a secret,' she said and laughed. Hey, she was legal. I was busy taking care of myself."

She gave a forced smile, but her eyes looked haunted by some inner anxiety. "How was I to know she was gonna be murdered?" She gave her long hair a toss and sat up straighter. "We weren't tight. Ours was just a friendship of convenience, Mr. Mahlon. Nothing else."

"Don't blame yourself for Karen's death," Mahlon said.

"Oh, I don't." She hesitated. "Don't think I'm morbid, but where did they find her?"

Mahlon told how he found Karen.

"For real, even? Her foot was like sticking out of the sand?" She wrinkled up her gumdrop nose at the thought. He nodded and told her about his efforts to identify Karen. She barely seemed to listen.

"How was she killed?" she asked as soon as he finished.

"Strangled."

"Hard way to go!" She touched her neck.

"Yeah, you could say that." He sat a moment watching the shade creep over the young female body across from him. Farther up, a beauty in a green halter top gathered her towel and padded away, the soles of her bare feet black as sin.

"What can you tell me about this guy Karen was seeing?" Mahlon asked when the young woman disappeared.

"Nothing really. He must have been a stud muffin because she'd get this dreamy smile whenever she mentioned him. Said I'd be surprised if I knew who it was. By the end of July she was out most nights. I'd be getting up for work and she'd be just coming in. All wanked out from partying. You know, losing it in the bathroom. A green look on her face. But she paid her half of the rent, so what the heck?"

"When did you see her last?"

"A morning or so before she disappeared. Hey, I didn't even know she was gone until her parents called one evening, asking for her." She stopped a moment, as if remembering something.

"Come to think of it, she was kind a spacey toward the end. Staring out the window, and all. I mean, it was, 'Come in, Berlin.'" She shook her head at the memory.

"That last morning she was tossing her groceries as usual. 'Too much partying,' I yelled as I passed the bathroom. When she came out, she apologized. Said she wouldn't be bothering me much longer. 'They' were leaving soon. Her and her man."

She turned to look at him. "When she left, I got really pissed off."

"Why?"

"I got stuck cleaning up the place." The note of irritation in her voice was unmistakable.

Mahlon changed the subject. "What happened to her personal things?"

"Parents took 'em when they came looking for her. She'd been gone more'n a week by then."

Mahlon looked at his watch. "Thanks. I hope I didn't keep you from studying for your next exam."

Rhonda gave a dismissive shrug. "My boyfriend helped me study all last night. I'm gonna ace it."

Mahlon could barely keep from laughing.

"If you think of anything else, give me a call." Mahlon handed her his card as they both stood. She gathered up her books and gave him the biggest grin.

"What do you know?" she said just as she walked away. "I'm a witness in a murder case."

The walk back to the parking area took only a few minutes, and he had the Plymouth moving through the parking lot exit when he heard someone call his name. Rhonda came running up to his window.

"I just remembered," she said.

"What?"

"Karen's parents missed some of her things. She had an autographed Led Zeplin poster. I kept it as payment for cleaning up. Her other things I put in a shoe box and took them home. I figured when she called, I'd tell her about them."

"Where's the shoe box?"

"Home. I'll call Mom and tell her where it's at if you want to look at it. It's nothing really, just odds and ends her parents missed."

"How do I get to your house from here?" Mahlon asked. She gave him directions.

"I gotta run."

The afternoon traffic on the Garden State Parkway was heavy, and Mahlon took more than an hour to reach the Raritan River. The day turned cloudy and by the time he pulled up at Rhonda's home in Red Bank the sun was gone for good. Mrs. Black invited him in for a glass of iced tea and insisted he tell her everything. Fifteen minutes later, he was on the road again with the unopened shoe box on the seat beside him.

When he arrived home, he opened a cold Molson and dumped out the contents of the box on the kitchen table. There was a bottle of suntan lotion, a half-empty jar of skin moisturizer, a black ball point pen from the Quinton Tavern in Philly, a white angel wing sea shell, a book of matches from Orbann's Lounge, a black and red bay scallop shell, one LBI post card, a jackknife clam shell, two perforated guitar picks, a slate black shark tooth, and a Led Zeplin concert program from the Spectrum in Philly dated early August 1970.

Sara had a meeting, so he ate supper at home. He scrambled some eggs and sat at the table, eating them right from the frying pan. The contents of the shoe box lay before him on the white Formica. He studied them where they lay, hoping inspiration would strike, but they were as meaningless a pile of junk after he ate, as they were before. When he finished eating, he dumped them into the box and set it on his mantlepiece.

The low cloud cover rolling over the rooftops toward the sea held the promise of rain, but Mahlon decided to take a walk down to the bay anyway. Pelham Avenue lay empty from the ocean dunes all the way to the bay, which was all right with Mahlon. He wasn't in the mood for company. The daylight was dying, and the flag at the Coast Guard Station snapped like a whip in the rising wind. Mahlon hardly heard it. His mind was focused on what Rhonda had told him earlier that day.

Karen had been seeing someone. And she acted as though Rhonda would be impressed if she knew who it was. Whatever that meant? Rhonda got the impression that Karen loved to party. But what if Rhonda were wrong? Maybe Karen's sickness wasn't from partying. Maybe she was pregnant. It would explain the morning sickness and her plans to run off. But suppose, for whatever reason, her lover didn't want to. Karen wouldn't be the first woman murdered for an unwanted pregnancy.

Speculation, my man. It's all pure speculation. He had to find out who Karen had been seeing. Otherwise, he was wasting his time. But where else could he look? If Karen's roommate didn't know who the guy was, who would?

He mounted the bulkhead at the end of the street and stood facing the rising wind and stark emptiness of the bay. The waves slapped against the bulk-head below his feet sending a thin spray of cold water into the night air. The boats in the marina beside him thumped and bobbed in their moorings like restless farm animals before a storm. He stood there until the house lights across the bay suddenly faded from sight. He had been living there long enough to know that could mean only one thing.

Mahlon started back toward the house at a brisk pace. The cold rain caught up to him a hundred yards from home. By the time he opened the front door, he was sopping wet. Like a drowned rat, he entered the house. The drenching left him with sodden spirits. He had been putting it off all evening and now the conviction came crashing down on him that his investigation was going no where. In fact, it was sinking rapidly, and he had yet to leave port.

Chapter 29

"You're not drinking Scotch and ginger tonight, I hope," James said over his shoulder, his face screwed tight with distaste. Though a gray business suit covered his broad shoulders, he still looked like a cop, yellow paisley tie and all. The meal and speeches were over, and the social part of the evening just beginning. Mahlon was right behind James, as he plowed through the throng of off-duty policemen right up to the bar.

"What the hell do you care what I drink?" Mahlon asked, as he slid into an opening beside his friend and looked around for some service.

"It's a waste of good Scotch. That's what it is."

"Well, tell him not to use 'good' Scotch."

James gave him a hard stare. "That's the trouble with you, Thomas. You don't know the first thing about Scotch."

"Come on, Hank. What's to know? When you're down enough, your troubles disappear. For a while at least." Mahlon got a perverse pleasure out of tweaking his friend's sense of drinking protocol. He was glad for the distraction. The thought of having to go out on that dance floor had his insides roiling.

Their good-natured banter was interrupted by the arrival of a black vested barkeep who took James' order without batting an eye.

"See," Mahlon said, "Scotch and ginger didn't faze him a bit."

"Hah. He probably thinks the Old Fashioned Sara ordered is yours."

When their drinks were served up, they worked their way out of the press of bodies to the open dance floor. On the way back to the table where Clare and Sara had been talking nonstop since they arrived, Mahlon nudged James. At another table not far from theirs, Chief Strickland was holding court. The man was pontificating to his dinner companions, and they appeared to be lapping it up.

"A missing person report gets misfiled," Mahlon said, out of the side of his mouth, "and it's my fault for pointing it out."

James answered with a grunt of disgust. "What do you expect from a stuffed shirt?"

Mahlon took a sip from his drink. "Damn, that tastes good."

James gave him a withering look, and they moved on. After they set the drinks in front of the ladies, James came around to Mahlon's side.

"Now, where were we?" James asked, after he took a sip from his glass. "Oh, yeah. Let me see if I got this right. You think the boyfriend did her in because she was knocked up. Right?"

"Yeah." Mahlon's said distractedly. The butterflies in his stomach were bouncing off the walls. Why, oh, why did he ever let Hank badger him into coming to this damn thing?

"It's a motive, all right," James said. "Only problem is how do you prove it? The autopsy didn't say anything about her being pregnant."

"I know. I know." Mahlon said. He wished Hank would go away. He was trying to make up his mind whether to just refuse to dance or to risk certain embarrassment with Sara on the dance floor.

"And this college girl you talked to. She didn't know the boyfriend's name. Right?"

Mahlon nodded, barely listening. He was swirling his drink and debating his alternatives.

"So where do we go from here, my friend?"

Mahlon didn't answer. James repeated his question, and Mahlon didn't appreciate the intrusion.

"Damn it, Hank, we are not going anywhere. My work for you is done."

James gave a start of surprise. "What the hell are you saying?"

Mahlon hadn't meant to announce it like this, but now that it was out, he couldn't take it back. "Hey, I ID'd the body for you didn't I?"

"Yeah?" James asked, his eyes narrowing with suspicion.

"And they nabbed that molester last week, so the rest is up to you and the county."

"So that's why you went all the way up to Montclair? Who are you kidding?"

"Well—" Mahlon raised his hand and scratched his beard. "—I figured I owed one to the Beauchamps, but I came up empty."

James moved off to digest this piece of news. The waitresses had cleared away the dishes by that time and the band started to play. With a stony expression on his face, James rose and asked Clare to dance. His wife excused herself and got to her feet. James turned to Sara.

"Thomas is a bit bashful about dancing. Get him out there and give him a lesson. And don't let him put you off, either." Sara turned and smiled broadly at Mahlon.

You son-of-a—. Mahlon's face was heating up.

James gave him a cold stare and, taking Clare's hand, led her out on the dance floor.

Sara rose, straightened her light green cocktail dress, and extended her slender hand toward him. "Thomas, let's give it a try."

Mahlon broke out in a cold sweat and looked around for an escape. Sara was waiting right in front of him when he turned back. He cursed under his breath, rose and took her hand. What else could he do? She led him onto the floor and turned to him, her arms open to receive him. Wiping his palms on his trousers, Mahlon took her left hand in his and placed his right on her hip. Sara took hold of his wrist and pulled it around to the small of her back.

"I'm not delicate, Thomas. I won't break." She moved closer to him, and they began to sway in time with the music.

"Bashful?" she asked with a mischievous grin. "A bashful Private Eye? That must be a first."

Mahlon gave her a thin smile. His mind was wrestling with the solid geometry of tangled feet. Each move he made seemed sure to send him stumbling. He was petrified. One misstep and Sara could limp off the floor.

Sara pulled away slightly and looked into his face. "Don't look so unhappy, Thomas. Take a deep breath and relax."

He took one and suddenly realized they were moving. Together. Dancing.

"You can let it out now, Thomas," she said trying to keep from laughing. He let his breath out.

"Yes, that's more like it." She placed her cheek against his. The clean smell of her upswept hair was bewitching. "Now, try to feel the music and move with it."

The vocalist with the five-piece band was singing now. One of last year's hits. The First Time Ever I Saw Your Face. Her voice was clear and mellow. The words conjured up that day last spring when a red head interrupted his R&R on the beach to hire him to find her missing handyman. And he returned and gave the red head in his arms a kiss.

Mahlon's steps were tentative, and Sara led for a little bit, showing him the way, and soon his feet found enough of the melody so that the two of them moved as one. And dear Sara followed every move. If people didn't look too closely, they might even think he knew what he was doing.

Sara was a miracle worker. How she did it, he didn't know. He was even beginning to enjoy himself. He ventured a look around at the other dancers. No one was paying him the least attention. A moment later, Hank and Clare glided by, executing a sweeping side-by-side step that impressed Mahlon. He had no idea Hank was such a good dancer. The two seemed totally absorbed in one another.

The dance ended, and Mahlon rewarded Sara with another kiss. "I don't know how you did it," he said, "but I actually enjoyed myself for a few moments there."

Sara smiled. "What you need is a few private lessons."

"And the beatings will continue until morale improves. Is that how it is?" Sara struck him playfully on the arm. They laughed and walked off the dance floor arm-in-arm.

Back at the table, the ladies teamed up for a visit to the powder room. James had been intercepted by someone on his way back from the floor and was now, thankfully, in conversation five or six tables away. Mahlon took it upon himself to replenish everyone's drink.

The dancers were on the floor again, and he had to skirt around them, following the ring of white tables to the other side of the floor. Halfway around, he spotted Sgt. Woodson sitting with a rather dour looking woman. Woodson locked eyes with him a moment and then studiously turned away.

The crowd at the bar was larger than before. As Mahlon waited his turn, he saw Steven Orbann talking to another man just ahead. Impeccably dressed in an expensive gray suit and silk tie, Orbann was holding forth, his face beaming confidence and his words just loud enough to reach Mahlon.

"No," Orbann said, arching his eyebrows in amused disdain at the speaker's last statement. "One of the best kept secrets is that LBI doesn't get back its fair share of state taxes." A campaign pitch, if Mahlon ever heard one. Damn. Politicians never take a night off. Mahlon turned away, not wanting to let Orbann change his mood, which was surprisingly light hearted now. At that moment someone yanked his sleeve and swung him around.

A black face loomed in front of him. "Tell that honky friend of yours, he got away with it the last time, but he ain't heard the last from me." The man's lips were curled back, and the words spilled out, well oiled with whiskey.

"Save that for the courts, Sanders," a bystander said, pulling the young black man by the arm. "Don't make an ass of yourself." Sanders shook him off.

"Red neck bastards like Chief James been doing us blacks wrong for a long time," Sanders said, poking his finger in Mahlon chest. "We ain't taking it any more. You hear? We got the law on our side this time."

Someone came to the aid of the first man, and together they pulled Sanders away from Mahlon. The young black officer gave way reluctantly. It was only as the three men disappeared toward the exit that Mahlon realized the second man was Sgt. Woodson.

"He's filing a discrimination suit," someone said.

"He keeps hitting the juice," the man in front said over his shoulder, "and the Chief will have grounds to throw his black ass off the force." Just then an opening appeared at the bar, and Mahlon slid into it and ordered his drinks. He wondered if Hank knew. Sgt. Woodson obviously did.

When Mahlon got back to the table, James was waiting for him. "I shouldn't have stomped off like that, Thomas, but you took me by surprise."

"I had things on my mind, Hank. I didn't mean to blurt it out like that."

"Well—" James paused. "—I've been talking it over with Clare. We think it might be for the better."

Mahlon's eyes widened when he heard that. "You two talked it over?"

"That's right. For some reason, she's taken a sudden interest in my situation." James looked Mahlon in the eye. "We appreciate what you've done. You kept the wolf from the door long enough for me to go on the offensive."

"Thanks, Hank. Speaking of politics," Mahlon said, "I hope you got a good lawyer."

"Now, what the hell do you mean by that?"

"I just had a brush with Ptl. Sanders. He's one angry, young black man." He told James what had happened and ended it with the comment made by the bystander.

"Sanders is just angry because I suspended him. That's all."

"He said you 'got away with it the last time.' What do you suppose he meant by that?"

James looked at him with an innocent expression. "I haven't the foggiest."

"I don't think this is something you can brush off, Hank."

"I'll handle it, Thomas. I'll handle it."

Sara got him out on the dance floor a second time, and he began to relax a bit. They returned laughing to the table. James stood up and gestured to Sara to dance. As they spun away, James wore a devilish grin. He said over his shoulder, "Why don't you and Clare join us?"

Mahlon wanted to kill him, but all he could do was manage a thin smile when Clare stood. On the dance floor, he was relieved to learn that she followed his awkward lead expertly. Before the song ended Clare had him talking about bird watching, and they continued their conversation all the way back to the table. It was the first time Mahlon had felt at ease in her company.

Mahlon and Sara took their leave of the Jameses shortly after that. Sara had a busy day tomorrow. As they strolled arm in arm out the door, Mahlon sighed with relief. The evening was over, and his anxiety about dancing was finally gone.

Inside the car, Mahlon switched on the radio and found some soft music for their ride home. He leaned over to kiss Sara when he saw something that brought him up short. Two car rows over, Steven Orbann was pumping the hand

and patting the back of Sgt. Woodson. What the hell were those two up to?

Chapter 30

The first hot breath of summer blew in from the southwest the third week of May and thickened the air over the pines with haze. By that time the tulips in Mahlon's front yard had long since withered like the leads in the Beauchamp case.

As it was, Mahlon had enough work to keep him busy, but the approach of summer always left him disgruntled. Each weekend brought larger crowds to the shore. More cars traveled the boulevard, and more power boats churned up the bay. High tide brought larger armies of wet-suited warriors tramping Pelham Avenue with surfboard shields on their way to battle Poseidon. Even his evening jog on the beach wasn't what it used to be. Fishermen now lined the surf, and Mahlon spent so much time ducking fishing lines that he never got into a running rhythm.

Even the local papers conspired against him, carrying nothing but articles on upcoming summer events. He couldn't open the paper without encountering schedules for community theaters, profiles of performers, and endless lists of entertainment schedules for the big watering holes on the island.

The last Wednesday in May, the Beach Haven *Times* ran a feature article that caught his eye. The name Ricky Gee had winked at Mahlon from shop windows and telephone poles for so long that he skimmed it to see what all the fuss was about. The article traced the "artistic" growth of this rising rock star from his humble start in small clubs in Philadelphia through an attention getting stint at

217

Orbann's Lounge on to his recent big label recordings in New York. To the writer's delight, Ricky Gee was kicking off his first national concert tour the week of July 4th at Orbann's Lounge, the scene of his first triumph. A cultural event Mahlon fervently hoped to miss.

So it was with churlish pleasure that Mahlon greeted the unseasonable return of cool weather that sent people scurrying for jackets and cleared the beach of even the most fanatical sunbathers that afternoon. A clammy mist rolled in at dusk and fogged the windows with its fetid breath. He invited Sara over, and they spent a quiet evening before the fire.

"What if this weather carries through to the weekend?" Sara asked. Memorial Day was Monday, and her mind was grappling with the last minute details of getting her business open by Friday.

"That's not going to happen," Mahlon said. He rose to prod the logs on the fire for some extra warmth.

"What if the putters don't arrive tomorrow? What will I do?"

"We'll hit the local stores and buy up what they have. We'll get them somewhere."

As it turned out, Sara's fears about the weather were unfounded. The next day dawned cool and overcast with a thin sliver of blue showing in the northwest. The morning was blustery, and by the time Mahlon sat down at his desk to do some paper work, Pelham Avenue was already dry. Shortly after nine, his phone rang, and Chief James called his name as soon as he lifted the receiver.

"Hank, what's got you on my line this early?"

"The other shoe just dropped," James said cryptically.

"What?"

"The rest of the dirt from my personnel file hit the streets this week."

"You want to talk about it?"

"Yeah," James said, "but not right now. I got lawyers coming in this morning about that discrimination suit Sanders filed." He hesitated.

"Thomas, Mrs. Andrews called again this morning. Yeah, pirates on the beach again. I hate to ask, but could you talk to her?"

"Damn, Hank, can't you detail one of your patrolmen to do it? I've got things to do."

"Sure," James said in a tired voice. "It's just that you know how to handle her, that's all. We could have lunch afterward. My treat."

Mahlon knew a call for help when he heard it. "Since you're buying, I'll see her. Beside, I haven't been chewed out by that woman in months."

"Thanks," James said. The note of relief in his voice was unmistakable. "We'll meet at Bernie's around noon."

Mahlon started for Barnegat Light at ten. The sky was brightening and a steady breeze carried clearing skies in from the west. He parked the Plymouth across from the Andrews' house. The untended shrubbery outside concealed much of the first floor, and all the shades were drawn on the upper floors, except for the windows of the widow's watch, which gazed down on him with stark disapproval.

The creaking of the porch boards announced his arrival. He tapped the weathered knocker three times, and the curtains parted. A second later, the door swung open.

"Humph," Mrs. Andrews said, her voice dry as dust, "only one this time. Where's the big one?" She raised a gnarled hand to silence any response. "Don't tell me. Too busy for the likes of me. I'm sure."

Mahlon just smiled and waited.

"Don't stand there smiling like an idiot. Come in! Come in!"

Mahlon did, and Mrs. Andrews shut the door behind him. The stained glass panels each side of the door gave the dim foyer a greenish glow. Nearby, a dark balustrade rose through the murky air into the shadows of the second floor.

Mrs. Andrews stood by the door appraising him for a moment. She wore an apron over the same blue paisley dress she had on the last time. Mahlon waited for her to speak.

"Found those poor men's bones last time, didn't you?" Her mouth drew into a tight line as if to add an "I-told-you-so" to her question.

"Not exactly."

She waved him quiet. "No need to explain. They were back again last night." Her eyes sparkled, as she punctuated her statement with a nod.

"Who?"

"The ghosts! Who else?" She looked at him over her silver-rimmed glasses and gave a disgusted shake. "They never send me a smart one."

Mahlon stifled a laugh. "Ghosts were on the beach again last night?

"Watched them carry their sea bags into the dunes, I did. Just like last time." She clasped her hands and waited for Mahlon to say something. Outside the day brightened as the sun broke through the clouds.

"I'll investigate, Mrs. Andrews." He knew his words obligated him to walk the length of the beach under her watchful eye. "We appreciate your willingness to do your civic duty."

"Oh, stop blubbering, will you?" She began shooing him out the door. "Get on with it."

Mahlon hid his laughter. He should have known better than to try to patronize her. She opened the door and impatiently ushered him out onto the porch. He trotted down the steps and across the street to his car and moved it thirty yards up the road to where the boulevard ended and Fourth Street intersected it from the west. He pulled off the road, leaving plenty of room for traffic to make the turn.

The beach entrance was a narrow breach in the snow fence. Mahlon trudged up the incline to the gap and looked around. An expanse of white beach rolled away toward the gray boulders that marked the edge of the inlet. Overhead, broken white clouds scudded out to sea, and a big herring gull sailed by, riding the tailwind east. Near the water two small lads, trousers wet up to their waists, ran and danced along the rushing surf.

Mahlon resisted the urge to look back. He already sensed Mrs. Andrews' skeptical eyes boring into his back. He should have worn his knee support. Traipsing all over the beach wasn't doing it any good. Since March, a new snow fence had been erected along the base of the dunes to discourage foot traffic. He followed it toward Old Barney, standing like a red jacketed sentinel beside the inlet. The desire to see where Karen had lain pulled him strongly.

"Don't get morbid," he told himself, and he slowed his pace. He put Karen out of his mind and began to wonder what scandal Woodson could have pulled from Hank's file. It was a wonder Hank managed to keep his temper in check. Woodson was lucky he hadn't collected a broken nose by this time.

In March the beach had been beaten trackless by the heavy rains. Today, the sand was dry, as his rapidly filling shoes testified, and pocked with footprints. He searched for some familiar feature, but the dunes all looked alike somehow, except for two which bore new "No Trespassing" signs.

When he came to the first dune with a sign, he saw something that brought him up short. A trail of footprints led right up the smooth sand of the slope between the dunes and out of sight.

"That's interesting." By the looks of it, more than one person had made the trek. And recently, too.

His eye came to rest on the snow fence in front of him. The upper wire had been cut, and someone had slipped a black wire loop over the staves on each side of the cut to hold them closed. He bent and examined the lower strand. It had been cut, too, and rewired together. There was no mistake about it. Mrs. Andrews' pirates weren't a figment of her imagination after all. Someone had deliberately cut the fence and crossed over the dunes. Why?

That would depend where the footprints led. Maybe it was a couple of lovers seeking privacy behind the dune. Mahlon realized at that moment that the lighthouse might help him satisfy his curiosity. He started toward it.

The dunes ended abruptly at the visitors' area near Old Barney, where packed gravel made the going easier. The beach ran on another forty yards to the dark stone jetty lining the south bank of the inlet. Mahlon mounted the high steps to the concrete apron that ringed the base of the lighthouse and sat on the nearest bench to dump the sand from his shoes.

To his relief, the lighthouse door lay open. The walk hadn't been for nothing. A young couple wandered into view while he was busy brushing the sand from his socks and disappeared into the lighthouse. As soon as he got his shoes on again, Mahlon followed them.

Climbing the yellow staircase was tiring, and when he came to the second window opening in the thick wall, he sat briefly on its ledge to give his knee a rest. The laughter of the couple ahead of him ran down the red bricks like water.

Finally, he emerged into a grey room with round windows that housed the drive mechanism for the old lamp. The door leading to the lamp chamber at the very top was padlocked. The others were no where in sight. He followed the sound of voices through another doorway leading to an observation platform, suspended like a circular cage on the outside of the lighthouse.

The breeze was much stronger up there and whistled softly through the iron mesh of the superstructure. Below him lay the green waters of the inlet, looking swift and deep.

White breakers rolled over the black line of rock on the other side of the inlet. The couple was busy taking pictures, so Mahlon circled in the opposite direction. On the ocean side, last night's rain clouds lay dark and sullen on the horizon.

When Long Beach Island offered up its rooftops for his inspection, he identified Mrs. Andrews' house without difficulty. But when he tried to spot the foot trail, the distance proved too great. His attention, however, was drawn to a line of houses that bordered the south edge of the park.

Black cherry and tall sassafras trees blocked the view of most of them. All he could make out on the ground were two shed-like structures near the beach. The shades on the second floor windows of the house behind them were drawn, and the old roof was missing a shingle or two. Mahlon wondered if it was occupied.

As if to prove him wrong, something moved at the back of the place. The trees made it difficult to see, but Mahlon caught a glimpse of a man in a white shirt moving around down there. The man was there one second and gone the next. Moments later, a car started up and drove away.

One thing was clear. The only way to find where the footpath went was to enter that fenced-off area behind the dunes.

Sure. And how do you get over that fence without the Park Rangers seeing you?

Mahlon studied the line of fencing separating the tourist area around the base of Old Barney from the woods and saw the answer. He headed for the stairs. The trip down was easier on his knee than the climb up.

When he stepped from the lighthouse, he glanced around. The bulkhead west of the lighthouse held a thin line of fishermen, but they were all facing the inlet. As for the Park Rangers at the entrance, the one-story comfort station over by the fence would provide all the cover he needed.

He waded through the knee-high weeds at the rear of the comfort station to the hurricane fence. It stood at least six feet tall, and the bushes on the other side grew tightly against the chain-link.

It took Mahlon three tries to scale it, and just as he got over, the hem of his shirt sleeve caught on the top and tore on his way down. He dropped into a narrow space between two bayberry bushes and stood with his back pressed against the fence, catching his breath. If the Park Rangers saw him now, he'd have some real explaining to do.

The only place to go was down. He let his back slide down the fence, and pushing branches aside, wiggled his way underneath the bushes. A minute later, he emerged from the undergrowth in a sandy clearing flooded with sunlight and alive with the sound of insects. He headed toward the sound of crashing waves with the idea that he would conduct his search for the foot trail by walking along the rear of the dunes.

Five minutes later, perspiration burned his eyes and sandburs clung to his trouser. He lifted his damp shirt from his body while he studied the narrow path. It came down the back of the dune, where torn ribs of Virginia creeper and trampled heather marked its course. It descended into a hollow where it disappeared into a tangle of brush, mostly young beach plums and red cedar. He followed it down, slipping and sliding on the loose sand and brushed past the young cedars and saw the trail bend from sight behind a huge holly.

Damn, it sure looked easier from the lighthouse. He wiped his face with his handkerchief and moved on.

When he rounded the holly tree, he expected to find an out-of-the-way spot, littered with empties and the like, but instead the trail continued on, dropping steeply down a sandy incline to the shaded floor of a forest. He entered the sun-dappled shade, glad to be out of the sun, and stood looking at the place. Holly trees with light green trunks and black barked wild cherry spread their branches above him.

A low brush grew at their base, and the path was a narrow, sandy line that snaked between the trees in the direction of the houses. He saw the rusty cyclone fence first at the end of a dark tunnel under the trees. The two structures he'd seen from the lighthouse stood just on the other side. They were wooden garden sheds and stood in someone's back yard. When he reached the fence, he saw that it was festooned with dead vines. Someone had cut them off at ground level and left them hanging on the fence. A closer look showed that the fence had been cut at a spot directly opposite the sheds. The two sides were wired together in three places with the same black wire that had been used on the snow fence.

Mahlon looked at the nearby houses but saw no one. Undoing the middle and lower wires, he slipped into the yard and closed up the hole behind him. The sand in front of the sheds was boot marked, and stout padlocks secured both doors.

Mrs. Andrews hadn't seen ghosts last night. That was for sure. Mahlon had a hunch that whatever was carried up from the beach was probably still in the sheds. But he had what he came for, and he wasn't going to add breaking and entering to the charge of trespassing. He'd tell Hank and see what he could make of it. The only thing for him to do was to get out of there before someone reported him to the police.

When he stepped from between the houses, he expected to find himself on Fourth Street, but he wasn't. Instead of the boulevard to his left, there was a dead end. He jotted down the house number in his notebook and hoped a street sign at the other end would tell him where he came out. Only a few houses stood on the park side of the street, and those on the opposite side hid behind a thick canopy of trees. The park fence on his right, overgrown with trumpet vines and poison ivy, pointed the way out to the main street. When he reached Broadway, the street sign said Third Street. A passerby, seeing an overgrown wall of vegetation, would think the place was uninhabited.

Mahlon slowed his pace when he saw no sign of Hank's patrol car in front of Bernie's. Hank had just about all he could handle. Leave it to Woodson to give him more. Mahlon couldn't help but wonder how his friend was going to handle it.

Minutes later, he was back on the boulevard staring at his car. A manila parking ticket fluttered on the windshield. With a curse, Mahlon yanked it free and turned it over. The name of the issuing officer was Sgt. David Schuyler Woodson.

I'll be damned!

Chapter 31

Looking neither right nor left, Chief James went straight to the table under the humming air conditioner and sat. He tossed his chief's cap onto the chair by the wall, and the beak hit the wooden back rail with a crack loud enough to turn heads. Ignoring the attention, James mopped his forehead with his handkerchief.

As luck would have it, when the morning clouds moved out to sea, the day turned warm. He was sick of summer already, and it hadn't even gotten here yet. The cool air in the restaurant felt damn good. When Thomas entered Bernie's a few minutes later, James managed a weary nod.

"Sorry to keep you waiting," Thomas said. He sat opposite James and looked askance at the rumbling A.C. in the wall over their heads. "Let's find another table, Hank."

"This one's fine," James said, with finality. The subject wasn't open to debate. "Look a little ragged around the edges today, Thomas. Mrs. Andrews take a broom to you or something?"

Thomas patted the torn ends of his shirtsleeve, wiped his glistening brow, and ran a hand over his beard. He detected a sandbur and, plucking the offending body from his person, dropped it in the ashtray.

"Now that's how a luncheon date should look," James said, with barely a smile.

"Hank, I'm in no mood for any of your crap. I've been chewed out by Mrs. Andrews. Slogged across the beach. Climbed the lighthouse. Jumped a six-foot chain-link fence, and clawed my way through bushes that would have torn the loin cloth off Tarzan's ass. All as a favor for you. And what do I get for my effort? Appreciation? No way! Insults? You bet!"

James was laughing by this time, in spite of himself, tears forming in his eyes. Then Thomas yanked something from his shirt pocket and tossed it on the table in front of him.

"Who's paying this, Hank? Tell me that?"

James looked down and saw the folded parking ticket, and his laughter dried up as quickly as it started. "Woodson?" James asked, his voice tight with anger.

Thomas nodded.

James wanted to swear at the top of his lungs, but he didn't. Instead, he pounded his fist on the table. When heads turned, he stared them down belligerently.

"Well, that wiped the smugness off your face," Thomas said.

"Don't push me, Thomas."

"Okay. Okay. Just order me a cold Molson's, and I'll be quiet."

James started to stuff the parking ticket in his shirt pocket, but Thomas plucked it from his hand.

"Hold on, buddy. Let's not give Sgt. Woodson another charge to bring up against you." He returned the ticket to his shirt pocket.

In spite of himself, James began to chuckle. "Did you really climb a fence?" Thomas nodded. "What the hell for?"

"All in good time, my friend. All in good time."

A smile grew on James' face. "That would be something to see."

"It was not graceful, let me tell you." Thomas shook his head sadly and began to chuckle. James joined in.

Bernie appeared, his taciturn face studying the two men. James asked about the day's luncheon special and then ordered the ale for Thomas and an iced tea for himself.

"You're a tonic for a troubled mind," he said when Bernie left. "I needed that laugh. So tell me what happened?"

Thomas described his visit to Mrs. Andrews and his walk on the beach. The cut fence wires and the foot trail over the dunes surprised James. Thomas explained why he climbed the lighthouse, and James had to chuckle when he heard about his efforts to scale the chain-link fence and his crawl through the brush on the other side. However, the foot trail leading to two storage sheds behind the house on Third Street lit his eyes up. At that moment, Bernie arrived with two large bowls of fish chowder and a small loaf of homemade bread.

"Well, the old gal wasn't imagining things after all," James said as soon as Bernie left. He began slicing the bread.

"If I wanted to bring contraband onto the island, Third Street would be the place to do it. No one but the residents seems to know it's there."

"Maybe so," Thomas said. He was busy slathering one of the slices with butter. "But the chances of being seen on the beach and crossing the dunes make it risky on clear nights. Third Street's a foul-weather backup. When the inlet's too risky to travel."

James considered this a moment while he tasted his soup. It was thick and hearty like he knew it would be. "What kind of contraband are we talking about here? She said they were carrying sea bags. My guess is they were carrying plastic bags filled with pot. It's the only thing that makes sense."

It was Thomas' turn to nod, now. He was working on his soup and the smile on his face told James he was enjoying every morsel.

"Right," Thomas said after he swallowed. "Let's take that idea a bit further. The pot's being ferried in from a ship. Those lights around Old Barney make a really good beacon, even in bad weather. They unload the stuff on the inlet beach and hump it over the dunes. And the sale of pot and who knows what else on LBI goes on uninterrupted."

"We're onto something, here, Thomas. I need the number of that house."

Thomas told him.   "You can see who owns the place at the Tax Assessor's office," he said. "Now let's eat."

James agreed. The men concentrated on eating and conversation lapsed. James knew he hadn't broached the matter he really wanted to discuss with Thomas yet, but he didn't want to ruin a good lunch with disturbing news.

Thomas finished his soup first, and he was buttering the last slice of homemade bread when he spoke up. "I saw something when I left the dance last month you might find interesting."

"What's that?"

"Sgt. Woodson was talking to Steve Orbann in the parking lot. They looked real chummy."

James curled his lip in disgust. "How am I gonna beat this guy? He's got Orbann's backing, too."

"You don't know that for sure. Maybe Orbann turned him down."

James gave an ironic laugh. "Guess who's been talking up Orbann candidacy around the station the last few weeks?" He gave a disgusted shake of his head. "Woodson's a dumb cop, but he knows how to play politics."

"Just what you need," Thomas said. "Something else to worry about. From your call, I gather you got a new mess on your hands. Want to talk about it?"

James gave a look at the patrons around him and then glanced at the air conditioner overhead. "It's noisy, but it will keep this conversation private." He set his elbows on the edge of the table and leaned toward Thomas.

"It's funny how things come out of the past that you thought were dead and buried. The rumor Woodson is spreading around now is that I'm a racist." James grimaced at the thought of it.

"On what basis?"

"It was in my file. It's a long story. Sure you want to hear it?"

"If you want to tell it. Sure."

James picked up his paper napkin and began folding it.

"In Newark, I was a foot cop. One hot night in a colored neighborhood, as we used to call them back then, somebody threw a party. Five, six people were drinking, including a mother and her son. When the party really got going, they went outside and started dancing on the top of some cars parked on the street. A neighbor reported it, and a radio car was dispatched.

"Naturally, the drinkers wouldn't come down so the officer called for the wagon. It arrived, and the officers started loading them on. That's when all hell broke loose." James ran his fingers up and down the crease he'd made in the napkin.

"A brawl ensued. The woman kicked one of the blues in the chest and knocked him down. The ones already in the wagon piled out, and the son pulls a knife and slashes at one of the officers. The officer pulls out his service revolver and orders the guy to drop the knife. He doesn't. He says he's gonna carve himself a cop and starts to advance. The officer shoots him in the leg. The bullet hits the femoral artery and blood starts spurting everywhere.

"Here comes the interesting part. The officer holsters his gun and tries to give the man first aid. He tries to use his nightstick as a lever in a tourniquet. But Mama won't let him. She's scratching and punching him. All the while her son is bleeding all over the street.

"I was two blocks over on my beat when I heard the shot. I took off running. When I came around the corner, I ran into a riot. Apparently, some bystanders joined in. All three officers were getting the shit kicked out of them.

Before it's over, the four of us are fighting twenty or so people."

James saw that his hands were balled into tight fists at the memory of it. He opened them and placed them on his lap.

"Help finally came. Some neighbor must have called because none of us could get to the radio. By the time we got the son to the hospital, he'd bled to death. Two days later, all four of us are up on charges. Some local Black ministers were demanding that we be punished." He gave Thomas a slow shake of his head to confirm the injustice of it all.

"The FBI gets into the act and investigates the incident. Fortunately, several blacks came forward and testified on our behalf. Eventually, we were all cleared. The investigation found that we had acted within the scope of our authority, and the officer who shot the son had acted in self-defense."

He balled up the napkin and tossed it on the table.

"Wouldn't you know it, Thomas? Woodson got the story from my personal file and is spreading it around. Only he leaves out the part about my being exonerated. One of Clare's friends gave her the story on Sunday. Clare's so mad she could kill him. I had to make her promise not to do anything foolish. Whooee! I'm glad she's on my side. If she meets Woodson, he'll think he's been hit by a buzz saw."

"What are you going to do about it?"

James shrugged. "Tell my side of the story to the papers?"

"They'll only use it to sell papers. You know that."

"But my reputation is at stake. How much does a cop have to show for his thirty years? Sciatica from sitting too long in squad cars, and the knowledge he's been an honest cop. Or not. I've been honest, Thomas, and I ain't about to roll over and play dead for anyone."

"Right," Thomas said. "Give Del Shannon a call. She'll give you a fair shake."

"I might just do that," James said rising from the table. He dropped some money on the table. "Thanks for taking Mrs. Andrews off my hands today. I hope the old gal has put us onto something because our antidrug campaign is going nowhere. We've made three raids this month and come up empty every time. Somebody's tipping 'em off. I swear."

Outside, James squinted in the bright sunlight. The last thing he wanted to do was go back to the station house. He'd been chief too long to start running from the job.

"Hank, a lot of people believe in you," Thomas said as they parted ways. "Don't forget that."

"Maybe so, Thomas. But it doesn't make it any easier to fall asleep at night."

Chapter 32

The putters arrived Thursday afternoon, so the "Grand Opening" of Sara's miniature golf course on Memorial Day weekend went as planned. Training her staff and ironing out last minute problems kept her busy well into the night. Mahlon didn't see much of her over the weekend, but the one time he did see her, he would like to forget.

He stopped by her business early Friday afternoon and found her inside the club house going over admission procedures with a young college girl. The holiday crowd was beginning to swarm the island, but the only ones on the course at that moment were five boys, brothers by the look of them, and two elderly women who giggled like a couple of teenagers.

When Sara finished instructing her assistant, she came outside. She wore a white sleeveless blouse and white shorts. Her long slender legs were already bronzed, and Mahlon had trouble taking his eyes off them. They stood side by side watching the young boys play.

"I used to be pretty good in my day," Mahlon said.

"How about a game?" Sara asked. "My treat. Loser cooks dinner for the week."

"Sure. Why not?"

She went into the club house and came back with clubs and balls. He got one of the new putters. Oddly enough, Sara's was a different design. He guessed she had brought over her own putter to test the course earlier in the week.

Being a gentleman, Mahlon let her go first. She sank three straight holes-in-one, while he over-shot the cups and ended up three-putting his way out of them. He smelled a setup but told himself it was just his suspicious nature. The next hole. He'd close the gap on the next hole. However, his timing was so atrocious, he hit the damn windmill blade four times in a row.

Sara set a wicked pace. She kept stroking the ball smoothly and sinking her putts with aggravating regularity while his score mounted. It was a competitive side of her Mahlon hadn't seen before. After every hole, she dutifully entered the strokes on their scorecard and flashed him that charming lopsided smile.

Three times his ball bounced off the putting green, and once it landed in the water obstacle. Sara administered the *coup de grace* when she stroked the ball into the bull's-eye on the last hole and won a free game. As if she needed it.

Mahlon finished with a respectable score—for thirty-six holes—but they had played only eighteen. He was humiliated.

"My instincts were right," he said, giving vent to his frustration. "This was a setup, if I ever saw one. You're just a miniature-golf shark." They both laughed at that.

"Why, Thomas," Sara said when they stopped, "did you think I would enter a business I know nothing about? I am too good a businesswoman to do that."

"This isn't over, you know," he said, putting his hands on her waist. "I want a rematch."

"I know a good pro on the mainland who can help your putting game," she said, laughing in his face.

"Ooh, that stung." Mahlon gave her a kiss and retreated to lick his wounds.

On his way home, he stopped at the book store in Beach Haven and bought a new copy of Birds of North America. His old one was falling apart.

Mahlon watched the local paper for James' story. He found it on the lower half of page one in the Sunday edition. Del's article described the vicious rumors circulating about

Barnegat Light's well known police chief. The incident in Newark was fairly presented. James' statement was well phrased and substantiated by the wording of the actual FBI report, which Del had somehow managed to obtain from the police files in Newark. Woodson's smear campaign backfired. The portrait of James that emerged was that of a hard-working, dedicated law enforcement administrator. Not a racial bigot.

That evening while he was annotating his new bird book with his previous sightings, he got a call from Chief James. Hank, apologizing for the lateness of his call, invited him and Sara up for a Memorial Day cookout the next day. Mahlon congratulated him on the article and accepted the invitation. Sara, however, wouldn't be coming. It was the last big day of her grand opening, and Mahlon didn't expect to see her until closing time that night. She'd wanted to see the day through to the very end.

* * *

Monday's sky, swept clean of clouds, was the blue of Venetian glass. Mahlon spent the morning and early afternoon birding at the southern end of the island where the sea, the sky, and the land fused into a oneness that was achingly beautiful. The highlight of his outing occurred just before he left for home. A white and brown Oldsquaw duck with exquisitely long pointed tail feathers splashed for a landing not twenty yards from the edge of the bay where he stood. If only Sara had been with him.

Around three he returned home to dress for his visit to the Jameses. On his way up the island, he was pleased to see that Sara's golf course was mobbed with players.

Traffic was heavy. Everywhere along the boulevard bathers were straggling down from the beach. Multihued and multilimbed, they flip-flopped over the macadam with beach umbrellas under an arm, towels draped around the neck, and crying little tots traipsing beside them.

Modesty fought its never ending battle with nudity, and Mahlon, studying the bodies passing by, wondered why those with the most flesh to exhibit invariably let it all hang out. Was it an unwritten law that the stout ones always wrapped their abundant charms in the gaudiest material? And why did it always cling to their ample hips like an afterthought?

Past Harvey Cedars, the lighthouse began its dance above the jumbled rooftops and island greenery. Each bend in the road sent it sliding this way and that across the treetops until he pulled into James' street.

Wondering what kind of reception he would get from Clare, Mahlon parked the Plymouth in the driveway behind two other cars. James had walked out to greet him. Looking more relaxed than he had since Mahlon first visited him in March, James wore a dark blue knit shirt, white trousers and white shoes - a common enough uniform among the male residents of the island. He possessed a handsome nonchalance that differed sharply from his customary rigid uniformed presence. He carried drinks in both hands and passed one to Mahlon before they shook hands.

"I mixed you an 'Abominable' when I heard you drive up," James said, pointing to the drink in Mahlon's hand.

"Abominable?" Mahlon held the drink up for inspection.

"One and a half jiggers of the best Scotch polluted with ginger ale." Laughing, they walked around to the deck on the oceanside of the house. Sunlight warmed the south corner and the stretch of sand between them and the dune heads by the beach. Redwood chairs and tables cluttered up the deck under the white canvas canopy that stood over the patio doors. Off to one side, a grill sent up smokey flames, and Mahlon guessed that they had been waiting for him to arrive.

Clare stepped forward to greet him, her high cheek-boned face held up to his for a social kiss. She asked about

Sara, and the welcome in her eyes and voice seemed genuine. He had been expecting a colder reception, and her manner relieved him. He complimented her appearance, and she turned to James.

"Hank, keep your eye on this one. He's making a play for me." Mahlon did a double take when he heard her say "Hank."

James chuckled and responded with something about Sara's absence which Mahlon missed. Apparently, Clare and James' relationship had undergone a change. Mahlon was glad to see it. Clare took his arm and introduced him to the other guests. One couple, a slim dour looking woman and her garrulous husband, were old neighbors of the Jameses. The woman shared Clare's interest in bridge, and her husband talked nonstop about his real estate business when he wasn't dunking his nose in an Old Fashioned. The other couple were relatives. The man sweated profusely in his 48 portly sports jacket. He taught high school. His wife had a jolly nature and helped Clare bring out the food.

After the meal, they sat talking on the deck while the daylight faded. Darkness settled over them, broken only by the glow from the kitchen like a brush of white paint across the boards of the deck. The mixture of now familiar voices webbed the dark with friendly talk. They grew quiet as they watched the moon rise like a gold watch from the pocket of the night.

The others left and while Clare put away things, James and Mahlon walked the deck smoking cigars.

"Del did you justice," Mahlon said between puffs.

James grinned in triumph. "Took the fire out of Woodson's charges, I'll tell you that." He spoke of all the calls he'd gotten yesterday. "Woodson's not beaten yet, Thomas. Not by a long shot, but I won that battle."

Eventually, their conversation turned to the house on Third Street. James said it was owned by a corporation called North Jersey Enterprises.

"What other properties do they own?" Mahlon asked.

"I'm looking into that, but I'd really like to know who the corporate officers are."

They puffed away on their cigars for a couple of more paces before Mahlon spoke. "I know someone who's good at that sort of thing. The only problem is it will cost money."

"Money, eh? If I give this lead to the State Police, it will be out of my hands. If I can crack this myself, Woodson will be left out in the cold, and believe me, I need all the help I can get to do that. Get your man on it. I'll find the money somewhere."

Clare came to the door. James was wanted on the phone.

She had a white sweater on her shoulders when she joined Mahlon on the deck. The yellow moon stood several spans above the horizon and cast a sparkling swath of light across the ocean waters. The moonlight softened the age lines on Clare's face, and Mahlon was less mindful of her attempts to hide her age than he was the first time they met. They stood gazing at the moon.

"I sense you don't like me very much," Clare said.

Mahlon felt a rush of heat to his face.

"Don't deny it. Our first meeting made that very clear." She turned and looked at him. "I can't say that I blame you. My husband's troubles were serious, but I wouldn't admit it. I didn't want them to touch me. I hoped that somehow they'd vanish overnight like a bad dream."

"I was rude and insensitive last time," Mahlon said. "I apologize."

"No. Please let me finish. Those ugly rumors about Hank." She smiled when she spoke the word. "Yes, Hank. When your home and happiness are threatened, social pretensions are meaningless. Well, those rumors hurt him more than he's willing to admit. Whatever my husband is, he is not a hateful man. He needed someone to confide in since this whole business started, but I was too busy to notice. You weren't. Thank you for that."

"He'd do the same for me."

"I know he would. I'd just like to think our past differences are ancient history, " she said, extending her slim hand.

Mahlon took her hand in both of his. "I'd like that, too." James emerged from the house and put his arm around his wife's shoulders.

"It's time I left," Mahlon said, checking his watch. "I promised Sara I'd ride with her to the night deposit."

"I'll let you know," James said, extending his hand, "if I find North Jersey owns any other properties. If they do, I'll have to call in the State Police Narcotic Surveillance Squad. I can't afford to run that kind of operation on my own."

"Maybe you should ask the Marine Police to check if they own any boats," Mahlon said.

"That's a good idea. Thanks, Thomas."

Chapter 33

The wooden hatch for the service counter on Sara's club house was closed and battened, but a light under the door told Mahlon Sara was waiting inside for him. She had the day's receipts all counted and the bank slip ready to go, so the lockup took only a moment and they were on their way.

On the car radio, Stevie Wonder was singing. The station was out of Atlantic City and played mostly soft rock. *You Are the Sunshine of My Life*, Stevie sang in the night. Sara settled back in her seat and let her head fall back against the head rest. He turned the volume down a bit before he spoke.

"Some weekend, eh?" he asked.

"Yes, it was," Sara said, "but I got my business off the ground and flying, and I'm going to work to keep it there." She hummed along with Stevie, and Mahlon listened. It was a good song.

"I should be exhausted," she said when the song ended, "but I'm not for some reason."

"Still running on adrenaline. How about something to eat and a little night life on the side?"

She lifted her head, a look of surprise on her face. "If you're up to it?" He shook his head and laughed.

Sliding sideways, Sara pressed her thigh against his and placed a hand on his arm. "This weekend has been nothing but work for me. I could use a little distraction. Besides, some man was supposed to cook dinner for me all this week, but he never showed up."

"Okay, okay. I want to check out a place not far from your bank."

Sara's bank was three blocks south of Orbann's Lounge. The return trip took only a matter of minutes. Parking spaces around the nightspot were nonexistent. Mahlon finally found one on a side street. As they walked back, he began having second thoughts about where they were going.

"We may feel a bit out of place here among the younger set."

"Who cares," Sara said. "I'm hungry."

They opened the heavy lounge door, and a wall of sound hit them. Sara made a face as she moved into the room, and Mahlon felt a strange sensation in his chest. It took a moment for him to realize he was experiencing the uniquely modern sensation of music made palpable through the miracle of electronics. Not only were the driving rhythms of amplified guitars assaulting his ears, they also vibrated his insides. Unprepared for this musical onslaught, he was about to motion Sara to leave when the guitars took a dive down the scale and the drummer punished the drums two more licks and the song, thankfully, ended. The band was about to take its break.

The lights were muted in the big room, and cigarette smoke hung above the diamond shaped bar as thick as Los Angeles smog. Almost every stool around the bar was filled. Talking couples and solitary drinkers of both sexes swirled their drinks, their restless eyes searching the crowd for that special someone. The noise level dropped dramatically when the music ceased, but now the hum and buzz of conversation began to rise.

"Can I help you?" a voice said behind him. Mahlon turned toward a stocky young guy in a dark blue T-shirt. "ORBANN'S LOUNGE" was printed in white letters over one breast. His hair was dark, though not stylishly long, and his wide-set eyes held a peculiar searching look.

"We came in out of curiosity," Mahlon said. "We'd like a drink and something to eat."

"Oh," the young man said, seeing Sara for the first time. "Sorry, I thought you were after some booty," he said out of the side of his mouth to Mahlon. "Believe me, this is the place for young stuff." He grinned and shrugged off his mistake.

"Just drinks and something to eat for the lady," Mahlon said again.

The young man gave him a long look. "You're not ABC or Vice, are you?"

Mahlon had to laugh. He took a better look at the guy. He appeared alert and capable. One of those college football players Myra mentioned. Taller than Mahlon by a full head, he possessed a tree trunk of a neck and the inflated-muscle look of a linebacker. His nose fell straight to the full mustache that accented the broadness of his face in a handsome way.

"Who are you?" Mahlon asked.

"Your friendly Orbann bouncer, Fred Fairfields."

"Sara Speilberg, business woman extraordinaire." Mahlon put his arm around Sara's waist as he spoke. "And I'm Thomas Mahlon, an ex-cop in search of food and drink."

Fred gave him a strange look. "I thought you looked like the law. Take that table by the wall. I'll send a waitress over. You know there's a cover charge."

"You got to be kidding," Mahlon said.

"Three dollars a head on weekends and holidays."

Shaking his head, Mahlon led Sara over to the table. The waitress showed up a second later, and Sara ordered a glass of wine and a cheese-steak sandwich, a combination that brought a smile to Mahlon's face. He ordered a bottle of Molson. Sara excused herself and went off to the ladies room.

Mahlon looked around. The place held more patrons than he expected. At three dollars a head, it more than covered the band's playing fee. Steven Orbann had a shrewd business sense. The waitress came back with their drinks. Fred was standing by the door not far from his table. Mahlon picked up his Molson's and stepped over to the bouncer's side.

"How long you been working here?" Mahlon asked over the rising din.

"Since the beginning of May. Weekends mostly."

"Under the watchful eye of Mr. Chance, no doubt?"

Fred looked at Mahlon. "Maybe he's Mr. Chance to you but he's 'C.C.' to the ladies." After a moment he added, "C.C. a friend of yours?"

"No. Met him one day when I stopped in to see Orbann on business. I got the impression Chance was Orbann's chief bouncer."

"Winter time maybe. He's seldom around now. He's into night fishing, or so I heard. When he is here—" Fred gave a disgusted shake of his head. "—he can't keep his hands off the waitresses. What's your business, anyway?"

"Private investigator."

"You're kidding. What kind of case were you working on? If you don't mind my asking?"

"It's okay. A murder case. One of Orbann's waitresses was strangled and buried in the dunes near Barnegat Light." A distressed look crossed Fred's face. He seemed on the verge of saying something, but didn't.

"Distressing subject," Mahlon said. "Especially, when you work in the same place." Fred nodded. A couple approached. The man was round like a barrel and held the wrist of a slim woman, pulling her along after him.

"You're hurting my wrist!" she said. "Let go!"

"Listen, bitch, I paid for your drinks. Now it's your turn to return the favor." The man's face wore a cheated look that lurked in his beady eyes and protruding lip. He wasn't much to look at and for that matter neither was she. She was well built, but a note of tiredness tugged at her eyes and mouth. Mahlon figured she'd been around the block one too many times.

"Tell him to let go of me," the woman demanded of Fred. Fatso gripped her wrist tighter with his right hand and belligerently eyed the two of them. Fred's eyes made brief contact with Fatso's glare and then dropped. To Mahlon's disgust, Fred turned away from the quarreling couple.

"He ain't gonna help you, honey," Fatso said, a victorious sneer on his face. "He don't want no trouble. Let's you and me finish our talk outside in my car."

Mahlon took a step toward him, but Fred blocked his way. The woman sighed as Fatso turned with her in tow toward the door.

Fred's hand shot forward, grabbed Fatso's left wrist, and jammed it up behind the man's back. Fatso let go of the woman's hand and tried to turn on his attacker. Using the man's momentum, Fred spun him around and rammed him into the door. It opened on impact and Fatso let out a sickened groan. Fred kneed him in the butt and sent him sprawling. He hit the pavement with a bounce and lay still. Fred stood over him a moment, but Fatso wasn't in any hurry to get back up.

The woman tottered over and looked down at him. "Gee!" she said in an awed voice.

"Go back and enjoy yourself, miss," Fred said as he straightened his hair. "If you want, I'll walk you to the car when you leave."

"Thanks, honey," she said, and she drifted back to the bar.

"For a moment there," Mahlon said, "I thought you weren't going to earn your keep."

"That was just to get him to drop his guard. Mr. Orbann doesn't want a big fight scene. 'Fast and efficient,' is his motto. Besides—" Fred's voice filled with anger. "—nobody uses force on a woman as long as I'm a bouncer here."

"Well, there's one less wise ass you have to prove that to," Mahlon said, as they watched the fat man get to his feet and stagger away.

"I don't care if she's a horsebag," Fred said, turning his attention back to the club. "She still has the right to say 'no' in my book."

"Can't argue with that." Mahlon spotted Sara coming through the crowd around the bar. Her steak sandwich had arrived, and she sat and started eating. Mahlon told her about Fatso man and Fred. She listened with interest but kept on eating. It wasn't until she finished her belated supper that she told him she'd met a young lady who used to work for her at the bath house. She was a waitress in the lounge. They reminisced a bit and that's why she took so long.

The sight of the band members picking up their instruments convinced Mahlon it was time to leave. Fred was back by the door.

"We're leaving," Mahlon said. "No one's paying me to listen to someone torture pigs."

Fred gave a polite laugh. "Stop in again sometime. Your the first private eye I ever met. Maybe you can tell me about some of your cases."

It was Mahlon's turn to laugh, but the band drowned his laughter. He opened the door for Sara. Fatso wasn't anywhere to be seen. As they walked to the car, Mahlon kept turning over what Fred had said about Chance. If Mr. Chance wasn't the head bouncer, what was he doing to earn his keep?

Chapter 34

Getting Smoky Harris on the phone took Mahlon the better part of that week. Smoky had spent fifty-five of his three score and ten playing the horses, and the opening of the summer racing season was sure to find him at the track. Mahlon didn't hit pay dirt until early Friday morning, when Smoky surprised him by answering on the first ring.

"Glad I found you home," Mahlon said. "What are you up to?"

"On my way to chase the ponies over at Liberty Bell with a lady friend." Smoky paused. Shifting the cigar to the other side of his mouth, no doubt. "What's it to you?"

The rustic timbre of the older man's voice made Mahlon smile. Smoky sounded like an insolent old country wag, but he was city born and raised and could tell you more about New Jersey politics than you cared to know. If there were anything he didn't know, Smoky knew who to ask to find it.

They first met at the county court house decades ago when Mahlon worked for him during the summers he was in high school. Smoky knew Mahlon's father and was well aware of the man's drinking problem. For some reason, he took a fatherly interest in Mahlon and kept tabs on him until Mahlon went in the service. Years later, when Mahlon made detective, he took advantage of the older man's expertise in one of his cases. After Mahlon left the force and went into business for himself, Smoky became his primary field man, adept at turning up information no one else could find.

"Might as well spend it as leave it," Mahlon said.

"I ain't dying yet, you young son-of-a-bitch," Smoky said, with a voice like a rasp of a file. "I got to get going, Tommy. What's on your mind?"

"A friend needs a rundown on a corporation."

"I'm too old to work for charity." Mahlon heard him puff on his cigar. Rarely was he seen without a cigar in his mouth. Mahlon stifled a laugh as he imagined they'd have to stick one in his mouth at his wake so friends could recognize him.

"Still there, Tommy? Or did you fall asleep?"

"I'm here. He's willing to pay."

"Good. My appetite for the fillies ain't slacked none with age, you know."

Mahlon gave him the information, and Smoky said it would take a few weeks. Without another word, he hung up. Liberty Bell Park was calling him away.

* * *

The following Monday, Mahlon had a meeting with a prospective client over in Forked River. He got on the road around ten. The day was bright but the ocean breeze kept it on the cool side. In the middle of Beach Haven's business district, he noticed a red flashing light in his rear view mirror. Mahlon checked his speedometer and confirmed that he was not exceeding the speed limit. He slid over to the inside lane to let the Beach Haven patrol car pass. Instead, it pulled up alongside him, and the officer waved him over. What the hell? Mahlon brought the Plymouth to a stop and waited for the officer to approach.

"Your license and car registration, please."

"Was I speeding, officer?"

Mahlon rummaged in his glove compartment for his registration and fished out his license and his old Trenton Police Department I.D. He held them out to the officer.

"Just license and registration." The officer refused to accept anything until Mahlon pulled back the I.D. card.

"How long have you lived on the island, Mr. Mahlon?" Mahlon told him.

"Remove the keys from the ignition and get out of the vehicle." The officer's voice was level and routine.

Several passersby stopped on the nearby sidewalk to watch. Mahlon felt his face redden as he left the car.

"Walk to the other side of the car, please." Mahlon stepped up on the sidewalk. "Now, Mr. Mahlon, place both hands wide apart on the roof of your car."

"What's this all about?"

"Mr. Mahlon, put both hands on the roof now and spread your feet."

Mahlon winced at the repeated mention of his name but did as he was told. The murmur of voices behind him grew. The officer pushed his feet apart and gave Mahlon a very thorough body search. Mahlon's face was a deep shade of red by the time the search ended.

"Remain in that position, Mr. Mahlon. I'm going to look at your car trunk for a minute."

"On what grounds?" Mahlon asked with a start of surprise.

"We're having a real problem with narcotics around here, Mr. Mahlon. We're stopping all suspicious looking characters."

"Suspicious looking characters?" Mahlon thought that over a second. When the answer dawned on him, he gave a start of surprise. "You're telling me I was stopped because I have a beard?"

The officer just smiled before he stepped around to the back of the car. Mahlon heard the trunk open and the officer rummaging around. The trunk closed with a jolt that shook the car. Next, the officer searched inside the car. He found a pair of binoculars under the driver's seat.

"What are these for?"

"Bird watching. Can I straighten up now?" Mahlon's shoulders ached, and his ego had absorbed all the embarrassment it would tolerate. The officer replaced the binoculars before he answered.

"Yes, Mr. Mahlon. Sit in your car while I run a check on your vehicle."

Mahlon slid in behind the wheel, feeling relieved to be out of the public's eye. Five minutes later the officer returned his credentials and keys. Mahlon looked at the man's badge number and saw that it was covered with a small piece of black tape. There were two small holes in the fabric of the man's shirt where his name tag used to be.

"You can go now, Mr. Mahlon," the officer said.

"You owe me an apology."

"Mr. Mahlon, I just enforce the law."

"Where's your name tag? Why is your badge number covered up?"

"Good day, sir," the officer said, backing away toward his patrol car.

Like any law-abiding citizen, Mahlon called the man every name in the book as he started the motor. He jotted down the patrol car's number in an effort to appease his anger and move into traffic. His first impulse was to drive to the police station and file a complaint, but a few moments later, common sense prevailed. Private investigators were not held in high regard by law enforcement authorities. Any protest he lodged would most certainly come back to haunt him later. Instead, he decided to drive by Sara's business and commiserate with her.

Sara's service hatch was open and that stupid windmill was spinning away, but no customers were playing the course. Mahlon ran a finger over his mustache. She must be inside. He stopped on the other side of the street opposite the club house and popped open the door. Something by the side of the club house froze him in place. Sara's motorcycle sat outside the club house door.

Giving it a frigid stare, he shook his head in disbelief. What the hell was that thing doing there? He'd never understand her fascination with that damn machine. She'd kill herself on it one of these days. He shut the door and restarted the motor. As he pulled away, Sara stepped from the club house and waved. He drove off as if he hadn't seen her.

If he couldn't talk to Sara, he sure as hell could bitch to Hank. Mahlon checked his watch. He'd have to hurry, or he'd be late for his appointment. But as soon as he finished in Forked River, he was coming straight back to Barnegat Light.

* * *

Chief James looked up from his desk in surprise when Mahlon stepped in. The Chief's secretary had just finished taking dictation when Mahlon entered the station, and she passed him right in.

"Thomas, what brings you here?"

"I got pulled over this morning in a traffic stop, and my car was searched for drugs," Mahlon said, as soon the door closed behind him. "When did you guys start that?"

"Us 'guys?'" James got to his feet.

Mahlon marched right up to his desk. "Come on, Hank. Don't play stupid. I'm talking about the island blues. When did you start random car searches."

"Are you crazy?" James asked, his face beginning to redden. "This is a resort island. The Chamber of Commerce would lynch us if we started pulling tourists over without probable cause."

"You haven't, eh?" Mahlon looked him in the eye for a long moment, scratched his head in bewilderment, and sat in the chair by James' desk. In a voice bitter with resentment, Mahlon explained what happened.

"The guy's overzealous," James said. He sat and reached for the phone. "I'll call his chief. What's his name?"

"Oh, that's the best part. His name tag was missing and his badge number was covered with tape."

James leaned back in his chair and thought for a moment. "This is beginning to smell. You better keep your nose clean until we get to the bottom of this. Somebody's got your number."

Mahlon gave a weary nod. "So what's new with you?"

"Not a hell of a lot. We've been chasing this drug thing, but we're always a day late and a dollar short it seems. The house is empty when we get there, or the stuff is nowhere to be found."

He lifted his pen off the desk and began to toy with it as he talked. "If I didn't know better, I'd say they got someone on the inside tipping 'em off. The State Narcotics Surveillance Squad says it isn't some nickel and dime operation. They claim it goes way beyond that."

James gave a sardonic laugh. "The politicians are having a field day with it. The word going around now is that I'm incompetent and too old for the job. Can you believe it?"

Mahlon shook his head. "Just how serious has it gotten?"

"They've taken a page right out of Prohibition. Back then it was Scotch coming in from Canada on boats. Today, it's pot and cocaine coming up from Florida. It's not just our little problem either. Drug arrests are up all along the Jersey shore.

"The young executive types in the expensive beach front homes think cocaine is adult candy. Something you pass around with the hors d'oeuvres to get things going. And pot is something you smoke after lunch in place of a fattening dessert."

"You turn up any more North Jersey Enterprises real estate?"

"You tagged that one right. They own another property here on High Bar Harbor, way out on Butler on the bay. And a bay front property in Surf City. The Sunset Trailer Park in Beach Haven Manor."

"Where our friend Diaz used to reside before someone enlightened him with a .222 magnum in the head," Mahlon said.

"One and the same. Diaz was a pusher. He must have been knocking down on the take, and someone didn't like it. We weren't so lucky with the Marine Police. North Jersey Enterprises doesn't own so much as a row boat. Hope your man comes up with something useful."

"I talked to him Friday morning. He said it will take about two weeks. If there's anything to turn up, he'll find it."

James threw his pen on his desk and stood. "Hate to rush you out, Thomas, but I've got work to do." Mahlon rose and headed for the door.

James came around the desk. "Any hot leads on the Beauchamps case?"

Mahlon gave a sarcastic laugh. "They're so cold, Hank, I've gotten frost bite. But at least I gave it a try."

Chapter 35

Friday of that week, Mahlon had to testify in court about the fraudulent back injury claim that he investigated over in Hammonton. When the lawyer for the defense saw Mahlon's photos of the defendant building a deck on his house, he advised his client to change his plea to guilty. Mahlon took the rest of the day off. At one o'clock that afternoon, he passed Sara's golf course on his way home.

Sara's motorcycle was nowhere in sight. On the spur of the moment, he turned at the next side street and parked. An elderly couple were enjoying themselves on the course. The man was trying to teach her how to putt, but she kept hitting the ball like she was playing croquet. As Mahlon neared the club house, the woman thwacked one off the back wall of the green and sank it on the rebound. Their laughter rang clear and far.

He stepped under the raised service hatch and placed both hands on the counter. Sara was sitting in a dark blue armchair reading the paper. She wore green shorts, and her tanned legs looked long and trim.

"Can I help you?" Sara asked without glancing up. She folded the paper and set it aside before she stood to wait on him. Then she saw it was he.

"Oh, it's you, Thomas."

Mahlon raised a hand in greeting and peeked around the side of the building. Good. The bike wasn't there. He looked back at her. "You got rid of it, I see."

"Rid of what?"

"Your motorcycle."

Her back stiffened. "So that's why you didn't stop Monday?"

He nodded. The laughter out on the course was beginning to annoy him. "I haven't seen it around in a while." He looked Sara in the eye. "I was hoping you got rid of it."

"Thomas, we had this conversation. I'm not giving up my bike."

He bobbed his head in resignation and turned to leave.

"What's gotten into to you, Thomas? I thought we had this all settled."

"Yeah, I thought so, too. But seeing it parked by the side there annoyed the hell out of me the other morning."

"Did you get up on the wrong side of the bed or something?"

He shook his head. "No, I got stopped by the police."

"Whatever for?"

"I'm a suspicious looking character. Don't you know?"

"Come inside, Thomas, and tell me about it. You'll feel better if you do."

She went to the side door and unlocked it. As Mahlon stepped around to the side, he glimpsed the red fender of the motorcycle half-hidden behind the club house. He scratched his chin and studied it a second. *She got here on it, and she'll get home on it. Whether you like it or not.*

"Some lemonade?" Sara asked when he entered. She pointed to a wooden chair next to hers, and he sat.

A small refrigerator stood on a table beside her armchair. Sara set out two paper cups and took out a container of lemonade. She poured their drinks and handed him one.

It tasted refreshingly cold and tart. "Just what I needed," he said, smacking his lips. He looked around at the room.

The inside walls were unfinished and still smelled of fresh lumber. A green cash box sat on the table beside the refrigerator. A barrel of putters stood in one corner with a carton of colored golf balls beside it.

"Not too busy today, eh?" Mahlon said.

"Oh, it will pick up later when the children get home from school. So tell me what happened."

"I was a victim of police harassment," he said with a sardonic laugh. Mahlon described the incident and the officer's missing name tag and covered badge number.

"It does sound strange," Sara said when he was done. "Why should a police officer harass you when you've had no previous contact with him?" She hesitated. "Maybe you did look suspicious?"

"Oh, give me a break." He chuckled at her mischievousness.

At that moment, an alarm rang. Sara reached into the cash box and pulled out a small card. The couple who were on the course appeared in the service window. They were laughing again. Sara rose.

"My wife won a free game," the man said as he returned their putters to the counter. "It was the only putt she sank outright on the whole course." The woman beamed proudly.

"Well, then you'll be back to play again soon," Sara said and handed the woman the card for the free game. When they were gone, she sat back down.

"You haven't mentioned that woman you found on the beach lately. Anything new?"

Mahlon shook his head. "Nothing's happened since I talked to her roommate."

"She worked at Orbann's Lounge, didn't she?"

"That's right."

"Is that why we made that little stop after the dinner dance?" Sara gave him a quizzical look. "And you didn't learn anything?"

"Not about the Beauchamp case, I didn't."

"About what, then?"

Mahlon finished his lemonade and placed the cup on the table. "When I went to see Orbann last spring, a guy named Charles Chance was running interference for him.

He was the head bouncer, according to Orbann. But a waitress who worked there said he isn't. The other night the bouncer said 'C.C.,' that's Chance's nickname, spends his nights fishing. From what I saw of him, 'C.C.' doesn't seem like the type. 'Bouncer' I can believe. 'Night fisherman' no way. You know what I mean?"

"Si, Si," Sara said with a grin on her lovely face.

"Oohhh!"

Three teenage boys approached the service window at that moment. Mahlon glanced at his watch. He had a report to write up before the day was over.

"Will I see you tonight?" Sara asked, when she finished waiting on her customers.

"I'll be over." Mahlon kissed her. "Thanks." She gave him a hug and he was on his way.

On his way back to the car, his thoughts were on Sara. She stood her ground like he guessed she would. He chuckled at the awful pun she'd made on Chance's nickname. He couldn't blame her. It was a natural connection to make.

Something suddenly slid into place that stopped him in mid-stride. It was a natural connection, all right. When he got the Plymouth rolling, he drove north. The report would have to wait. He had a witness to interview in Barnegat Light.

* * *

The one story bungalow on Bayview Avenue sat near the road, Mahlon noted, which explained why the woman had seen and heard so much. He knocked on the screen door of the porch, and after a short interval a middle-aged woman came to the door.

"Ma'am," Mahlon said, "my name is Thomas Mahlon. I work for Police Chief James. Could you answer a few questions for me about the murder of Carlos Diaz?"

"Who?"

"The man who was shot across the road there."

Her hand flew to her mouth, and she gave an involuntary shudder. "I don't like talking about that."

"It won't take long," Mahlon said. "I promise." ·

She wore a sleeveless white blouse and blue shorts, which matched the blue mottling on her legs. Her hair was pulled back, making her plain face look all the plainer. She stood in the living room doorway and did not appear eager to come any closer.

"Are you a lawyer?"

"No, Mrs. North. I work for Chief James. Will you answer a question or two?"

"Ask me from there."

"Thank you. What exactly did you hear that night?"

"Not much, you understand. The evening was nice and I'd left this front door open. While I was knitting, I heard a car pull up. I didn't look out to see who it was. A moment later a man's voice said something which sounded like 'Yes!' 'Yes!' in Spanish. Then I heard two loud pops, and the car drove off. I set down my knitting and came to this door. First, I thought someone was trying to set the reeds on fire, but I couldn't see any flames. It's happened a couple of times, you know. Young people will do anything for a thrill nowadays."

"What happened next?" Mahlon asked.

"A car came by, and its lights flashed on something that looked like a body. I wasn't about to cross over there and make sure, so I called the police."

"Are you sure the man said, 'Yes', 'Yes'?"

She looked at him uncertainly for a moment. "I thought that's what he said. Why?"

"Think about it, ma'am. Do you remember whether there was a pause between the 'yeses' like 'Si - Si'? Or did he say the sounds one after the other like 'C.C.'?"

"Now that you mention it, the 'yeses' did come close together like the last one." She gave a convinced nod of her head. Then a worried look swept across her features. "Did I tell the police something wrong? God, I hope not."

"Don't worry," Mahlon said. "You couldn't have done any different under the circumstances. Thanks for your help." Mahlon went back to his car and drove off.

Moments later he parked his car alongside the Barnegat Light Police Station. When he entered Ofc. Richardson smiled in recognition and waved him on through the railing gate toward the Chief's office. James looked up from his work.

"Two visits in one week, Thomas? What brings you back? Not another traffic stop, I hope."

"It's a long shot, Hank," Mahlon said, as he sat, "but I think I've got a suspect for the Diaz murder."

"The hell you say! Who?"

Mahlon told him about his late night visit to Orbann's Lounge and his conversation with the bouncer who told him Chance's nickname is 'C.C.'

"On my way home from here, I stopped to see Sara and got to talking about Chance. Orbann said 'C.C.' was his head bouncer, but the bouncer said he isn't. According to him, 'C.C.' spends his nights fishing. While Sara and I were talking, she punned on Chance's nickname. You know, 'Si, Si' for 'yes.'" Well, that got me thinking. I spoke to your witness on Bayview Avenue a few moments ago. She now thinks Diaz could have been yelling 'C.C.' and not 'yes' in Spanish. It's possible Diaz was begging Chance for mercy."

James gave his head a scratch. "That sounds pretty thin, Thomas. Can you imagine what a defense lawyer could do to a story like that in court?"

"I said it was a long shot, didn't I? Just suppose Chance murdered Diaz. Diaz was a pusher, right? So maybe Chance is the local enforcer or something. He goes fishing at night, and we know that drugs are being delivered by boat. It all fits."

"But suppose Chance is a surf fisherman. They fish at night. What then?"

"Crap, I never gave that a thought," Mahlon said, his enthusiasm waning for a moment. Then he said, "Wait a minute, Hank. One way to prove my point would be to see if Chance owns a boat. It's stretching a bit, I admit, but it's worth a try. Give the Marine Police a call and see."

James shook his head in disbelief as he picked up the phone and dialed the number. He made his request to someone on the other end and then spent a short while waiting for an answer. He listened a moment and thanked the person and hung up.

"Let me tell you something, Thomas," he said in a tired but patient voice. "I don't know where your ideas come from sometime, but this one is a beaut." His face broke into a broad smile as he said, "Chance owns a hundred footer that is docked here at Barnegat Light. You son-of-a-gun, how do you do it?"

"Just put it down to simple genius," Mahlon said with mock humility.

"You're too modest."

"Hank," Mahlon said, "the connection between Chance and the Diaz murder is still tenuous. It does, however, raise some interesting questions about Orbann. Our Republican candidate for Freeholder."

"Damn right it does," James admitted. "But until we get something more concrete, I'm leaving his name out of it. I'll ask the Narcotics Surveillance Squad to watch Chance's boat. Let's see what that turns up."

James made a note on a pad and then continued. "We had some good luck ourselves yesterday. An elderly man was hit by a van on—"

"You call that luck?"

"No, Thomas, I don't. It was unfortunate for the old man but lucky for us. He was cycling in the bike path when the hophead in the van ran him off the road. The old man was killed outright, and the van plowed into a telephone pole. Of course as these things go, the driver escaped injury." James expelled his breath dis-gusted-ly. "And they say there's a God."

"Get to the lucky part."

James paused and gave Mahlon a warning look. "The driver was so full of snow he couldn't see straight. Well, earlier this morning when he heard the charges against him, he offered to make a deal. I got the call before you came in. He's talking to an Assistant Prosecutor. He'll trade the name of his pusher for a lighter sentence. He's a local and this may get us started in the right direction toward cleaning up this whole mess."

"Let me know what you learn about Chance," Mahlon said as he got up to leave. They shook hands and then Mahlon went home.

The primaries were held the next day. On Wednesday, Mahlon read The Beach Haven Times while he drank his morning coffee. Orbann won a slot on the November ballot very convincingly. Mahlon brushed the coffee from his mustache with a paper napkin. Orbann would be tough to beat in November, unless someone shook a skeleton out of his closet.

Chapter 36

The next Monday, Mahlon spent the entire day on the road doing background checks for a local attorney. He didn't get home that evening until well after ten. The phone was ringing when he entered the house.

"Mr. Mahlon, this is Paul Beauchamps." The sound of the man's voice brought back a vision of Karen's mother, horror-stricken by her daughter's death. The man spoke his name twice before Mahlon shook off the image and answered.

"I hope I didn't awake you." Mr. Beauchamps sounded tenta-tive and uncertain.

"Not at all."

"Sorry to be calling so late. I had to wait until my wife went to sleep."

"How is she?"

"The funeral was very hard on her. Before there was always a shred of hope but afterward—" He left the sentence unfinished.

"My visit put the two of you through hell. Didn't it?"

"You mustn't blame yourself. I knew it couldn't go on like that forever. Not knowing what happened to Karen was torture, too."

Mr. Beauchamps cleared his throat. "I'm calling to ask if there is anything new to report. Your letter said you talked to Karen's roommate and learned she was dating someone. Have you found out who he was?"

"No, I haven't. Karen never told Rhonda her, eh, boyfriend's name—" The word "lover" was on the tip of his tongue, but he caught it just in time. "—and I haven't been able to track him down."

He made no mention in his report of his suspicion that Karen was pregnant at the time of her death. He saw no need to add to her parents' burden.

"I was afraid of that. My son came home this afternoon, and we've been talking. We both want Karen's murderer found. We have some insurance money left, and we'd like to use that to continue your investigation."

"I don't mean to be rude," Mahlon said, "but her killer's long gone. Wouldn't it be wiser to use the money for your son's education? He's in college, isn't he?"

"Yes, but he doesn't need it. He wants justice and so do I. Will you help us?"

The prospects were very poor to say the least, and Mahlon didn't like taking money he hadn't earned. On the other hand, Mr. Beauchamps and his son needed some hope that justice would be done.

"I suppose I could give it one more try. But for the life of me, I don't know where to begin."

"We will be most grateful. What is your retainer fee?" Mahlon told him. "I'll send you a check tomorrow."

"I'll tell you what," Mahlon said. "I'll hold onto it. If nothing turns up in ninety days, I'll return it. How's that?"

"Fine," Mr. Beauchamps said. "I have your address. My son will drop off the check. He works down there somewhere, but you know how young people are nowadays. They don't tell you a thing." He paused for a second.

"By the way, my wife wouldn't approve of this. If you call, ask for me."

"I will."

"Anything else you need?"

"I could use a recent picture of Karen."

"I'll get one to you."

"Mr. Beauchamps, I'll give it my best, but I won't take your money needlessly."

"I'm sure you won't. You understand this is something we have to do."

When he came home the following afternoon, he found an unaddressed envelope in among the mail. Inside at his desk, he opened it and found a check and Karen's picture. Mahlon switched on his desk lamp to study it.

Karen stood near a picnic table holding a food-laden plate. A light blue tube top outlined her small breasts, and tight shorts emphasized the ripeness of her thighs and the shapeliness of her lower legs. Mahlon saw no sign of the provocative stance Rhonda had described. Perhaps the Karen in the picture had not yet become the Karen Rhonda came to know.

Opening the top drawer, Mahlon removed a magnifying glass and bent over the picture to examine her face more closely. Her large eyes smiled at the camera as though they were used to smiling. The longer he studied her the more he sensed an attractiveness that belied the thinness of her face and the narrow fullness of her mouth.

He set the picture down and groomed his mustache with a forefinger. For months, the only face Karen had was that of a sand-coated skull grinning up from the bottom of a grave. For the first time that skull was fleshed with smiling lips and eyes lit with happiness. The picture somehow made her death more personal.

He tucked the picture in his wallet and put the check in his desk drawer, where it would stay until he had done something to earn it. If he only knew where to begin.

Mahlon picked up the phone. Maybe Hank would have an idea or two, besides it was high time the two of them paid Agnes another visit.

* * *

Talk and laughter rippled through the Tuesday lunch crowd as Mahlon sat at one of the two available tables. Chief James arrived minutes later and moved toward him with a spring in his step Mahlon hadn't seen for some time. James wore his summer uniform, and the thick sun-bleached hair on his tan forearms lent him a healthy look that Mahlon envied. James removed his sunglasses and took the chair opposite Mahlon.

"Well," Mahlon said, "aren't you the tanned golden boy of Barnegat Light."

"Don't get testy, Thomas. Clare and I enjoy the beach. After all our house is practically on the dunes."

"Yours and too many others, if you ask me. Things are better on the home front, I take it."

"Much. So lunch is on you for a change. What gives?"

"The Beauchamps want me to continue my investigation."

James nodded and opened his mouth to speak, but the arrival of Agnes at their table closed it again.

"Can I get you something?" she asked, her voice distant and reserved.

"Agnes, how are you?" Mahlon asked.

"Fine. Would you like something from the bar first?" She was all business, and her look dared Mahlon to try to thaw her.

"We dropped in just to see you."

"Surprised you could still find the place."

"How could we forget the one person who helped us identify that body in the dunes?" James asked.

"You mean the waitress found up at Barnegat Light?" The frost melted from her voice.

Mahlon nodded.

"How did I help?"

"You steered me to Sammy's Shoe Shoppe." Mahlon laid a hand on her arm. "That's how I traced her to Orbann's Lounge."

"It's the truth," James said.

"Me? I did that?" she asked in pleased disbelief.

"Would I lie to my favorite waitress?" Mahlon said.

"What ya know about that?" Agnes rested a hand on her ample hip and looked about in amazement.

"We've been busy lately or we would have been here sooner. Right, Hank?"

James agreed.

"What would you like for lunch, hon?" They placed an order. When she waddled away on her large white-stockinged legs, she was still shaking her head in disbelief.

"Where do I begin?" Mahlon asked out of the blue.

"Begin what?" James asked. "Oh, the Beauchamps case. The only place you can start is at Orbann's Lounge."

"I'm buying lunch and that's all you can suggest?"

James grinned and nodded.

"Why did I ever think you could help?"

"Hey, there are no guarantees in our kind of business. Beauchamps understands that. Just get out there and make something happen."

"Okay, okay. You came in here looking very pleased with yourself. What's new with you?"

James glanced about before he answered. "C.C.'s boat is *very* interesting. Called the 'Xanadu II.' Used for all night fishing parties. Leaves in the evening and goes way the hell out. Hundred miles or so. Doesn't usually dock until the middle of the next morning. Takes half-day trips on Saturday, too. According to the surveillance team, C.C. boarded her three times last week. Brought a lady friend along. I understand they spend most of their time in the captain's cabin."

"Now, that's my idea of fishing," Mahlon said with a laugh.

"The 'Xanadu's' large and carries the latest radar and navigation aids. If we could only get a lead on the next delivery date, the Coast Guard could snatch them on their way in with the goods."

Agnes appeared with their order—chef's salad for James and a roast beef and horse radish sandwich for

Mahlon. While they ate, Mahlon thought about the problem of learning the next delivery date.

"Hank, did C.C. go out last Saturday?" He asked between bites of his sandwich.

"No, just nights. Why?"

"I've been thinking. A party boat like that probably keeps some kind of log. We already know two nights when deliveries were made."

"How do we know that?"

"The two nights Mrs. Andrews saw ghosts. If someone took a look at that log, he might be able to learn the date of the next delivery. The last time the ghosts appeared was right before Memorial Day. Odds are that the next delivery is right before the Fourth of July. Right?"

"Yeah," James said, "but who's going to do it?"

"The surveillance squad can't or they risk exposing their operation. And you can't, so that leaves me."

James' eyebrows shot up in surprise. "What the . . . "

"Don't get flustered, Hank. I can go out this coming Saturday."

"Don't get flustered?" James shot back. "Just what do you know about fishing? Will you tell me that?"

"Nothing and that's a mark in my favor."

"Mind explaining that?" James demanded.

"Yeah, I mind." Mahlon said flashing a superior grin. "Us Private Investigators have our trade secrets, you know."

"If they suspect you're onto them, you're dead. And what if 'C.C.' decides to go along for the ride?"

"He probably won't recognize me. But if he does, I'll have only wasted a morning of my time and twenty or thirty dollars of your money," Mahlon said matter-of-factly.

"My money!" James almost yelled. "I've got to finance this hare-brained scheme?"

"Can't expect an ordinary citizen to pay for police undercover work. Can you?" Mahlon laughed at the look of disbelief on James' face.

"I don't know, Thomas. Can you bring something like this off?"

"I won't lie to you, Hank. There's a good chance I'll fail. Nothing ventured, nothing gained. You just said that to me about the Beauchamps case in so many words."

"Okay. What gear will you need?" asked James.

"An ice chest that'll hold two six packs, tackle box, pole and reel."

"I can take care of all that."

"I'll also need some fried chicken to serve as a peace offering. Can Clare fry up a chicken or two?"

"What the hell do you mean by 'peace offering'?"

"Patience, Hank. Now can Clare do the chicken for me?"

"I guess so. The 'Xanadu' is docked at 16th Street on the bay. It leaves at eight. Pick up the chicken before you go. I'd feel better about this if I knew what you had in mind."

"I'll tell you all about it when I get back," Mahlon said.

Agnes walked up. "Everything all right, hon?"

They thanked her and Mahlon paid the bill. The day outside the hotel had grown hot and sticky. James had an afternoon meeting. Mahlon watched his patrol car head north on the boulevard. On impulse, Mahlon followed in his wake minutes later. The "Xanadu II" rated a once over.

Mahlon didn't know one type of boat from another. In his mind, anything that floated and carried people was a boat. Later, when he pulled off Bayview Drive onto the gravel parking area that stretched for several blocks along the docks, he realized how great his ignorance was. All manner of boats pointed their prows toward the island and held aloft their jumble of antennas, masts, and poles.

The bone dry smell of the gravel couldn't mask the stink of fish guts and dead crabs that filled the air on the dock. Above him, men moved purposefully about a large craft with an open top deck cluttered with benches. At the edge of the dock a sign advertised evening cruises.

The sun disappeared behind one of the smudged gray clouds littering the sky over the bay. The haze that hung above the island melted all distances, blurring even the roof tops of nearby High Bar Harbor.

Wiping his damp forehead, Mahlon sauntered along the dock. Oil-slicked water slapped against the hulls, and the mooring ropes creaked and complained as the boats rose and fell. Some boats wore open sores that dripped long blood-red rust stains. Decay was an irreversible principle of nature and only man seemed stubborn enough to fight it.

Midway along the dock he spotted "Xanadu II" riding handsomely in the chop of a passing boat. Newer than most of the surrounding boats, "Xanadu II" obviously had a captain who believed in maintenance. From the dark gray paint on its hull to the radar pod and array of antennas etching the humid sky above it, the boat looked impressive. A bench ran the length of the cabin wall before which lay the wide expanse of the newly washed deck. Above the long deck cabin, Mahlon noted the captain's bridge or whatever it was called on a boat that size. The glass enclosed area afforded the captain an excellent view of the deck and the sea ahead.

With the pretense of examining the next boat, Mahlon moved on far enough to view the rear deck area of the "Xanadu II." Steps with a handrail linked the main deck to the upper level and Mahlon guessed he'd have to climb it if he expected to see the boat's log. He already had an idea of how he'd do it. The captain of this boat would be no fool, and Mahlon almost wished he hadn't been so damn cute about volunteering for the job after all.

272

Chapter 37

Smokey Harris got back to Mahlon on Thursday evening. He had a trip scheduled to the Atlantic City Race Track the next day. If they could meet somewhere on Rte. 9 for lunch, he'd hand over what he had on North Jersey Enterprises. Of course, payment was due on delivery. Mahlon suggested Chuzzlewit's Cafe in Manahawkin for their rendezvous. He hadn't been there since last summer when Chuz helped him with the Barnes case.

The drive over to Chuz's the next morning was an unpleasant one. With the day hot and traffic heavy, the Plymouth's AC decided to act up, giving Mahlon yet another reason to rue the approach of hot weather. More vehicles clogged the roads, and the increasing appearance of New York plates on the rear bumpers ahead of him did not escape his notice. It explained why the Sunday evening drive north on the Garden State Parkway in summer had become a nightmare the last couple of years.

Three battered pickups, the vehicle of choice for Stafford Township locals, stood side-by-side on a stretch of new paving stone in front of the diner. Though the mustard yellow sign still read "Chuzzlewit's Cafe," the fresh gray stone and pressure washed chrome exterior had Mahlon wondering if the diner had under-gone a change of management,

Once inside, however, his fears were quickly put to rest. The same worn green linoleum lay on the floor, and the dark line of grime around the base of the counter stools hadn't been disturbed since his last visit.

Chuz, with a pencil sticking from his gray head and his jowls shaking with every step, bounded back and forth between the four men sitting at the counter. He stopped in mid-stride when he saw Mahlon.

"Well, look who it is."

"I spotted the new stone and shiny chrome outside," Mahlon said, "and came in to meet the new owner."

The man's face turned serious. "Hey, you gotta keep up in this business, partner, or you lose customers." Which brought a snort of laughter from Mahlon. The dig had sailed right over the man's head.

"I got something special on the menu today, partner. Take a seat. I'll be right with you."

"Actually, I'm meeting someone here for lunch. I'll be at one of the tables in case you lose sight of me in the crowd."

With a chuckle Chuz disappeared into the kitchen. Mahlon went to the table farthest from the others and sat. A moment later, Chuz popped through the door and set a tall, sweating glass of ice tea before him.

"I didn't order that."

"I know, but you look hot. This ought to cool you off until your friend comes."

A new fire-engine red Chrysler station wagon rumbled across the stones outside the front window and came to a stop near Mahlon's car. A moment later, the driver's door opened, and Smoky Harris stepped stiffly out. He had a light summer fedora on his head, a cigar in his mouth, a crisp white shirt on his back, and a pair of yellow trousers hanging off his skinny hips. A look at the diner brought an instant frown to his face. Shutting the door behind him, he crossed the stones toward the door, knees bent and heels tentative as they touched the ground.

"Smoky, how are you?" Mahlon said when the man entered.

"Keeping one step ahead of the undertaker, thank you," Smoky said, his voice reedy and dry.

He sat opposite Mahlon and looked the place over with a critical eye. He opened his mouth, but Mahlon cut his complaint off.

"What are you doing, Smoky? Planning to start a family?" Mahlon gestured toward the red station wagon outside.

Smoky took a puff on his cigar and blew smoke toward the ceiling before he answered. "Now, don't get snotty, Tommy. Nobody, but nobody likes a smart-ass.

"If you have to know, I won the Trifecta last month over in Philly. Wanted a red car ever since I was kid, so I decided to celebrate and get me one. That big beauty was the only red one on the lot." He raised his chin defiantly. "And I took it." His eyes challenged Mahlon to say something.

Mahlon took another look at the station wagon and then turned to Smoky. "Well, nobody should wait that long for a dream. Hope you enjoy it for a long time."

"Why, thank you, Tommy. I intend to. Now, is this a diner, or just a poor imitation o' one?"

At that moment, Chuz pushed through the kitchen doors and set two large salads and an ice tea on their table. The greens heaped on the plates ran thick with pink Russian dressing,

"How did you know I wanted Russian dressing?" Mahlon asked.

"I didn't, partner." Chuz gave a high-pitched laugh. "It's the only dressing I got." He hustled back to the kitchen.

"Well," Mahlon said, as he plunged his fork in the salad, "what did you learn about North Jersey Enterprises?"

Smoky pushed the salad away with his forefinger, rested his elbows on the table and went on smoking.

Mahlon stopped chewing. "What's wrong with it?"

"Don't eat rabbit food."

"Why not?"

"Gives me indeegestion."

275

With a shrug, Mahlon went back to eating.

"A friend at the State House," Smoky said between puffs, "got me a copy of their annual report. Officers' addresses were all mail drops. Trustees, too, but I tracked one of 'em down. A driver for a trash hauling outfit outside Jersey City."

Smoky threw one spindly leg over the other and settled back in his chair before he went on.

"Hudson County friend told me an interesting story about that one."

"The driver?"

"No, the trash hauling outfit."

Taking the cigar from his mouth, he studied the ash closely. "Want to hear it?" He eyed Mahlon, and the dried old skin around his mouth slipped into a smile.

"Does it cost extra?" Mahlon asked. "Or does it come with the basic service package?"

"Trouble is you got no sense of humor. Now, get me some sugar for my tea, like a good boy." Mahlon reached for the sugar on the next table and set it before him.

"Never dreamed when I was a young guy starting out there was money in garbage. Hell, it was just somethin' you want to be rid of." He started spooning sugar into his tea, and five spoonfuls later a white mound lay at the bottom of his glass.

"They ain't garbage collectors anymore, you know? Waste disposers. That's what they are. This particular one is operated by a certain North Jersey family, if you catch my meaning."

Mahlon nodded.

"Didn't always, though."

Chuz was back with two steaming platters that he set on the table. The smell of broiled flounder and heaped steak fries tantalized Mahlon's nose and made his stomach yearn for a taste.

"Something wrong with the salad?" Chuz asked.

"Don't eat no—," Smoky started to say. Mahlon cut him off.

"Gives him indigestion." Chuz picked up the dish with a shrug and went back behind the counter.

"So what's all this got to do with North Jersey Enterprises?" Mahlon asked as the two men began to eat. Smoky shook ketchup on his fries and tasted his fish before he answered. He nodded his head in appreciation and got back to his subject.

"Maybe nothing and maybe everything, Tommy. You tell me when I'm done. As the story goes, a bright young lad made a fortune during the Korean War. Kept the black market one step ahead of the Inspector General, where he just happened to work. When it was time to come home, he changed his cash to diamonds. Carried them to the States in a rectal tube, and invested in real estate and a waste disposal company.

"Damn, this is good fish, Tommy," He forked another piece into his mouth and ate it with pleasure.

"Now, where was I? Oh, yeah. A little pressure here, a little pay off there, a merger or two. Soon his trucks are hauling garbage for several communities.

"A strike or two later, and trash is suddenly an expensive item up in those communities. This family I didn't name starts to take notice."

"They put the squeeze on him. Right?" Mahlon asked.

Smoky frowned. "Wrong. This guy joins in with them, and a few years later sells them his share of the business. Sinks the money into several shore properties including a slum block in Atlantic City. They say casinos are coming to A.C. one of these days. That property is right on the boardwalk.

"The other properties he sold to North Jersey Enterprises two— three years back."

"What's his name?"

"Oh, he changed that when he sold the waste disposal company. Well, he didn't change it, really. Just knocked off the Eyetalian part, if you know what I mean."

"No, what do you mean?"

"He used to be Stefano Urbani."

"Stefano what?"

"Life ain't never the same once your hearing goes," Smoky said. "Stefano Urbani. Maybe you know him by his new one."

"Steven Orbann," Mahlon said.

Smoky nodded and pushed his empty plate away. He looked out the window for a minute. "I'll be hitting the road as soon as you cross my palm, Tommy." He named his sum.

"You said last night you had something to hand over. Where is it?"

"The only thing I want to see handed over is money. If I told you last night on the phone, I wouldn't have the cash to go to the races this afternoon. Would I?" Mahlon handed him his fee.

Minutes later Mahlon watched the old man drive away in the red station wagon. Smoky sat behind the wheel with the fragile stiffness conferred by old age and failing eyesight. When he turned back to throw some bills on the table, he spotted Smoky's iced tea. It sat untouched.

That afternoon Mahlon phoned Chief James and told him Smoky's story.

"Puts Orbann in the middle of things. Don't it?" James said.

"We got what we're looking for," Mahlon said. "Chance was his enforcer. Orbann's the brains."

"Got to pass this on. Who knows what kind of records Orbann keeps in that penthouse of his. How much do I owe you?"

Mahlon told him Smoky's fee. James' curse rang in his ears.

Chapter 38

Saturday morning dawned gray and cool. The horsetail reeds at the entrance to James' driveway were dancing in the wind when Mahlon pulled in. He left the warmth of the car and zipped his gray windbreaker against the morning chill before he made his way up the steps. He wondered if the old blue shirt and jacket would keep him warm enough when he got out to sea. The rest of his fishing outfit consisted of old levis, a white floppy hat, and frayed tennis shoes.

James, dressed in a white T-shirt and brown slacks, opened on his knock. He stood for a moment, looking Mahlon over from head to foot.

"Hired help to the back door, fellow."

"Quit the crap, Hank. You got fifteen minutes to teach me something about fishing, so let's get started."

Inside, Mahlon helped himself to the coffee on the stove while James went for the fishing equipment. A moment later James returned with a tackle box, boat pole, and hemp sack.

"Did Clare fry that chicken I asked for?"

"It's in the fridge," James said. "First time fishing and the only thing you're worried about is your stomach."

"Henry, what did that woman of charm and taste ever see in a lout like you?"

"One more 'Henry,' and you'll be wearing a black eye under that hat of yours. Now listen carefully because I'm only going to explain this once."

He demonstrated the operation of the reel and went over the contents of the tackle box. After fixing a basic rig for boat fishing, he showed Mahlon how to attach the hooks and lures to the line.

"Keep it simple," Mahlon said. "I intend to ask one of the hands to help me out."

"Hands?" James said disgustedly. "You're going out on a boat, Thomas, not to a ranch."

"You know what I mean."

"They're called mates."

"Okay. Okay. One of the mates." Mahlon tucked the package of fried chicken under his arm and picked up the rest of his gear. James held the door open for him.

"Good luck," James said as he left.

"Thanks. I'll need it."

He loaded the rod and tackle in the car and put the fried chicken in the ice chest. Less than five minutes later, Mahlon pulled up at the dockside not far from the "Xanadu II." Some fishermen were already aboard, and several tackle-laden men were crossing from car to boat, loading their equipment. The air on the open dock was cool.

With pole and tackle box in hand, Mahlon boarded the boat, paid his money to the mate, and moved along the side rail toward the rear. On the aft deck two young men were cutting up fish on a waist-high table. The stench of fish guts roiled the air. Several fishermen stood by watching, having already marked their fishing spots with inserted poles in the holders along the rail. Mahlon spotted an empty slot near the steps that led to the top deck and stuck the handle of his pole in the holder.

He returned to the car for the ice chest and stowed it under a bench that ringed the cabin wall. With his mind on his mission, Mahlon stuck his cold hands deeper in his pockets and looked around. He'd gotten a place near the steps to the upper deck, which at the back was more of an open-sided roof. It would provide some shade if the sun was out, but at the moment he would have preferred some warmth. Now, all he had to do was wait for the right moment to get a look at that log book.

Talk of fish and bait and lures soon filled the air while the deck heaved beneath him from the occasional bow wave of a passing boat. The mate announced that yesterday bluefish were biting on some-thing called bucktails.

"What's that?" Mahlon asked.

The mate had him open his tackle box. "That thing there." He pointed first to a white feathered object and then touched a long silver lure with trailing green rubber-like tubing that masked a hook. "This one's good, too."

Shortly before eight the motor started, sending vibrations through the entire craft, and eased out into the channel, heading north for the inlet. The weather hadn't improved any, but the cold clean air sweeping across the boat blew away the foul smell of ground up fish. The engine throb increased when they rounded the Coast Guard Station, and soon the lighthouse and the inlet channel appeared off their bow.

By this time the wind on deck was chilling. Mahlon followed the other men into the cabin. It was warm there, and he knew it was the place for him. Men slept on benches despite the throbbing race of the ship's engine and the rumble of exhaust from the rear. Outside, gray clouds still stretched from horizon to horizon. Mahlon found a bench and closed his eyes.

An hour later the thundering motor suddenly stopped, and everyone filed outside. Mahlon began fastening the silver lure to his line as the others were doing. Then the horn tooted and everyone dropped his line over the side into the olive green sea. Soon, someone at the back rail called for the gaff, and a mate ran by with a long wooden pole topped with a large hook.

Mahlon's rail mates were a *Mutt* and *Jeff* team who traded jibes and jokes about fishing trips of the past. The taller one was red headed and spoke with the easy nonchalance of a man who never rushed anything. His side kick was a short stocky man in gray work clothes and a Day-Glo orange hunter's cap. Mutt's name was appropriately, "Big Roy," and his tall friend was "Red."

When his lure reached bottom, Mahlon began reeling it up. As he worked the reel, he saw off to the west a bright blue rift in the gray sky. Better weather was on the way. Suddenly, his pole bent, and Mahlon jerked his pole back and up.

"Reel it," Red said in his slow drawl.

Mahlon began turning the reel. The line went slack, and he was sure he lost it.

"Reel! Reel!" Big Roy shouted. "He's turning toward you that's all."

He reeled as fast as his hand could turn. Then the weight pulled on his line again, and he was surprised by the resistance. The fish was fighting the upward pull of his pole. Someone yelled for the gaff as the fish started to cut small circles in the water below. A wooden pole plunged past Mahlon's side. The fish swerved toward the boat, and the gaff shot upward, hooking it through the stomach. The fish sailed over the rail and hit the deck flapping and hopping. Blood oozed from the hole in its side. Red stepped on it and expertly pulled the hook from its mouth with a pliers.

The fish was bluish silver and shiny against the gray deck. Red inserted his hand into the gill slit and lifted it. The fish resisted feebly.

"Caught yourself a blue," Red said with a big grin. "Where's your bag?"

Mahlon pulled it out from under the bench and held it open. The fish disappeared into the dark burlap interior. He pushed the bag under the bench. He stood looking at the bag. The fish sure seemed bigger when he was fighting it to the surface. The difference must be the pull of the fish's desire to be free. The bag moved a few more times and then lay still.

The rest of the morning passed without him making another catch, which didn't bother him. His mind was grappling with the problem of getting himself up to the captain's cabin. Just before eleven the horn tooted and the men reeled in their lines for the last time that day.

Big Roy on his right hooked a fish. He reeled it in, trading jibes with Red who stood at his side grinning and shaking his head. When the fish came over the rail, Big Roy laughed delightedly.

"Some luck," Red said. "Last fish of the morning, too."

"You betcha," Big Roy said, hoisting the big fish by the gill slit for all to see.

"Yeah," Red said, "by tomorrow his arms won't be long enough to describe it." Everyone laughed.

After putting his tackle away, Mahlon opened the ice chest and began munching on a chicken leg. When the mate walked by, Mahlon offered him some chicken and a can of beer. The man accepted them and offered to clean Mahlon's fish.

When he finished the chicken, the mate put Mahlon's fish on the cleaning table. Mahlon watched him work and began asking about his work. The mate was a college student. He said the captain paid well even though the hours were long. He worked the all-night trips during the week and the half-day Saturday trip.

"Doesn't leave much time for a social life," Mahlon said.

"Yeah, but the captain sometimes takes out a private party, and I get the night off."

"How often is that?"

"Not often enough," the mate said. "The last time was near the end of May." He chuckled to himself. "That must have been one awful trip."

"Why?"

"Well, it turned foggy as hell before midnight and the radar was on the blink. They spent the night out here praying some big ship wouldn't hit them. Didn't get in until dawn."

Mahlon reset the hat on his head. A foggy night near the end of May, eh? When the mate finished cleaning the fish, he rinsed the filets with water from the hose and put them into a plastic bag. Mahlon gave him a generous tip.

"I want to take some fried chicken up to the captain," Mahlon said as the mate began working on the next man's fish.

"No one's allowed top deck."

"The hell you say. What man doesn't like fried chicken and cold beer? I'll just say I climbed the ladder when your back was turned. Okay?"

"It's your neck, mister," the mate said and went on with his work.

Slipping two beers and some foil wrapped chicken into his jacket pocket, Mahlon hauled himself up the steep steps to the upper deck. The wind felt stronger on the exposed deck and the roll of the boat intensified, as did Mahlon's fear of falling overboard. He took a firm hold of the rail and looked toward the shore. The island grew more distinct with each passing minute. The rift of blue sky had widened. No doubt the afternoon would be sunny and warm.

Through the cabin window, Mahlon could see the captain's broad, muscular back seated before the wheel. The man's hair was trimmed close to his skull like a Marine's. With butterflies banging around in his stomach, Mahlon slid the door open. The captain turned and stared hard at him.

"No one's allowed up here," the man barked.

"I know," Mahlon said. "I slipped up when the mate turned his back. Thought you might like some fried chicken and beer." Mahlon held the foil package out to him.

"You did, eh?" the captain said without changing the appraising look in his dark eyes. "Don't like people up here. Mate knows that."

"Like I said, I slipped up here behind his back."

"So you did. Fried chicken?"

"And a cold beer," Mahlon said, pulling a can from his jacket. His eyes swept the cabin for a sign of the log book.

"Sit. We'll make the inlet in ten minutes anyway." He took the chicken. "You hold the beer. Coast Guard doesn't like drinking on the job."

While the man ate, Mahlon looked him over. There was a tough outdoor look to him. A two-day beard darkened his wide face, and an old thin scar ran from his left sideburn straight down his brown neck. He took the beer from Mahlon and swallowed a mouthful. Rolling his hard mouth in appreciation, he handed the can back. Between bites, however, the corners of his mouth dropped into a look of mistrust and hostility.

No logbook was in sight, and Mahlon's heart sank. The instrument panel teemed with control knobs, dials and scopes. Several electronic devices hung from the cabin roof. Everything but a log book. Mahlon took a deep breath and his heart shifted gear. The sweat began to trickle down from his armpits. He'd have to come right out and ask for it.

"Much paperwork with a boat like this?" Mahlon asked trying to sound matter-of-fact. The captain looked at him for a moment. Mahlon resisted the urge to avoid his gaze.

"Account books," said the captain.

"You don't have to keep a log book or something like that?"

"What for? Take people out to fish and bring 'em back. That's all."

The marker buoys for the inlet slid past the boat and the captain throttled back the engines. A sense of despair settled over Mahlon. He had reached the captain's cabin only to learn that the entire trip was a wasted effort. The lighthouse eased by on their left and the "Xanadu II" cruised through the fleet of small boats anchored in the inlet channel.

On the bulkhead to the right of the captain hung a calendar bearing the name of a local boat repair firm. The months were listed vertically in two columns. Everyday of the year to date was crudely crossed out with a pencil. Mahlon had to smile. For all his tough exterior, the captain counted days on his calendar like a school boy awaiting the end of the term.

The boat would dock in minutes and Mahlon was starting to resign himself to failure. July 4th was two and a half weeks away and Hank's chances of breaking the drug operation were disappearing fast.

Then Mahlon noticed something. The crudely penciled X's on the calendar almost hid the fact that some dates had been circled in ink. He couldn't believe it. The dates in March and May when Mrs. Andrews had seen the ghosts were both circled. His eyes slid to the end of June. Thursday, June 28th, was circled too.

The Coast Guard Station slid past on his left, and the boat entered the channel leading to its deck. If the delivery dates were circled, he'd better find out damn quick.

"I'd like to go out on an all-night trip sometime," Mahlon said. His voice sounded thick in his ears. The captain didn't seem to notice. All he did was grunt.

"I can make it down on the twenty-eighth, I think."

The captain glanced at the calendar and then spoke, "Not on this boat. Booked for a private party." Mahlon almost shouted for joy.

The dock came into view off the port bow. As Mahlon downed the last of his beer, he saw something that sent a sudden stab of anxiety through his gut. Charles Chance stood waiting on the pier.

With a quick goodby to the captain, Mahlon headed for the door. Darting across the top deck, he scrambled down the rear steps just as the boat nudged the dock. His stomach knotted up. How was he going to get past Chance when he left the boat?

The other fishermen had already gathered up their equipment and were queuing up to leave by the bow. Mahlon pulled his cap lower on his face and thrust the tackle box inside the ice chest on top of the filets. One of the mates ran past him to secure the aft line. The engines revved momentarily and then shut down. The boat was docked.

From the rear of the line Mahlon could see Chance waiting just to the right of the gangway. The men began to file off the boat, and soon only a few heads separated Mahlon from Chance's gaze. Mahlon swallowed dryly and quickly shifted the ice chest onto his right shoulder. The man ahead of him moved past Chance, and holding his breath, Mahlon followed. Only thirty yards of dusty gravel separated him from his car.

''Hey, mister,'' the mate's voice called behind him. ''You forgot your pole.'' Mahlon swore to himself but kept walking.

"Hey, wait a minute!" The man yelled louder this time.

Fearing he'd attract more attention if he continued ignoring the call, Mahlon stopped and turned slowly. The young man trotted up and handed him the pole.

"Thanks," Mahlon said with a forced smile. "That was stupid of me."

"Anxious to get home and eat that fish, I bet," the mate said and turned back. Over the man's retreating shoulder, Mahlon watched Chance saunter toward the rear of the boat. He hadn't been recognized.

Mahlon's hand shook a little when he inserted the key in his trunk lock. He stowed away the ice chest and pole. Inside the car he took a deep breath and let the tension of the last twenty minutes drain away. The trailing edge of the cloud cover sailed overhead and sunlight brightened his world.

Chief James opened the rear door in answer to his knock. He had lunch waiting and while they ate Mahlon described his trip. Though there was no log book, they both agreed that the calendar served the same purpose.

"June 28th looks like the most likely date for the next delivery," Mahlon said, remembering what the mate had said.

James nodded. "Who do you know at the DEA?"

"I made a few friends up there when I was in Trenton. Why?"

"If we could pull a few strings, you could go out with the Coast Guard and me to bust that boat on the twenty-eighth."

"You think so?"

"I'll do what I can from this end," James said. "After all, you've worked this one, too."

"Great."

"By the way, that pusher the van driver fingered has been under surveillance for more than two weeks. Operates out of that house over at High Bar Harbor with half a dozen others."

"What's he dealing?" Mahlon asked.

"Oh, he's a real candy man. Whatever your particular sweet tooth craves. Heroin? Coke? Speed? Barbiturates? That place is a regular delicatessen, and the other two down the island use the same menu. Thomas, it's a money making enterprise."

"When will the State Narcotics Squad put them out of business?"

"Hopefully, before the Fourth."

James went back to eating his sandwich. When Mahlon told how he left the rod and reel on the boat, James almost choked. Mahlon offered him one of the filets as a peace offering before he went home.

Chapter 39

That evening Mahlon and Sara dined on grilled bluefish lightly dusted with dill and topped with sliced lemon. He served heaping salads in side dishes and kept a chilled bottle of sauvignon blanc within easy reach. The white, moist fish and the green dill complemented each other perfectly. After the meal they lingered at the table until the wine was gone. He told her the day's events, and they sounded even more productive with the pleasant bite of the wine on his tongue.

Sunday afternoon Mahlon came down to earth. He was cleaning his wallet in a fit of restlessness when he dropped Karen's picture on the table beside the dollar bills. Her picture and the thought of her father's check in the drawer stabbed at his conscience, and he had to admit to himself that he had put off seeing Orbann long enough. Tomorrow he'd drive up to Brant Beach and get it over with.

Shortly after ten the next morning, Mahlon opened one of the iron studded doors of Orbann's Lounge and entered the dimly lit room. The smell of stale beer and cigarette smoke hit him the moment he stepped inside. A few of the regulars sat at the bar, nursing their morning beers while the lone bartender busily restocked the bottled beer. He didn't look up until Mahlon spoke.

"Give a call upstairs and see if your boss has time to talk about Karen Beauchamps."

"Who?"

"Karen Beauchamps."

The man gave an annoyed sigh and lifted the phone behind the bar. He spoke a few sentences in low tones and motioned Mahlon toward the stairs. A moment later, Mahlon stood at the top of the dark stairs, knocking on Orbann's door.

"Enter," said a voice on the other side.

Steven Orbann, wearing slacks the color of celery and a white open-necked shirt, looked out his window at the blue expanse of morning sky and the sunlit strip of ocean beyond the rooftops.

Orbann held a small Oriental tea bowl that he placed on a black lacquered tray between a matching tea pot and bamboo wisk. He turned to his guest.

"Mr. Mahlon." Orbann bowed his head in greeting. "Karen Beauchamps' murder still haunts you, I see." He gestured toward the tea set. "Will you join me for tea?"

"Yes, I'd like that."

"Sit if you like," Orbann said, as he bent over the tea set and with unhurried movements fixed a bowl of tea. Finally, Orbann straightened and carried the small tea bowl to Mahlon and set it ceremoniously before him on the edge of the desk.

"You do that well," Mahlon said.

"Outside—" He made a sweeping gesture with his hand. "—is chaos. In here, I take comfort in simple ritual. It helps me maintain order in my life." Orbann brought his bowl to his lips and Mahlon followed suit. The tea tasted strong but Mahlon enjoyed it.

Orbann took his seat behind the desk. "Miss Beauchamps was an unfortunate victim of the aggression this society generates. It may sound heartless put that way, but it's true nevertheless. Our culture caters to our senses not to satisfy them but to manipulate us." He raised a questioning eyebrow, and Mahlon nodded.

"Those who can't sublimate their aggressiveness find violence their only deliverance. Why, it's the very food we

Americans feed on. We inflict it on each other daily. On the athletic field and in the home."

Orbann's voice had lost some of its reserve and now rang with conviction. "Senseless as her death may seem, that girl was murdered by our own chaotic society just as much as she was murdered by the one who took her life." He caught himself and smiled apologetically. "Excuse the diatribe. I feel strongly about this."

Orbann's outpouring caught Mahlon by surprise. He had expected the same cool rejection he got on his first visit.

Instead Orbann had turned passionately philosophical. Mahlon didn't know whether to pursue the original purpose for his visit or take up the philosophical issue at hand. He sipped his tea and thought it over.

"And the remedy for this chaos," Mahlon said, "is a personal sense of order. Right?"

Orbann nodded. "Up here I'm a man of ritual. Downstairs, I'm a man of business who happens to sell something that makes people forget the chaos of their lives."

"Do you?"

The man smiled as if he knew what Mahlon was thinking.

"Liquor has always made man forget his troubles."

"True," Mahlon said.

"In such a world the wise man protects his own interests. I'm a candidate for Freeholder because I know that a bright economic future for this island is the best guarantee that I'll realize my own goals. Simple as that." He sat with his tea bowl suspended between the fingers of both hands as though waiting for Mahlon's next blunder.

"I came to ask about Miss Beauchamps, but if you don't mind I'd like to ask you about something else."

Orbann smiled condescendingly. "Ask what you please."

"What do you think of David Schuyler Woodson?"

Laughing softly, Orbann placed the tea bowl on his desk. "I know what you are driving at, so I'll answer that instead. Age always yields to youth sooner or later. This island will face unimaginable problems in the years ahead. I just want to see young talent situated in positions where it can meet those problems head on. Chief James is of the old school, and it's time he moved aside in the name of progress."

"And you think this 'someone' should be Sgt. Woodson?" Mahlon asked. "Woodson has talents, all right. He's expert at the art of slander, innuendo, and character assassination. I'd think twice about championing that man if I were you."

"Thanks for the advice. Can we get to the real purpose of your visit? I've several matters to attend to when you leave."

Agreeing, Mahlon told Orbann what Karen's roommate had said about the girl and her unknown lover. Perhaps Karen was pregnant. Had her lover been married, it might have been motive for her death.

"I did not then," Orbann said, "nor do I now involve myself in the personal lives of my employees. Why, I can't even remember what she looked like let alone tell you about her love life."

Mahlon removed Karen's picture from his wallet and pushed it across the desk toward Orbann. The man glanced at it briefly and pushed it back.

He shook his head and rose from his chair. "Statistics indicate murders are committed by someone the victim knows. Find her lover and most likely you'll find your murderer. Now, if you'll excuse me."

Mahlon picked up Karen's picture and rose from his chair.

"Sgt. Woodson's only qualification is his youth. A business man of your experience ought to know how unimportant that is."

On the way home, Mahlon tried to fathom Orbann's motive for supporting Woodson. Either he needed Woodson for his political plans or he wanted someone he could own. If Orbann and Chance were really partners in the drug business, that would make some interesting headlines.

Thinking about Orbann and Woodson was much easier than thinking about Karen. He had failed again. He couldn't uncover another lead, and her killer went unpunished. When he entered his home, he took her picture from his wallet and tossed it disgustedly on the mantle. For the rest of the week his gut lurched every time he saw them. Eventually, he covered them with an envelope and brought the punishment to an end.

Chapter 40

Mahlon phoned his friend at the DEA on Monday morning. Approval wasn't received until late the next morning. James called with the good news. The Coast Guard patrol boat was scheduled to cast off at eleven Thursday night.

"We think," James said by way of explanation, "the 'Xanadu' will rendezvous with the supply ship about thirty miles out. They leave dock around nine, but we don't expect them to rendezvous until around midnight. Say it takes a half-hour to transfer the pot and whatever else they have. At thirteen or fourteen knots an hour, it's a two-hour-plus return trip. We'll be in position to intercept them around one-thirty a.m."

"It's a big dark ocean, Hank," Mahlon said. "How will we identify them?"

"Thirty miles is beyond the coastal shipping range, I'm told. Ships sailing out of New York either go east along Long Island or southeast along New Jersey. The shipping lane lies fifteen to twenty miles offshore. 'Xanadu' should be the only boat coming in from nowhere."

"We hope. What about the supply ship?"

"We're just a small link in a long chain. The Feds want more time before they close down the whole operation for good. Meet me at the Coast Guard Station at ten-thirty." With that James rang off. Mahlon ran a hand over his beard. Thursday night was beginning to look interesting.

Tuesday brought the scorching heat, and thousands of day-trippers descended upon LBI. Boulevard traffic reached an intolerable density as all of Philadelphia and Camden came down to sweat by the sea. Mahlon toyed with the idea of taking an early afternoon dip, but the thought of those naked masses crowding the beach made him cringe. No thank you. He spent the day working at his desk, wishing fervently for the cooler days of fall.

The frontpage that morning ran the story on John Dean's testimony at the Senate Watergate hearings the day before. Dean testified that Nixon was involved in the cover-up. In fact he told Dean that raising $1 million in hush money was no problem. The "smoking gun" was in Nixon's hand at last, and Mahlon felt it was only a matter of time.

After supper he walked along West Avenue. The humidity had increased and a drooping sun gave off its sluggish heat above a hazy bay. He passed Sara's house. The weather was great for her business, but he missed their evenings together. He turned back when he reached the yacht club tennis courts and returned home hotter and sweatier for his effort.

By eleven a stale southwest wind worried the kitchen curtains, but the thermometer remained stuck in the high seventies, discouraging thoughts of sleep. When he finally did go to bed, he tossed and turned. An hour or so before dawn, a breeze cooled his room, and he fell asleep. It was almost nine when he awoke.

The promise of another scorcher hung in the air like an ominous threat. The thought of another sleepless night set Mahlon dressing with a purpose. After breakfast, he rode up to Ship Bottom to buy a window fan. The trip took only ten minutes, but what he witnessed on his way home gave him something to think about.

After stowing his new fan in the trunk of the car, Mahlon turned up Twenty-fifth Street toward the beach with the intention of crossing through the municipal parking lot over to Twenty-sixth. At the entrance he saw something that made him stop. Two patrol cars sat side-by-side in the center of the otherwise empty parking lot. One bore the seal of Beach Haven and the other Barnegat Light.

"I'll be a son-of—" Mahlon couldn't believe his eyes.

He moved into the parking lot and stopped beside the Barnegat Light patrol car. Sgt. Woodson was doing the talking. The officer in the other car was the same man who had harassed him several weeks back. So this is where that traffic stop came from.

"Good morning, officers."

Sgt. Woodson turned and gave a start of surprise.

"So this is where covert drug stops are planned, eh?" Mahlon said with a harsh laugh. "It's a sneaky job, but you guys are up to it."

The other officer, his face flushed with embarrassment, took off with squealing tires. Woodson's face went from red to purple, and Mahlon started laughing. He was still chuckling by the time he got back to the boulevard. Oh, that felt good!

* * *

A low front rolled across the island Thursday afternoon. With it came cooler weather and a light, steady rain. Mahlon stood at his doorway watching the rain puddles spread across the gravel. The smell of summer rain scented the air. By supper time, the clouds had clamped down on the island like a dirty gray lid. Would "Xanadu" change its departure time? If it did, Hank would call. Night came like a pencil smudge on the gray sky, and the rain's light patter carried on into the dark.

He ate supper and tried to read, but his eagerness to get started left him restless and unable to concentrate. Finally, it was time to don his windbreaker and be on his way. His hand no sooner touched the doorknob when the phone rang. With a feeling of disappointment, Mahlon picked up the phone.

"This is Pam Richardson," a woman said. Her voice was hushed and low.

"Who?" Mahlon had to strain to hear her.

"Pam Richardson, Chief James' administrative assistant. I haven't much time. Fifteen minutes ago, I let slip that the Chief and you are going on that intercept tonight. Sgt. Woodson hit the roof. He didn't know a thing about it. I'm really sorry."

"That's all right."

"He's been in a bad mood all week. I think he's planning to stop you on your way up."

"How do you know that?"

"Right after he found out, he got on the phone with someone. He said something about a surprise he had planned for that 'smart-assed detective.' Officer Sanders showed up just a moment ago, and Woodson took off in a patrol car."

"Thanks for—"

"Sanders is coming. I got to go." The line went dead.

Mahlon put down the phone and looked at his watch. It was nine-forty-five. Woodson knew his car, and with only one road north, Woodson would have not trouble spotting him. Mahlon picked up the phone again and dialed Sara's number.

"Thomas," Sara said when she heard his voice, "I thought you'd be on you way up to Barnegat Light by now."

"I would be, but I ran into a little problem. Can I borrow your car?"

"Of course you can."

He breathed a sigh of relief.

"The only problem is, it's in the shop. My transmission's acting up."

"Oh, hell!"

"What's wrong with yours?"

"Nothing." He explained that Woodson was trying to stop him from reaching the Coast Guard Station.

"I'll get you a ride," Sara said and hung up.

Five minutes later, Mahlon was pacing back and forth at the mouth of his driveway, the pebbles crunching wetly under his feet. The light mist that fell was cool against his face. He held up his wristwatch and tried to read the time in the dim light of the street lamp. Where the hell was she? He looked toward the bay, hoping to catch some sight of her approaching headlight on the glistening street.

Then he heard it. The staccato exhaust of a motorcycle rumbled in the distant reaches of the night. It grew louder. He rubbed his nose in exasperation. She's got to be kidding. This was no night to go riding on a motorcycle.

The glow of a single headlight rounded the corner from West Avenue, flooding the street with a raucous rumble that rattled windows on nearby houses. Mahlon looked around self-consciously. Curtains parted and faces peered out into the misty night. Sara brought the bike to a stop and eased back on the throttle. She wore a white helmet and a dark leather jacket.

. "Here," Sara yelled over the throbbing motor and held out a helmet with a pair of goggles strapped to it. Mahlon didn't take it from her.

."You expect me to ride up there on this?"

Sara pulled the helmet back and shifted her body to balance the bike. A jean-clad leg and cowboy boot stabbed the road next to his foot to steady the machine.

"Thomas, you called me for a ride. This machine is all I have. Take it or leave it." Her words were clipped and her chin was raised defiantly. She thrust out the helmet again.

Mahlon thought for a second. If he wanted to make that intercept, this cycle was his only way of getting there. With a rueful shake of his head, he took the helmet from her. Inside it, he found a long, white silk scarf. He held it up and looked at her questioningly.

"Let it trail over your shoulder," Sara said. "Maybe he'll take us for two women."

Mulling that over for a second, Mahlon shrugged and wrapped the scarf around his neck, letting one end trail as she had directed. When he donned the helmet, Sara motioned for him to climb on behind her. He swung a leg over the rear fender and settled onto the damp seat. His goggles took a second to adjust. Reaching behind her, Sara pulled his left hand around her waist. He slid his right hand forward and hugged her.

The staccato rumble swelled. They rolled forward and were on their way. The seat tilted to the left, and Sara made a smooth turn onto the boulevard. His added weight didn't seem to affect her steering a bit. She gave it more gas. With a slight kick in the seat, the bike shot forward as the roaring of the motor increased.

The tugging wind ballooned his jacket out behind him, and the mist now washed coldly against his lower face. He began to wish he had worn something warmer. He hugged Sara for warmth. The sensation of holding her close on a moving bike proved very agreeable. The compensations for making this trip were beginning to look pretty good.

The mist quickly beaded up on his goggles, and he used his fingers to wipe them clear. The problem of how they would pass unmolested by Woodson's patrol car began to nag him. If Sara tried to outrun him, she could lose her license. And there was no other way to go around. Somehow they would have to pass right under his nose.

Occasionally, Sara changed lanes to avoid standing pools of water or to pass a turning car. Her movements were smooth and sure, and she kept her speed moderate. Mahlon's apprehension eased considerably.

He stole a glance over her shoulder. In front of the mist-streaked faring, the road lay straight and empty. The house lights slid across his wet goggles like one blurred halo after another. They wove through the sinuous intersection in Harvey Cedars and into the dark stretch beyond, the tires hissing on the wet macadam as they went.

They reached a deserted stretch of road in Loveladies where the homes on the dunes were just light points in the mist. Mahlon caught the reflection of a single pair of headlights in Sara's mirror. Otherwise, the road was empty of vehicles. Sara squeezed the handbrakes and brought the machine to a stop.

"What shall we do when we pass him?" she asked, turning to look at Mahlon.

"He ought to be waiting just over the Barnegat line. I say, we look him right in the eye like we got nothing to hide and hope we get by."

Sara nodded, and they moved north again. A traffic island separated the twin roadway in Loveladies. At its very end stood a wooden sign announcing Barnegat Light. Behind it glowed the strobing red lights of a waiting patrol car. Mahlon's stomach contracted into a tight ball. Sara stiffened when she saw it, too. She eased back on the throttle.

When the patrol car came fully into view, the door opened and out stepped Sgt. Woodson. Mahlon tapped Sara on the shoulder and gestured toward him. She made a show of nodding and gave Woodson a small wave. He studied both of them intently, as they drew abreast of him. Then the rapid approach of the headlights behind them caught his attention. He stepped to the middle of the road and began waving down the approaching car.

Sara took advantage of the distraction and increased her speed slightly. Throttling back, she made a coasting left turn into the nearest side street. A moment later, they rounded onto Bayview Drive, and Sara gave the engine the gas. The center of the road was torn up for the installation of a new sewer pipe-line.

Four minutes later, Sara made a wide U-turn in front of the square, beige brick building that housed the Coast Guard Station. She killed the engine. Mahlon checked his watch. They had made it with time to spare.

He swung off the bike and removed his goggles and helmet. The quietness was a relief. The muffled burble of a boat engine drifted through the damp night air. Sara sat watching him, her hands trembling a bit from the chill. Mahlon unwound his scarf and looped it around her neck. He took her two hands in his to warm them.

"I was wrong," he said, looking into her eyes. "You're one hell of a driver, and I owe you for this."

"It's always nice to hear a man admit he's wrong," Sara said with a smile. Mahlon nodded, and a sheepish grin spread across his face.

He leaned down and kissed her. "Too bad we haven't the time to warm up."

She pulled a hand free and slapped him lightly on the arm. "Get on that boat before they leave without you." She busied herself tucking in the scarf and securing the helmet to the back seat.

Mahlon looked back the way they'd come. A mile down the road he saw the flickering lights of an approaching patrol car, its siren just starting to wail in the night.

"Woodson finally figured it out," Mahlon said with a laugh.

Sara blew him a kiss, jump-started the bike, and roared off. Mahlon trotted toward the building. When he reached the door, he took one last look. Sara was driving on the opposite side of the excavation. When she passed the patrol car, she raised her hand and gave Woodson a tiny "goodby" wave. Mahlon laughed and shook his head. That is *some* lady.

The laugh died in his throat. The patrol car slowed, made an awkward K-turn, and took off in pursuit of the motorcycle. Sara was long out of sight.

Chapter 41

The dark aroma of brewing coffee seeped through the mess deck of the "Point Batan". Seaman Apprentice Forney, who just made the fresh pot in the galley, was now pounding up the companionway.

The mess deck was snug, even with the tables collapsed, but that didn't seem to bother Chief James. He lay snoring on a bench-seat, his head swaying as the sixty-five-foot Coast Guard patrol boat rode the ocean swells. Mahlon wished he was asleep, too, but wondering what happened to Sara kept him awake.

Once they came aboard, they did their best to stay out of the crew's way. In fact, James dropped off as soon as his head hit the seat. His snores and the rumble of diesel engines were the only company Mahlon had for the past hour or so. Staying cooped up below decks was not Mahlon's favorite way of passing time. A breath of fresh air right now would be wonderful.

Footsteps clanked on the metal companionway, and freckle-faced SA Forney in battle helmet and life jacket appeared in the doorway.

"Gentlemen, the skipper has the ship on radar. Time to go topside."

James opened his eyes, sat up and gave a noisy yawn. They filed out of the room on the seaman's heels and headed up the companionway. Half way up, the engines roared and the boat surged forward. James, still fighting off sleep, staggered backward and bumped into Mahlon. He

303

recovered, muttered an apology, and continued slogging top side.

There were no stars visible from the main deck, but the damp mist felt good on Mahlon's upturned face, and the fresh air smelled wonderful. The patrol boat was hurtling through the dark at top speed. Mahlon hoped fervently that the radar was work-ing.

When they reached the pilot house, SA Forney ushered them to a spot away from the two other men on the bridge. The only light came from the instrument panel and the green glow of the radar scope on the helmsman's left. A green line swept the face of the scope tirelessly, trailing tattered points of light in its wake.

"The blip at twelve o'clock," SA Forney said in a half-whisper, "is our target. The one moving up at four is the 'Garfish' out of Beach Haven. They got a late start."

Another green blip inched toward them from ten o'clock. Judging by its size, the ship was massive.

"And that big one on our left?" Mahlon asked.

SA Forney shrugged. The officer in charge overheard the question. "The blip off our port side is an oil tanker out of Port Elizabeth."

"I'll leave you gentlemen here," SA Forney said. "I have to report to the forward M60 machine gun." He was out the door.

The skipper hailed the "Garfish" on the marine phone and spoke for a minute. After that, the seconds ticked away, and no one on the bridge spoke. The only sounds were the racing diesels and the snick-snack of the wiper blades on the pilot house windows.

Mahlon studied the radar scope. The blip that was the "Xanadu" looked to be moving in their direction and would pass slightly to the south of them. The "Garfish" and the tanker were coming on fast. From the way the center point of the radar sweep kept edging forward, he could see that the "Point Batan" would have to cross the tanker's heading before they could intercept the "Xan-adu. They would cross the tanker's bow with scant room to spare. An uneasy feeling grew in the pit of Mahlon's stomach. He hoped the skipper knew what he was doing.

The distance between the blips on the radar scope continued to shrink. On the skipper's orders, the helmsman changed their heading to starboard, opening the distance they would have when they crossed in front of the tanker, and Mahlon breathed a sigh of relief.

Before they crossed the tanker's bow, the "Xanadu" abruptly altered course and raced straight for the cover of the tanker.

"They've spotted us," the skipper said.

The "Xanadu's" blip was there one second and then disappeared from the screen, as the tanker's larger blip moved between them.

"They're making an end run," the skipper said. He barked an order.

"Hold on!" the helmsman shouted as he spun the wheel hard to the left.

Mahlon managed to get a hand on the railing before the deck tilted steeply under him. The "Point Batan" veered left. Instantly, Mahlon feared they would collide with the oncoming tanker.

The breath caught in his throat, as the barn red bow of the big ship rushed out of the dark and seemed to fill the entire starboard window. James uttered a loud oath. The "Point Batan" held its turn. An eternity passed before the red hull retreated back into the night.

"Sorry about that, gentlemen," the skipper said. "I really didn't mean to cut it that close."

"Warn us next time," James shot back.

The deck righted itself, and they were dashing toward the rear of the tanker with their diesels wide open. The big ship kept sliding by their starboard window. Then the "Point Batan" hit the tanker's boiling wake with a thump, and they swung to the right. The "Garfish's" blip left their radar screen. Another thump and they come out on the other side of the tanker. The skipper gave an order, and the engines were throttled back.

Mahlon saw nothing out of the pilot house window. The "Xanadu's" running lights must have been turned off. When the radar reacquired the "Xanadu," the blip was moving south parallel to the tanker's course. It suddenly altered course and headed for the tanker's bow.

At that instant, the "Point Batan's" search lights lit up the darkness, sweeping the water ahead of them. A small bale and some black lumps floated in the distance.

"They're dumping contraband," the skipper said. He gave an order. The searchlights lifted, caught something white in the distance and began tracking it. The "Xanadu" slid through the mist at the far reach of the searchlight with the eerie glow of a ghost ship.

Boom-boom-boom, the forward machine gun let go a short warning blast. Fiery tracers sailed away into the night. Like it was stung by a bee, the "Xanadu" leaped in the water and vanished into the mist. The "Point Batan" surged forward to take up the pursuit. The game of tag went on.

"Hold your fire," the skipper said. He spoke into the marine phone. "'Garfish', he's making a run for it and coming your way."

On the scope the "Xanadu's" blip crossed the bow of the tanker. With their forword light sweeping the water, the "Point Batan" took up the pursuit. Mahlon shook his head. Playing tag with a tanker like this was insane.

The radio crackled. "Batan, he's ours!" The skipper turned to them and flashed a grin.

"Wait!" the radio squawked again. "He's turning back."

They had the bow wave of the tanker in their search lights by that time. The "Xanadu" popped into view just as the tanker hit it. The boat plowed sideways through the water for a second or two, and then rolled under the bow of the big ship.

"God Almighty!" the skipper said, yanking the throttle back. Mahlon blinked in disbelief.

A crunching, thumping sound rose over the dying drone of the diesels. Horn blasts from the tanker pierced the night, and the "Point Batan" swung in a tight circle away from the tanker. Outside, running feet pounded the deck. James, his face glazed with shock, looked at him.

"The 'Garfish' must have spooked him," the skipper said with a shake of his head.

"Poor bastards," James said. "Maybe we can lend a hand on deck." He didn't wait for the skipper's okay. He was out the door in an instant, and Mahlon followed.

The stern of the oil tanker was already sliding into the misty dark, its red and green running lights faint specks in the night. Search lights crisscrossed the roiled waters of the tanker's wake. Seat cushions, papers, styrofoam cups, splintered parts of the superstructure popped to the surface, but no survivors were spotted.

The lights of the "Garfish" were a hundred yards or so away. They were fishing someone out of the water. Crewmen stood at the "Point Batan's" rail peering into the dark. One of them leaned over the side with a grappling hook and brought up a black plastic bag. A jagged slash on its side spilled a quart of oily water onto the deck.

"Quiet!," one of them shouted. "I think I hear something."

Someone ran forward. A moment later the engines died and the boat started to drift. Everyone strained to listen.

"There it is again," one of them shouted. A low moan floated to them across the water. They rushed to the seaward side of the boat. All heard it this time. The search lights began sweeping the surface on that side, and a few moments later they spotted a man's body floating in the oil-slicked water twenty yards away.

One of the crewmen grabbed a flotation ring and jumped into the water. The motors surged to life and the boat reversed direction, swinging the stern closer to the men in the water. Mahlon and James lent a hand hoisting the injured man on deck. It was Charles Chance, and he was breathing.

While the others pulled the crew member back on board, Mahlon helped carry Chance over to a lighted part of the deck. Blood oozed from a nasty wound in the man's upper arm. When they laid him down, Chance shuddered and let out a gasp. The bosun's mate ordered the others back to work.

A corpsman pushed Mahlon aside and began tending to Chance. He called out for a stretcher while he cut away the man's shirt, exposing a deep, jagged tear in his biceps. The corpsman applied a pressure bandage that seemed to stop the bleeding. He administered a shot of antibiotics and felt Chance's throat to take his pulse. A worried look crossed the man's face. That's when Mahlon saw the blood seeping out from under Chance's back.

They rolled Chance over on his side. The corpsman ripped open the man's shirt to reveal the bloody end of a large splinter protruded from his back. Grabbing it with some compresses, the corpsman tried to ease it out of the wound. It was in too deep. The stretcher arrived just as Chance gave a shudder and stopped breathing. The corpsman started mouth-to-mouth resuscitation immediately, but Chance never revived.

James came over to Mahlon's side. "How's he doing?" Before Mahlon could answer, the corpsman covered Chance's face.

"Orbann will be looking for a new enforcer in the morning," Mahlon said.

James nodded. "The 'Garfish' picked up two of the crew. Chance and the captain were the only two others on the boat. No sign of the captain so far."

"Isn't this going to tip off Orbann?" Mahlon asked.

"I hope not," James said. "I was just talking to the Drug Task Force. We'll give the papers a story about a tragic collision at sea. There will be a hearing, of course, but not for at least three weeks. By that time, the raid will be history. We got what we wanted out of this."

James stretched and yawned. "I got a full day ahead of me preparing affidavits for the search warrants we'll need. I wanted to do them ahead of time, but Chief Strickland insisted on helping me. He's got me penciled in for 10 a.m." They both laughed at that.

"There's three island communities involved," James said. "The County Judge is going to be a busy man tomorrow afternoon."

"When are you going to hit the houses?"

"If everything goes all right, early Tuesday morning, July 3rd. Strickland's going away for the weekend or we'd hit them sooner."

Mahlon watched them put the dead man into a body bag and zip it up. Chance was no longer a problem. C.C.'s enforcing days were over. What did worry him, though, was Sara. What happened when Woodson stopped her? There was no telling what trumped-up charges that officious creep might bring against her. Mahlon couldn't wait to get back to port to find out.

They spent the next three hours scouring the area for the captain. All they got for their efforts were seven slashed garbage bags and one sealed plastic bag of antphetamines that somehow floated to the surface. The captain, it seemed, went down with the boat. By the time they sailed back to port, dawn had come, bringing with it a cold, stippling rain.

Chapter 42

"Then he said my bike hadn't passed inspection," Sara said, as the last couple coming off the course laid their putters on the counter. She thanked them and moved the clubs to the barrel inside the counter before she continued her story.

"I just smiled and gave him my registration." She looked immensely pleased with her self. The glow of the overhead light on her red hair held him spellbound for second. She was one beautiful woman.

Chuckling, Mahlon went about unhooking the service hatch and lowering it. After Sara secured it on the inside, he walked around to the door.

"The man was absolutely furious," Sara said when he entered. She was busy counting the day's receipts. "Whatever did you do to him?"

"Witnessed too many of his screwups. That's all. Enough about Woodson. I'm glad he let you go. I was afraid you'd end up in jail for the night."

Sara stopped what she was doing and turned to him. "After the camps, Thomas, did you really think it would bother me?"

He ran a hand through his beard and frowned back at her. Her white summer blouse and tan slacks were very becoming, but beneath that lovely exterior was a strength he should never underestimate. "I didn't look at it that way."

"So," Sara said as she went back to her counting, "what did you and the Coast Guard do out there last night?"

311

Mahlon told her about the drug intercept and the drug boat's collision with the tanker. She pursed her lips thoughtfully as she listened.

"Did anyone drown?"

"Well, Chance didn't drown. He died of injuries. Only the captain went down with the ship."

"How splendidly masculine of him," Sara said, the contempt in her voice thick enough to cut with a knife. She had finished her counting by this time. Filling out the bank slip only took her a minute.

"Follow me to the bank. Then we'll go to my place."

"Glad to, but it will take me a while."

"Why?"

"I'm on foot."

"What happened to your car?"

"Nothing. I got a lift from my neighbor."

She thought this over a moment. "And how were you planning to get home?"

He smiled sheepishly. "On the back of your motorcycle. How else?"

Her eyes glinted with pleasure when she heard that. Sara stepped forward and kissed him lightly on the lips. "That's sweet of you. Let's celebrate a little before we go home. My treat."

He held the door open for her. "After you, my dear. Your steed awaits outside this door." Her laughter, light and lyrical, rose like music through the dark.

On the boulevard their motorcycle joined the restless flow of vehicles that patrolled the island every summer night. Sara slid into line while he held her waist, enjoying the closeness of her and the smell of her hair. In Brant Beach the brightly lit front of Orbann's Lounge slid by. Mahlon hardly gave it a glance, knowing it would be a mad house this last Friday night in June.

They made the deposit at the bank, but instead of continuing south toward Beach Haven, Sara turned back the way they had just come. In a few minutes they were back at Orbann's Lounge, and Sara was slowing the bike as though it was their destination. A white banner with red lettering hung above the great arched doorway.

Catch the Fireworks of

RICKY GEE

June 29th to July 8th

Sara turned up the side street to Orbann's parking lot. A moment later they were standing by the cycle, unbuttoning their chin straps.

"Why this place?" Mahlon asked.

"His name has been in every store window since early spring," Sara said, shaking her hair free of the helmet. "I want to see what all the fuss is about."

The loud driving music hit them before they even reached the entrance. Mahlon hesitated, and Sara pushed past him and opened the door. Clenching his teeth, he followed. She paid the cover charge, and the two of them moved into the smokey interior. The lighting was low, and the room upholstered with moving bodies. Once again it was the music that got to him. It was sound made palpable. Revelers swayed and danced on every side.

Behind a wall of barstool drinkers and hustling bartenders, a slim blond man belted out a song. Awash in a cone of bright light and wreathed in cigarette smoke, Ricky Gee pranced and sang, and the crowd loved it. When the song ended, the whole place clapped and cheered, and Ricky quickly launched into his next song.

Mahlon and Sara wedged their way through the bodies to the bar. The tap handles were gone, and Mahlon knew he'd have to settle for bottle beer. Sara placed the order, and a few minutes later with drinks in hand, they found a vacant piece of wall to lean against and watched the star perform. The music meant nothing to him, but Mahlon noted the energy and concentration that Ricky put into his performance. Grudgingly, Mahlon had to admit that there was more to the man's talent than just a blue silk shirt and crotch-tight jeans.

"Move along, mister," a loud voice said in his ear. "No one over thirty is allowed in here."

Mahlon turned and looked into the grinning face of Fred Fairfields. "Says who?"

"Mr. Orbann's new assistant. That's who. What brings you here?" Fred nodded and smiled at Sara.

"Curiosity." Mahlon had to shout over the noise to make himself heard. "Hers, not mine. She wants to see Ricky Gee in action." The swelling music made talk impossible for a moment.

"When did you get promoted?" Mahlon asked when the noise dropped as the song ended.

"This morning. Mr. Orbann said he might need my services on the campaign trail, too. What do you think of that?"

"Congratulations. It's all very interesting."

Fred stood by his elbow looking the crowd over.

The drummer gave a flourish, and Ricky picked up his guitar. He slid something from a wire necklace around his neck and kicked into his next number.

"Last number of the set," Fred said at a shout. In Mahlon's time the song would have been called a ballad. The accompaniment, discordant to Mahlon's untutored ear, ran like a sour counterpoint to the love lyrics Ricky sang. When the song ended, Ricky hopped down from the small stage and moved toward the line of drinkers watching him from the other side of the bar. He did something which brought cheers and shouts from the crowd. The combo went into its finale and then filed off the low stage behind the bar.

"What the hell was that all about?" Mahlon asked Fred who was still standing beside him.

"Ricky Gee's trade mark."

"How's that?"

"Carries guitar picks on a gold wire around his neck. Drops 'em down some broad's blouse after every set. If she wants to party, the pick gets her into his bed."

"Into his bed?"

"The guy's a stud. What can I tell you?"

"Obviously, nothing I would understand."

"Got to get moving" Fred said. "See you around." He slipped into the crowd, and Mahlon turned back to Sara only to discover she was no longer beside him. A moment later, he spotted her talking to a young woman at a nearby table.

"One of my workers," Sara said when she returned to his side. By then the band was making their way back to stage.

Sara nudged him. "Let's go. I've seen enough to satisfy my curiosity. Besides I don't want you falling asleep on me when we get back."

"Oh, don't worry about that," he said, grinning. "I spent most of the day catching up on my rest. Hey, I'm good till morning."

Sara pushed him away playfully. "Oh, you are, are you? We'll see about that."

The music followed them outside, and the rumble of the cycle as they pulled away was almost a welcome relief to his ears.

It was after midnight when he left Sara's house. The stroll home through the pleasant June night should have been refreshing, but Mahlon could not get his mind off what Fred had told him earlier. Ricky Gee's conquests were the spoils of fame, but the casualness of his sexual conquests was a mystery. Women slept with guys they really liked, but no woman he ever met went to bed for a guitar pick.

315

He must be getting old. The world no longer resembled the place where he grew up. Young women went to bed with a man for a guitar pick. He couldn't change that, but he didn't have to like it.

At that moment he hit on an interesting coincidence that halted him in mid-stride. He just might earn that money Mr. Beauchamps sent him after all. Among Karen's things that Rhonda Black had given him were two perforated guitar picks. Ricky Gee might just be the Mr. Right he'd been looking for all this time.

Chapter 43

Mahlon left for Orbann's Lounge shortly after nine Saturday morning. The sun was a dusty yellow medallion in a hazy blue sky. The car was as hot as a furnace. It was going to be another scorcher, but Mahlon hardly noticed. He had the two picks from the shoe box and Karen's photo in his shirt pocket, and he hoped the candidate was in a cooperative mood.

When he entered Orbann's Lounge ten minutes later, Fred Fairfields was waiting on the other side of the diamond shaped bar to greet him.

"Mr. Mahlon, how are you this morning?"

"Sleep here all night, Fred?"

"No; just filling in for a friend." The tap handles were back in place. Fred was drawing a beer for one of the morning regulars. When he returned, he smiled at Mahlon. "What brings you here?"

"This," Mahlon fished a guitar pick from his shirt pocket and dropped it on the bar.

"Damn," Fred said, scratching his head and laughing, "Who'da thought old Ricky Gee's a switch hitter. Did he drop that down your shirt last night or what?" Fairfields chuckled at his own joke.

Mahlon smiled thinly and waited for the young man to stop laughing before he spoke. "Why don't you call Mr. Orbann on the house phone and tell him I'd like to see him." Mahlon returned the guitar pick to his shirt pocket.

Fairfields' smile disappeared. "I didn't know you were here on business. I'll ask him right away."

Fairfields spoke to Orbann and then gave Mahlon the sign to go up. A moment later Mahlon pushed open the door at the top of the steps and walked in. Sitting behind his desk, Orbann gave Mahlon a quick look and continued with his paperwork. He wore a crisp white sport shirt. He didn't look up when he spoke.

"Haven't you taken up enough of my time? What is it now?"

"I want to see the list of entertainers who performed here in the summer of 1970 and 1971."

"I've no such list. Now please leave."

"Don't con me, Orbann," Mahlon said hotly. "The Alcholic Beverage Commission requires such a list, and you know it."

Orbann looked up in surprise and then smiled faintly. "It will take me a few minutes to find it." He got up and went to his files. "What are you looking for?"

"For now let's say I'm playing a long shot."

"Here." Orbann handed Mahlon a file and sat.

The file contained a list of the entertainers and the dates of their performances for each month of that summer. Mahlon studied them a few moments.

"One performer was very popular here that summer. Let's see. You booked him twice in June and, oh, eight or nine times in July. He also played here the whole month of August except for four nights."

"Who's that?" Orbann said disinterestedly.

"Richard Gerald Testa," Mahlon said. He slid the file onto Orbann's desk.

"Ricky Gee?" Orbann stopped working and sat back in his chair. "It isn't often that I hear him called by his real name."

"No one goes by his real name these days."

Orbann sat forward as though he had taken offense. "What exactly do you mean by that?"

"Nothing." Mahlon thought quickly. There was no sense tipping his hand. "'Thomas' isn't my real first name.

Mother stuck me with Aloysius, and I've spent a lifetime dodging it."

"Oh, I see."

"What do you remember about Ricky Gee that summer?"

"Well, he'd been playing small clubs outside Philadelphia, and my booking agency scheduled him as a replacement that June. He caught the crowd's attention, so I had him return in July. He's an extraordinary performer."

"His career really took off after that, I suppose," Mahlon said.

"Indeed. He made his first album that fall and has been going up the charts ever since."

"Makes a big hit with the young ladies, right?"

"Rock musicians attract females like sugar attracts flies. Ricky Gee, however, has the most voracious appetite of anyone I've met." A look of understanding swept Orbann's face, and he leaned forward. "Surely, you don't consider him a suspect in the murder of that waitress, do you?"

"It's beginning to look that way." Mahlon fished a guitar pick from his shirt pocket. "Two of these were found among Karen's effects after she disappeared. She may have been pregnant, too. Perhaps she tried to lay the blame on him."

"People have killed for lesser motives."

"He was on his way up. A pregnant girl would really be a drag."

"Yes," Orbann said, his voice taking on a thoughtful note. "Put in that light, I'm reminded of something else you may find interesting." He stopped for a moment and looked out his office window at the clouds building up over the mainland.

When he resumed speaking, his voice had a confiding tone. "I try to mind my own affairs and let the world do what it likes. My candidacy, however, requires a change of philosophy."

"I'm sure it does."

"Because Ricky might have had a motive to kill her, I...."

"Her name was Karen Beauchamps." Mahlon cut him off.

"Right." Orbann paused and seemed lost in thought for a moment. "What I'm trying to say is that sometimes I gave Ricky the key to a house in Barnegat Light."

"Why?'"

"So he could take his women there. He didn't want them hanging around where he lived." Orbann watched Mahlon closely. "Miss Beauchamps' body was found on the beach at Barnegat Light, wasn't it?"

"Yes, in the dunes."

"The house is on Third Street. Not far from the beach."

"So?" Mahlon said, trying to hide his rising excitement.

"Third is the last street before the State Park."

"That's not far from where I found Karen," he said, feigning surprise.

"I thought so." He told Mahlon the house number.

"That sheds a different light on things," Mahlon said with a nod. He slapped his thighs and rose to his feet. "Thanks for telling me this. Make sure Ricky doesn't hear about it."

Orbann smiled and then stood. "Glad I could help." He extended a hand. "If this information helps you solve the case, I hope the press hears about it."

Mahlon grinned. "'Freeholder Candidate Helps Solve Murder Case?' Would a headline like that do?"

Orbann laughed. He knew when his leg was being pulled.

On his way downstairs, Mahlon was grinning from ear to ear. The tiger had tried to hide his stripes. Not that it would do Orbann any good, now. After the raid, he'd have all the publicity he wanted. But not the kind that would get him elected.

When Mahlon reached the bottom of the steps, he hesitated. Someone in the bar was shouting angrily. He opened the door to the lounge and stepped through it.

"I want those burned out lights replaced, too," Ricky Gee shouted. He stood by the bar. Fred was behind it, writing everything down on a clipboard. "We played the last two sets last night in total darkness. My fans want to see me. Can't you get that? They want to see *me*."

"And that platform rug." Ricky pointed to the stage. "Look at that damn thing. It's threadbare." He backed off and threw his hands up. "Why did I ever come back here?"

Fred was getting it all down on paper, but his face was red with anger. Ricky looked a little ragged around the edges. His long blond hair was mussed in the back like he had just gotten out of bed, and a day's growth of beard darkened his face. Ricky turned and stomped toward Mahlon.

"Mr. Testa," Mahlon said. The opportunity was too good to pass. "Can I speak to you a minute?"

"Yeah, get that lazy bastard over there working. I've made the whole scene—garage bands in Philly, American Legion Halls rented out twice for the same date, smelly little downtown bars—the whole scene, I tell you. And I'm not putting up with any of that shit, now."

The skin under Ricky's eyes was dark as were the roots of his blond hair. His nostrils were red with irritation.

"Do you recognize her?" Mahlon held out Karen's picture.

"Don't waste my time. I wanna see the boss." Ricky tried to step around Mahlon, but Mahlon blocked him.

"What the hell is this?" Taken by surprise, Ricky stepped back.

"Mr. Testa." Mahlon had a hard edge to his voice. "Look at this girl and tell me if you recognize her."

Ricky started to object, but the look in Mahlon's eyes changed his mind. He glanced at the photo.

"Man, in my business I meet thousands of chicks a year." He pushed the picture aside. "I can't remember every one. What's so special about her, anyways?"

"Karen Beauchamps. Remember her?"

He pulled the picture back and took another look at it. "Yeah, but she looked better when I knew her."

"How well did you know her?" Mahlon asked.

Ricky gave a dirty laugh. "Right down to her little panties."

Mahlon bristled, and Ricky held his hands up defensively.

"Nothing to get worked up about, man." Ricky looked toward the men at the bar. "She got what she wanted. I banged her a couple times and sent her home to Mamma." The crash of a liquor bottle behind the bar cut Ricky's laughter short.

Mahlon turned. A red flush colored Fred's face and neck, and his mouth was crimped angrily at his careless mistake. With a muttered expletive, Fred bent down to clean up the mess at his feet. Ricky used the diversion to slip around Mahlon and open the door. Mahlon had half a mind to yank him back to tell him that Karen never made it home to Mamma. Fearing that might scare Ricky off, Mahlon let Ricky pass and pocketed Karen's picture. Fred was still cleaning up the broken bottle when Mahlon left the lounge.

Mahlon drove north looking for a public telephone. The hazy sky now looked flat and depthless, and the car's interior felt like a steam bath. He finally spotted a fast food place that he knew had a pay phone, and he pulled over and parked.

Inside the smell of hoagies under construction was everywhere, but the air felt cool and refreshing. Mahlon dropped a coin in the phone slot and dialed Chief James' number.

"Hank," Mahlon said when the receiver was lifted. "I got some good news."

"Well, I've got some for you, too," James said. "Strickland will be back tomorrow. The raid has been moved up twenty-four hours. We're go for five a.m., Monday morning."

"You are?"

"Yeah, since the "Xanadu" didn't make its delivery, we've some concern about sufficient evidence being available if we wait longer."

"Wouldn't you know it?" Mahlon asked disgustedly.

"You sure sound thrilled."

"Your raid will nab Orbann, but it will send Karen's murderer out of town."

"What the hell are you talking about, Thomas?"

Mahlon told him the whole story, starting with his visit to Orbann's last night and ending with his talk with Ricky Gee ten minutes ago. "He's the 'Mr. Right' I've been looking for, Hank."

"Damn!" James said. "I'd like to give you a little more time, but this thing is too big to change now. I can't jeopardize our chances of closing the entire drug operation down."

"But what about Karen's murderer?"

"You win some. You lose some. You know that as well as I do."

"Yeah, but it isn't easy to swallow. Not when you're as close as I am," Mahlon said.

"I know. Look, I gotta run. We expect to see you two on the Fourth. Clare's counting on it."

"Don't count on Sara. She'll be busy," Mahlon said, and he hung up. Before leaving, he ordered himself a large ice tea. While he waited for it, his mind began racing. He had to find a way to crack Ricky Gee. There was no way that guy was going to walk away free.

Chapter 44

Just after one Sunday night, Mahlon worked his way through the crowd at Orbann's bar and ordered a Molson. He was going to confront Ricky and make him incriminate himself. He had his service revolver strapped to his right ankle in case Ricky objected. As ideas go, it had all the subtlety of a punch in the mouth.

Outside, the night was close and moonless. The weather report said something about a cold front passing through before morning. Mahlon hoped the weatherman had it right for a change. The air inside Orbann's was slightly drier, but the cigarette smoke started his throat itching.

He paid for the sweating bottle of Molson's and raised it to his lips. Icy cold, the ale scratched that itch just fine. Fortified for the moment, he retreated to a spot by the wall where the rest of the wallflowers stood.

Ricky's last performance of the night had yet to begin. Apparently, his complaints had been heeded. The platform was now brightly lit and covered with a new green rug. The crowd was the same as last night, only the faces were different. The same sun-burned noses, the same languid eyes trying to make contact, and the same loners reading their fortunes in bottle marks on the shiny wood of the bar.

A waitress, laden with a tray of empties, slipped past Mahlon, and right behind her came Fred Fairfields, his broad chest covered in a blood red Orbann T-shirt. Mahlon touched his arm.

"Working overtime?"

Fred turned and broke a nervous smile. "Thought you might show up tonight."

"How come you're here?" Mahlon asked. "Don't you know the old saying about 'All work and no play'?"

"Sure, but I'm saving up for new wheels."

Fred looked around to see who was listen-ing, and when he spoke his tone was confiding. "Thought you might like to know. Mr. Orbann and Ricky had one flaming argument after you left this afternoon."

"About what?"

"Ricky was all spazzed out. We could hear him down here. Yelling he'd leave when he damn well pleased."

"I knew it!" Mahlon said. "He's going to run."

"You think he offed that girl. Don't you?"

Mahlon looked at him. Fred stared right back, his mouth tightened into a stubborn line.

"Look, I never said that," Mahlon said.

"He's gonna get away. Isn't he?"

"Not if I can help it. I'm going to talk with him again after his last set."

"Can you use a hand?"

"No, thanks, Fred," Mahlon said, patting Fred's well-muscled back. "I've handled tougher characters than him."

"Well, if you do, I'll be around." Fred stood there thinking for a minute. His eyes started to scan the crowd. "What kind of wheels you got, Mr. Mahlon?"

"'68 Plymouth. Suits my needs. Just had the AC fixed. What are you looking for?"

"Haven't really decided," Fred said. He leaned closer. "By the way you didn't park it out back, did you?"

"Yeah. Got the last available space by the exit."

"Hope nobody plows into you. These hairballs do some fender bending getting out of here. You know."

"Not tonight, I hope," Mahlon said.

"I'll be seeing you," Fred said and edged off into the crowd.

Whistles and cheers greeted Ricky Gee as he stepped onto the platform. His combo took their places, and Ricky mouthed a few garbled words into the mike and began a rhythmic hand clap. The audience quickly picked it up, as the band kicked into its first number. Bodies began to sway while the more enthusiastic did little dance steps. Midway through the number, the combo shifted into high, and a louder, more strident rendition that brought cheers from the audience.

Mahlon's ears hurt, but he endured the next forty-five minutes in stoical fashion, replenishing his Molson a second time just as the last song ended. Ricky, wearing his patented leer, stepped from the platform and dropped a guitar pick down the blouse of a stunning brunette. Her girl friends cheered as he leaned over and nibbled her ear. Before he pulled away, he said something. She nodded and tried to throw her arms around his neck. Ricky intercepted her hands, winked at her, and returned to the band.

The applause brought the group back for an encore. Just as they started the song, the doorway to Orbann's penthouse opened. Mahlon caught a glimpse of Orbann above the heads of the bartenders who were hustling to set up the last drinks of the night. The man closed the door, watched Ricky a moment, and then disappeared into the kitchen area.

When the song ended, Ricky and his combo filed off the stage. All around the large room, young people started drifting toward the door in pairs.

Mahlon finished his beer. As far as he could see, Ricky didn't seem the least bit agitated. A moment later, Ricky popped out the door of the men's room dressed in a black and gold print silk shirt. It was unbuttoned at the top and showed his tanned, hairless chest. He gestured to the brunette to meet him around back. She smiled giddily and began taking leave of her two girlfriends.

Mahlon set the empty on a nearby table and wiped his mouth. Once Ricky left, he'd never return. Hank's raid would see to that. It was now or never, and the fact that Ricky's mind was on something else wouldn't hurt at all. Mahlon started walking toward the door. The brunette was right behind him.

Outside, the wind had risen, driving the loose sand and litter across the sidewalk and into the street. As Mahlon rounded the rear corner of the building, he guessed that Ricky planned to use the house on Third Street one more time before he left. Otherwise, why would he bother with the brunette?

The parking lot was almost empty. Ricky stood by a van parked near the rear service door. The brunette's sandals were slapping the pavement smartly in her impatience to join Ricky. Mahlon approached the singer, but Ricky only had eyes for the young woman.

"Where you going to bury this one, Ricky?" Mahlon asked.

The singer looked at him with narrowed eyes. "Get lost, you creep." Ricky turned on his smile again for the brunette.

"Miss, be careful with this man," Mahlon said, turning to the young woman. She hesitated. a look of uncertainty crossing her tanned face. "Not every girl he takes out lives to brag about it."

"Hey!" Ricky yelled. "Stop that shit." He shoved Mahlon aside and took the girl by the arm. "Don't listen to him. He's crazy." A gust of wind blew her hair across her face. She brushed it aside and gave Mahlon a worried look.

"Go ahead," Mahlon said, "but while you're at it, ask him what happened to Karen Beauchamps."

"Maybe I shouldn't do this," the brunette said.

"Forget this creep, babe," Ricky said. "We've got some sweet balling to do. Don't we?" He pulled her toward the passenger door of the van.

"Enjoy yourself while you can," Mahlon sad. "Hope I don't read about you in tomorrow's paper." With that the girl yanked her arm free and began backing away. She took three steps before she turned and ran.

Ricky swung at him, but Mahlon pulled back. The punch missed by inches. Before Ricky could deliver another, Mahlon had his fists up. With the chance for a sucker punch gone, Ricky tried kicking him. The tip of his Italian leather shoe seared across Mahlon's thigh. Mahlon caught the man's foot on the upswing and pushed it higher. With a yell Ricky went sprawling backward. He landed on his back with a thud that knocked the wind out of him. Mahlon moved forward, rolled Ricky onto his stomach, and got him in an arm lock. Then he hauled the gasping singer to his feet.

Mahlon pushed him against the van. It had gone easier than he expected. He heard footsteps behind him. As he turned to look, the side of his head exploded in pain. His legs gave way and darkness came with jarring abruptness.

Chapter 45

Someone was groaning, and Mahlon wished he'd shut up. Didn't he have an awful pounding in his own head to deal with? As the timpani in his skull lessened, he opened his eyes and realized the groaning voice was his own.

On the blacktop ten inches from his nose stood a shiny black tire and a silver hubcap. Mahlon worked himself into a sitting position with his back against the door of the nearest car. Damn it! Ricky's van was gone. He remembered pushing Ricky against the van just before his head imploded. He fingered the growing lump above his ear. Ouch!

Thunder boomed over the bay, and a rising wind sent debris scudding across the parking lot. The smell of rain was in the air. With one hand on the door to steady himself, Mahlon got to his feet. He breathed in the cool air, trying to clear his head, before he headed to his Plymouth on shaking legs.

Easing himself behind the wheel, he tried to think what to do next. Ricky had used the house on Third Street the summer he killed Karen. It was a long shot, but what choice did he have? Maybe he was going there now. Mahlon fished the keys out of his pocket.

At that moment, two bartenders exited the rear door of the lounge and scampered to their cars. A second later, the door swung open again. Fred stepped out, locked the door, and without hesitating, headed for Mahlon's car. This was no time for amateur night, Mahlon decided, and he turned the key. The starter cranked, but the engine didn't catch. He pumped the gas and tried again without success. Fred was by the door by then, and Mahlon had no choice but to crank the window down.

"Where's Ricky?" Fred asked.

Mahlon shrugged in disgust. "Gone."

Fred cursed. "I should have been out here to help, but Mr. Orbann's gone, and I had to lock up. How did he get away?"

"I was encouraging him to cooperate when someone hit me."

Fred slammed his fist into his open hand. "What the hell are we gonna do now?" The anger in his voice was unmistakable.

"Go after him," Mahlon said, giving the key another turn. The engine still refused to start.

"Forget it, man!" Fred said, yanking open the door, "I'll drive." Rain splattered against the windshield. "Haul ass, or you'll get wet."

Mahlon didn't argue. He took the keys from the ignition and followed Fred back to the car he'd left just minutes ago. Now that he looked at it, Mahlon saw that it was fairly new. Why did he say he needed new wheels? Pelting rain ushered him in the passenger's door.

"Where do we go?" Fred asked, as he started the car.

"Barnegat Light. Third Street."

A minute later, they were driving north on the boulevard, Fred having taken the corner on squealing tires.

"Damn, Fred! Don't kill us in the attempt."

"What if he's not there?" Fred asked, ignoring his comment. His foot stayed on the gas.

"Then he's gone," Mahlon said. With those words, despair hit him in the gut like a fist. Tomorrow's raid would surely send Ricky packing. If only his damned car hadn't conked out.

Surf City passed in a blur. Halfway through it, lightning struck the water tower and lit the houses and the road like a strobe. A split second later, the clouds ripped open with an earsplitting boom and torrents of rain fell. Fred swore and reluctantly slowed the car to a crawl.

"Thanks for the lift," Mahlon said, taking a look around the car. The inside smelled new. "So what's wrong with this car that you want another?"

Fred didn't answer. A driver in front of them yielded to common sense and pulled over, but Fred pressed on. Around them flashes lit the dark, and thunder hammered the car roof like an anvil.

"It's my sister's," Fred finally said when things quieted down. "She lets me use it."

"Sounds like a nice sister."

"Yeah." Fred sounded as though he wasn't exactly sure.

Suddenly, headlights flared in the rain-washed windshield. With an oath, Fred swerved to miss a pickup that had wandered over on their side. They yelled insults at the driver as the vehicles splashed past each other.

With a shaky hand, Mahlon cleared the mist from the side window. Blobs of yellow house lights bobbed in and out of view, but everything else was lost in a dark blur. Mahlon hoped he wasn't wrong about Ricky's destination, or this crazy ride was for nothing.

Outside Harvey Cedars the rain slackened, and Fred increased their speed. By the time they reached Barnegat Light, the rain was hammering the roof again, and blinding squall lines swept over them like moving waterfalls. On Third Street, Mahlon had trouble spotting the house in the rainy darkness. He ordered Fred to stop and back up. Finally, he spotted it under a shrouding overhang of trees. A stab of disappointment pierced his gut.

No van was outside, and the windows were dark. Mahlon hopped out of the car and ran up the steps of the small porch. Cold rain plastered his hair to his head. The front door was locked. He trotted around to the back, splashing through puddles along the way. Damn! That door was locked, too.

When he got back to the car, his beard was dripping, and his soaked shirt chilled him to the bone. "Ricky's gone!"

"Shee-it!" Fred yelled, smacking the steering wheel. "That bastard's got to be somewhere."

Mahlon gave a hopeless shake of his head. "This is where he stays." He looked again at the dark house. "But without a woman, who knows?" Then something occurred to him. Ricky could be over at Orbann's place in High Bar Harbor.

"Fred, there's one more place we can look. Get moving."

Without hesitation, Fred threw the car into reverse, and back they went until a hollow crunching made them stop. A porch light went on. Fred spun the wheel, and they shot down the street. Mahlon looked back. The porch light winked from sight as they skidded around the corner. Mahlon wrapped one arm over the back of the seat and braced the other on the dash.

"Sounded like a garbage can," Mahlon said. "Hope there's no damage."

"Who cares? Where is this place?"

"Over on the bay." Mahlon gave directions. Fred drove the dark streets with an angry intensity, and Mahlon kept a white-knuckled grip on the dash the whole time. Fred's anger made him uneasy. The storm really had him on edge.

Moments later, Fred slowed as they turned right off Arnold Boulevard onto a side street. They went to the end before Ricky's rain-slick van glistened in their headlights. Fred pulled over and killed the motor and the lights. The street light above the van dripped rainwater like a leaky faucet. In the house behind it a single light burned. Mahlon prayed it was the right one.

"Stay put, Fred. This isn't your business."

"The hell it isn't. I'm—"

"Listen!" Mahlon cut him off. "You're staying here. Understand?"

"Yeah, sure," Fred said, resentment bitter in his voice.

Mahlon peered through the wet windshield again. "If I'm not back in fifteen minutes, get the police." With that he stepped out into the storm and crossed the street. His head protested a bit when he tried to trot, so he slowed to a walk.

The house was a white, one-story bungalow with a screened porch on the front. An empty lot, overgrown with tall horsetail reeds, stood between it and its neighbor. The tall wall of reeds were a convenient screen for drug dealing.

Rain-stippled puddles in the front yard seeped into his shoes, and water trickled down his back. Using Ricky's van for cover, he studied the house. The light inside came from a middle room. Mahlon moved to the porch steps and heard voices coming from inside. His heart started to race.

Inside the screened porch, the front door of the house was open. Bingo! There was Ricky sitting at a table with his head in his hands. Well, it wasn't such a long shot after all, was it? Looks like the pressure is starting to get Ricky-boy. Let's go in and make him really sick.

Mahlon eased open the screen door and slipped onto the porch. Ricky didn't hear him. Mahlon tiptoed to the doorway, paused for a moment, and then entered. Ricky sat at the dining room table with a pencil poised to write.

"Writing your confession?" Mahlon asked when he stepped into the room. The rock star jumped at the sound of his voice.

"Precisely," a voice said, and it was Mahlon's turn to jump. Steven Orbann was standing on the far side of the room.

"What are you doing here?" Mahlon asked.

"I was about to ask you. Besides trespassing, that is." Orbann's crisp white shirt and tie were visible in the open neck of his tailored grey windbreaker, and the look on his handsome face was composed. The fright in Ricky's eyes, however, was unmistakable.

"He's going to kill me," Ricky said. "He's got a gun."

But Orbann's hands were empty.

"Our man here just confessed to killing Karen Beauchamps," Orbann said. "I want him to write a full confession."

"That's a damned lie!" Ricky screamed back at him. "He's going to shoot me and make it look like suicide." A flash lit up the night outside the window behind Orbann, the boom followed on its heels. Orbann glanced at the ceiling as the drumming on the roof increased.

"Ricky, you're too excitable for your own good," Orbann said, as the last rumble died away. "And your excitability cost that young woman her life."

"I'll show you excitability," Ricky yelled and jumped to his feet. Mahlon's punch caught Ricky in the jaw. With a startled gasp the singer sprawled to the floor.

"You had that coming," Mahlon said, shaking his hand, "but it felt so damned good. Why don't you jump up again?"

Ricky clutched his pain-ridden jaw. "What are you talking about?" he said in an injured voice.

"I've been dogging your trail since March," Mahlon said. "Karen Beauchamps didn't deserve to die because she was pregnant."

"I didn't kill her, I tell you." Ricky pointed at Orbann. "He's trying to frame me!"

Orbann smiled confidingly from across the room. "She was pregnant, Ricky, and you were too ambitious to let her ruin your plans. We figured that out in my office today. Didn't we?" He looked to Mahlon for confirmation.

"Yeah," Mahlon said, keeping his eyes on Ricky.

"She wanted you to marry her," Orbann said.

"Yeah, but . . . "

"It would've screwed up your chance to go big time. So you met her and killed her. Didn't you?"

"No," Ricky said looking to Mahlon for some sign he was believed. "The last night I saw her, she came up between sets. I told her to get lost. Yeah, I didn't want anything to do with her. But I didn't kill her. I swear!"

"Don't they all say that?" Orbann said with a sneer.

"I was with another broad that night," Ricky said. "Brought her to this dump, as a matter of fact." He gestured at Orbann. "You said I couldn't use Third Street. You needed it for your own woman."

"How do you know it was the same night?" Mahlon asked.

"'Cause she stopped coming around after that. And I remember something else. It was so damned foggy I ran off the road. We left the car on Arnold and walked."

Mahlon nodded at the mention of fog.

"You expect us to believe that?" Orbann asked, dismissing the explanation with a sneer.

"And what were you doing on Third Street that night?" Mahlon asked, turning to Orbann.

Orbann gave his man-of-the-world smile. "I had something going with a friend's wife. Discretion is always a must in situations like that."

"So Karen's showing up made things awkward?" Mahlon asked.

Orbann's face reddened with anger. "I'm a respected businessman. Don't cross-examine me." He pointed a finger at Ricky. "He killed her, not me."

Mahlon crossed to Orbann. "Not after tonight, you're not,"

"What's that supposed to mean?" He waited for Mahlon to explain. When Mahlon didn't answer, he went on. "Well, we'll let the police handle it."

"That could prove downright embarrassing." Mahlon stood face to face with Orbann now. "There was no woman. Just drug runners."

Orbann stiffened. "Utter nonsense!"

"Karen didn't know Ricky was coming over here. She went to Third Street to talk to him and stumbled on your drug delivery. That's why you strangled her. Isn't it?"

Orbann shot a nervous glance over Mahlon's shoulder. "Look out!" he yelled. At the same time, his hand reached under his jacket.

The move was quick, but Mahlon had been expecting it. As the revolver came out from under the windbreaker, Mahlon grabbed Orbann's wrist and swung it clear of his own body. The gun fired, and Ricky cried out. Mahlon took a step forward, shoved an arm around Orbann's chest, and threw him over his hip. Orbann hit the floor with a jolt, the revolver clattering from his hand. Mahlon gave it a kick that sent it spinning beyond Orbann's reach just before the man yanked his legs from under him.

The impact with the floor started the drums beating in Mahlon's head again. Orbann scrambled across him toward the gun while Mahlon clawed at his jacket to hold him back. Suddenly, Orbann's elbows and knees stopped driving.

"He's trying to kill me," Orbann said in the silence that followed. Mahlon shoved Orbann aside and got to his feet.

"Keep it right there, Mr. Mahlon." Fred stood in the doorway holding the revolver in his hand. It was pointing in Mahlon's direction. Orbann slowly got to his feet.

"Give me the gun, Fred," Orbann said, holding out his hand. "I'll keep them covered while you call the police."

Fred looked at Ricky and then at Mahlon. Orbann took a cautious step forward. Mahlon started to go for his ankle holster, but Fred shook his head and began waving the gun for him to stay still.

"Shouldn't we call your lawyer?" Fred asked.

"We can do that, too." Orbann grew more confident and moved a step closer. "You'll get a bonus, I promise."

"Don't give it to him, Fred," Mahlon yelled.

"But I am," Fred said. "I am."

The first shot drove Orbann back a step. The next two dropped him at Mahlon's feet. The look of surprise on Orbann's face lingered long after he stopped moving.

Mahlon stood in stunned silence. When he recovered, he knelt and touched Orbann's neck. Two pulse beats and then nothing. With a shake of his head, he looked at Fred. The revolver now hung by Fred's side. His face was impassive. Over at the table, Ricky cowered against the wall, his arm bleeding through the fingers of his hand. His horrified gaze was focused on Orbann's body.

Mahlon straightened. "Why, Fred?" He stepped toward Fred and took the gun from his hand. Fred shook himself from his stupor.

"He killed my sister," Fred said in a distant voice. "He'd have gotten away with it, too." His mouth twisted in a grimace of a smile. "There's nothing his big shot lawyers can do for him now. Can they?" He reached into his trouser pocket, pulled something out, and pressed it into Mahlon's hand.

Mahlon galanced down. In his palm lay a distributor rotor. He looked in Fred's eyes.

"Mine?"

Fred nodded.

"Damn you, Beauchamps," Mahlon said. "You suckered me."

"It wasn't that hard," Fred said.

Outside, the rain-lashed reeds whispered to the dark.

* * *

Hank rose to check the steaks on the grill. The sun had dropped behind the house, taking the heat from the back of Mahlon's head. The chairs and the deck stood in shadow, but the dune-studded oceanfront before them still burned brightly in sunlight. Mahlon tossed the newspaper he was holding onto the round white table beside him and snorted in disgust.

"Damn it, Hank, he comes off like the hero of it all."

"I know," James said. He gave the thick vidalia onion slices a final turn and came back to his seat. "Orbann's out

339

of business and, thanks to that Fairfield guy, permanently out of breath, too."

"Don't start on me, Hank. How was I to know he sabotaged my car?"

"Okay. Okay. Karen's murder is solved and our drug problem contained for the moment." James propped his feet up on the railing and took a sip of his drink.

"The mayor called this morning." James held the glass up for inspection and made a face.

"Yeah, and?" Mahlon asked, turning to look into his friend's face.

"Explaining Orbann's death wasn't easy. Next case you solve, don't let a family member kill the suspect. It's so damn messy that way."

"Don't joke about it," Mahlon said. "I keep thinking about the Beauchamps. First, their daughter disappears and that breaks their heart. Three years later, I find her body and break their hearts all over again. Now, Fred's up on murder charges. It's enough to kill them both."

James pursed his lips. "I never gave it a thought. For what its worth, the mayor's happy at last. The search for a new chief is off until I retire." A sea breeze stirred the beach grass on the dunes, bringing with it the smell of the sea.

Mahlon took a sip of his "Abominable" before he picked up the Beach Haven *Times* again. "Strickland's mug on the front page burns me up." He read the front page head-line aloud.

"FREEHOLDER CANDIDATE MURDERED:
CHIEF STRICKLAND'S RAID PUTS
DRUG KINGPIN OUT OF BUSINESS.

How the hell does he do it?"

"Guys like Strickland have a knack for being at the right place at the right time," James said with a philosophical nod. "But I know something that will cheer you up. Woodson tendered his resignation yesterday. Moving to Florida. Looking for greener pastures."

Mahlon raised his glass. "May he never find them."

James tapped Mahlon's glass with his, and they drank to it.

"The steaks are almost done," James said, dropping his feet to the deck. He went to the grill just as the phone rang inside the house. A moment later, Clare appeared at the doorway and called his name.

When James stepped inside, Clare came to Mahlon's side. "I'm sorry Sara couldn't join us, Thomas." She looked out toward the sea. "We owe you a great deal. Hank isn't very good at saying 'Thank you.' I want to do it for us both."

"Consider it done, Clare," Mahlon said and smiled up at her.

James returned. He wore a frown on his face.

"What's wrong?" Mahlon asked.

"Oh, that was the officer on duty," James said before he lifted his glass and drained it. "Mrs. Andrews has been on the phone all day asking for me." He wiped his mouth with the back of his hand and looked out to sea. "She saw ghosts on the beach again last night."

"Oh, hell," Mahlon said.

About the Author

James M. Maloney, a retired educator, taught creative writing for most of his thirty-five years in the classroom. His writing has appeared in regional publications and the op-ed page of the New York Times. He attended Trenton State College and Rutgers University and was named NEH Independent Study Fellow in 1986. He resides with his wife, Helen, in Whiting, New Jersey. His first novel was DARK MOTIONS, featuring private investigator Thomas Mahlon. THE STUMP MAN, his second novel, introduced Vietnam vet turned private investigator, Ward Dundee.